Praise for Jacqui Rose

'A gritty, thrilling page-turner.'
Kerry Barnes

'Raw and in your face, *Sinner* grips you by the throat and never
lets you go.'
Heather Atkinson

'A captivating read from one of my favourite authors.'
Mel Sherratt

'Gritty and gripping.'
Kimberley Chambers

'A hard-hitting, edge-of-your-seat story full of suspense, twists
and turns. Gripping until the end, I loved it!'
Stephanie Harte

'A gritty and compelling read from start to finish. Fast-paced
gangland at its finest. Loved it!'
Edie Baylis

'A rollercoaster of a story line, with so many twists and turns. I
highly recommend this as a must read.'
Reader Review, 5 stars

'A brilliant and mind-boggling book. Once you start reading
you can't put it down.'
Reader Review, 5 stars

'I finished this book in one day. Jacqui Rose's books just keep
getting better and better.'
Reader Review, 5 stars

'Jacqui Rose is one of my all-time favourite authors. This book
has you gripped from the opening page, it starts with a boom
and ends with a boom. I couldn't turn the pages
quick enough.'
Reader Review, 5 stars

'I could feel the blood pumping through my veins with the
tension this story brings. Talk about keeping me on the
edge of my seat!'
Reader Review, 5 stars

SINNER

Jacqui Rose was born in Manchester but grew up in South Yorkshire. She spent her childhood daydreaming and writing plays and stories for anyone who would listen.

She trained as an actress but eventually decided to focus on her love of the written word and became the bestselling author of over a dozen gritty British crime novels. She is now collaborating with Martina Cole on her new novels.

Jacqui is also a children's author and has been nominated for several awards.

Jacqui has three grown up children and when she's not writing, she is busy running around after her dogs, cats and horses.

If you'd like to find out more about Jacqui Rose, follow her on twitter @jprosewriter.

Also by Jacqui Rose

Taken
Trapped
Dishonour
Betrayed
Avenged
Disobey
Toxic
Fatal
Poison
Rival
The Streets
The Women

Collaboration

Loyalty – Martina Cole with Jacqui Rose

SINNER

JACQUI ROSE

avon.

Published by AVON
A division of HarperCollins*Publishers* Ltd
1 London Bridge Street
London SE1 9GF

www.harpercollins.co.uk

HarperCollins*Publishers*
Macken House, 39/40 Mayor Street Upper
Dublin 1
D01 C9W8

A Paperback Original 2023
5
First published in Great Britain by HarperCollins*Publishers* 2019

Typeset in Minion Pro by HarperCollins*Publishers* India

Printed and bound in the UK using 100% Renewable Electricity
by CPI Group (UK) Ltd, Croydon CR0 4YY

To my readers, with thanks x

'What's done cannot be undone.'

Lady Macbeth

1

SOHO

LATE LAST NIGHT

Alfie Jennings gulped down the last drops of the bottle of whiskey as he watched the orange and yellow flames of the fire dance about. Pulling his gaze away he stared at the letter he held in his hand, reading it once more as he tried to stop himself from trembling whilst feeling the same clawing terror he'd felt over the past ten months or so since the letters first started to arrive.

Leaning over the neatly cut-up line of cocaine that sat on top of the black, hand-carved mantelpiece in the front room of the large Georgian house in Soho, Alfie snorted it up greedily. He hoped the coke he'd bought from his friend would somehow make him feel better. Get him high and make him forget.

Closing his eyes, he swallowed as the white powder hit the back of his throat. He tasted the bitterness as a rush of euphoria raced through his bloodstream and for just one fleeting moment, his crippling fear subsided, only for it to return a few seconds later as it came crashing back all too hard, all too quickly.

About to snort another line at the same time as making a mental note to pull up his mate for selling him low-grade coke, Alfie felt his phone vibrate in his pocket. Pulling it out, he stared at the screen. Number withheld. He frowned as he answered.

'Hello? . . . Hello?'

Getting no reply and trying to ignore the cold, clammy dread creeping over his body, Alfie attempted to convince himself that his racing heart was just down to the bad batch of coke. He spoke again. 'Hello? *Hello?* Listen, whoever this is, let me tell you something: I don't appreciate being prank called, and when I find out who you are, I will make sure I get . . .' He stopped suddenly, hearing slow breathing on the other end of the line. But not wanting to show alarm, Alfie cleared his throat, now aware of his own breath; short and shallow, his voice smaller, quieter, fear mixing into his words.

'Who is this? Look, this isn't funny anymore. You hear me? I don't know what you're trying to do but if you think you're going to scare me by playing the old heavy breather game, think again, cos you're wasting your time. You don't scare me. You think a few phone calls and a few letters are going to get me going? Do me a favour. You seriously can't

2

know who I am. I'm Alfie Jennings. You hear that? I'm Alfie, and I never get frightened about anything, so why don't you just do one and call someone else?'

Hurriedly, Alfie clicked off his phone, throwing it across the room as he took deep, long breaths, wiping the prickles of sweat off his face, trying to calm his trembling, *trying* to stop the wave of nausea overwhelming him as he swallowed the vomit back down along with his panic.

It was stupid. So stupid. How could a few letters and calls make him feel so jumpy? Maybe it was just the coke making him twitchy. Paranoid. Christ almighty.

But as Alfie stood – his handsome face pale and strained – in the large, newly decorated front room, still holding the letter in his hand, the second one he'd received that day and feeling like it was burning a hole in his palm, he knew the real problem wasn't the substandard coke. The real problem was he was scared – *really* scared – and he hated himself for it. He was disgusted at his fear, and God knows he'd never admit it to *anyone*. The worst thing was, no matter how much he drank and snorted coke to take away the panic, the fear still sat there like a stone in his stomach.

He couldn't even tell Franny – his long-term lover – about it, although it was clear she knew something wasn't quite right. She'd asked him on several occasions if there was some kind of problem, even going as far as suggesting that he took a break, went back to Spain, set up again there, anything to make him feel better. But all he'd said to her was that he was fine. That everything was just fine, but fine couldn't be further from the truth.

It was a joke. *He* was a joke, and the shame of it all sat on his shoulders like a weighted barbell. And besides, even if he wanted to tell Franny, what would he actually say to her? *How* would he say it? And how could she look at him afterwards with any kind of respect when he told her he was afraid? Afraid of the calls. Afraid of a letter. A flipping four-line letter. It was pathetic because after all when it came down to it, he *was* the *great* Alfie Jennings, the *same* Alfie Jennings who'd put fear into so many men over the years and the *same* Alfie Jennings who'd taken on gangs and notorious crime families to become one of the biggest faces there was. Yet here *he* was trembling like a girl over a poxy note, which this time had been left on the window of his car. But then, it wasn't just any note, was it? Because the note wasn't from just anybody, was it? No, because he was certain he knew exactly who the note was from.

Shaking and with his thick, dark hair stuck to his sweating forehead, Alfie glanced down again at the letter.

Roses are red,
Violets are blue,
I'm your worst nightmare
and I'm coming for you.

Screwing it up tightly and throwing it into the flames, Alfie rested his head against the fireplace.

The letters had been one of the reasons he'd moved back up to Soho from Essex; it made him feel safe, or rather he'd hoped it would've done. He'd thought the familiarity of the

4

place, seeing the people he'd grown up with and throwing himself back into his old ways would make him feel better, make him forget. But he hadn't. Not one little bit. He was still looking over his shoulder, still drinking more than he should to stay as sharp as he would've liked to, and still taking too much coke, all behind Franny's back.

The only thing it had helped him do was forget Bree Dwyer, an old friend who he'd bumped into last year, and when he'd stupidly thought that Franny had ripped him off in a business deal and wasn't coming back, he had sought comfort in Bree and very quickly they'd become lovers. Then just as he was beginning to settle down with her, Franny had come back, explaining the reasons why she'd done what she'd done, but by that time it was too late, because he'd already fallen in love with Bree without bothering to fall out of love with Franny.

But over time, Franny – who'd always been the strong one – did something that if he'd been in the same position, he knew he couldn't have done; she'd become friends with Bree, trying to make the three of them work. And Jesus, it'd been complicated, *especially* when Bree had found out she was pregnant. Not that she'd been certain if it was his or her ex-husband's baby, though ultimately it hadn't mattered whose it was, because Bree had had a miscarriage. Afterwards, she'd decided she didn't want anything to do with him and once again his heart had been broken when she'd moved away without saying goodbye and without leaving a forwarding address.

And through all of it, and although Franny had been hurt, *really* hurt by his relationship with Bree – albeit he'd never set out to cause her any pain – Franny had been kind. Supportive. Worrying about him. Suggesting he took time out in Spain whilst she stayed in England to run the businesses. Not that he'd taken her up on it and anyway, when the first letter had come all those months ago, Bree and his broken heart were soon forgotten, overshadowed by his own debilitating fear.

A sound in the hallway cut into Alfie's thoughts. For a moment he froze before quietly stepping back towards the hearth, his eyes fixed on the lounge door.

Feeling his heart begin to race again, Alfie carefully slid his hand behind the bronze clock on the mantelpiece, and pulled out a large jagged knife. He paused, listening again, then made his way slowly around the room, quickly turning off the light, leaving him in darkness save the glowing embers of the fire.

He could feel the tightness in his chest as he gripped the leather handle of the knife. Moving across the room in the darkness, careful to avoid banging into anything, afraid to make a noise, Alfie stiffened as he heard the sound again. Someone was coming. They were getting nearer.

Nervously playing with the knife in his hand, he twirled it around and around in his palm, which was now wet with sweat as he stared into the darkness, just waiting. He let out a breath he hadn't known he was holding, and there it was again. Just outside the door now.

As the door began to open, Alfie pushed himself as far back as he could then without hesitation he jumped forward, grabbing the person in a neck lock, spinning them round and with as much strength as he could, he threw them hard against the wall, kicking at them brutally as they fell to the floor.

In the darkness, Alfie, enraged, slammed their head against the wooden floorboards over and over again at the same time as ignoring the punching and struggling from the person beneath him. With one hand, he grabbed their throat, pushing down hard as he brought the knife to their cheek, pressing it into their flesh. He could hear choking as he held their neck. 'You haven't got nothing to say now, have you? Let me show you what happens when you think you can take me on. Thought you could frighten me, did you? Well I'm going . . .'

'Alf . . . Alf . . .'

Horrified, Alfie suddenly let go, scrabbling back as he dropped the knife, frantically leaping up to turn the light on. 'Franny? Oh my God, Franny. Jesus, what have I done?'

Sickened at himself, he stood transfixed as Franny rolled around in pain, the small nick on her face oozing with blood. Then shaking himself out of his trance, Alfie dropped to his knees, cradling Franny's head in his arm as he pulled up her top to reveal the angry bruise on the side of her ribs. 'I'm sorry. I'm so, so sorry. Are you all right? Jesus Christ, I could've killed you. What were you thinking of creeping about like that?'

Rubbing her throat, Franny began to sit up, wincing at the pain, her voice croaking from the chokehold as she stared at Alfie in shocked bemusement. 'Me? What I am doing? Alfie, I live here!'

Turning his shame into anger, Alfie snapped, 'I know that, but you could've been anybody!'

'Like who? Like who, Alfie?'

Alfie shrugged, not wanting to hold eye contact. 'I don't know, like a burglar.'

'Are you kidding me? When was the last time you knew a burglar to use a key? What is *wrong* with you?'

Although he knew he was out of order and should be full of apologies, her tone bristled him. 'There's nothing wrong with me. Why would there be anything wrong with me? What are you trying to say, Fran?'

Standing up with great effort and holding her side, Franny shook her head, strands of her long chestnut hair covered in blood from the wound on her cheek. 'Have you heard yourself? Are you . . .' About to say something else, she stopped as her eyes caught sight of the lines of cocaine still sitting on the mantelpiece. She spoke coldly. 'What is that?'

Alfie glanced towards where Franny was staring. Shit, he'd forgotten about that. Irritated, but aware it was more about being caught out, he said, 'What do you think it is? Can't a man have a bit of downtime?'

Stepping towards him, Franny matched Alfie's tone. 'Not when that downtime turns you so paranoid you think you need to attack me for coming into my own home!'

'Turn it in, Fran. I hate it when you exaggerate . . . Look, I'm really sorry, okay? I thought you were . . .'

'Thought I was who, Alf? Talk to me.'

Alfie shrugged, aware of his anxiety as he tried to sound casual. 'I dunno. Does it matter?'

'What matters, Alf, is that you were so high you could've killed me. You didn't even wait to see who it was . . . Baby, what's going on? I mean you haven't been yourself for a long time now. I'm worried about you. I know I've said it before but why don't you think about getting away? Take some time out. Set up again in Spain if that's what it takes. You were happy there and we can make that work. We've done it before; after all Spain is only a couple of hours away . . . What's that you're burning?'

Franny looked at the fire and again, Alfie shrugged. Uncomfortable, he mumbled, 'Nothing.'

Franny's voice was soft. 'Alfie?'

'Don't look at me like that.'

'Like what?'

Rubbing his chin, Alfie snapped, 'Like I'm hiding something.'

'Well are you? Because I can clearly see something burning.'

Angrily and unable to deal with his emotions, Alfie grabbed his coat before turning to stare at Franny with as much hostility as he could muster. 'What is this, the Spanish Inquisition? You'll be wanting to know what time I went for a piss next.'

'Alf . . .'

Alfie cut in, leaning in to Franny's face. She recoiled at the smell of the whiskey on his breath. 'Don't flipping Alf me. I already told you, it's nothing. Like the coke is nothing. It's *my* nothing. It hasn't got anything to do with you, so why don't you just leave it? Now unless you've got anything else to say, I'm off to the club. Someone around here has to earn the money you seem to spend like water.'

And with that, Alfie Jennings slammed out of the room, leaving Franny to stare at the dying flames of the fire.

2

Shannon Mulligan was on her knees. It was only 8pm and she'd already lost count of the amount of blow jobs she'd given that day in the small members-only club in Mead Street, Soho. Though on analysis, she reckoned it must be a lot on account of how painful her knees were and how much her jaw was aching – those were two good indicators in her book. Her rule was, if she didn't feel the burn in her knee joints and the throbbing in her jaw, well she hadn't done enough, which ultimately meant her pimp, Charlie Eton, would have something to say. And one thing that Shannon Mulligan knew all too well was that Charlie's first language wasn't English when it came to money.

Charlie talked in bust lips, black eyes, broken ribs and knocked-out teeth. Not that she was particularly bothered about her teeth – they'd started falling out a long time ago, long before she'd started working for Charlie and around about the same time she'd moved from heroin on to crack. Besides, she didn't think it was half bad not having all her front teeth: it made the blow jobs easier and stopped the punters' pubic hairs getting stuck in them, which was one of her pet peeves.

Bored and glancing up, Shannon's view was blocked by her client's enormous pasty white wobbly belly as he thrust into her mouth one final time before he let out a loud squeal – reminding Shannon of the pig she'd seen on TV last week – as his legs gave way underneath him, and he collapsed satisfied to the floor.

Staring in disgust, Shannon stood up and sighed. Today was her sixteenth birthday.

Charlie Eton was one of life's bastards and he prided himself on this self-proclaimed title. If anyone called him a *bastard,* rather than be offended, he took it as a compliment, knowing that he must be doing something right, because to Charlie being a *bastard* showed strength. It showed aggression. It showed he'd wound somebody up enough for them to be upset. Everything he aspired to do and be – that word said it all.

He didn't ever want to be called *nice, kind, warm, loving,* not by anyone. Not by his ten kids he never saw, not by any of his ex-wives and certainly not by the people who worked for him. Though after being in the business for as long as he had, he doubted *anyone* who knew him would call him those names. And he was comfortable with that. *Very.* Because *those* names were synonymous with weakness.

Weakness to him was a disease. A disorder. It was what

his mother had been, night after night when instead of fighting back, she'd allowed his father to beat her up and then done nothing when his father's attentions turned towards him and his younger sisters. Attentions that not only included kicks and punches, but also long, painful, drawn-out attentions in the bedroom, day or night.

And it'd been after one particular night when Charlie Eton was just twelve years old, when the friends his father had brought home – to join in with his perversions – had left, that Charlie had first heard his father call him a *bastard*. And it'd been a revelation to Charlie. Like listening to the sweetest music. He'd seen it as a coming of age. His own version of a bar mitzvah. Because that winter's day in the cold, cramped, damp two-bedroom house he shared with his parents and four sisters, Charlie discovered that he too had power.

His father had been sprawled naked on top of one of his sisters whilst their mother drank herself into a stupor in the next room. Charlie had seen the fear in his father's eyes as he held the coal fire's burning red poker against his neck, and right then Charlie had understood that his father, the man he'd spent his whole life terrified and cowering from, could also be afraid. Could also be weak.

And the weakness exuding from his father had spurred Charlie on, exciting him. Making him feel alive. Making him feel worthy. Strong. Powerful . . . Untouchable. And for the first time in his life, Charlie had felt a glimmer of happiness. A glimmer of peace. And the more fear, the more *weakness* his father had shown him, the more it had encouraged Charlie to use his new-found courage to burn and blister his father's flesh further, smelling the sizzling, stubbled skin mixed in with the smell of his father's fear. Then it'd happened. The moment when the words, '*You bastard*,' were screamed from his father's lips and the moment Charlie Eton knew life would be different.

Although he'd got the beating of his life, ending up in hospital with a broken arm, fractured skull and dislocated jaw, he'd learnt a priceless lesson that had helped his bruises and broken limbs hurt less. He'd learnt that weakness was a man's enemy.

'Hey, boss! Boss?'

Sitting on the gold-leafed toilet seat, trousers around his ankles with his bloated body falling over the lavatory bowl in waves, Charlie's thoughts were sharply interrupted by one of his men who stood in the entrance of his expensive, black-tiled bathroom. Annoyed by the intrusion, Charlie snarled.

'Can't a person go to the frigging carzey in peace?'

'Sorry, Charlie, I just . . .'

'Watch your manners!' Throwing the nearest thing he could reach, which just so happened to be the toilet brush, at the man's head, and fuming, Charlie stood up, pulling up his trousers without bothering to wipe.

'Sorry, *Mr Eton*, it's just that you asked me to let you know when I saw Alfie going into his club.'

Narrowing his grey eyes, Charlie glared. 'Yeah, but I don't remember that including disturbing me when I'm having a shit.'

'Yes, boss. Sorry.'

Sighing and deciding there and then that he was going

to give the man his marching orders, Charlie asked, 'How long ago?'

'Must have only been about ten minutes ago. He didn't look so great to tell you the truth. He looked a bit ill.'

Stepping forward, Charlie breathed into the man's face. The sticky aroma of unbrushed teeth wafted between them. 'When I want a medical diagnosis, I'll call 999, but in the meantime, just shut the hell up. You understand?'

'Yes, boss.'

Satisfied, Charlie nodded. 'Good, now off you trot . . . oh and whilst you're at it, get your things and *go*.'

'What?'

'You heard me, go. Leave. You're sacked. I don't want to see you around here again. Got it?'

'But why? I don't understand.'

Bemused, Charlie brought back his leg, kneeing the man hard in his balls. 'Why? Because I'm Charlie Eton, that's why. And for your information, I don't need a reason to sack you, and come to think of it, I don't need a reason to kill you either. So, if I were you, I'd piss off out of my sight before I count to ten.'

Fifteen minutes later, Charlie Eton sat on the large blue leather sofa, dressed in designer jeans and a pink Ralph Lauren shirt, in the crisp white back room of his club, deep in thought and ruminating about Alfie Jennings whilst Shannon attempted to work on his limp penis.

Fed up and feeling a bit of chafing, Charlie kicked Shannon away, sending her crashing into a pile of beer crates.

14

Indignantly, she screamed, her big green eyes filling up with tears as she looked down at her laddered black tights, which she'd only just bought cheaply from one of the shoplifters who regularly came by the club selling their goods. Looking through the fringe of her red curly hair, Shannon's bottom lip quivered as she wailed. 'What did you go and do that for?'

'Turn it in, Shan – or at least turn it down. I'm not in the mood for any of your whining and blubbering. I've already had enough shit tonight, and that's before I decide what needs to be done about Alfie. I mean, who the hell does he think he is setting up a club right on my doorstep? He must think I'm a flipping mug. Do I look like a mug, Shan? Come on, be honest. Do I look like I've got idiot written on my forehead?'

Wiping away her tears, Shannon shook her head. 'No, Char, he's the one who's the mug.'

Charlie stared at his niece and smiled. He liked her loyalty. That went a long way in his book. Okay, so she moaned a lot, she chewed off his ear more than the other girls that he had working for him, but when all was said and done, Shannon was a good grafter – he'd give her that. And underneath the thick, exaggerated make-up, there was a beautiful girl and even though she was just sixteen, there was still the look of a child about her. A vulnerability. When she wiped off the cack from her face, she could easily pass for as young as ten. A ten-year-old with a woman's body. Punters paid a lot for that.

The other thing he'd always liked about Shannon was that she seemed grateful. Grateful for the care he gave her.

He supposed there was something to be said about having family working for him. Not that his sister, Shannon's mother, had been much use to anybody. Far from it.

Like their own mother, she'd been weak, spending most of her life in and out of mental institutions before she'd been found dead from an overdose of heroin in a back alley off the Old Kent Road. As a result, Shannon had gone to live with one of her aunts who, in his opinion, had done a good job with the girl. She'd prepared Shannon for the harsh realities of life. She'd made her strong. She hadn't wrapped her up in cotton wool, which didn't do anything for anybody apart from making them weak.

No, what his sister had done was get Shannon out there. Exposing her to how life really was. Getting her to earn her keep from the start by pawning her out, before putting her full time on the *game,* and Shannon had not only earned his sister a crust, but she'd also made a little bit of pocket money for herself too. If his memory served him right, he recalled his sister telling him once that Shannon had been earning at least fifteen pounds a week for herself when most eight-year-old girls would be lucky to have a couple of pounds. Shannon certainly was a lucky girl.

To Charlie, a strong work ethic was one of the most important things in life because nothing in life came free. He of all people should know that, and now Shannon, thanks to his sister, knew that as well. Still, even he knew on occasion there were exceptions to those rules.

He grinned, digging into his trouser pocket, and winked at Shannon as he pulled out a small off-white rock of crack cocaine, throwing it to her gently.

'You'd thought I'd forgotten, didn't you? Well I hadn't . . . Happy birthday, Shan. Now you can't say I don't give you anything . . . Come on then, come and give your uncle a birthday kiss.'

3

Another person who seemed to have Alfie on their mind was Franny Doyle, but it was another couple of hours before she'd cleaned herself up and found herself walking slowly along the bustling streets of Soho towards their club just off Sutton Row.

Although Soho had changed a lot over the years, she still felt at home here. It gave her a certain kind of peace like nowhere else did.

She'd been raised in the small square mile of Soho and around each and every corner were memories. Happy child-hood memories, and she could almost feel the ghosts of the past.

She smiled sadly to herself as she walked past St Anne's Church on Dean Street, remembering how her father Patrick, a number-one face, had once raced her home from there to their large house in Soho Square; him running, and her pedalling away on the new pink bike he'd given her, like her life depended on it. And they'd laughed hard and hysterically whilst the rain lashed down, and they'd been soaked to the skin but it hadn't mattered, not one little bit.

Until those days had become complicated, they were happy ones. And she supposed that's what she missed most of all. The simple pleasures. The laughter, something that was certainly absent from her life of late, though one thing that being back had done was reconnect her with the past, and take away any doubts she had. It made her see even more clearly what was important to her, and that was family. Family came in all different ways and in all different manners. Family didn't need to be about blood, but that didn't mean she wouldn't protect them like they were. No matter what it took. No matter what she had to do.

So yes, even though life at the moment was difficult and stressful, and at times it felt like she wasn't coping properly, she was pleased to be here among the vibrant streets of Soho. Not that it had been her idea to come back – it had been Alfie's. Nor had it been her idea to get back into the club business – again that had been Alfie's – but considering the state of mind he was in, she couldn't have persuaded him otherwise even if she'd tried.

Though hopefully, very soon, Alfie would realise what was best for him. Realise he really did need to get away. Properly away. To Spain. To Mexico. To Brazil. To anywhere but here. He'd looked ill earlier, a shell of his former self, and no matter what, she still did care about him. She always would. Just because he'd be in one country and her in another, it wouldn't mean the end of them, but right now, her and Alfie's relationship was the least of her worries.

Taking a deep breath, Franny closed her eyes for a moment, the enormity of everything washing over her. She had to keep on believing that things would work out in the end. In fact, they had to, because it wasn't just Alfie feeling anxious. If things didn't work out very soon, she wasn't sure what she was going to do.

Opening her eyes and regretting not putting a warmer top on, Franny, once more beginning to feel the pressure build up, started to walk again, still with Alfie firmly on her mind.

Ten minutes later, having stopped for a quick catch-up chat with one of the old prostitutes who'd worked the area for as long as she could remember, Franny arrived at the club. She walked down the stone basement stairs towards the discreet entrance and as she did, her phone rang.

She answered quickly. Her tone was hushed and cold as she stood in the shadows of the night, her gaze darting around anxiously.

'Yes? . . . What? . . . For God's sake, haven't I told you not to call me unless it's an emergency? . . . No, you listen to me. I said that I'd come round and I will. I've never let you down before have I? . . . No, that's right. You know I've got a lot on so I don't appreciate you making everything harder . . . I'm going to check on Alfie first, but like I say, unless you want us both getting into trouble, don't call me again on this number.'

'Who shouldn't call you again?'

Franny jumped, turning round and letting out a small scream as she clutched the phone to her chest, backing away. 'Jesus Christ, you nearly gave me a heart attack. Don't go around creeping up on people like that.'

Vaughn Sadler stepped out of the shadows into the light, staring at Franny, his green eyes twinkling with suspicion. 'I wasn't. Not my style, darling. Sneaking about has never been my thing.'

He held her stare and, annoyed, she waved him off. 'Whatever, Vaughn. You carry on telling yourself that.'

Vaughn tilted his head, finishing off his large cigar. 'You seem jumpy.'

Wiping away the tiny beads of perspiration on her brow, Franny snapped, 'Well yeah! Because you've jumped out on me.'

Vaughn leant in, a smirk spreading across his handsome face. 'You carry on telling yourself that . . . So go on then, who was on the phone? Who shouldn't call you again?'

Franny bristled with anger, desperate to get away. 'Sorry to tell you this, Vaughn, but you're not my keeper. Now if you don't mind getting out of my way, I'm here to see Alfie.'

She turned to head for the entrance but felt the firm grip of Vaughn's hand on her arm.

'Not until you tell me.'

Franny shook her head, pushing her long chestnut hair out of the way. 'Not a chance, and not because I'm hiding anything, but because it's none of your business. Now I'd appreciate it if you'd take your hands off me.'

Vaughn dropped his hold. The coldness in his tone turned to ice. 'I don't like you, Franny, and I certainly don't trust you. If it wasn't for Alfie, after that *stunt* of yours you pulled last year, you'd be six foot under.'

'Is that a threat?'

'No, it's a regret. We should've got rid of you a long time ago because I know as well as you do that behind that pretty face of yours and those big innocent eyes, you're a scheming bitch and come to think of it, you still owe me a lot of money. I don't forget, and I certainly don't forgive people who rip me off.'

Trying to keep her temper under control, Franny chewed the inside of her bottom lip. 'You know it wasn't like that.'

'Like I say, you're a scheming bitch. You might have Alfie fooled, darlin', but sweetheart, I know your game. You are so like your father it's unreal. Gangster through and through aren't you?'

Irritated, Franny sighed. There was no love lost between her and Vaughn, who'd been Alfie's business partner for a long while now. And no, she didn't entirely blame him for being pissed off with her. But he knew as well as Alfie did that the *stunt* he was always referring to, the *ripping off* he often spoke about, simply wasn't true. Okay, she'd taken his and Alfie's money without asking them last year. A lot of money. Two million pounds to be precise. But it wasn't about conning or cheating anybody. The fact was she knew if she'd asked them they, or at least Vaughn, would've said no. And *no* would've meant two people who were very dear to her would've likely been killed by the notorious Russo brothers, who'd demanded the money in return for her family's safety. Not that it'd ended up being as simple as that, far from it, but she would defy anyone not to do the same in her position, and that included Vaughn.

'I didn't rip you off, you know that, and I'd do it again if I had to.'

Vaughn nodded. 'I know, and that's the problem. You aren't to be trusted, and if Alfie can't see that, then I'll make it my business to *make* him see.'

'Keep out of my business, Vaughn, you hear me?'

'Not a chance. I'm going to bring you down, Franny.'

Franny barged past Vaughn, pushing down her anxiety and doing her best to ignore what he was saying.

'I'm watching you, Franny Doyle. You hear me? I'm watching you!'

As Franny walked into the overheated basement club, her mood wasn't helped when she saw Alfie slumped across the bar with one of the women who worked for them almost sitting on his knee. The minute she saw Franny, she blushed, tottering off quickly in her too high stilettos and shorter than short mini skirt muttering an apology under her breath.

Stony-faced, Franny sat on the Perspex bar stool next to Alfie as she looked around the club full of wealthy punters. Punters who were happy to flash their black Amex cards and pay well over the odds for the middle-of-the-road Champagne they served. And in return for their money, they got to wind down and chat freely to the pretty girls who worked there, away from their wives' prying eyes.

Not that their *girls* were actual underage girls, not like Charlie Eton's. That wasn't even a possibility. To Franny,

Charlie was the scum of the earth. She'd seen first-hand how young they were as well as seeing how badly he treated them, and in truth, it made her sick to her stomach. They were all vulnerable or runaway kids who saw Charlie and his club as an escape. Somewhere better than where they had come from. And Christ, that was the most depressing part of it all.

Franny had always been strict with the recruitment process. The youngest girl who worked for them at the moment had just turned twenty, and on account of it being almost impossible to know how old someone was just by looking at them, she always insisted on seeing the girls' passports without exception.

The other thing she was strict on was making sure the girls understood from the get-go that the place wasn't a knocking shop, or an escort business, nor did it have a room at the back for giving clients sneaky blow jobs.

All that was required of them was to look pretty, to be friendly, and to keep smiling, in addition to getting the punters to buy drinks. Lots of drinks. Obviously, what the girls did in their spare time with the clients wasn't any of her business, but she warned them from the outset that if she heard them offering the clients sex, they'd be out on their ear before they could say *the full works*.

Membership for the club was in excess of ten thousand pounds a year, and so far, not only was the place doing very well, they also had a waiting list. The clients seemed to appreciate the air of discretion and sophistication, so having Alfie looking like he was about to vomit all over the expensive, plush black marble floor any minute was not a good look.

For the clients' benefit, Franny kept a wide smile on her face whilst hissing a whisper. 'For God's sake, just sit up, Alf. You look a mess. This isn't the time *or* the place.' Half-cut, Alfie stared up at Franny. He winked at her. It always surprised him that even when she was angry she looked beautiful. In truth, she looked even more beautiful when she was annoyed, which didn't mean to say she pissed him off any the less. In fact, it just added to his irritation.

'Oh, that's nice, ain't it? No hello, no kiss, just straight in chewing me ear off.'

'I wouldn't have to if you carried yourself properly.'

Alfie shook his head. 'Jesus, Fran, leave it out. All I'm doing is having a drink in my own club. No more, no less. It's not a crime.'

Still holding her smile as she seethed, which she knew was more to do with her encounter with Vaughn, than Alfie, Franny snapped, 'Like I say, you look a state, and you're embarrassing yourself. Having the girls fall over you isn't the way to run a place, not this kind of place anyway. And before you ask, Alf, I'm not jealous – far from it. This is about business and this business is supposed to be a classy joint. Now I get that something's going on with you, but *don't* bring that something to work.'

'Cometh the ice maiden.'

'Grow up, Alfie!'

With Franny's arrival acting like a bucket of cold water, Alfie sat up, glaring, his blue eyes piercing from underneath his fringe of thick black hair. 'Listen to me, if you only came down here to give me grief, why don't you just turn your pretty backside around and go home. I can do without another lecture.'

Franny sighed, her voice softening as she touched his hand gently. 'If you must know, I came here to see if you were all right. I was worried. You haven't been yourself. Look what you did earlier. I just want to know what's happening . . . Come on, talk to me, Alf.'

Alfie stayed silent for a moment before shrugging, trying to dispel his gnawing unease.

'I'm fine. How many times do I have to tell you?'

'Alf, it's me you're talking to. There's something going on, I know there is. You're distant. I can feel you pushing me away.'

Alfie looked at her evenly. 'You think this is about Bree and you, don't you?'

Franny bristled, her voice tight. 'What . . . what are you talking about?'

Gently, Alfie took her hands. 'I'm talking about *you*. You think I still miss her. That I'm still in love with her, don't you?'

A flicker of relief crossed Franny's face and more relaxed she said, 'I don't know – are you?'

'No, and you know why?' Franny shook her head but let Alfie continue to talk. 'Because why would I want to waste my time on someone who didn't love me back? I mean, she can't have cared. She can't have given a damn about me if she just dropped me the way she did. Going off like that without even a goodbye. I don't know what I was thinking getting together with her in the first place.'

Seeming slightly distracted as if wanting to get on with

what she had to do, Franny said, 'You were hurt, Alfie. I understand. You thought I'd left you. It's as simple as that.'

Alfie shook his head, genuine warmth and regret in his tone. 'No, I was wrong, Fran. I'm surprised you don't hate me. I put you through shit and hurt you badly, yet it's not Bree sitting here, is it? It's you . . . And I know this sounds bad, but it's a good job that the pregnancy didn't work out, otherwise if the baby had turned out to be mine, I'd have been lumbered with Bree for the rest of my life.'

'Exactly, and I'm not holding any grudges, Alf. Bree is in the past now. She's forgotten. What's done is done. We don't have to mention her again.' Franny squeezed his hand and gave him a kiss on the cheek, indicating that the topic of conversation was now closed.

With the cocaine in his system making him flick from one mood to another, Alfie growled as he pulled away from Franny, snatching hold of the glass of whiskey on the rocks in front of him. He raised it.

'Well let's drink to that. Good riddance to her, that's all I can say. I had a lucky escape from that bitch . . .' Alfie paused, his demeanour once again changing as he thought about the letters. 'But the point is, Fran, what's going on with me, it isn't about her. I've just got a lot on my mind. You know, making a go of this place, all the long hours, it catches up on a person. I'm not as young as I use to be.'

Seeing an opportunity, Franny stared at Alfie. 'That's why you should get away. Take a break. Go back to Spain. We could even open another club out there. You were happier when we were living out there. Think about it, Alf, it could work out great.'

'You're keen on getting rid of him all of a sudden. That's all I seem to hear these days. If you ask me, it seems a bit odd.'

For the second time that evening, Franny jumped as she turned around to see Vaughn again, and like before he stared at her coldly.

With Vaughn making her feel paranoid, Franny hissed, 'Well I didn't ask you, and it's not about being *keen*, Vaughn, or about it being odd. It's about what's best for Alfie, and in case you haven't noticed, he's not himself at the moment. If you want to see something else in that, be my guest, but let me tell you something, you're wasting your time.' She turned back to Alfie. 'Look, Alf, I'll see you later.'

Franny began to walk away through the crowd of noisy, milling people, but she stopped in her tracks as Vaughn caught up with her, speaking out of earshot of Alfie. 'Where are you going, Fran?'

Slowly, Franny turned on her heel to stare back at Vaughn who stood inches away, his muscular body rigid with anger.

'What?'

'You heard me, where are you off to?'

Franny's expression spoke hatred. 'You're like a dog with a bone, aren't you, Vaughnie? What's your problem?'

'Just answer the question, Fran. It's not that hard.'

Expert at keeping her temper even, Franny's voice was devoid of emotion. 'I'm going home. It's been a long day. Happy now?'

'Home? Are you sure about that?'

Snorting with derision, Franny shook her head. 'Whatever it is you've got to say, just say it.'

Giving a cloying smile, his handsome face twisted with a hatred that matched Franny's, he leant forward to whisper in her ear. 'Oh, I will, when the time's right, that is. When I've worked out what exactly it is you're up to.'

Franny laughed scornfully, and then said above the music, 'You've clearly got too much time on your hands, Vaughn, or maybe you just need to go and get laid. Now if that's all, I'm going home.'

'Not quite all . . . Tomorrow I think you and me should go over the club's accounts and then you could explain to me *why* there's a lot of unaccounted money going out of the business.' Franny didn't turn to acknowledge Vaughn's words; she continued to walk straight out the door.

Outside in the street, Franny leant on the black, wrought-iron railings, welcoming the cool. Shaking, she closed her eyes, breathing deeply, feeling the beginning of a tension headache. There was no way she could meet Vaughn and go over the books because he would want answers, and she had none to give him. The last thing she could do was tell him why she'd been taking money out of the business without telling either him or Alfie. But she knew Vaughn well enough to know he wouldn't back down, and very soon he'd cause her real trouble, which was one thing she couldn't afford to happen. So she had to work out what she was going to do about Vaughn. One way or another she was going to have to stop him.

After taking a couple of minutes to compose herself, Franny pulled out her phone and dialled a number. It was answered after only two rings.

'Hi, it's me . . . Look, I'm sorry about earlier. I didn't mean to be so angry, it's just that you know you shouldn't call me on this number; anyone could've picked up, and things are becoming really difficult. I think Vaughn's on to me . . . Anyway, I'm coming now, okay? See you soon.'

As Franny pushed down her sense of guilt, she slipped the phone back in her pocket, hurrying along Sutton Row, not noticing Charlie Eton and his men striding towards the club.

4

Charlie smiled as he held a small machete in his hand. 'So, come on then, ladies and gentlemen, who's first?' He tapped the weapon in his palm as he nodded to one of his men to lock the door. Terrified by the intrusion, the club girls and clients began to scream, running in panic towards the fire exit, but their way was soon blocked by a handful of Charlie's men, who herded them into the corner like sheep.

Having just come back from the bathroom located at the back of the club, it took Alfie a few moments to realise what was happening. Directly, he jumped into action, catching a glimpse of Vaughn smashing a bottle into the face of one of the intruders on the far side of the room.

About to go and help, Alfie felt a hard punch to his head, which had him spinning round to come face-to-face with a short, Mediterranean-looking man, holding a large knife. Undeterred, Alfie grabbed the chair next to him. He swung it round, hitting and opening the side of the man's face who cried out in agony, but spurred on from the pain, the man, now covered in his own blood, threw his weight on top of Alfie, sending them both crashing to the floor.

Quickly, Alfie scrabbled along the polished floor on his knees, lunging forward to grab the man's neck and twisting him round in a headlock. He forced his fingers into the man's eyes until he heard the squelching of flesh. Panting, he shoved the man away and watched for a moment as he squirmed about on the floor in agony. Then Alfie barked, 'You prick – who sent you? You think you can come into *my* club and try to scare off *my* punters? I'll show you.' Raising his fist ready to finish off the job, Alfie froze as a piercing scream filled the air. He turned and was shocked to see Charlie Eton – who he hadn't realised was behind this until that very moment – standing and grinning as he held his machete against the neck of one of the girls.

Seeing the expression on everyone's faces, Charlie filled the room with a wheezing laughter. 'At least now I've got everyone's attention . . .' He stopped as he noticed Alfie on the far side of the club. 'Hello there, Alf, good to see you. I thought for a moment I'd miss you . . .' Charlie sniffed then drew the machete slowly down the woman's chest.

'Pretty little thing, isn't she? I must say, Alf, you know how to pick your women.'

Alfie stood up, eyes firmly fixed on Charlie who walked slowly towards him. Alfie was aware that Vaughn, as well as the other men who worked for him, had been blindsided by Charlie's attack.

'Leave her alone, Charlie. I don't know what this is about, but I do know your beef isn't with her.'

Charlie Eton grinned again, his fat cheeks folding up in layers. 'You're right, but that doesn't mean I don't want to cop a feel.' Still holding the machete in one hand, Charlie's other hand went under the woman's skirt and between her legs. She shuddered in disgust, tears beginning to roll down her face as Charlie's lardy fingers pulled and grabbed at her knickers.

Sliding his fingers inside her, a lecherous smirk on his face, he groaned in pleasure.

'*Mmmmm,* that's right baby, big daddy's here. Does that feel good, sweetheart?'

Alfie's face screwed up in rage. 'For God's sake, Charlie, let her go! Whatever it is you want, I'll give it you. Just name it.'

'Now that is a big promise, Alfie.'

Alfie, feeling desperate but trying to sound calm, said, '*Please*, Charlie. I'm begging you, just leave her alone. Come on, mate, what do you say?' Getting no response, Alfie brought down his voice to a warm murmur. 'Charlie. Charlie, for me . . . just let her go . . . as a favour, to me . . . you *know* what I'm talking about.'

A tiny flicker of acknowledgement passed over Charlie's face for the briefest moment before it disappeared again. He considered the girl for a second, sneering, then pushed her forcefully aside, sending her flying into the bar and causing her to hit her head on the sharp corner.

Ignoring the blood now pouring from the girl's head, Charlie stared hard at Alfie. A small vein pulsated on his temples. 'I don't know what you're talking about, but I do know that you're getting soft and maybe that's why you think it's okay to run this club right underneath my nose. You know me, I don't like anyone taking away my business, so I thought I'd come and pay you a visit. Aren't you going to offer me a drink, Alf?'

In the silence of the club, Alfie, feeling the pressure beginning to mount and knowing he had to play the game before someone got really hurt, walked behind the bar, his eyes still on Charlie, and grabbed a whiskey bottle off one of the silver shelves.

He unscrewed the top and poured a large measure into one of the glasses before walking back across to Charlie, offering him the drink as he struggled to control his trembling hands. 'What are you on about? I'm not taking your business. We haven't got the same clientele, and we certainly haven't got the same kind of girls as you. I'd say yours were rather *specialised,* wouldn't you?'

Knocking the whiskey back in one, Charlie winced as the burn of the drink reached the back of his throat. 'You must be doing well if you can serve this stuff, which goes back to my point really. There isn't room for two of us. Times are hard, it's not like it used to be, so the way I see it is, *I was here first.'*

Fighting his sense of alarm, Alfie tried to play it down. 'Come off it, Charlie.'

Charlie narrowed his eyes, giving Alfie a cold stare. 'No, *you* come off it. You and I go back a long way, Alf, and that means something, so I'm going to do something I wouldn't normally do; I'm going to give you a choice. You either shut this place down . . . or you work for me.'

Amazed, and knowing this was the last thing he needed to deal with, Alfie cut in. 'What the hell are you talking about?'

Glancing around, Charlie smiled. 'If you let me finish, Alf, then you might understand. The fact is that even I can see it'd be a shame to see this place closed down. I mean it's got a bit of class; you and Vaughnie have done a good job with it. So, I reckon – and this is only because I like you, Alf – that if you kept this place open and do what you gentlemen do best, then we could split the profits, say seventy-thirty to me, then everyone's laughing. Well, I will be anyway.'

Alfie spoke bitterly through gritted teeth, his head beginning to pound. 'You're having a bubble. I would never give you a penny.'

Straight-faced, Charlie lowered his voice, his tone toxic. 'That's where you're wrong. I'm afraid, Alf, whether you like it or not, you've got a decision to make . . . Let me know as soon as possible what you decide. The offer won't be on the table for long.'

'And if I don't?'

'You've known me long enough to realise that *wouldn't* be a good idea.' Then without warning, Charlie purposefully dropped the empty glass he was holding onto the floor, shattering it into tiny fragments before inexplicably leaning forward to give Alfie a kiss on the cheek. 'It's good to see you, Alf, it really is. Next time we shouldn't leave it so long.' And with that Charlie turned and left, and as Alfie watched, stressed and tense, his mind wandered to the anonymous letters and a shadow of fear crossed his face.

* * *

Five minutes later, Alfie was running down Frith Street, pushing past a large crowd of Chinese tourists who were busily taking photos of the outside of Ronnie Scott's jazz club with their iPhones.

Catching up to Charlie's leisurely stroll, Alfie breathlessly blurted out his words. 'Charlie, hold up. Wait! I need to talk to you. It's urgent.'

Surrounded by his men, and looking surprised, Charlie turned around, beads of sweat pricking at his forehead, his overweight body heaving from the exertion.

'I've already told you what the deal is, Alf, it's non-negotiable. I'm not going to change my mind, but of course if you've already made a decision and you know what's good for you, then I'm all ears.'

Turning pale, Alfie shook his head. 'It's not about that.'

Charlie shrugged his shoulders, the weight of his body making it look like a strain. 'Then what?'

Glancing at Charlie's men, Alfie stepped closer in, not wanting anyone but Charlie to hear. He spoke in what was almost a whisper. 'Have you got them? Have you got them as well?'

Unable to fully turn his head to look at Alfie due to how close he was, Charlie, clearly curious whispered back, 'Got what, Alf?'

'You know: Have you got them?'

There was a long pause from Charlie before he said, 'Are you asking what I think you're asking? You want some young, fresh meat?'

Charlie's words were like an electric shock to Alfie. He

36

jumped back, staring at him in horror. 'Jesus Christ, no! Who do you think I am? You know I'm not into that shit.'

Chuckling, Charlie spoke leeringly as he licked his lips. 'Things change. People change. *Tastes* change.'

Wiping his face almost as if he could wipe the strain away, Alfie snapped, 'Well not my tastes, and certainly not for that.'

Stepping back to let a kid on a bicycle go past, Charlie laughed, though his expression showed interest. 'Then what are you talking about?'

'I just . . . I just . . .' With his hands in his jacket pockets, Alfie stopped, nervously curling his fingers around one of the anonymous letters he'd received last week. 'I just . . . well I just wanted to know if you'd got them as well. If he'd sent . . .'

'Got what, Alf? Sent what? For God's sake, you aren't making any sense.'

Retreating and feeling overwhelmed, Alfie, unable to bring himself to say what he wanted to, shook his head. 'You know what, it doesn't matter.'

Charlie stared at Alfie as he backed away. 'Are you okay? You don't look so good. In fact, mate, you look terrible.'

Feeling his heart race, Alfie shrugged. His voice was small. Tight. Strained. 'I'm fine. Are you? Are you fine?'

'Well I'm certainly not acting weird, if that's what you mean.'

Almost in tears, Alfie gave the tiniest of headshakes. 'You know it's not, Charlie, but you know *exactly* what I'm talking about. You know why I'm asking if you're okay.'

Again, another flicker of acknowledgement crossed

Charlie's face and again, it disappeared as quickly as it had appeared. Then matching Alfie's small, strained voice, Charlie mimicked, 'No, Alf, I don't know. I have no idea what you're talking about, and if you want my advice, I'd lay off whatever it is you're sticking up your nose. I'll see you around . . . Oh, and make sure you come to that decision soon.'

As Charlie quickly turned around, feeling a stab of anxiety, he knew *exactly* what Alfie Jennings had been talking about.

At the same time as Alfie Jennings was heading back to his club, Franny was on the other side of town. Panicked, she hurried along the deserted street that ran parallel to King Henry's Dock in Woolwich, checking behind her every few yards as she made a right turn into Ruston Road.

As she crossed a small bit of wasteland, a loud rustling noise coming from near the derelict warehouse startled her. Her chest went tight, and her breathing became shallow as she nervously took a step back, crouching down behind a large discarded oil drum and feeling the chill of the wind coming from off the river Thames.

Hearing the noise again, Franny tried to slow down her breathing, desperate to stop panic overwhelming her. She pushed herself further against the rusty oil drum, not moving for fear of being seen by whoever it was. She stayed crouching for a moment, listening carefully. There it was, and it seemed like it was getting nearer.

Trembling and bracing herself, she slowly peered around the drum, still trying to keep herself as far back as she could, but suddenly she let out a long sigh of relief as a brown, mangey cat rummaged in a pile of rubbish.

Standing up, relieved but annoyed with herself at how on edge she was, Franny felt her phone vibrate. Quickly pulling it out of the pocket of her beige suede jacket, she saw it was Alfie. She ignored it, but it rang again . . . And again. Deciding it was better to take the call, Franny took a deep breath, answering as casually as she could.

'Hey, Alfie! You okay? How's it going?'

'How many frigging times does it take for you to answer?'

Sensing the irritation in his voice, Franny held her own temper and kept her tone as light as possible. She trilled at him. 'Sorry, babe, I didn't hear it. Anyway, what's up?'

'Where are you?'

Absentmindedly, Franny spun around, staring at the small new-build block of flats in front of her. She could hear the tension coming into her own voice. 'Me? Where am I?'

'Well who else do you thinking I'm talking to?'

'I'm . . . I'm . . .'

On the other end of the line, Alfie impatiently cut in. 'Look, it don't matter. Just get yourself down to the club straightaway. We've had a bit of trouble. How long will you be anyway?'

Awkwardly, Franny said, 'The thing is, Alf, I'm a bit busy right now. I mean, do you really need me? Can't you and Vaughn handle whatever it is?'

There was a long pause and Franny could hear Alfie's breathing down the phone as he seethed. Eventually he spoke.

'Listen to me, Fran, I ain't in the mood for this, so whatever the hell it is that you're doing at this time of night: having a bath, painting your toenails, watching a bit of Netflix . . . *I. Don't. Care.* Because all I care about is *you* getting yourself down here asap. *Understand?*'

'Alfie, like I say . . .'

Franny frowned at her phone as Alfie cut off the call. Sighing, she glanced at the time. It was just gone one-thirty in the morning. The night-time traffic in London was almost as bad as it was during the day, so she knew it'd take her at *least* an hour and a half to get back to Soho, and by that time, she had no doubt Alfie would be gunning for her, and that was even before Vaughn got involved. As she saw it, it would be pointless even *trying* to rush back and pretend she'd just been in the bath. And okay, when she did finally get there, Alfie would have a hundred and one questions for her. Still, what else could she do? She'd just have to man up and face that when she saw him, but for now, she figured she might as well stay and do what she was here to do, because after all, she was already in trouble. *Big trouble.*

With her mind made up, Franny defiantly turned off her phone, shoving it back into her pocket as she headed for the row of maisonettes across the road. She tried to push the thought of Alfie, and the guilt, from her mind.

Realising she'd forgotten to bring the key, Franny pressed the silver buzzer on the black wooden door, checking over her shoulder nervously. Getting no answer and not wanting to stand there longer than she had to, Franny pressed again agitatedly, holding down the buzzer this time as she stared directly at the doorbell camera. A second later, she heard the click of the lock and she hurried into the communal entrance where another door just in front of her sprung open, taking her into a private stairwell that led up into a bright, spacious flat overlooking the Thames.

Bree Dwyer stood smiling at Franny. 'Thank you for coming.'

Forcing down her irritation, knowing that a lot of it was caused by her own guilt, something her father had always tried to teach her not to feel, Franny smiled as she looked back at Bree. 'No problem, it was just a bit difficult to get away. I'm not in the best of moods because Alfie . . .'

Bree cut in, concern etched across her face. 'Is he okay?'

Franny nodded as she took off her jacket at the same time as noticing how much weight Bree was losing. 'He's fine, just under a bit of pressure, like we all are. You know how it is.'

Bree's big blue eyes widened. 'So, what's wrong with him?'

With her irritation returning, Franny, not wanting to be reminded of Alfie, snapped, 'I said he's fine. Anyway, I'm not here to talk about him, I'm here to see you, and of course . . .' Franny trailed off and turned around, walking across to the pink cot in the corner of the room. She bent over the hand-carved bar rails. '. . . And of course, this little one.'

Behind Franny, Bree ran her hand through her long blonde hair as she rolled her eyes. She spoke wearily. 'She's only just got to sleep, Fran. Leave her, will you?'

Ignoring Bree, Franny scooped the baby into her arms, bringing her in to her chest, stroking her silky mass of hair. 'Don't be stupid, she's fine; she can sleep anytime.'

'You don't have to snap. I was only saying.'

Rubbing her head, knowing that she shouldn't really take how she was feeling out on Bree, Franny tried to sound warmer. 'Then don't make it difficult for me to see her every time I come here, because unfortunately for me, I can only get away at certain times. You're not looking so good by the way. I hope you're looking after yourself. You can't get ill. What would happen to Mia if you did?'

Bree gave a tight smile as she gathered up Mia's cuddly

toys from the floor. 'Like I said before, I'm eating fine, but maybe if I was able to get out now and then, get some sunshine, perhaps I'd feel better. I feel like a prisoner here, Fran. It feels like I'm back in my old life.'

Triggered again, Franny's hostility returned as she stared at Bree, seeing the dark rings underneath her eyes. The *old life* that Bree was referring to was with her ex-husband, Johnny, who along with his mother, Ma Dwyer, had abused Bree and kept her a virtual slave. And it'd been when she was still married to him, and on one of the few occasions he had let Bree out, that Bree had bumped into Alfie after not seeing him since she was a teenager.

Though what happened next was something that none of them could've predicted. Alfie believed that Franny had left him and stolen his and Vaughn's money, and wasn't coming back, and Bree was desperate for someone to take care of her. Alfie and Bree had quickly got together, wanting each other to help heal their broken hearts.

And of course, it had been a shock. A real shock when she had finally returned to Essex to explain the truth to Alfie about what had *really* happened with his money, to find out that he had already set up with Bree. It had felt like someone had punched her in the stomach. Hurting her more than she cared to admit. So she had done what she always did when something hurt her; she had put up her defenses, coming across as cold and unfeeling. And she was good at doing that. What she *wasn't* good at was feeling, and especially feeling hurt. But being numb to pain was just how she liked it, and that way it was easier for her to forgive Alfie for breaking her heart.

Surprisingly, amid the mess of it all, her and Bree's friendship had blossomed and when Bree had discovered she was pregnant, more than likely with Alfie's baby – though there was a possibility it was Johnny's – Bree had been somewhere between happy and scared.

Bree had told her that she wanted the baby but hadn't wanted the lifestyle that came with Alfie, and she of all people had understood that, because even though she'd been born into this life of crime, there were times, *many times*, that she wished she could get away herself.

Her heart had gone out to Bree, and of course she'd wanted to help, but both of them knew if Bree did go through with the pregnancy, Alfie would never just let her leave with his child to get on with life as she wanted to. So they'd, or rather *she'd* come up with the plan to allow Bree to have her baby in peace. And it'd seemed so simple at first: tell Alfie that Bree had lost the baby, and then afterwards she would help Bree get a flat so she could get on with her life, and she would get on with her life with Alfie, and everything would go back to the way it was. Though the best laid plans always had a way of messing up.

And the way she saw it, Bree had a lot to do with it all going wrong by not having the patience to see this out. All Bree seemed to do now was put pressure on her, something she just didn't need.

Sighing with exasperation, Franny snapped again, 'What are you talking about? Why are you talking about being a prisoner? This is *nothing* like your old life. You've got everything here. And don't forget you were part of this plan as much as I was. You agreed to it all. I never forced you, Bree, you wanted this. But now you're making out like I'm the bad guy here.'

'I'm not. It's just that before Mia was born, it was okay staying here, but it's got worse and worse. This wasn't the plan, Franny, this . . .'

'You're right, this wasn't the plan, because the plan never included you being so ungrateful.'

Bree's face crumpled. 'I am grateful, Franny, though whether you like it or not, I'm a virtual prisoner. You've got to see this is messed up. It isn't right.'

Franny cut in, refusing to feel guilty when all she was doing was trying to help. Her anger rose as she bounced Mia gently on her shoulder. 'What I see is I've put everything on the line for you. I pay everything for you, I've even got Vaughn wanting to go through the accounts because I've been taking money from the club right under their noses. And you know as well as I do that if Alfie found out what I'd done, he'd kill me. You do realise that don't you? But all I seem to get from you is complaints. What do you want from me, Bree? Don't you understand how much *I'm* risking by doing all this? I've *literally* done everything possible to make your life easier, and all it's done is make my life harder. Jesus, Bree, I'm even paying for your other daughter to go to boarding school in Ireland until . . . well until you get your life sorted.'

'You mean, until Alfie goes away.'

Angrily, Franny nodded. 'Yeah, I do mean that, but that's just the way it is.'

'But he may never decide to go. Have you thought about

that? And what then? Am I supposed to be stuck here forever?'

Fuming, her tension headache returning, Franny's face turned red. 'For Christ's sake, Bree, don't whine. Alfie *will* go, just trust me.'

'How?'

'Look, I'm working on it okay? That's all you need to know, and then you can have all the freedom you want, but for now I'm doing this to not only protect myself but you as well. I'm protecting you, Bree, never forget that.'

The two women fell silent, but Franny continued to stare hard at Bree, resenting the pressure she was under.

In one way she understood what Bree was saying, but unfortunately, these things took time. She knew Alfie needed to go away and that's *why* she'd kept encouraging him, but she had to be clever about it; Alfie wasn't stupid, and Bree complaining about it wasn't going to make it happen any quicker.

She just wished Bree could stop being so selfish and realise she was doing all this for her. *All* this because of Bree . . . and of course Mia . . . yes, baby Mia, she would do *anything* for her, which in itself was strange, because she didn't think she'd *ever* get attached to a baby . . . To Mia.

She'd never cared that she wasn't able to have children herself, and she'd certainly *never* felt anything like love for other people's children, until now that was. And it made her feel odd, as if she wasn't in control of her own emotions – which she was always able to keep in check. But somehow, Mia felt part of her, and she honestly didn't know why, but what she did know was that, for Mia's sake, she *had* to make this situation work. But it was getting more and more difficult by the day, and she could feel the pressure coming in from every angle. Vaughn, who didn't trust her before, trusted her even less now. He was on to her big time.

But whatever happened, she knew Alfie could never find out what she was doing. He would kill her, and not just say it or threaten it, he would *actually* go through with it. Although she was a woman, she knew the rules of the life they led. Betrayal and lies came with consequences.

But she'd sacrificed too much already for it to go wrong now, and besides, what would Mia do without her? Yes, she had Bree, but Mia needed someone stronger than Bree to look out for her in life. Loving her was one thing, but loving her *and* being strong was something entirely different.

Trying not to let her exasperation get the better of her, Franny broke the silence. 'Bree, have a little bit more patience, okay? It's going to work out one way or another so just try to remember that everything's for you. Everything I'm doing here is for you.'

'I wonder sometimes.'

Infuriated by Bree again, Franny paced the floor. Her voice was scornful as she asked, 'What's that supposed to mean?'

Looking pale, Bree swallowed hard before speaking quietly. 'You're always so angry with me and you seem . . . you seem to be more interested in Mia than me.'

Franny walked across to Bree and leant down into her face. 'Are you being serious? Are you really jealous of a baby?'

Bree shook her head. 'No of course not! I'm not saying that.'

'Then what are you saying?'

'It's just that you seem different from when we started all this. We were friends and now . . . I just don't know how to explain it.'

Guilt and stress and uncertainty rushed through Franny. 'Maybe because it's bullshit and there is nothing to explain. You need to grow up, Bree, and appreciate what's around you, and if you haven't realised already, this is a really difficult situation I'm in. Don't forget, if it wasn't for me, you wouldn't have Mia. You were happy to run off and get an abortion.'

The shock on Bree's face didn't mar her beauty but the sadness in her eyes shadowed it. 'Franny, *please* don't say that. It wasn't like that, you know I was desperate. I didn't want to bring a child into the life that Alfie leads. All the violence, all the crime. The people that come with it. All the drugs and guns, even the money laundering he does, well it all comes at a price. It's dangerous and I know what it's like to live in fear and I didn't want to bring a baby into that. I *know* it was you who helped me, but being cooped up here, it's difficult. The only person I see is you. I just want to go out, even to the park.'

Playing with Mia's tiny fingers, Franny shook her head. 'I've already told you, we can't risk it, not at the moment.'

Wrapping her blue silk dressing gown round her, Bree appealed, 'When then?'

As Mia started to become grizzly, Franny rocked her, the sound of her cries filling the room. 'The subject's *closed*, okay? I don't want to talk about it so just drop it, Bree.'

'Then maybe it would be better if we just told Alf . . .'

Franny angrily interrupted, 'If we told him? If we told him that we went behind his back, that we've lied to him, that we've been taking money from the business so you can stay here? Are you stupid?'

'No, I . . . I . . . all I'm really trying to say is look around you, Franny; we're in the middle of nowhere, no one will see me if I go out, and if anyone *did* find out, I'd never say it was you. I'd never say you were involved.'

Franny gave Bree a cold stare. 'Bree, unlike you, Alfie's not stupid. He knows you had no money, no real family, and suddenly you have a flat and your daughter's in a good school. He'll know someone helped you, and it won't be long before he works out that someone was me.'

'Then what about Mia? It's not good for her to be kept inside like this.'

'She's fine.'

'No, she's not. I know what's best for her, Franny, she is *my* baby.'

With the expression on her face tight and taut, Franny walked across to Bree, gently giving Mia back to her. She glared at Bree before picking up her jacket to turn away, but at the door Franny stopped, speaking quietly. 'No, Bree, you're wrong, she isn't just yours. You can't push me out of her life that easily.'

6

Shannon trembled as Charlie stood above her in the back room of his club. She was stoned, but not so stoned she hadn't felt the hard kicking Charlie had just given her. The blood ran from her mouth as she gazed up at him. 'I'll do some more okay? I'll work harder, I promise, Char.'

The boot to the side of her head sent her flying back against the table and the ringing in her ear almost muted out what Charlie was screaming at her. 'Too fucking late! You call yourself family and then you have the cheek just to hand me four hundred quid! You cheeky bitch. I can't believe it. I mean, there's me thinking that you're pulling your weight and it turns out you're just mugging me off . . . Four hundred quid for a whole day's work.'

In serious pain, Shannon hugged her knees to her chest as she sat against the wall. 'I tried, I really did.'

Charlie's bellow filled the entire room as he charged

towards Shannon, lifting her up from the floor by her hair. He stuffed the money she'd given him into her mouth, pushing it down her throat, making her gag, making her face turn from red to blue. Her eyes opened wide in terror as she struggled to breathe.

'Tried! Are you being funny? All you have to do is open your mouth or open your legs and bingo! You hardly have to be a frigging genius, but what you want is a free ride ain't it, Shan? You don't want to do any work. You're taking the piss because you think I'm soft for family. Well think again, darlin', because I warned you before about handing over this sort of money.' He shook her hard, and her head flicked back and forth, before he dropped her back on the floor, watching in disgust as she vomited up the contents of her stomach along with the money he'd stuffed in her mouth.

Void of any sympathy, Charlie raged, 'I hope you're going to clear that up. This ain't a free boarding house, Shannon. You're no better than a dirty dog.'

Pulling off her top and quickly trying to clean up the vomit with it, Shannon nodded fearfully. 'I know, Char, and I'm really sorry . . . Look, there, that's better, it's gone. It's all clean now.'

Charlie crouched down to Shannon, curling up his nose at the smell of bile. 'Stop the crying, for God's sake. I don't know what you expect me to do, Shan. I mean, seriously, tell me how I'm supposed to pay for all you girls, *and* pay for this place *and* all the other expenses I have, when all you give me for a day's work is this?'

Unable to stop crying, Shannon wiped her mouth with her top, which was now covered in vomit and dirt. Mucus and snot stuck to her cheek. Then looking so much younger than her sixteen years, she trembled, gazing at Charlie through her swollen, black eye. 'Char, I'm so sorry, you got to believe me. I won't do it again.'

Grabbing another handful of Shannon's hair, Charlie pushed his face onto hers. He spoke in a hiss. 'You say that every time, and every time I give you another chance. Maybe if you spent less time sucking that crack pipe and more time sucking cock, there wouldn't be a problem.'

Shannon nodded her head, but she flinched as Charlie pulled her hair harder and continued to talk. 'It's no good, Shan. If I give you special treatment, all the other girls will want special treatment too, and I can't be doing with that. I can't do with the grief, so you need to say ta-ta.'

Shock crossed Shannon's face, her eyes full of fear. 'What . . . what are you talking about?'

Standing up, Charlie wiped his hands on his tailor-made dark blue jeans. 'I'm letting you go, Shan, I'm not anybody's mug.'

Panicked, Shannon crawled towards Charlie, grappling at his trouser leg. '*Please, please*, Uncle Charlie, I'll try harder. I'll do anything you want, just *please* don't get rid of me.'

Trying to shake her off his leg, Charlie bellowed. 'For God's sake, get up!'

Shannon continued to beg, her voice becoming louder and more high-pitched as hysteria set in. 'No! No, Char, please. I love you. I don't want to go, please don't make me go, I want to stay here and work for you. Please, Uncle Charlie, I'm sorry.'

Turning to one of his men who was sitting reading a magazine in the corner, Charlie spoke abrasively. 'Get her out of here, Frank, *now*!'

Whereupon, Frank picked up Shannon – who scratched and fought like a tomcat – and took her outside to the dark streets of Soho, dumping her still crying and half naked in the alleyway.

'Do you have to do that shit?' A few streets away in the empty club in Sutton Row, Vaughn stared at Alfie as he hoovered up another line of finely cut cocaine.

Standing up straight, Alfie squeezed his nostrils between his fingers as the powder burnt the inside of his nose. He glanced at Vaughn, feeling the numbness at the back of his throat as he spoke. 'I get enough grief from Franny, I don't need you acting like me mother as well. Just lighten up – it's a few lines, that's all. Maybe you need to take a toot, help you chill out more.'

Grabbing Alfie's expensive shirt, Vaughn twisted him around. Both their handsome faces screwed up in rage as they stared at each other, full of hostility. Vaughn's green eyes narrowed. 'I don't need to get out of me head and neither do you. In case that shit has made you forget, we've got a problem with *Charlie*, and I'm not talking about the stuff you put up your nose.'

Pushing Vaughn's hands away, and biting down the rising feeling of stress, Alfie glared. 'I know what we have, and winding yourself up more ain't going to help.'

'Oh, and that shit is, is it?'

Exasperated, Alfie walked around the bar to pour himself

a glass of vodka, trying to even out the buzz of the coke. 'Look, let's just wait for Franny, and then we can decide what we're going to do.'

Vaughn laughed scornfully as he tapped his special-edition diamond Rolex. 'It's twenty past three, mate. Franny ain't coming – not here, anyway . . .'

'What's that supposed to mean?'

Vaughn looked immaculate – despite the altercation with Charlie's men earlier – in his silk grey shirt and Jacob Cohen jeans. He sat down on the bar stool. 'You called Franny almost *two* hours ago and she's still not here. Don't you get it?'

Aggravated, partly by Vaughn and partly by the fact that the cocaine wasn't giving him the high he wanted, the pulse on Alfie's jaw began to throb. 'Get what?'

'What do you think she's been doing?'

Alfie shrugged. 'She was in the bath, or doing her nails, all that crap that girls like to do.'

Bemused, Vaughn stared at Alfie, his voice mocking. 'Is that what she said? Is that what she told you?'

'Well kind of, she said that . . .' Alfie trailed off, remembering that Franny hadn't *actually* told him anything. 'Look, does it matter what she said? She'll be here.'

Reaching for the bowl of cashew nuts, Vaughn popped one into his mouth. He pointed at Alfie. 'Yes, actually it does matter. If she was at home when you called, why isn't she here already? Even me old mum could walk it in fifteen minutes, let alone Franny.'

'You need to back off – that's my woman you're talking about, and I don't like what you're getting at.'

Not interested in doing anything near to backing off, Vaughn continued. 'I don't like it meself, but she ain't to be trusted. You know that, but you just don't want to admit it.'

Knocking back the vodka and immediately pouring himself another drink, Alfie said, 'You've just got it in for her. Ever since she took that money, you've been looking for something to hang on her.'

'Well do you blame me? She's screwed us over once and she's capable of doing that again.'

Angrily, Alfie threw the glass to the side. He rubbed the stubble on his chin. 'She ain't like that.'

'Oh, please, Alf, that's exactly what you said last time, yet she took two million quid right from under our noses.'

'She did that to save her family.'

'Whatever the reason she still did it and even to this day we ain't got our money back. Wake up, son, and see what's in front of your face.'

Trying his hardest not to grab Vaughn and give him a good hiding, Alfie slammed his fist down on the bar. 'First off, never call me son, and secondly where do you get off trying to cause trouble? Don't get me wrong, it pissed me off as well and it caused us a whole load of grief, but just cos someone's late don't mean they're up to no good. Fuck me, that would mean most of the population at one time or another were mugging each other off.'

Vaughn snorted with derision. 'Why all of a sudden the rose-tinted glasses, eh? You need to smash those fuckers up and see what's going on in front of your nose.'

'So where's your proof then? You ain't got any have you?'

'If you must know I heard her on the phone earlier, telling someone not to call her. She was well agitated. She's up to something.'

Alfie fell silent as he sat in the empty club trying to process what Vaughn was telling him. There was no way Franny would go behind his back. Mug him off. Do the dirty. No way at all. Okay, she'd taken the money but as he kept telling Vaughn, that was different. It was to save somebody's life. He couldn't be angry for that. And it'd been a one-off. In all the time he'd known her, over all the years, she'd never once given him reason to mistrust her. *He* was the one not to be trusted. Him, not her. *He'd* been the one who'd broken Franny's heart with Bree. He'd also been the one who'd slept about at the beginning of their relationship and he'd been the one who'd gambled money and invested in projects without telling her. But her? Franny? No, she was loyal. Loving. Faithful . . . Honest. Yes, she could also be cold and hard, but that was only because of the way she'd been brought up among the gangsters and faces of London. She wouldn't have survived or made it to the top any other way than being the way she was, which meant at times she had to be ruthless, but none of that equated to her hurting him or Vaughn, none of it spelt that she was going to betray him in any way, and it pissed him off that Vaughn thought it was okay to insinuate that. 'Wind your neck in and shut the fuck up about Franny.'

'I will, when you can tell me where she is, because clearly she ain't at home. If you ask me . . .'

Cutting in straightaway, Alfie roared, 'I didn't ask you, so *leave* it!'

Vaughn's eyes glinted with anger. 'I know you didn't, but I'm telling you anyway. She's obviously boning someone at the same time as planning to rip us all off.'

That was it. Unable to control his temper any longer, Alfie dived over the bar, grabbing hold of Vaughn, bringing his fist hard into his face. 'Say that again and I'll kill you. You hear me?'

He banged Vaughn's head against the bar but, undeterred, Vaughn fought back. His face red, his words harsh.

'So go on then, Alf, tell me where she is. Tell me where she *fucking* is!'

'Where's who?' Franny stood at the entrance of the club, looking at the two men. She gave a small smile to Alfie before walking up to kiss him, then turning to Vaughn, her gaze full of hatred, she said, 'Where's *who*, Vaughn? I hope you weren't talking about me?'

'Where've you been, Franny?' Vaughn smirked as he questioned her.

Calmly, but with her heart racing, Franny answered him. 'I've been at home, doing me nails.'

Alfie, having let go of Vaughn, pushed his fringe out of his eyes. 'Told you.'

'Let's see then.'

Incredulously, Franny continued to glare at Vaughn, her chest tightening as she tried to keep down the panic. 'Excuse me?'

'Let's see your nails.'

'What the fuck is wrong with you?'

Slowly, Vaughn sauntered across to Franny. He grabbed her hands roughly and examined them.

'Don't look like you've been doing your nails to me.'

Locking eyes with Vaughn, Franny pulled her hands away. Her voice icy cold, she said, 'I did my toenails. What? Are you going to pull off my shoes now to see my polish?'

Matching Franny's animosity, Vaughn nodded. 'If I have to.'

From behind Vaughn, Alfie stepped in. 'Of course he's not. Not unless he wants to go through me. Well do you? Cos I'm in the mood for a fight now.'

Turning to Alfie, Franny shook her head. 'Alfie, don't. He ain't worth it. He's got a problem with me because of what I did. I get that, but it's stupid to fight among ourselves.'

'How noble of you.'

Ignoring Vaughn, Franny continued to speak to Alfie. 'I'm sorry I took so long – I wasn't feeling so great – but I'm here now and I'm all ears.'

As Alfie went to sit down, Franny followed but was held back by Vaughn grabbing her arm. He whispered in her ear, 'You and I both know you weren't at home, and I'll find out what you're up to, Franny Doyle, and then I'm going to bring you down and watch you burn like a towering fucking inferno.'

Half an hour later, Alfie, agitated, having explained what had happened with Charlie said, 'So that's the bottom line, Fran, it's a fucking mess. The last thing we want to do is fork out money to him, but at the same time, no one wants a war. This is already going to have a knock-on effect with the punters. Who's going to want to come to a club when there's a possibility of some fucker coming through the door with a machete?'

Taking a sip of her lemonade, Franny, not looking the best herself and having listened intently to what Alfie had been saying asked, 'But can't you talk to him, Alf? You've known him since you were kids. You two used to hang out together.'

Fighting being distracted by what Vaughn had said about her, Alfie shrugged, hating the fact that jealousy and doubt were beginning to creep over him. Everything seemed like it was out of control, and he didn't like that feeling one little bit. 'When we were little, and that don't hold any weight anymore – not really. This is Charlie we're talking about. Once he's made up his mind, that's it. It proper feels like we've been snookered. Have an all-out war with the geezer or . . .'

Vaughn interrupted, his gaze firmly on Franny as it had been for the last half an hour, wanting to make her feel as uncomfortable as possible. 'You're not thinking about actually paying him, are you? Cos that ain't ever going to happen on my watch, Alf. This is my business as well, and I'm not handing my money over to some nonce.'

With the stress beginning to weigh heavy, Alfie slammed his fist on the bar in front of him. 'Do I look fucking stupid? We just have to work out another agreement with him, cos he ain't going away. If we can bring down how much he wants . . .'

Vaughn snapped, 'I already told you, that's not going to happen. Look, I think the best thing we can do is get some kip. We'll talk tomorrow when we're all thinking straight . . .

Oh and, Franny, don't forget I want to go over those accounts with you.'

Back in Soho Square, in the large, cream and gold decorated bedroom of Alfie and Franny's townhouse, Alfie lay on the king-size bed, smiling at Franny as she got undressed. He'd decided he wasn't going to tell her what Vaughn had been saying about her. It was stupid for him to even get wound up by it. No doubt the cocaine, useless as it was, had played a part in his paranoia. In all that was happening. The letters. The club. Franny was his constant. Beautiful and loyal, but more importantly, Franny was his, *all* his, and no one was going to try to tell him otherwise. But as Alfie watched Franny climb onto the bed, a sudden unease crossed over him as his gaze wandered down to her feet and he noticed her unpolished toenails.

7

It was just past 6am and Alfie couldn't sleep. Hadn't slept. Though it was less about the cocaine that ran around his veins and more about the feelings that rushed around his body.

He'd stayed awake all night watching Franny sleep fretfully, tossing and turning, and it'd taken all his willpower *not* to wake her up and ask her a thousand questions about the truth of where she'd actually been. More to the point, *who* she'd been with. *Shit. Shit* . . . He hated feeling like this. Jealousy was not something he wanted to deal with; the last time he was jealous, he'd done someone a serious injury.

He didn't have the headspace to cope with it, not on top of everything else. Jesus, this was the last thing he needed, and part of him was pissed off with Vaughn for making him feel like this. The man hadn't had any solid evidence about anything, yet he'd just piled a whole heap of doubt in his head.

Annoyed, Alfie got up and pulled on a pair of jeans and a jumper. He needed to get some fresh air. Lying in bed thinking was only making everything worse – a lot worse – and the last thing he wanted to do was have a blowout row with Franny.

After striding outside, Alfie stood, leaning against the wall, taking long, deep drags on his cigarette before stubbing it out on the wall of Barclays bank, situated on the corner of Greek Street. He felt the chill of the early morning air as he watched a dustcart speed down the road, seeing it scrape against the wing mirror of a badly parked black cab, but it was good to get out.

Turning away and immediately lighting another cigarette, Alfie crossed the street, heading for one of the cafés in Rathbone Place to get himself a coffee.

He couldn't think straight. Maybe he *should* get away. As much as it was good to be back in Soho, especially this particular part of it – the small square a hideaway from the bustle of the West End – it hadn't brought him the peace of mind he'd hoped for. Everything was becoming a mess. The letters. The tension between Vaughn and Franny. And now Charlie had his dog in the fight, it was becoming one big fucking nightmare. And as much as he hated to admit it, he just wanted to run.

Maybe it was best if he threw in the towel at the club, or maybe like Franny had suggested, he should go and speak to Charlie on his own. There was a lot of history between Charlie and him. There was even a time when he'd helped Charlie out and he'd never asked anything in return. So maybe – though it would rile him to have to – if he went and *really* pulled the favour card, then maybe Charlie might think again . . . Fuck, he didn't know what he . . . A sound broke into his thoughts. He spun around. The street was now deserted but he waited for a moment, trying not to let his jumpiness overwhelm him.

He took a deep breath to calm himself down, steadying his breathing before continuing to walk, but then he stopped again, listening intently . . . There it was, and it was coming from over there. He stared at the trees in the near corner of Soho Square Gardens. He could see someone hiding there.

His heart thumped and prickles of sweat beaded on his forehead as he walked towards the black gates of the gardens, which were still locked, but he knew another way in. Alfie walked around to the south side, climbing up on the bench, which gave him easy access to vault over the railings.

Cautiously, he walked towards the middle of the square, creeping around the back of the mock-Tudor, black and white timber building in the centre of the gardens. Feeling the cosh in his pocket, Alfie brought it out as he slunk along.

He listened again for the sound, and making sure nobody was behind him, he followed the noise, creeping past the trees and shrubs to crouch down behind the old oak in the corner of the square as the mist of the early morning lifted.

Still gripping the cosh tightly, Alfie craned around the corner of the large and gnarled tree trunk. Taken aback he stared, placing the club back into his pocket. 'Jesus, are you all right?'

Shannon Mulligan stared at the man, dried blood and crusty mucus caked onto her face. She squinted through her swollen black eye as she shivered with cold, her words slightly muffled as her torn lip made it difficult for her to speak. 'I'm fine.'

He moved nearer, crouching down to the girl. 'You don't look it, love – is there anybody you want me to call?'

Shannon shook her head, wishing the person would just disappear. She wasn't in the mood for chat, especially from some posh-looking geezer. Not that he sounded posh; he sounded as common as she did. Still it was obvious by the way he dressed that he had a bit of money.

Looking worried, Alfie spoke again. '*Please*, there must be something I can do.'

'Yeah, piss off!'

Unoffended and clearly not one to be put off, he tried again. 'Have you been here all night? Look, you can't stay here.'

A flash of annoyance crossed Shannon's face. 'I can do what I bleedin' want, mate – who are you anyway, the park police? No, you ain't, so now you've done your do-gooding, you can fuck right off and leave me alone.'

He grinned. 'Fiery ain't you?'

'Nosy, ain't you?'

'What's your name?'

Shannon curled up her face in a sneer but instantaneously

regretted it as pain shot through her injured lip. 'What's yours?'

'I'm Alfie.'

Shannon shrugged, her voice dripping with sarcasm. 'Well that's very nice for you, now like I said before, *Alfie*, can you piss off?'

'You look cold.' And without waiting for a reply, Alfie took off his jacket and tried to wrap it round Shannon's shoulders, but she scurried away, pushing herself back against the tree. 'My name ain't Oxfam, you know. I don't need your skanky jacket.'

Alfie laughed. The jacket in question had cost him a couple of grand. At the thought of it, he laughed again, something he couldn't remember doing for a long time. 'Then why don't you just tell me your name, and after that, I can buy you a cup of tea. You've made me laugh, which I can't remember doing for a long time, so it's the least I can do for you.'

Shannon scowled. 'Am I some sort of fucking joke to you?'

Lighting up yet another cigarette, Alfie shook his head. 'No, of course not. I like you, that's all.'

'Weirdo, you don't even know me. You going to give me one of them or what?' Shannon gestured to Alfie's cigarettes. He handed her the box and with her dirty, bitten-down fingernails she grabbed one eagerly, putting it into her swollen mouth before allowing Alfie to light it for her.

'So, are you going to let me buy you something to eat then?'

Shannon, feeling more at ease with this stranger, cocked

her head as she looked at Alfie. 'No, but you could give me a tenner.'

'Why do you want a tenner?'

'Cos I ain't got one.'

Going into his pocket, Alfie pulled out a wad of money. He winked at her. 'That's a good enough reason as any. I like a person who can be straight.'

Amazed, Shannon said, 'You're *really* going to give me ten quid?'

'Yeah, that's what you asked for isn't it?'

She looked at Alfie suspiciously. 'I'm not giving you a blow job if that's what you're after; for starters I charge *twenty* quid, but anyhow, my mouth hurts too much to do it.'

Alfie shook his head sadly. 'No, darlin', that's not what I'm looking for . . . I tell you what, why don't you take this.'

'Fifty quid!' Shannon looked at the money and then at Alfie, then back at the money before saying, 'You really are weird, mate. Is this how you get off, get your kicks?'

Alfie laughed again. 'It certainly isn't.'

'But no one gives money away for nothing.'

It was Alfie's turn to shrug. 'I do. Go on, darlin', just take it.'

As he pushed the money into her hand, caught underneath the ten-pound notes was a piece of paper. It fluttered down to the muddy ground. Frowning, Alfie picked it up but when he did so he physically recoiled as if an electric bolt had gone through him. His head swam, and a wave of nausea passed over him. He'd forgotten he had one of the letters in his pocket.

Spotting the change in Alfie's demeanour, and seeing how ashen he'd suddenly become, Shannon asked, 'What's that?'

Beginning to tremble, Alfie rubbed his chest, feeling the familiar tightness return as a cold sweat ran down his back. Scrunching the letter up and pushing it as far down in the pocket of his jeans as possible, Alfie tried to sound as casual as he could. 'Nothing . . . it's . . . it's just a letter.'

'Must be something bad to make you look like that. You've gone proper pale, mate. Go on, what is it?'

Glancing back at her, Alfie pulled himself together. 'Now who's the nosy one?'

Something like a shy smile touched the corners of Shannon's mouth. It was the first time anyone had been nice to her in longer than she could remember. In fact, when she really thought about it, apart from Charlie giving her the odd free rock of crack now and then, there'd been no one in her life who had been particularly kind to her. The only thing she remembered of her mother was her being out of it on heroin. And as for her auntie who took her in, well, she would hardly describe her as the warmest of women.

Not wanting to think too much about the past, Shannon turned her attention back to Alfie, wiping her nose on the back of her hand as flakes of dried blood fell out of her nostrils. 'Suit yourself, don't tell me then.'

Changing the subject completely, Alfie asked, 'How old are you anyway?'

Shannon paused, contemplating her reply, before confidently saying, 'I'm twenty.'

'You look younger than that.'

Trying to appear casual, Shannon shrugged again. 'You asked me how old I was, not how old I looked, and I couldn't care less if you believe me or not.'

Feeling the twinge in his knee from crouching, Alfie stood up. 'Okay, well if I can't persuade you to let me buy you a cup of tea, I'll be off . . . But look after yourself, little miss nameless, and like I say, I'm Alfie, and if you ever need a chat or just somewhere to have a drink, pop into my club. It's on Sutton Row. It's just before you get to the corner of Falconberg Mews . . . And here, if you won't take my jacket at least take my jumper. It's going to be cold today.'

Back in Woolwich, Bree had made up her mind. Even though it was cold, the sun was shining through the window, and there was no way she was going to spend yet *another* afternoon cooped up inside.

Yes, she'd promised Franny not to go out, but then Franny had promised her that the days wouldn't run into weeks and the weeks wouldn't run into months. What was she expected to do? And besides, it wasn't hurting anyone, not if she was careful, and one thing she was good at was being careful; she'd spent all her married life having to sneak and creep about, just so she was able to get out for a few hours here and there, so she was now somewhat expert at it.

Smiling at her daughter who was fast asleep in the cot, Bree picked her up, careful not to wake her as she wrapped her up tightly in a pink cashmere blanket. She gently placed her in the baby stroller Franny had bought from Harrods, when she'd first found out she was pregnant. Before things had got tense between them.

Checking she'd got her keys, Bree bounced Mia down the stairs in the stroller. At the bottom, before walking into the communal area, she took a deep breath. She shouldn't feel guilty about going outside. There was nothing wrong with it, nothing at all. But then, why did she feel like she was doing something so bad? It wasn't a crime, and it wasn't Franny who had to stay indoors day in and day out, seeing and speaking to nobody, and as much as Franny refused to hear her when she said that living this way reminded her of her old life, that's exactly what it felt like, and all the old triggers, all her old demons seemed like they were coming back.

She felt down, lonely. She'd even go as far as saying she was depressed, and she wanted out, but at the moment it seemed like Franny was holding all the cards, not just because she was indebted to her for what she'd done by helping her to keep Mia, but also financially. And she was certainly grateful, but right now she refused to let the thought of Franny stop her taking Mia out for some fresh air. After all, she was a grown woman and she could do what she liked.

With a renewed sense of determination, Bree stood in the communal hallway of the maisonettes, pushing away her guilt and hesitating only for a moment before she stepped out into the sunshine, feeling the warm wind on her face.

She closed her eyes and took a deep breath. The last time she'd been outside was when she'd gone into labour with

Mia, and Mia had come early, so that made it almost four and a half months ago.

It was crazy, she knew that and she was embarrassed to admit even to herself that over time she'd become slightly wary of Franny, even going so far as to say she was *afraid* of her. Not that she thought Franny would actually hurt her, but there was an intensity about Franny that hadn't been there before, as well as an unhealthy concern for Mia.

On the odd occasion when she *had* tried to stand up for herself, well she was no match for Franny, and before she knew it – and maybe she was just being silly to think it – but in some strange way she felt Franny was keeping her prisoner.

Sighing, Bree crossed over the road in the direction of Woolwich Church Street, not wanting her thoughts to ruin the day. She pushed the buggy along the pavement, minding the potholes, strewn rubbish and discarded pieces of well-chewed gum, and taking in the surroundings she'd never really explored before.

She'd managed to find a five-pound note in one of her jacket pockets, which must have been there from before the birth, and now she was going to get herself a McDonald's. It was stupid really, but she couldn't help smiling at the idea of being able to order a cheeseburger without anyone telling her she wasn't allowed.

Cutting through a back alleyway, Bree sighed heavily as she unsuccessfully tried to stop thinking about her situation. How things had come to this, she didn't know. One minute she was with Alfie thinking about their future, and the next? The next his long-term girlfriend was helping her hide out. It was all such a mess.

Although she'd walked out on Alfie, that didn't make her stop caring . . . or stop loving him for that matter. Not that she'd *ever* tell Franny that. That was the last thing she would do, and she'd no doubt that it was possibly the last thing Franny would want to hear. The problem wasn't Alfie, the problem had always been his lifestyle. And there was no way he was ever going to give it up. It was what made him tick. It was in his DNA but bringing a baby into that life and all that came with it – the danger, the people, the uncertainty – it just wasn't the way she wanted to live.

It hadn't been an easy decision and as much as it hurt to the point it felt at times like a sharp object was pressing into her chest, it'd been the right one, and she knew however much she missed, loved and adored Alfie, doing the right thing for Mia had to come first.

Having cleaned herself up in the public toilets, Shannon was now almost skipping down the road. She smiled to herself as she felt the money that Alfie had given her in her pocket. He'd been a strange guy. An odd guy. He hadn't been bad-looking, actually he'd been really handsome, but it was weird that somebody, *especially* a bloke, had given her something for nothing.

She'd half expected him to be waiting around the corner for her, playing out some pervy role-play, a fantasy; him acting as her stalker and chasing her along the streets, only for it to end up with them having sex down some dirty, cold alleyway. But he hadn't been there. He was nowhere to be seen. And although she hadn't wanted to get off with him and be forced to earn out the fifty quid he'd given her, she'd actually been slightly disappointed because it'd been nice just to talk to somebody who didn't treat her like she was something nasty stuck to the bottom of their shoe.

Still, it didn't matter because now she'd be able to buy some decent crack off her dealer, and not just one measly rock.

Just the thought of it made her lick her lips, but they were so sore. Bloody Charlie. Maybe she'd give him a few days to calm down and then go around and see if he would take her in again. This wasn't the first time he'd thrown her out and she doubted it'd be the last. Anyhow, she wasn't going to worry about it because today had turned out better than she'd ever expected it to. If she'd been with Charlie right now all she'd have been doing was sucking some stinking old fellow's cock, but as it stood, she was going to be able to get high. She giggled to herself. Life really wasn't so bad after all.

She didn't even mind that she'd have to travel further this time, as her dealer had moved. Yes, she could get some stuff from round Soho but the problem with that was all the dealers knew Charlie, which meant he'd find out she'd bought some rocks, which would mean he'd want to know where she got the money from. Besides, her dealer's crack was some of the best around, and that's all that really mattered.

Delighted at the thought of what the rest of the day held, Shannon crossed over Samuel Street by Woolwich Dockyard, making her way to Warspite Road, which was on the other side of the dual carriageway.

Running across the busy road at the same time as her sticking two fingers up and screaming obscenities at the passing lorry beeping its horn, Shannon hurried along, pulling up the sleeves of Alfie's jumper.

As she turned into the quiet road full of derelict houses and empty factory units, Shannon stopped in her tracks, before running around the side of an old empty warehouse. She stared, squinting through the bright sunshine as she watched a woman pushing a buggy along the alleyway.

She continued to stare, and she couldn't be sure, but she thought it was . . . yes, it was. It was her. It was Bree. She hadn't seen her for quite a while but now she was looking properly, there was no mistaking that face. The last time she'd seen Bree was ages ago. What was she doing round here?

About to wave, Shannon paused, and having thought for a moment, she stepped back into the shadows. Then, keeping her eyes firmly on Bree, Shannon pulled out her phone and dialled a number.

'It's me, I thought you might be interested . . . Guess who I've just seen pushing a pram.'

8

I've got a bit of time, I'll be around in about half an hour. See u soon. Kiss to Mia. F x

Bree stared at the text in horror as she sat in the corner of McDonald's finishing off her meal deal. Her heart raced and she didn't know if it was the cheeseburger that was suddenly making her feel queasy, but she was overwhelmed with nausea as she got up and rushed out into the street.

She ran back across the road, pushing the buggy with Mia crying loudly as she sprinted past the grey railings at the top of Ruston Road, passing a young girl, who was clearly out of it on drugs and sitting with bloodshot eyes, sweating and shaking, slumped over on the pavement.

With the buggy bouncing all over, Bree dashed down the road, panic setting in.

Getting to the door, Bree's hand shook as she rummaged

in her bag for the keys. God, where were they? She didn't have them. *Shit* . . . Alarmed and panic making it difficult for her to think clearly, Bree's heart raced as she looked again at the bottom of her small clutch bag. She glanced nervously over her shoulder as she checked her pockets.

'Mia, please don't cry, Mummy's trying to find something.' She tried to smile at her daughter who was still screaming and, annoyed at herself for even thinking it was ever going to be okay to go out without Franny's permission, she rocked the pram. 'Sshhhh, Mia, it's okay, darling, Mummy will get you inside soon.' Her voice cracked with emotion and she fought back tears. She had no idea what she was going to do, and she was genuinely afraid of what Franny would say – what she'd *do* – if she found her out here.

Looking back down at her daughter, Bree suddenly gripped the pram and closed her eyes, an overwhelming sense of relief hitting her. The keys. Of course, she'd put them under Mia's blanket. Grabbing them quickly, Bree fumbled and hurriedly put the right key in the lock, opening the outer entrance before rushing over to the door that led up to her flat.

Inside and aware that the clock was ticking, Bree tried to heave the buggy up the stairs, but it was too heavy and quickly she took Mia out, taking the stairs two at a time.

Throwing off the blanket, Bree placed Mia back into her cot before charging back down, dragging the empty buggy up and pushing it into the corner of the room where it was always kept. Checking she hadn't missed anything, Bree heard her front door open.

'Hi, only me!'

'Hi, Fran.' She could hear her voice on edge as she tried to calm herself, then looking down, horrified, she realised she still had her jacket on. Hearing Franny's footsteps getting nearer, she furiously tugged it off, throwing it on the floor before kicking it under the chair.

Wiping the perspiration off her face and drying the sweat from her palms on the sides of her trousers, self-consciously, Bree smiled as Franny stepped into the room carrying a large shopping bag.

'Hey, good to see you. It's a nice surprise.' Her voice trilled, and Bree wasn't sure if it was paranoia, but it somehow sounded too loud for the small space. With all the running around the pressure was getting to her.

'You look hot,' Franny said gruffly.

Bree could hardly get her breath and it felt like she'd been stripped of air. 'Me? Do I? I'm fine. Yeah, God yeah, totally.'

Franny's gaze was unwavering. 'If you're fine, why do you look so flustered?'

Animated, Bree waved her hands around. 'It's just Mia, she won't stop crying. Gets a bit much after a while.'

Cutting her eyes in annoyance at Bree, Franny, unable to deal with having to prop Bree up emotionally on top of everything else, snapped, 'She's a baby, Bree, what do you expect? I hope you haven't just left her there crying?' She walked towards Mia, scooping her up in her arms, and immediately Mia fell silent. 'See, that's all she needed, a bit of TLC. I sometimes wonder about you and where your head's at. You can be so selfish. Don't leave her like that, you hear me? And why are her hands cold again? Have you had this window open?'

Bree nodded. She didn't care what Franny thought as long as she didn't think she'd been out. 'Yes . . . er . . . it was a bit hot.'

'Well that's stupid to have it open by her, she'll get ill. She'll get a chest infection. It's common sense, Bree.'

Bree gave a tight smile. 'I'm sorry.'

Agitated, partly from the guilt she felt from what she was doing not only to Alfie but also to Bree, Franny walked over to pour herself a glass of water as Mia nuzzled happily in her neck. She shrugged. 'Well it ain't me you need to say sorry to . . .' She trailed off before begrudgingly adding, 'Anyway, how are you?'

Not seeming so much on edge, Bree sat on the chair by the window. 'I'm okay – the usual.'

The tension in the air between the two women was palpable as the room fell silent. Eventually Franny said, 'Look, I can't stay long, I just brought some shopping for you and there's a few bits for Mia as well. I better go. Alfie will be wondering where I am and I've got to speak to Vaughn today, which I'm not looking forward to. Anyway, I'll call you.' Kissing Mia, Franny handed her back to Bree, walking out of the room and down the stairs without looking back.

Letting out a long sigh of relief, Bree turned and put Mia back in her cot. She smiled at her daughter, who was attempting to chew on her own hand.

Although going outside hadn't gone as smoothly as it

could've done, thinking about it she felt better than she had done in a long while. She'd needed to get out and so had Mia. Maybe next time she'd go to the park. She had to be careful of course but that . . .

'Bree?' Franny's voice behind her made her jump, cutting into her thoughts. She swivelled around to come face-to-face with Franny who stared at her coldly, her eyes dark and emotionless, her face drawn and taut.

'Bree?'

Pushing herself back against the cot, Bree began to shake, unsure quite what was going on as Franny repeated her name with a tone that forced a chill through her body.

'Bree . . .'

Bree's voice was only just audible. 'Yes?'

Stepping in closer, Franny towered above Bree. 'What have you done?'

Still shaking, Bree shrugged. 'Nothing, I don't know what you're talking about.'

'Don't lie to me, Bree.'

'I'm not. What's this about, Franny? You're acting really strange.'

Franny's voice held an ominous tone. 'Don't pretend, Bree, you know exactly what you've done.'

Giggling nervously, Bree tried to lighten the mood. 'This is silly – just tell me.'

'You've been out, haven't you?'

Feigning shock, Bree shook her head furiously. 'Of course not! No way! That's absurd. It's crazy, I don't know where you got that idea from.'

'You dropped the receipt, Bree. You should've been more

careful if you wanted to fool me.' From behind her back, Franny produced the McDonald's receipt and waved it in the air. 'I told you not to go out, didn't I?'

'That's not mine, it's . . .'

Franny shouted, giving Mia a start, causing her to begin to scream again. 'Enough, Bree! I'm not stupid! That's why you looked so flustered, isn't it? That's why you looked so guilty when I came in.'

Bree pushed Franny out of the way, stepping around her. 'Yes, yes, it is, and I shouldn't have to feel guilty.'

Franny's face flushed red. 'That's right, you shouldn't, and if this was a normal situation you wouldn't, but it ain't normal. I have put my *life* on the line for you. You hear that? My *life*. And all you've done is gone out and risk it. It's a joke – you talk about not having to feel guilty, well that's exactly what I do. I feel guilty. You try lying to Alfie and then have to see him every day. Even keeping you here, well the truth is, I felt bad. I knew it was for the best, but you know something, Bree, I ain't going to feel bad anymore. Why should I? Especially if you don't care, and let's face it, I shouldn't even be helping you because when it boils down to it, all you are is some woman who fucked my man.'

Bree looked hurt. 'Franny, please, you know that's not how it went. I didn't know about you, and I'll always be sorry, but I thought we got through that.'

Franny's face screwed up. 'You got through it, I just have to learn to live with the hurt.'

'But . . .'

'I don't want to talk about it anymore, you hear me? The

only thing that I want to talk about is you becoming a liability to me.'

'But . . .'

Hating the fact she'd shown her emotions by opening up about Alfie, something she'd been taught by her father never to do, Franny cut Bree off in anger. 'What did I say? No fucking buts, Bree! If someone sees you, I'm at risk. Me. Not you. Me. I'm the one who'll have a bullet in their head. You obviously don't care what happens to me.'

'I do, of course I do.'

'Well let me tell you, you have a funny way of showing it. And what about Mia? What would happen to Mia if I was dead?'

Bree looked shocked. 'I . . . I . . .'

Pacing around the room, Franny's eyes narrowed. 'You haven't thought of that, have you? Mia needs me, Bree. You're fine as someone to change her and hold her but what real use are you to her?'

'What are you talking about, Franny? I'm her mum.'

Another flash of anger crossed Franny's face. 'That's just a title, Bree. I've seen the way you've been these past few months. Weak. Needy. Mia doesn't need someone like that around her.'

'Franny, this is crazy, she needs me.'

'Keep on telling yourself that, Bree, if it makes you feel better. But I don't think she'd appreciate you risking everything so you could have a fucking Big Mac.'

'That's not why I took her out.'

'You're a selfish bitch. You keep forgetting that you agreed to this. I didn't force you.'

Trying her best not to cry, Bree chewed on her lip. 'I didn't know it was going to be this long. You've got to see it from my point of view, Franny. Think how you'd feel.'

'I know I'd do whatever it was that was needed, no matter how long that took.'

'Well Mia needed some fresh air.'

Hollering at Bree, Franny's eyes blazed with fury. 'Then open the fucking window because what Mia needs above everything else is to be safe, and by you taking her out, you have risked everything you wanted for her. How can I protect her if I'm dead, Bree? Because if Alfie finds out that's what will happen, and then you won't have a chance, sweetheart, because you're no match for Alfie. You can't stand up to him. You're not me, and not only that, Alfie will hate you. He'll take his daughter and it'll be him who's calling the shots. It'll be him who decides on Mia's life. You'll just be some pretty thing in the corner watching your daughter become something you don't want her to be, and there'll be nothing that you can do to stop it. Do you want Mia to end up like me?'

Bree sounded puzzled. 'What do you mean?'

It was Franny's turn to fight back the tears. 'Look at me, Bree . . . *Look* at me! What do you see, hey? You see someone who's strong, right? Who's tough. Who's hard. Who's cold. Yeah, you do, but that's all you see because that's all there is to me. There's so much missing because I don't feel, not the way most people feel, and I don't love, not like you. I don't have that thing inside me to know what it is to be a woman. And you know why? You know why I don't? Because I was brought up by someone like

Alfie, in the kind of life that Alfie leads, with the kind of people that Alfie has around him. And I don't want that for Mia, and if you had any sense neither would you. You wouldn't risk going out. You'd wait, however hard it is, you'd wait. Because if I'm not here, if I'm not around anymore, believe me that little girl will be fed to the lions . . . And maybe this is the reason.'

'Reason for what?'

Franny gazed at Bree evenly. 'Why Mia is actually one of the few people I can truly feel in my heart. Because I *know* better than most people what it's like to live that life, and I can stop it happening to her. I can stop her ending up like me . . . So at least now you'll understand and hope-fully realise why I *have* to do what I'm going to do. It's best for both of you.'

Bree began to sound panicked. 'What is?'

'I wish I didn't have to do this, Bree, but you've given me no choice, and in the long term, I know you'll thank me.'

Bree began to step away as Franny walked towards her. A strange look crossed her face.

'What are you doing? What are you going to do?'

'Bree, look, you've got nobody to blame but yourself, so until I can get Alfie to take a break, this is what's going to happen . . .' Suddenly Franny grabbed Bree's arm, twisting it behind her back before marching her towards the bedroom. With Bree no match for Franny's strength, she was powerless to stop Franny throwing her in, and locking the door from the outside.

Hammering on the door, Bree screamed in distress. 'Let

me out! Let me out! Franny, you can't do this! Franny, this is crazy!'

Walking across to pick Mia up who'd settled herself down, Franny smiled at the baby, calling out to Bree as she did. 'Stop shouting, you're going to upset Mia.'

'Franny, have you heard yourself? This is madness. Just let me out.'

Cradling Mia in one arm, Franny began to unpack the shopping with her other. 'Save your breath, Bree.'

'You can't keep me in here forever.'

Bemused, Franny kissed Mia's head, her voice full of bafflement. 'I've no intention to! And I never wanted to do this. You make it sound like this is what I want. Believe me, I'm not getting any pleasure out of this and if you'd listened to me, then none of this would've happened. Look, you'll only be in there when I'm not here.'

'And what about Mia? What's she supposed to do? You're just going to leave her out there in the cot?'

With a wide grin, Franny mouthed silently to Mia, '*Your mummy's crazy*,' before answering Bree and saying, 'What's wrong with you? You'll have Mia in there with you. You'll have everything you need. You've got the en-suite bathroom and you can have the kettle to make yourself a tea. I'll cook you some food, so you won't be hungry, and Mia will have her bottles.'

Bree's voice dripped with anger. 'You've got it all worked out, haven't you?'

'Well someone has to, and anyway, you should be thanking me that I'm going to so much trouble. And when Alfie does go away, which I'm working on, then it'll all be over. You won't have to live like this anymore, and maybe we'll even look back on this and laugh.'

But as Bree Dwyer sank to the bedroom floor, putting her head in her hands, one thing she knew for certain was that she'd never look back and laugh.

9

'Where is she? Where the fuck is she?' Vaughn Sadler said the words that Alfie was thinking, not that he was going to admit that to him, but he'd been looking at his watch for the past few hours wondering the exact same thing.

He'd left Franny sleeping and by the time he'd come back to the house, she'd gone. He hadn't been that long either. Okay, he'd stopped to chat to the girl in the park but after that he'd just made his way along Rathbone Place to get a bit of breakfast before sauntering back. At the most he'd been out for an hour and a half, which meant Franny had been AWOL *again* for *several* hours. Her phone was off. *Again*. She'd left no note. *Again*. And even if he tried, he wouldn't be able to begin to guess where she'd gone. *Again*.

'You need to fix up your bird, Alfie. Are you finally going to believe me that she's up to something?'

Knowing full well it was too early to start on the whiskey,

but not giving a damn, Alfie poured himself a large double shot and knocked it back. 'What exactly are you accusing her of? All this agg between you is doing my head in.'

Vaughn gazed at Alfie. He didn't look in a good way; come to think of it, he hadn't looked in a good way for a long time. He'd looked positively ill since Bree had left. And although, personally, he hadn't been particularly keen on Bree, he had to admit she'd made Alfie happy, and she was certainly a lot more trustworthy than Franny, not that that was very difficult to do. Jesus, next to Franny, the Kray twins would've looked trustworthy. Somehow, she needed to be put in her place.

But there were two problems when it came to him dealing with Franny. The first was that she was a woman, and *that* fact pissed him off no end. He couldn't just go in and give her a hiding like he'd normally do when someone was blatantly mugging him off. He couldn't just slap her around and give her a good kicking she wouldn't forget, which led him on to problem number two: Franny was well aware that this was the case, and God, didn't it just play right into her hands. She was having a proper laugh at his expense.

He had to admit, there was part of him that was tempted to ignore his own rule book, ignore the bottom line of her being a woman, because after all, Franny was as much a part of this life as he was, as Alfie was, as any of the other faces were, and there was no way he'd ever dream of giving them special treatment, so why would he give it to Franny?

Franny knew the rules of a life of crime; she knew the consequences as well. Jesus, the woman had been born into the business; her father had been a number-one face and he'd taught her *everything* he knew.

Instead of playing with dolls and doll's houses like other little girls, Franny had been taught how to pick locks and pick pockets by her father. *Party tricks*, he'd called them. So, when the criminal fraternity met up at Patrick's house, Franny, at the age of only eight or nine, had been the star attraction, delighting in showing off her skills, her *party tricks*, much to the amusement of everybody assembled and to the great pride of her father.

And as a result, there was no mistaking the fact that Franny knew how it *all* worked. No mistaking that she knew if she played with fire, she'd get well and truly scorched, and that's *why* Franny always played the female card. She hid behind it, saw herself as untouchable because of it. And to a point, as much as it irked him, got under his skin, she was right. Therefore, no matter how much he wanted to knock whatever it was she was hiding out of her, he couldn't quite bring himself to raise his hand to a woman. Though he supposed *killing* her would be a different matter. After all he wouldn't have to touch her. He wouldn't have to lay one finger on her. He wouldn't even have to go very near her. A bullet travelled far . . . Oh yes, killing Franny Doyle would be easy. It might even be the solution.

Suddenly snapping himself out of his thoughts, Vaughn answered Alfie, 'Like I said before, I don't know exactly what she's up to, but I do know that the books aren't balancing. She's spending money like water.'

Trying to play it down, Alfie shrugged. 'She's a woman ain't she. They love shopping and all that shit.'

'Come off it, Alf, this is Franny we're talking about. When was the last time you saw her tottering along the street in a pair of Louboutins, carrying shopping bags? That ain't her style. You know that, and I know that. She might have a beautiful face and – no disrespect here – a banging body, but she's more fucking geezer than most geezers I know. She's weird. She's different to any woman I've ever met, but she's clever; fuck me isn't she just? Ruthless as well, which in my mind means she's fucking dangerous.'

Alfie waved Vaughn away, dismissing what he saw as melodrama, though he still felt a nagging doubt, but he couldn't quite put his finger on why. 'Turn it in, you sound like a pussy boy. This is Fran, she ain't the eighth battalion you know.'

Looking serious, Vaughn leant in. 'Have you never heard of a silent assassin? That's who we're dealing with.'

Pouring another shot of whiskey and knocking it back as quickly as he had done the first one, Alfie roared with laughter. 'You need to have a word with yourself, Vaughnie. *Silent assassin.* Jesus Christ, what TV show have you stepped out of?'

Not to be cut off, Vaughn continued, 'Maybe I'm not putting it right, but what I'm saying is, whilst we're looking at Charlie and keeping our eyes out front, and whether you believe it or not, Alf, if we're not careful, one way or another when we're not looking, we're going to get stabbed in the back by your missus. *Again.*'

Rubbing his head, Alfie, not feeling great, said, 'Listen, I know you won't ever be able to trust her after what she did with our money. I get it, but this obsession you've got with her has to stop. You're creating something that's not there. Every time you're in the room together, I'm having to referee you both. It's Charlie we need to be thinking about.'

'You're right we do, and that's the point – we can't have anybody that ain't trustworthy in our fold. That's the last thing we need. Keeping it tight and all together is difficult enough without having to look over our shoulders.'

Thinking that a line of cocaine might be more helpful than the whiskey, Alfie pulled a face, feeling the stress beginning to build. 'I dunno, it's not like you've got anything concrete to base it on.'

'So, why's she not here? She knew we had a meeting to discuss the accounts. It's obvious she's trying to avoid it.'

'That's ridiculous.'

Vaughn stood up and walked across to where Alfie was tucking into the whiskey. 'Okay, then look me in the eye and tell me that you trust her. Go on, say it, Alf. Say that you trust Franny *and* mean it, and I promise you that I'll leave it. I won't ever mention anything about Franny again. I'll drop my beef with her. How's that for a deal? So, come on then, do you or do you not trust her?'

Alfie swallowed. He could feel the side of his jaw pulsing from tension and he stared at Vaughn. What the fuck was he going to say, because the problem *he* had was that Vaughn knew him too well. He would see if he was lying, and he *would* be lying if he said that he trusted Franny completely, because at the back of his mind, he knew there was something not quite right. But then, maybe it wasn't her, maybe it was his own state of mind, his paranoia, and it certainly didn't help that Vaughn kept sowing seeds of doubt. Shit. He had no idea what to think, and if he thought that Vaughn was bad now going on about Franny, if he admitted anything close to not trusting her, he'd never hear the last of it.

The one thing though that all of this *had* made him decide, was he was going away. Once he'd had a word with Charlie, he would take Franny's advice and shoot off somewhere and get his head together, but right now he was going to be careful what he said to Vaughn.

He opened his mouth. 'Okay, here's the truth, Vaughnie, I . . .'

A loud crash from the entrance of the club stopped Alfie saying any more. He nodded his head to Vaughn, who took the signal, pulling out two small handguns from a chrome bucket full of ice underneath the bar. He threw one to Alfie.

Carefully catching it, Alfie whispered, 'Take the other exit; I'll go and see who it is.'

Nodding, Vaughn moved quietly towards the back of the club leaving Alfie to switch off the lights and make his way as silently as he could to the front of the club.

Just before he got to the entrance, Alfie pushed flat against the wall, readying himself but hearing nothing more. He tapped the door with his boot to push it open, craning to listen, though all he could hear was the distant sound of traffic coming from Soho Square.

Flicking the safety latch off the gun, Alfie moved outside, the cool air hitting him hard.

About to walk up the basement stairs, he stopped abruptly, seeing something on the floor. He picked it up. It was a letter addressed to him. With shaking hands, Alfie ripped open the envelope, feeling his legs begin to give way as he read what it said.

> *Roses are red,*
> *Violets are blue,*
> *You sent me to prison, Alf,*
> *now I'm coming for you.*

'Alfie?' Vaughn's voice behind Alfie made him jump. Strung out, he began to fire his gun over and over again, the bullets ricocheting in the small entranceway.

'Fucking hell, Alf! Jesus Christ, what are you doing?' Vaughn grabbed Alfie, slamming him hard against the wall, knocking the gun out of his hand before he pushed his forearm against Alfie's throat.

His face red with fury, Vaughn spat out his words: 'What do you think you're doing? Do you want every single copper descending on this place?'

Alfie shook his head, his eyes wide open with fear, and managing to push Vaughn away from the tight hold he was in and spluttering. Alfie rubbed his neck. 'No, fuck's sake, no, of course not!'

Alfie turned to go back into the club but Vaughn, raging, blocked his way. 'I want an explanation. Now!'

Bending over to rest his hands on his knees, Alfie, shocked by his own actions, tried to play it down.

'I dunno, mate, I just thought I saw a rat, that's all. I hate the fucking things.'

Pulling him up and twirling him round to face him, Vaughn furiously shook his head, speaking through gritted teeth. 'No, no, no, no, you're not going to try to tell me that you risked the fucking flying squad swooping in, just so you could kill a rat. You need to come up with something better than that, Alf.'

As he spoke, Vaughn glanced up the basement stairs, seeing a stranger curiously looking down at them both. He pulled Alfie inside, immediately punching him hard at close range in the face.

Staggering backwards, Alfie tasted the blood in his mouth but there was something about the physical pain that he welcomed at that moment. His head was a wreck, and anything was better than thinking about those letters. 'I'm sorry, okay? I fucked up.'

Furious, Vaughn strode up to him, pulling and shaking him roughly. '*Sorry!* Are you kidding? I ain't going down for you, not for this, not for you shooting a gun out there like you're cowboy fucking Jo. You need to lay off that coke, Alf. You're acting crazy and you're looking rough as fuck. One druggie in the place is bad enough.'

Puzzled, Alfie looked at Vaughn. 'What are you talking about?'

Grabbing hold of Alfie's arm, Vaughn dragged him towards a door marked, *staff only*. He pushed it open, but as soon as he did, a girl pounced on him, trying to scratch at his face, screaming at the top of her voice.

'Who the frig are you to lock me in here, hey? I ain't your fucking dog.'

With ease, Vaughn pushed her off, keeping her at arm's length. 'I found her round the back. She says she knows you . . .'

10

Shannon stared indignantly at Vaughn. 'I do know him! I was just bringing his jumper back.'

Alfie's eyes flashed angrily. He ran at Shannon, grabbing hold of her. 'It was you wasn't it? You left it for me. Is this your idea of a joke? You think it's funny?'

Upset, Shannon shook her head. 'What are you talking about? Get off me, I ain't done anything.'

Clearly unconvinced, Alfie pushed Shannon hard in the chest. 'You think it's funny to play with people, do you? Well I'll show you what I do to funny.'

Shannon's eyes filled with tears. She'd thought this *Alfie* bloke was all right, but it was turning out he was like every other man she knew. 'I . . . I don't know what your problem is, mate! I only came here to give you your jumper back.'

Alfie's voice raised the roof. He bellowed at Shannon as he lunged at her. 'Liar!'

'Leave it out, Alf, she's just a kid.' Vaughn put his hand on Alfie's shoulder, but he shook it off and continued to shout.

'I'll leave it out when she tells me about *this*!' Alfie waved the letter in the air as he pushed Shannon again in the chest. She stumbled, falling backwards, landing sprawled on the floor.

'You're fucking mental, mate. How could it be me? I don't know even know what's in it.'

Her crying was like a hard slap to Alfie's face, snapping him out of his rage. He scrabbled down to the floor, picking her up and cradling her in his arms. 'Oh Jesus, what have I done? I'm so sorry. Are you okay? Of course, it's not you. I don't even know what I was thinking.'

Distressed, Shannon pushed him away, burying her face into her knees. She already felt terrible. Her dealer had ripped her off and charged her more than double the price for a rock, so she'd only been able to afford one, and the high had worn off quickly, leaving her feeling miserable and agitated, which was why she'd come to see Alfie. He'd been nice to her, and she didn't really have anywhere else to go, but it was obvious that she'd made a big mistake thinking Alfie would be any different to anyone else. 'Piss off! I hate you! I *hate* you!'

'I don't blame you, darlin', and if it makes you feel any better, I hate me as well right now.'

'You didn't have to push me. I've hurt me knee now.'

Shame rushed over Alfie and it was only made worse by how young and vulnerable she sounded. 'I know, and I was wrong. Well out of order. I'll never do that again, I promise. You're safe here . . . Can you forgive me?'

Warming to his tone, Shannon glanced at Alfie, wiping away her tears. His eyes were kind and maybe it'd turn out that she *could* trust him, maybe he *wouldn't* hurt her again, but then, what did she know? For a long time she'd believed that her uncle Charlie and her auntie were kind and trustworthy until she realised that most other girls at eight didn't have to sleep with men who were old enough to be their grandfather.

'What's your name, sweetheart?'

Against her better judgement, she muttered, 'Shannon.'

Alfie smiled, seeming pleased that she was talking to him. 'That's a nice name. It suits you, and I'm glad you're here. Thank you for bringing my jumper back. You didn't have to. Can I get you a drink or . . .'

'Hello? Alfie? Hello?'

Alfie looked at Vaughn. 'Shit, it's Franny. Look you stay here with Shannon, make sure she's all right, and I'll go and speak to Franny. The last thing I need is for Franny to see Shannon here . . . Look after her will you?' And without waiting for an answer, Alfie quickly got up and left the room.

Seeing Franny standing in the middle of the empty club, Alfie feigned a smile. He wasn't in the mood to start questioning her about where she'd been, and he certainly wasn't in the mood for her to start questioning *him* about Shannon. That could all wait, because he had to admit it was good to see her. Really good. She was just what he needed. He walked towards her, then touched her cheek, before giving her a gentle kiss on the lips. 'Hey, Fran.'

Franny pulled away and frowned as she looked at Alfie's

face: strained, his mouth bruised and bloody, completely dishevelled.

'What's been going on? What happened to your face, and what happened outside? The crate of empty bottles is all shot up. Has Charlie been again?'

'No, nothing like that . . . Just leave it.'

'Alf, clearly something's happened. Just tell me.'

'For a minute there, I was happy to see ya, but you just can't help chewing me ear off, can you? I'll see you later.'

Alfie grabbed his key from the side and stormed towards the exit and up the basement stairs with Franny close behind. He marched down Sutton Row but halfway along he stopped as he heard Franny calling him. 'Alf! Alf, wait a minute, please. What's happened?'

He shouted over his shoulder. 'I don't need this shit now.'

Continuing to run after him, Franny called out, 'What is *wrong* with you?'

'I asked you to leave it. Can't you just do that one simple thing?'

Catching up, Franny touched Alfie's back. 'How can I, when I see you in this state?'

He turned to look at her, fighting the emotions that were overwhelming him. He felt the tightness in the back of his throat as he tried to hold back the tears. It was a joke – he was a bloke and yet here he was standing in the heart of Soho, blubbing like a girl. He couldn't speak; he just squeezed his eyes tightly, listening to Franny talk, her voice quiet and warm.

'Oh my God, Alf, *please*, you've got to tell me what's going on. I want to help you.'

Instead of answering Franny, Alfie pulled out one of the letters from his pocket, handing it over to her. She read it then gazed at him.

'Alfie, why didn't you tell me about this before? Is this what it's all been about?'

Still unable to speak and unable to make eye contact, Alfie nodded as Franny continued to talk.

'I know that a while ago you said something about a guy being released from prison, but you never told me *who* it was. Even when you told me, you seemed on edge about it . . . worried. Do you think it's from him?'

Alfie's voice broke. He looked up to the sky feeling the rain beginning to fall. 'It's got to be. There's only one person I've ever ratted on . . . Like I told you before, I ain't a grass. It's not usually my thing to go around snaking people out and landing them in prison, and besides, it was a long time ago.'

'I know! But what I don't understand is, *who is he*, Alf? Because this ain't like you. Not the Alfie I know. Why don't you just tell me who it is?'

Alfie shook his head. 'Trust me, it's best you don't know.'

'Well whoever it is, this guy must be a pretty big face to get you acting like this, though you know what I think, Alf? I think that all that gear you're taking is making you more paranoid – jumpier. It's making everything seem worse.'

Sniffing and wiping his face, Alfie looked down. 'Maybe you're right. My head's a mess and I can't seem to snap out of it, so what I think I'm going to do is take your advice: go away for a bit; perhaps I'll end up investing in Spain again. Things seemed simpler out there, we were happy. And the Costa is hardly the other side of the world, is it? Oh, I dunno, but I'll talk to you all about that later . . . Look, I've got to go.'

'Where to?'

'No more questions, Fran, I can't deal with it.'

Franny nodded as she squeezed Alfie's hand. 'Okay, baby.'

Then finally managing to look at her, Alfie smiled, though his eyes were full of pain. 'I love you, Franny. You hear me? You're the best thing that ever happened to me . . . I'll see you at home. I've just got to go and see someone.'

And with that Alfie turned and ran down the street.

11

Charlie stared in the mirror, something he tried not to do often. Not that he was anywhere near worried about his balding head, nor did he care that his body folded over in huge waves of fat, and neither was he bothered that his nose and face were a ruddy red map of veins. No, the one thing that he couldn't stand was the fact he looked like his father. Almost a carbon copy of him. It was like his father was staring back, taunting. Mocking. Reminding him of his childhood filled with abuse, which he thought would never end.

When he looked in the mirror he could remember what happened as if it was yesterday, but above all he remembered the smell of his father. Alcohol mixed with charcoal. Always charcoal. His father would have a constant fire burning on the rusting barbeque. Getting rid of any incriminating evidence. Bloodstained sheets. Bloodstained underwear. Photographs of him and his sisters that his father and his sick friends would take of them. Anything and everything went on the fire. To this day he couldn't bear the smell of charcoal.

Turning away, he looked down at his phone. He hadn't heard one peep out of Shannon. Not one text. Not one phone call to tell him that she was sorry. He'd even got a couple of his men to go around all the crack dens in Soho, thinking that she'd be there. But she was nowhere to be seen. Well he would make her fucking sorry when she came crawling back to him.

Who did she think she was? He'd put a roof over her head, food on her table and she earned a wage. What more did the little bitch want? But he supposed he shouldn't blame her because *he* was the mug. He'd been the one who'd been soft on her, trusting her because she was family. Thinking she was better than the other girls who worked for him. He'd been weak. He'd been kind. And what did she go and do? Throw it all back in his face. And when she did come back – and she would – the little runt would regret *ever* trying to take the piss out of him again.

The one thing Vaughn Sadler hated more than crackheads were chatty crackheads and since he'd turned right into Shaftesbury Avenue, Shannon hadn't stopped talking. The only thing that he'd contributed to the conversation was to ask if it was left or right at Sanford Street. Not that she'd known – the only thing she did seem to know about was which drug dealer or nonce to avoid. Though the one thing, the only thing of interest she'd said all night was she worked for Charlie Eton, and not only *that*, but she was also Charlie's niece.

He'd no idea if Alfie knew this piece of information or not, and when Shannon had first said it, his immediate thought was, Charlie must've sent her. But as quickly as that thought had come to him, it disappeared. The girl was just a vulnerable druggie who Charlie had used and abused, and as such, he'd found himself feeling sorry for her, which is how he now found himself stuck in a car with her chatting ten to the dozen, having given her some money and volunteering to drive her to her friend's house. Shit!

Sighing, Vaughn flicked on the wipers of his Range Rover as it began to pour with rain. He pulled over to where Shannon was pointing at the same time as noticing how few teeth she had for such a young girl. 'Over here, mate. That's lovely. Right here will do. Cheers for the lift.'

'No worries. You'll be all right?'

Nodding, Shannon jumped out of the car, once more delighted at having some money in her pocket, though this time round, she'd make sure her dealer didn't mug her off. But she could get used to this; not having to sleep with men and playing all their pervy games for a living felt good, and she had to admit, although at first Vaughn had been a bit moody, and hadn't really been much of a talker, he'd been nice to her, like Alfie had. Two people being nice to her in twenty-four hours – that really did take some beating. By her reckoning, this might be the best day of her life. 'Yeah I'll be fine, Vaughn. See you around. Oh, and tell Alfie, I hope he's all right.'

Absentmindedly, Vaughn watched as Shannon skipped down an alleyway. He had to give it to her, she was made of tough stuff. He didn't know if he'd be able to cope with all that she put up with, and underneath the hard exterior, she seemed like a sweet kid who just needed someone to look out for her. It was a shame she was so bang on the gear.

Turning his attention away and looking into his wing mirror, Vaughn indicated to pull out, wanting to do a U-turn rather than have to drive the whole way around, but he froze as he caught sight of a dark blue Porsche Cayenne Turbo at the traffic lights of Warspite Road. He stared at the driver and through the pelting rain, he could just make out who it was. It was Franny.

What was she doing around here? It was only a couple of hours ago she'd been at the club. He'd assumed she'd gone somewhere with Alfie, but clearly she hadn't, and whatever the reason she was here, well maybe this was his opportunity to find out *exactly* what Franny was up to.

Pulling into the lane, Vaughn cut across the road being careful to keep a couple of cars' distance from her. It helped that it was raining hard. He doubted the visibility was good enough for her to see him. He only hoped that the traffic would stay busy. But at the main roundabout, she turned left into Ruston Road, driving past the large plumbing store and several derelict warehouses. With no other cars about, Vaughn was forced to slow down, hanging back as he watched Franny pull over.

Turning off his lights, he frowned. She'd never mentioned knowing anybody living in Woolwich, and he knew most of her and Alfie's friends and acquaintances.

Continuing to watch, deeper puzzlement crossed

through him as he saw Franny taking out a set of keys from her bag to open the front door of the smart block of flats. Suddenly, he ducked. She was looking his way. Shit. He hoped that she hadn't seen him. Breathing hard, he waited a couple of moments before he sat back up. Watching and waiting.

12

Inside the flat, Franny, having taken off her jacket, unlocked the bedroom door to Bree. She had been going to leave coming to see her until tomorrow afternoon, but with Alfie going off the way he had done, well that had given her a window of opportunity to come and see Mia . . . *Bree.*

'Hi, Bree.'

With her blonde hair scraped back, Bree looked at Franny, relief overwhelming her. She hadn't known how long it was going to be before Franny decided to come back, especially as she'd let her imagination run away with her. Somewhere between being locked in the bedroom and now, she'd convinced herself that she'd be held there forever, especially with the mood Franny had been in. She hadn't even got her phone to call, Franny had taken that as well. Simply put, she was at Franny's mercy.

'You're back quickly, Fran.'

Franny stared at Bree. She looked like she'd been crying, which to her was ridiculous. What was there to be upset about? Bree had everything. It was almost as if she was staying at a five-star hotel, and like she'd told her on numerous occasions it wasn't going to be forever – but as usual, Bree had to make a drama of everything. She narrowed her eyes coldly. 'Have you got a problem with that because I can turn around and go if you'd prefer?'

'No, no of course not. I'm just surprised, that's all. You don't usually come so soon between visits . . . Thank you.'

Stern-faced, Franny nodded, not particularly interested in having a long discussion with Bree, but her mood suddenly lifted, and her expression changed, a huge smile spread across her face as she glanced at Mia asleep on the bed. 'She looks content.'

'She's been good.'

With nothing near patience, Franny, still smarting from the argument they'd had before and having been left feeling raw after seeing Alfie, snapped, 'She's a baby, of course she's good. She's not going to be anything else, is she?'

Admonished and looking glum, Bree spoke flatly. 'No, no of course not.'

Sitting on the edge of the large king-size bed, Franny seemed to pull herself together and with her tone slightly lighter, said, 'Anyway, I've got some good news for you. Alfie's going to go away.'

A rush of emotions ran through Bree. It was the strangest of things, but the thought of Alfie leaving somehow upset her. 'When? Why's he decided to go all of a sudden?'

Shrugging, Franny yawned. 'He hasn't told me any

details, but he hasn't been himself lately . . .' She trailed off, hinting to Bree that she wasn't in the mood to chat about Alfie.

'Is he all right, Fran?'

With the tension between the two women always just under the surface, a flicker of annoyance came into Franny's eyes. 'Why do you care?'

'Well I don't hate him if that's what you mean. He's never done anything wrong to me, quite the opposite. The only reason I left . . .' Bree stopped, feeling Franny's intense, hostile glare.

'Are you telling me you still have feelings for Alfie?'

Knowing there was no way she was going to admit the truth to Franny, especially after the earlier conversation, Bree shook her head, emphatically saying, 'No, Jesus, Fran, not like that anyway. Obviously, I don't want anything bad to happen to him, but I was just curious.'

Franny continued to stare but said nothing as she thought about Alfie. Although she'd wanted him to go away, she'd actually felt for him tonight. She'd known he was in a state, but what she'd seen this evening had surprised even her, and it hadn't made her feel particularly good. Perhaps that's why she'd needed to come and see Mia . . . *Bree*. She'd needed a distraction but sitting here was anything but. Bree looked terrible, and she was hardly what she'd call good company.

Sighing and glancing down at the Limelight Gala watch Alfie had bought her a couple of months ago, Franny saw it was just past one in the morning. A sudden thought rushed through her mind. Why not? It wouldn't do any harm now. Not at this time of night anyway, and perhaps it would break the tension between them.

'What do you say to a drive out?'

Bree's face lit up. 'Do you mean it? Really?'

'Yeah, I can't sit here. I've had more laughs at a funeral parlour. We can just drive out along the river. My car's right outside and it's got blacked-out back windows, so no one will see you. And then we can come back, but don't think I'll make a habit of it . . . and, Bree, don't make any stupid moves, understand?'

The warm feeling Bree had had, suddenly faded. An ominous chill ran through her.

'No, of course I won't.'

'Okay, then let's go . . . Get Mia and *hurry up*.'

Outside in the car, the rain was getting heavier and Vaughn was in two minds whether to put his wipers on or not. He didn't want to risk being seen. Deciding it was probably best to keep the engine turned off, he leant closer to the windscreen. Shit, he wished he could see better. Maybe he should step out of the car to get a clearer view, but he'd have to be careful.

Reaching for the door handle, Vaughn squinted. There were two people coming from the flats. That one was definitely Franny. But who was the second one? He couldn't quite make out who she was with.

As Vaughn watched them jump into Franny's car, the rain making it difficult for him to see easily, another person who was watching had a much better view. Shannon saw it all.

13

'Mr Eton, I'm sorry I couldn't stop him.' Charlie Eton turned around to see one of his men trying to pull back Alfie Jennings from entering the room. Puzzled, he looked at Alfie, who stood drenched to the skin.

'It's fine, you can leave us now.'

'Are you sure, Mr Eton, because I can get him out if you like?'

Charlie, as was his habit, picked up the nearest object – a chair – and threw it in the direction of his henchman. 'Get the fuck out of my sight before I do something you won't like!'

The man scurried away leaving Charlie, red-faced and breathing hard, with Alfie.

'This is a nice surprise, Alf. I take it you've come to a decision.'

Alfie shook his head, hardly able to speak as he stared

at Charlie, who stood only in a pair of white faded under-pants.

Pulling on a Ralph Lauren purple velvet tracksuit, Charlie gave a sideward look to Alfie.

'Then to what do I owe the pleasure, because as you told me the last time, my merchandise is a little bit too young for you . . . You look fucked by the way. Jesus Christ, Alf, what's going on?'

Pallid and sweating, Alfie's voice was strained. 'You need to tell me the truth, Char. I promise it won't go further than these two walls. Please, just tell me. I don't want you hiding anything from me.'

'Alf, calm down. You're not making sense, mate.'

Trembling, Alfie stared at Charlie, wiping the sweat and the rain off his face. 'Just *tell* me if you've got one of these as well.' He pulled out the letter he'd shown Franny, shoving it into Charlie's hand.

Charlie read it, and shrugged. 'This is a joke. Some muggy prankster.'

He pushed it back to Alfie, who began to pace.

'It ain't a joke, I just know it.'

Still none the wiser, Charlie said, 'Well who do you think it's from?'

Alfie's face turned into a picture of bemusement. He clutched his head, his whole body tense and strained. His voice shaking, loud and anxious, he said, 'Are you fucking kidding me? Are you being serious? There's only one person it could be from, and you know it as well as I do. I know it's from him, and you're probably gonna get one too—'

'Alfie mate, it ain't from him.' Charlie's voice held an

unusual warmth. 'Jesus Christ. Look, I know you and me have a lot of agg at the moment over the club, but I don't want to see you like this. You're losing it, mate. You need to go home, have a shower and a shave. You're looking terrible, and I swear, Alf, I don't know anything about any letters.'

Ignoring what Charlie had to say, Alfie charged over to him, grabbing hold of his tracksuit top and shaking him hard. 'Char, you're lying! I know it!'

'I'm not, and do you know why, mate? Listen to me carefully here. Because they ain't from him. Now let go of me.'

Blinking, and with a manic, faraway look in his eye, Alfie nodded, dropping his hold. He began to pace up and down again at the same time as Charlie went over to the large black locker in the corner.

Opening the top drawer, Charlie pulled out a bag of cocaine, tapping some out on the side before cutting it up finely. He waved a silver toot at Alfie, still speaking gently to him. 'Here, mate, take some of this – it looks like you need some.'

Sounding broken, Alfie walked over to where Charlie was standing. 'Yeah thanks.' But about to snort a line, Alfie stopped, staring intently at Charlie. 'You really think it's not from him?'

'Jesus, Alf, how many times – of course I don't.'

A shallow exhalation came from Alfie as he tried to get his breath, shame rushing over him. 'Cos I'm scared, mate, and I know it's stupid, but I'm scared.'

Charlie gave a small but genuine smile. 'I know you are, but it'll be fine, Alf . . . I'm here. It's going to be fine.'

And almost to himself, Alfie nodded, the tears falling down his cheeks as he leant his head on Charlie's shoulder. 'It's going to be fine . . . it's going to be fine . . . it's going to be fine.'

'For fuck's sake! Jesus Christ!' Vaughn banged on the horn. Fuck! What the fuck did she think she was doing?

'Get out of the way! Get out of my way!'

Shannon stood in front of the revving car, smiling a semi-toothless grin at Vaughn. She'd seen Bree come out of the flat and although Bree had been with some woman she didn't know, she'd made up her mind to go and say hello – after all, at one time they'd known each other pretty well – but when she'd seen Vaughn's car turning around in the street, the thought of getting a lift back to Soho was more inviting than a quick chat with Bree.

It was an absolute touch that she'd seen him. The weather was shit plus she'd spent all her money, so she couldn't even get a night bus back to town.

She shouted warmly, raising her voice above the pelting rain. 'What you still doing here, mate? I thought you'd pissed off home?'

Vaughn stared at Shannon and sighed. He'd no hope of catching Franny up now. She was well and truly gone because of some stupid kid. Shit, as sweet as Shannon was, he'd thought that he'd seen the last of her. He certainly didn't need to babysit some crackhead . . . Maybe that was a harsh thing to think. He was being unfair. It wasn't her fault she'd had the life she did, but that didn't make it any less of a bitter pill to swallow that for one sweet moment, he'd thought he'd got Franny right where he wanted her.

But Christ knows, he couldn't see the kid out in the street in this weather and especially as it seemed she didn't really have anywhere to go.

So, with a heavy heart and trying to push down his irritation, Vaughn signalled for Shannon to come around to the passenger side. He shouted back, though not as warmly as she had done. 'Come on then! Come on if you're coming! Jesus!'

Jumping in, wired and smiling, Shannon, soaked to the bone, giggled. 'I thought it was you. You don't get many gold-coloured Range Rovers round here. You going back to Soho, mate?'

Flatly, Vaughn nodded, smelling the distinct, acrid aroma of burnt crack cocaine coming off Shannon's breath. 'It looks like I am, doesn't it?'

Shannon looked at him oddly, her words slurred from the drugs. 'You all right? You seem a bit pissed off.'

'I'm fine. I just saw someone I knew. I was hoping to catch up with them, that's all.'

Looking out of the window, Shannon absentmindedly murmured, 'That's funny.'

Vaughn scowled as he turned a right, heading towards Blackwall Tunnel. 'What is?'

'That we both saw someone we knew . . . not that I've seen Bree for ages. One day she just . . .'

Vaughn slammed on his brakes, sending Shannon flying forward. He swivelled round in his seat to stare at her. 'Who? Shannon, who did you say?'

Nonplussed, Shannon shrugged. 'Bree. Back there. I saw her just before I saw you.'

With his mind racing, Vaughn spoke slowly. 'Shannon, do you know this person's second name?'

Looking at Vaughn strangely, Shannon nodded. 'Of course I do. It's Dwyer. Bree Dwyer.'

14

Back in Soho, it was Vaughn's turn to hit the whiskey. He knocked it back in one, straightaway pouring himself another drink. He looked at the clock. It was just gone four in the morning but there was no way he could sleep.

Of all the things he expected, it wasn't this. He'd never dreamt that Franny was still in contact with Bree because anytime that Bree's name had come up, Franny had acted in one of two ways: blasé or vitriolic. Yet there she was with keys to what was probably Bree's front door. But why? Why keep it from him? More to the point, why keep it from Alfie? That's what he didn't understand. There was no reason on earth for Franny not to tell Alfie. Bree and Alfie were long over. She didn't want to be with him because of his lifestyle; even he got that. So why all the hiding? The secrecy?

Although, there could be another reason why Franny was being suspicious lately. Maybe it wasn't to do with Bree at all; perhaps they'd just bumped into each other and she was in Woolwich purely for a social visit . . . Who knew?

With most people, he'd probably think there was a simple explanation. An innocent one. But this was Franny he was dealing with. And the word *innocent* could never be linked to her.

He had been trying to question Shannon some more about Bree, but by the time they'd driven through the tunnel, she was crashed out. A drug-induced nap. He'd even had to carry her inside the club, laying her on the couch opposite the one he'd found Alfie collapsed on, who also seemed to be in a drug-related sleep.

Feeling the burn from the whiskey, Vaughn heard the door open. He whipped around. It was Franny.

Wanting to play it cool until he'd worked out exactly what was going on, he said, 'You're up early, or haven't you been to bed yet?'

Not expecting to find anyone here, Franny was shocked. She'd only come back for some cash. She'd made it her business not to use her bank cards whenever she was in South London in case Alfie saw any statements, but annoyingly, Bree hadn't told her yesterday that she'd run out of nappies, which meant coming back to get some more money.

It was a nuisance to have to drive back and forth to Woolwich, but the traffic was light for once, and she had hoped she could get away without anyone seeing her. That's why she hadn't gone home to pick up her purse in case Alfie had been there, but now she wouldn't be able to go in the safe without Vaughn asking her a million questions.

Tightly, she said, 'I could say the same about you . . .' About to continue, Franny frowned, turning to look at Vaughn directly. 'Who's that, and why the hell is she asleep on the couch? Come to think of it, why's Alfie here too?'

'You tell me, Fran. You seem to be the one who holds all the answers.'

Not in the mood to have to deal with Vaughn, Franny stepped closer, smelling the whiskey on his breath. 'I'll ask you again, who's that on my couch?'

'A friend.'

Franny's voice was hostile. 'I don't know what the hell's been going on, but I don't want some stray in here. This is a business, Vaughn, and I'm not going to get it shut down because of some underage kid you've picked up.'

Seething, Vaughn knocked back another whiskey. 'For fuck's sake, Franny, I haven't picked her up. Like I say, she's a friend.'

'Whatever, Vaughn. Just get her out of my club, understand?'

'But it's not just *your* club is it? From what I remember, we're all partners here, with Alfie and I having the lion's share, so I'll have who the hell I want here.'

Having been awake for the past few minutes, Shannon had heard the conversation and with her head still spinning, she sat up blurry-eyed.

She stared at Franny, recognising her as the woman from outside the flats in Woolwich. She hadn't liked the look of her then, and although she was very beautiful, she certainly didn't like her now. Stuck-up cow. Who did she think she was, talking about her like that?

With a sneer on her face, Shannon, full of confrontation, glowered at Franny. 'You were that woman out . . .'

She stopped as she saw Vaughn shake his head. She didn't know why, but she did know that he wanted her to keep her mouth shut, and she was more than happy to do it for him, partly because she'd taken an instant dislike to Franny, and partly because Vaughn had called her his *friend*, and in her entire life she'd never heard anybody call her that.

Franny stared. 'I was *what* woman?'

Biting her nails, Shannon shrugged. 'Can't remember what I was going to say now.'

Tutting, Franny impatiently turned back to Vaughn. 'Tell Alfie to call me when he wakes up, and when I come back, I want her gone. Understand?'

As Franny slammed the door, Vaughn looked at Shannon. 'I'm sorry about her.'

'Nasty cow, I don't know how you put up with her.'

'Me neither, and you know something, Shannon, I ain't going to put up with her any longer.'

Whereupon, Vaughn followed Franny out of the room.

Shannon felt edgy. Agitated. Itchy. That was the problem with crack. The high never lasted any time at all and the low felt so bad all she wanted to do was get high again. Sometimes, sleeping directly after the buzz helped, but on this occasion it hadn't, and Shannon didn't know if she could cope with the way she was feeling for very much longer.

Looking at Alfie still asleep on the couch, she smiled. He was nice, but he wasn't as nice as Vaughn. Vaughn was special. He was her friend and she hoped that one day she could show him how much that meant to her.

Rubbing her face and feeling like it was crawling with ants, she wondered when Vaughn would get back. Shannon began to pace the room. She looked down again at Alfie who was snoring loudly. Nervously biting on her lip, a thought crossed her mind.

But then he'd been so good to her and she didn't want to seem ungrateful, but she supposed, it wasn't as if he couldn't afford it. And maybe he wouldn't mind; after all he'd been willing to help her before, so why not now? And she was sure that he wouldn't want her to feel the way she was; she could always pay him back, couldn't she?

Two minutes later and having talked herself into it, Shannon bent down by Alfie's side, whispering his name. 'Alf? Alf? You awake, mate?' There was no response. She could see he was bang asleep. Then, as carefully as she could, Shannon began to slip her hand down the front pocket of Alfie's jeans, feeling gently with her fingers, not wanting to wake him up.

She smiled as she pulled out a five-pound note, but knowing it was far from enough, Shannon cautiously went into Alfie's other pocket. Touching what felt like a wad of notes, eagerly, Shannon gripped them, slowly pulling them out, checking every few seconds to make sure that Alfie was still asleep.

But she frowned, disappointed when she saw that instead of it being a roll of twenty-pound notes as she'd first thought, it was actually several pieces of paper . . . Letters in fact.

The same letters that Alfie had accused her of leaving for him.

With her interest now swelling, Shannon gave Alfie another quick glance before sitting on the wooden floor to read the letters. She unfolded the first one, then the second, shaking her head as she went on to read the third and fourth. They were all poems. Creepy poems. She shuddered, a chill coming over her. No wonder Alfie had been so freaked out by them.

Going to put them back, Shannon's hand hovered over Alfie's pocket as she saw him beginning to stir. She held her breath, terrified he was going to wake up, but seeing him settle back down again, as quickly and gently as she could, Shannon began to slip the letters back into his pocket.

She screamed as Alfie suddenly grabbed her arm. He sat up, bleary-eyed. He stared at her, his voice full of hostility when he spoke.

'What the hell are you doing?'

Shannon's eyes filled with tears. 'I'm . . . I'm sorry, I was just . . .'

Alfie interrupted as his gaze rested on the letters that Shannon held in her hand. Anger surged across his face. 'What are you doing with those . . . *Answer me!*' He bellowed the last part of his sentence.

Shaking, Shannon said, 'I was putting them back. I was just . . .' She stopped as shame rushed over her.

'You were what?'

'I was just looking for some money and I'm sorry, Alf, I didn't want to rob from you, you've been so good to me, but I began to cluck, and I couldn't stand it any longer.'

Still glaring, Alfie snapped, 'Okay, but then what are you doing with those? Have you read them?'

Thinking it was pointless to attempt to lie at this stage, Shannon nodded her head sullenly. 'Yeah, and they're pretty weird. Who are they from?'

Dropping hold of Shannon's arm, Alfie shrugged. 'There was this guy, a long time ago . . . I got him put away.'

Wide-eyed, Shannon said, 'You're a grass?'

Alfie gave her a small smile. 'Not exactly, but the point is, he's out now and, well . . .'

It was Shannon's turn to interrupt. 'He wants to do you some damage?'

Closing his eyes just for a moment, Alfie nodded, sounding breathless as he said, 'I think so.'

'You scared?'

Certainly not wanting to admit how he felt to Shannon, Alfie pulled a face. 'Me? No! What do you take me for? Of course not.'

Shannon sniffed, the effects of the crack low making her shake. 'You look it.'

Needing to shut down the conversation, Alfie, not particularly unkindly said, 'Well I ain't, and anyway, don't change the subject. I want to know why you thought it was okay to nick from me.'

'I never thought it was okay, it's just that I feel so shit.'

Alfie sighed, feeling not too clever himself. Whatever kind of coke Charlie had given him, well it was certainly stronger than what he normally took. He looked at Shannon. How could he be angry with her? Not that it made it all right for her to steal from him when he was asleep, but the least he could do was give her a break.

'Look, you're out of order, but I'm not angry, just a bit disappointed that's all. Here, take this twenty, and I ain't giving you any more – not so you can feed your habit anyway . . . Come on, I need to go home for some sleep and you can't stay here. How did you get in by the way?'

'With Vaughn, and that snotty bird was here too.'

Alfie frowned. 'Who are you talking about?'

'Franny.'

Alfie laughed. 'Oi! Watch your mouth, that's *my* snotty bird you're talking about.'

Smiling shyly, Shannon took the twenty that Alfie was handing her. 'Well more fool you, mate!'

Outside in the street, Shannon watched Alfie walk away. She liked him a lot. He was kind and funny, so she had no idea how he'd ended up with Franny. What he saw in her was beyond her. She was a prime bitch. No doubt about it.

She sighed. Thinking about Franny made her think about Bree. How did they know each other anyway? When *she'd* known Bree, she'd never mentioned anything about Franny, though she did suppose it was a while since they'd spoken, and even back then, Bree had always seemed secretive.

Frowning, Shannon pulled out her phone and pressed dial, knowing that someone else would be interested to hear about the events of the night. Not only that, but they'd probably have all the answers.

15

Franny cursed Vaughn. She was angry, and she could feel it in every cell of her body. She had no idea what the hell Vaughn was up to with that girl, but what she did know was she looked like trouble, and having her sniffing around the club, well that just wasn't an option.

It was bad enough they had to deal with Charlie. Even once Alfie was gone, they had to try to come to some kind of compromise. Certainly, at the moment they couldn't afford to pay what he was wanting, especially as she was forking out for Bree. She already knew that word had got out about the attack on the club with some of the clients wanting to cancel their membership, so having a girl looking like she'd stepped out of a crack house lying in their staff room wasn't going to help matters.

The problem was, she'd taken her eye off the ball thanks to Bree's constant demands, though hopefully, now that

Alfie had decided to take a break, life would get a lot easier.

All the running around and looking over her shoulder had become a strain, and with Vaughn on her back, it was getting risky. With any hope, Vaughn would eventually decide to join Alfie abroad as he had done in the past, though perhaps that was just wishful thinking on her part.

Sighing, she pulled up outside Bree's house. Apart from anything else she knew she needed to get more rest. She was tired, and it was certainly making her irritable. Though the one good thing was she'd been able to get Mia's nappies. Whilst Alfie was sleeping off whatever he'd indulged in, she'd been able to pop home and get some money before running in to the late-night supermarket. The truth was, Alfie couldn't go away soon enough.

Inside the flat, Franny, having thrown her keys and jacket onto the side, unlocked the bedroom door. A wave of exhaustion hit her as she longingly glanced at the bed. 'Hey, I've got the nappies you wanted.'

'Thanks – I appreciate you going for them, and I'm sorry I forgot to tell you before. You look tired. Come and sit down.' Bree smiled as she stood holding Mia in her arms.

Taking up the offer, Franny sat down on the bed, lying back and sinking deep into the pillows, but the minute she did, Bree, still holding Mia, charged for the door, slamming it closed behind her before quickly turning the key and locking Franny in.

Bree breathed deeply, closing her eyes partly in relief and partly in fear. She spoke through the door, her voice shaking slightly. 'I'm sorry, Franny, I never wanted to do this to you, but I just can't go on like this.'

Furiously, Franny, having jumped up from the bed, hammered on the door. 'You're making a big mistake, Bree – just open the fucking door, and then we can forget all about this.'

'But we won't forget it, will we? If I let you out now, you'll only lock me in again, and who knows for how long this time?'

With a hiss, Franny snapped, 'I've already told you: Alfie is going away. He'll be gone soon so all you needed to do was have a bit of patience. It's me who's had the hard time – you've had it easy.'

Walking across the room and placing Mia on her changing mat, Bree was shaking. She shouted back at Franny, 'But that's the thing, Franny. I've had patience, don't you see? And when I didn't, when I just wanted to get out for a bit, what did you do? You locked me in the bedroom. Don't you see how wrong that is?'

Hitting the door with her fist, Franny seethed, 'I took you for a drive, didn't I? Even after you went against me. I *still* took you out.'

'Listen to what you're saying, Franny – it's crazy.'

'Crazy? This was all for your own good, all of it. None of this was about me. The only thing I didn't want to happen was for Alfie to find out, because then something would happen to *me*. Why is that so hard for you to understand?'

Bree's eyes filled with tears, guilt running through her. 'It's not, but like I said before, this isn't normal. It's wrong, Franny.'

'Well it's a good job I didn't say it was wrong when you wanted me to help you get away from Alfie, isn't it? I've spent thousands on you and for what? Thanks for nothing, Bree.'

Turning her back on the door, Bree, not wanting to be drawn into any more conversation, saw Franny's car keys lying on the side. She immediately grabbed them before rushing across to the small kitchen off the lounge to grab Mia's tin of formula milk. Her thoughts raced as she grabbed what she could. Biscuits and crisps, a few cans of Coke, a loaf of bread, before pulling open a drawer to where the plastic bags were kept, and throwing the collected items inside a bag. What else did she need? Think. She had to think. Blankets, she had to get Mia's blankets. Quickly turning around to get them, Bree froze.

'Who did you think you were messing with, Bree? You should've known better than that.'

Bree could hardly breathe as she stared into Franny's cold and angry face.

'How . . . how did you get out?'

Franny laughed, harsh and bitterly. 'Didn't you listen to anything I said about my childhood, about my father? I was turning locks before you could even ride a bike.'

'Stay away from me, Franny.'

Franny tilted her head to one side. 'Why does it have to be like this? We were friends, Bree, and now look, you're telling me to keep away.'

'Just let me go, okay? Let me walk away with Mia and whatever happens, I'll take responsibility. No one will ever know you've been involved.'

Franny's tone was disconcerting. 'It's not as simple as that though, is it?'

'It can be. It can be whatever we want it to be.'

Franny's eyes narrowed. 'And what about Mia? Are you just going to walk away and take her out of my life forever?'

Bree shook her head. 'No, no of course not. You can see her anytime you want.'

'The minute you leave this flat, both you and I know you'll change your mind.'

Feeling uncomfortable, Bree, still holding Franny's car keys, went to walk out of the tiny kitchen, pushing past Franny. 'I wouldn't do that to you, but believe what you like. I'm not going to live like this any longer.'

Following her through to the lounge where Mia was still happily lying on the changing mat, Franny snapped angrily, 'You're going to ruin everything. All you have to do is wait a bit longer.'

Feeling a renewed strength, Bree spoke firmly. 'No, I'm sorry, Franny, but I ain't listening to you anymore. This has to stop, *now*. So here's how it's going to go: I'm going to take your car, but I'll let you know where I'm going to leave it, and I promise I'll be in touch.'

'Look, just stop being stupid. You haven't got anywhere to go. You can't just go out in the middle of the night with Mia.'

'Anywhere is better than here.'

'You're being ridiculous, Bree. You sound like a spoilt child. Just give me my keys back!' Franny snatched towards Bree, who pulled away her hand and raised her arm, dangling the keys high in the air. Franny lunged towards

126

them, and as she did so, Bree took a step back, but she stumbled. Her arms began to flail, her face paling as she tried but failed to reach for the banister, unable to stop herself from falling backwards down the open staircase. She screamed Franny's name as she fell, but Franny was frozen to the spot. In shock she couldn't move, let alone answer.

There was a loud thump and a bang, then nothing but silence.

Horrified, Franny stared down the stairs at Bree's body lying sprawled and broken, her arms twisted, her legs bent, her eyes staring wide open. Then snapping herself out of the trance, Franny ran down the stairs, kneeling by Bree, speaking quietly. 'Bree? Bree, honey? Bree, wake up, darlin'. It's okay, you've just had a nasty fall. Bree?' There was no response and desperately, Franny put her ear against Bree's chest before feeling for a pulse. Nothing. Gently, she lifted Bree's head up, but it lolled back like a broken doll's. 'Bree, come on! Come on! Don't do this to me. Please, baby, wake up.'

As Franny spoke, she looked at her own hands. They were covered in blood. Scrambling away from Bree's body, she pressed herself against the wall, breathing heavily, wiping her hands on the carpet in the small downstairs hallway of the maisonette.

In shock, Franny closed her eyes, but the image of Bree was still there in her mind. Hearing Mia begin to cry, she opened them, but going to stand up, a sense of nausea engulfed her. She swallowed hard, trying to steady herself, then took a deep breath before trying to get up again.

Mia's cry got louder before it turned into a scream. Forcing herself to get up, Franny unsteadily began to walk up the stairs. Speaking more to herself than Mia, she said, 'It's okay, it's okay, I'm here. It's going to be all right.'

Scooping Mia up, Franny gently bounced her up and down. She walked past the top of the stairs, looking down, hoping that somehow Bree's body wouldn't be there. Somehow the events of the last ten minutes hadn't happened.

She glanced around, her eyes darting wildly. She had to pull herself together. She would be no good to herself let alone Mia if she crumbled, and besides, she was a Doyle and being weak wasn't the way she'd been brought up. There was nothing she could do for Bree now, but she could still help Mia.

Quickly, Franny grabbed Mia's coat, putting it on her and placing her in the baby seat. Her heart raced as she worked out what she was going to do. There was money in the club, and her passport was there as well, and okay, she didn't have one for Mia, but she knew people who could sort that out, and she knew people who could get her out of the country safely. She just had to hurry. Time certainly wasn't on her side.

Rushing down the stairs as she carried Mia, and stepping over Bree's body, Franny raced for the front door. She opened it.

'What are you doing here?'

Vaughn stared at Franny as she began to push the door closed, but with the baby in one hand and with Vaughn's strength, she was no match for him as he pushed it easily open.

'I could ask you the same thing. I followed you because I wanted to know . . .' He stopped. Stared. Looked at Bree lying motionless on the floor before his gaze went to Franny, and to her jeans smeared with blood.

'Vaughn, it ain't how it looks.'

'I don't think even you can come up with a decent explanation. What the fuck have you done?'

'It was an accident.'

Not answering, Vaughn's eyes went from Franny to Mia. 'Whose baby is that?' He glanced down again at Bree, his mind beginning to race, beginning to piece it all together.

Franny spoke matter-of-factly, her breathing staggered. 'My friend's.'

Vaughn shook his head, his tone disbelieving. 'No. That's Bree's baby, ain't it? Which means . . . Oh my God, that's Alfie's baby. This is why all the cover-up. All the secrets.'

Suddenly, Franny lashed out, kneeing Vaughn hard in the balls. Taken by surprise, he cried out, doubling over in pain and giving Franny the split-second opportunity to run out of the door and into the communal hallway before heading outside.

She jumped into in her car, her eyes focused on the front door as she strapped Mia in but a moment later, she saw Vaughn rushing out. He threw himself against the car, bashing on the window furiously. 'Stop the fucking car, Franny!'

'No chance!'

Reversing wildly, Franny saw Vaughn's car in the rear-view mirror. She put her foot on the accelerator and crashed into it, hoping the damage would slow him down. The next moment, Franny sped off into the night.

Under a pile of jackets in the boot of Vaughn's Range Rover, Shannon was startled awake. Wanting to know what the bang had been, she cautiously sat up, just high enough to peer through the crack of the boot cover to see a car speed off before catching a glimpse of Vaughn charging towards the 4x4.

She lay back down, curling up again, not wanting Vaughn to find her there.

When Alfie had gone home and made her leave the club, she'd had nowhere to go – not that she'd told Alfie that, but she wasn't ready to go back to Charlie's yet, though neither did she want to sleep rough in a park, being hassled by strangers. She knew what that was like. So, she'd walked around and when she'd seen Vaughn's gold Range Rover parked off Soho Square with him nowhere to be seen, but with the doors unlocked and the engine still warm, she'd taken the opportunity to get in, thinking that she would hide in the back for a couple of hours before shooting off. That had been the plan but within minutes, Vaughn had come back and she'd found herself being thrown about in the boot as he sped along.

Hearing Vaughn get in the car now, Shannon listened with interest to the call he was making.

'Alfie! Alfie! For fuck's sake, pick up the phone! I need to talk to you! Call me back as soon as you get this. If you don't hear otherwise, I'll meet you at the club. Make sure you call me back!'

16

Looking in her rear-view mirror, Franny caught sight of Vaughn, his car engine blowing out black smoke. She sped up, hoping to lose him altogether as she hit the accelerator at sixty, wanting to go faster but knowing that it was stupid to risk getting pulled over by a bored officer roaming the streets in the early hours of the morning.

Turning left, she drove through the tunnel, all the time keeping an eye out for Vaughn. It looked like she might've lost him. She slowed down as she came to Bush Lane, turning a sharp left and jumping the lights.

She glanced over at Mia in her car seat. She'd woken up and now was screaming. She tried to comfort her as well as driving, but found it impossible to do both. The sound of Mia's cries filled the car as the vision of Bree came into her head.

'No, no, no, no, no!' She spoke out loud as she attempted

to push all thoughts away. She needed to focus. Just focus. Focus, and get the fuck out.

Coming towards Shaftesbury Avenue, with Mia finally having fallen into a grizzly sleep, Franny turned into Dean Street then turned right into Carlisle Street. She drove clockwise around Soho Square before taking a left down Sutton Row, stopping directly in front of the club.

Checking Vaughn was nowhere to be seen, Franny jumped out of her car, running down the stairs of the club.

A few streets away, Vaughn raced along. He'd kept well back and once he'd seen Franny turn towards Temple Church, he'd decided to hold completely back, following his gut, believing she was heading for the club.

'Fuck's sake, mate! Come on! Get out of the way!' A large lorry was now blocking the entrance to Dean Street, full of sand for the nearby building site. He honked his horn, waving out of the window. 'Come on! Come on! How long you going to be?'

The lorry driver chewed on his cigarette, staring at Vaughn. He shrugged, looking amused. 'However long it takes, mate!'

Resisting the temptation to get out and do the builder some serious injury, Vaughn knew he had to get to Franny. Seething, he reversed down the street, pulling into the nearest parking space before jumping out and running down the road.

In the back room of the club, Franny knelt down and began to unlock the safe, quickly turning the combination, hoping and praying that Vaughn hadn't got around to changing the code. She could break into most safes, certainly the one they had, but the one thing she couldn't do was buy more time.

Without realising she'd been holding her breath, she let out a sigh of relief as she heard the safe's lock click and the door spring open.

She could feel the sweat running down her back, and she could see her hand shaking, still stained with Bree's blood. Taking a short, sharp inhalation of breath, Franny muttered to herself, knowing she had to think of Mia. 'Come on. Come on, don't give in now.' She began to empty the safe. The money. The gun. The passport. The credit cards in different names. Throwing them all into the large canvas rucksack.

Getting up, Franny, feeling agitated and trying not to panic, quickly closed the safe door, glancing up at the clock. It was still early and thankfully the mornings were still very dark. At a rough guess she had a couple of hours before it became light but by then, she'd be well away. Heading to Scotland and from there she could sort out a passage to Norway. Just her and Mia.

The thought of it spurred her on and she began to run through the small corridor and into the staff room door, her heart pounding, but she paused and gave a quick look round, satisfied there wasn't anything else she needed. She stormed through the door . . . and straight into Vaughn.

'Franny, this is becoming a habit.'

'Get out of my way.'

Vaughn shook his head. 'Not until Alfie arrives, and then you can explain to him what you've been up to.'

'Just leave him out of it. This has nothing to do with Alfie, you understand?'

Vaughn's bitter laughter filled the club. 'Why don't you let him be the judge of that? What's that?' He pointed to the canvas bag that Franny was holding. His face twisted up in anger. 'Are you robbing from us, *again*?'

Holding Vaughn's stare, Franny's voice was full of hostility as she said, 'No, I ain't, because this money's *mine*. I worked just as hard for it as you did.'

'You stupid bitch! I don't know what's going on in that head of yours but you're not fucking normal. You've got a screw loose.'

'Go to hell.'

'As long as you're joining me, and I've no doubt you will, the shit you've done in your life . . . So come on, whilst we're waiting, why don't you tell me exactly what happened to Bree.'

Franny's voice was small and tight. 'I'm not telling you anything. Now I'll ask you again, get out of me way.'

Vaughn leant forward, his tone menacing. 'What did she do to you, Franny? What did she say to you to make you kill her?'

'It wasn't fucking like that! You don't know anything about it.'

'I know you've got blood on your hands.'

With precious time ticking away, Franny snapped, knowing she couldn't be there when Alfie arrived. 'Move! Now!'

Vaughn's eyes flamed with anger. 'No, I already told you, I ain't going anywhere and neither are you.'

Quickly slipping her hand into the canvas bag, Franny pulled out the gun. She pointed it at Vaughn, her eyes flashing with anger. 'Move!'

Vaughn glanced at the gun, then at Franny. He sneered. 'You don't frighten me, Fran. I've been around long enough to have a thousand guns stuck in my face and I'm still standing.'

Full of hatred, Franny hissed, 'Do me a favour, Vaughn, save the trip down memory lane and realise I'm not messing around.'

'And neither am I.' Vaughn stepped forward towards Franny, a smirk on his face. 'You ain't going to use that.'

It was Franny's turn to smirk. 'Isn't it you who always says the apple doesn't fall far from the tree? Remember who I am, Vaughn. Don't make any stupid moves.'

'Problem is, Fran, I think *you're* forgetting who *I* am!' He stepped even nearer, not taking his eyes off Franny for a moment.

'I've already told you, stay back!'

Ignoring Franny, Vaughn stepped even nearer. He reached for Franny, grabbing her wrist but she pulled it away and tried to shake him off. Undeterred, he leapt at her again. Suddenly there was a loud sound ringing in her ears, a loud bang echoing in the room, and Franny stood staring, holding the gun as Vaughn dropped to the ground in a pool of blood from the wound just above his chest.

Trying to keep her emotions down, she carefully used her foot to tap him, then leapt back as Vaughn began to speak, his words staggered. 'You'll pay for this.'

Glancing around before she crouched down, Franny

spoke in a whisper. 'I don't think so, Vaughn. Looks like you're the one who'll pay for it. You should never have crossed me. If only you'd left it well alone, none of this would've happened.'

Vaughn, struggling to talk, grimaced in pain. 'Just wait until Alfie finds out.'

'But he won't find out, will he? And even if he does, I'll be long gone.'

'I . . . I . . . I . . .'

She stared at Vaughn watching him fall into unconsciousness. She had to think. Think. Think and move. She could hear the sound of her own breathing. Noisy. Filling the air. She had to get out. She had to go. But as she continued to stare at Vaughn, Bree came into her mind and it felt again like she couldn't move. Once more she was frozen to the spot . . . But what about Mia? She had to think of Mia. Alfie would be here soon. The thought of that hit Franny hard. He couldn't find her . . . and he couldn't find Mia.

Suddenly motivated, Franny dropped the gun back in the canvas bag and began to sprint for the door, charging through the entrance hall and up the basement stairs to where her car was parked, to where Mia was still fast asleep.

Opening up the boot, Franny threw the bag in, but her gaze landed on something. A thought rushed through her mind. Yes, yes, that was it . . .

Looking over her shoulder and checking the small narrow street was still clear, Franny, still breathing hard, grabbed the petrol can from the back of the boot, immediately turning to run back down the stairs of the club, charging into the main dance room where Vaughn was lying.

She ran over to him, bending down before slipping her hands under his, dragging him backwards, using all her strength to pull him, a trail of blood smearing the floor.

Panting, Franny stopped, not knowing if she'd have the strength to pull him into the office but digging deep, she began to pull again, dragging him into the staff room. At the door, she used her foot to roll him inside before running back to the main room to grab the petrol can.

Charging back and listening out for any sound, Franny began to pour the petrol over the whole room, dousing the furniture, dousing the blinds . . . Dousing Vaughn.

A lighter! Shit! She didn't have a lighter! Quickly her eyes darted around the room, then her glance landed back on Vaughn. Of course! She bent down, going into his front pocket to pull out a solid gold lighter, a present from her and Alfie two years ago. She shook her head at the irony.

Going over to the other side of the room, Franny flicked open the lighter and stared at the flame, pausing just for a moment before she touched one of the couches with it. Directly, it set on fire; the material and the petrol a combustible mix.

A sudden rush of panic coursed through her. What was she doing? What the hell was she doing? But as she went to try to fan out the flames, she abruptly stopped and thought about Bree again. She thought about Alfie, and of Mia, and she realised there was no going back. This was her chance to get away, to go through with the plan. To take Mia to a place of safety. If she didn't do this and she let her emotions get the better of her, then everything would've been for nothing. Bree's death would've been for nothing.

With that thought in her mind, Franny jumped back into action. Dousing the rest of the furniture and with the fire now well underway, she picked up the can, running back into the main room, throwing the last of the petrol over the velvet chairs in the corner and the electricity box, seeing it spark with flames before she hurled the entire can into the fire.

She turned to run, shutting the door behind her, making her way as quickly as she could out of the club and up the stairs.

'Franny, what's going on?' Alfie stood at the top of the basement stairs, looking down at her from the road. She couldn't breathe. She couldn't think straight. *Oh God.*

She glanced behind her and breathlessly said, 'Alfie. You're here.'

He looked at her oddly. 'Are you all right?'

She walked towards him, her eyes full of emotion as the fear and panic bubbled below her falsely calm exterior. 'Alfie. Alfie.'

'Has something happened? Vaughn called me – it sounded urgent. Franny, what's going on?'

'Alfie, listen to me, I should've told you. I know I should but then Vaughn . . .' She trailed off not knowing what to say.

Alfie rubbed his head as Franny walked up to where he was standing. He felt terrible, his head was pounding so any drama was the last thing he needed, but he spoke quietly, worried about Franny. 'You're not making any sense, babe. What about Vaughn? All this shit has to stop between you two.'

'I can only . . .' Horror suddenly crossed Franny's face. Fear filled her eyes as she stared at her car. The doors were open. She hadn't left them like that but now they were wide open. She ran around to the passenger seat and let out a scream, loud and full of pain. 'Mia! Mia! Where's Mia?'

She turned to stare at Alfie, desperate, and beginning to shake. 'Where is she, Alfie? Did you take her? Did you?'

Shocked to see Franny in such a state, Alfie shook his head. 'Who's Mia? What the fuck are you talking about? You're frightening me, darlin'.'

Franny charged up to Alfie and began to hit his chest, tears streaming down her face as terror ran through her. 'Tell me where she is! Please tell me where she is!'

Grabbing hold of Franny's hands, shaking his head, Alfie's eyes were full of concern. 'Sweetheart, I've no idea what you're talking about. None.'

Franny stepped back, the words almost unable to come out. 'Mia. She's a baby. She was here, right here. I left her here.'

'A baby? Whose baby? What the fuck are you talking about? Fran, I can't help you if you don't tell me what's going on.'

Franny stared at Alfie. Pale and with waves of nausea rushing through her. Her whole body shaking. 'She's . . . she's my friend's baby . . . I . . .' She trailed off again.

'Fran, I don't understand. Why was she with you?'

Franny screamed at the top of her voice. 'I was just helping out, for fuck's sake. She asked me to look after her for a while . . . and now she's gone. Alfie, help me, Mia's gone!'

She ran around to the driver's seat, jumping in the car as Alfie slammed down the boot.

'Where are you going?'

'To find her – she can't have gone far.'

She began to reverse, spinning around as the still-open passenger door swung open and closed. 'Stop! Fran! I'm coming!' Without hearing Franny's answer, Alfie jumped in as Franny sped off. And as they drove away, neither of them saw the club bursting into flames.

17

As Shannon sat opposite Charlie and his sister in the club, she felt shaken about the events of the morning, and it hadn't helped that she hadn't been able to find any dealers who'd been up to sell her any crack. But as was always the case, the fear she felt from Uncle Charlie and Ma – Auntie Margaret – made everything else fade into obscurity.

Chewing on her thumb, Shannon wished she hadn't bothered calling her auntie or done what she'd done. At the time it'd seemed like the right thing to do – after all, Ma was Bree's ex mother-in-law – but as she sat with Auntie Ma, who was staring daggers at her, the right thing to do was certainly turning out not to be the *best* thing to do.

Charlie sniffed. 'So come on, Shannon, spit it out – what else do you know about Franny and Bree?'

Sullenly, Shannon said, 'I don't know anything else. All I know is what I told you.'

Pointing his fat finger at Shannon, Charlie snarled. 'Listen, by rights I should give you a good hiding, but Ma here persuaded me not to, for now anyway.'

'I only saw them together that once I called you about, Ma. That time in Woolwich, but I didn't know who Franny was until she came into the club. I recognised her as the woman who was with Bree.'

'And where's Bree now?'

Shannon shrugged. 'I dunno. I've told you everything.'

Ma Dwyer stood up from behind the table. She wore a green tight jumper and a pair of black leggings, which did nothing to hide her bulging waistline. She struggled to move her grossly obese body as she waddled over to where Shannon was sitting. Shannon stared down at her aunt's oedema-swollen ankles and feet pushed tightly into stained, white canvas trainers. She clipped Shannon hard about the head. 'Watch your cheek. You're becoming a stuck-up little cow. If you're hiding anything . . .'

'I'm not, I'm not!'

Ma nodded, her hard, cruel demeanour oozing from her. 'Don't get smart!'

Shannon looked up at Ma. She remembered a time when she'd thought that all little girls had aunties like Ma. After her mother had died, she'd gone to live with Ma and her sons in Essex. And quite quickly, the problems that she'd had when she'd been with her mother seemed nothing in comparison to what happened when she was with Ma.

Not that she could really remember her mother – the

woman had been in and out of mental institutions all her life – but she did know that she had loved her. There'd certainly been no love for Ma, though, and when she'd had the opportunity to go and work for Charlie, she hadn't looked back, having very little contact with Ma and none at all with Bree. Though through the odd conversation she'd overheard Uncle Charlie having, she knew Bree had run away. She also knew that something bad had happened to Ma's sons, but she'd been too afraid to ask. The one thing she'd learnt growing up was never to ask Ma or her uncle their business unless of course you wanted to feel the hard edge of their fist.

But even to her it'd come as a surprise, *shocked* her to know that Bree had left her husband to be with *Alfie*. Alfie! Not that she blamed her. Though how he ended up back with Franny, she didn't know. In fact, there was a lot she didn't know, but if she *had* known any of it, she certainly wouldn't have called Ma.

Alfie had been good to her, and the more she thought about what she had done, the more miserable she felt. It was clear that Ma hated Alfie, but she'd only done what she'd done because of Franny, who'd been mean. But now she wasn't sure how she was going to put things right.

Poking Shannon in the chest, Ma said, 'I know what your head's like. That crack has sent you stupid. You sure there isn't anything else you've forgotten?'

Giving Ma a small smile, Shannon shook her head, knowing full well there was *one* thing. But she hadn't forgotten it; it was simply that she'd never talk about it. Not to Ma. Not to Charlie. Not to anyone. She'd made a promise.

And no matter what happened, she'd never breathe a word. 'No, there isn't anything else, I swear.'

Suitably satisfied, Ma sniffed. 'Right, well you know what you've got to do, don't you? Go on then, Shannon . . . Move!'

18

'Keep looking! Keep looking!' Franny screamed as tears continued to fall down her face. It felt like she couldn't breathe. She took a left turn down Regent Street, jumping the lights, driving too fast, not caring about anything else but finding Mia.

'This is crazy, Fran, we won't find her like this. She could be anywhere.'

'Keep looking!'

Alfie's voice was full of concern as he gazed out of the window. 'I hate to say it, but we need to call the police, darlin'. You need to call your mate and tell her what's happened.'

'I can't! I can't . . . We just got to find her! We just got to find her . . . There! Look over there! That woman, with a baby.'

In the dark of the morning, at the edge of Regent's Park,

Franny pulled over, skidding the car to a halt, her wheels bouncing up on the kerb.

Dashing out of the car, Franny charged at the woman, dragging at her clothes as she screamed in her face.

'Mia! Mia! Give me my baby!'

Terrified and confused, the woman began to step back, falling against the black metal railings whilst trying to fend Franny off as she continued to pull the baby out from her arms.

'Give her me! Give her me! I said *give* her to me! She's mine!'

Petrified, both the woman and the baby began to scream.

'Franny, Franny stop! For fuck's sake! What's wrong with you!' Alfie grabbed Franny, dragging her off.

In shock, Franny stared at Alfie and then at the woman and at the baby: black straight hair instead of soft bouncing curls. Olive skin instead of pale skin. A boy instead of a girl. Somebody else's baby.

Tears ran down Franny's cheeks as she called after the woman who'd rushed off, holding her baby tight to her chest.

'I'm sorry, okay . . . I'm so sorry, I made a mistake. I don't know what I was thinking.'

Gently, Alfie put his hand on Franny's shoulder. 'Get back in the car, Fran. Come on, babe, let's go.'

Franny nodded and climbed back into the car in silence.

As she drove off again, speeding round the outer circle of Regent's Park before taking a left into Chester Road, Alfie spoke. 'Franny listen to me, this is madness. You nearly killed that woman back there! We can't just drive around.'

He frowned and reached across to the dash, something catching his eye. He grabbed it and instantly a chill rushed over him. Terror. His words were barely audible.

'Franny . . . Franny . . . Stop the car. I know who's got her.'

Franny glanced across at Alfie at the same time as she slammed on the brakes. 'What?'

Swallowing hard to try to get his breath, Alfie whispered his words. 'I said, I know who's got her.'

'How? What are you talking about? Tell me . . . Tell me!' she screamed at Alfie as he began to read the letter out loud, which'd been left tucked on the dash.

'*Roses are red, Violets are blue, I've got the baby, what ya going to do?*

Oh, and don't call the police, I'm warning you!'

Drained of colour and feeling traumatised, Alfie gazed at Franny. 'It's from that guy I was telling you about. It's from him. He's got her, he's got your friend's baby.'

Franny stared at Alfie strangely. Her voice tight. 'No, no, it can't be.'

He crumpled up the letter in his hand. 'It is, whether you like it or not, Fran.'

'No.'

'It *is*, I know it is.'

Franny shook her head, hysteria tingeing her tone. 'It can't be, it just can't.'

'I'm telling you it is!'

'It ain't, Alf!'

Angrily Alfie raised his voice. 'I know what I'm talking about. He's got Mia.'

147

'He hasn't! He hasn't!'

'He has!'

Franny screamed at the top of her voice. 'He ain't, Alf, he ain't because they were from me.'

'What?'

'The letters were *all* from me! Not this person you think. So you see, whoever has got her can't be him, because I wrote them. *All* of them.'

The car filled with silence as Alfie tried to comprehend what Franny had just said. He spoke in a hush. 'You?'

'Yeah.'

His eyes flickered with anger. '*You* wrote them?'

Franny gave a tiny nod along with a tiny reply. 'Yes, all of them.'

Alfie's voice was tight. 'Even the letters I got when we were in Essex?'

'Yes . . . I'm so sorry, Alf.'

'Sorry?'

Franny nodded.

Alfie slowly turned to look at her, his face darkened as he stared in hatred and spoke in a measured tone. 'I'm going to kill you.' Then, incensed, he lunged at Franny. She screamed as he grabbed for her throat, but she managed to hit him off and scrabble out of the car, running towards the entrance of Queen Mary's rose garden with Alfie only metres behind her.

With her heart pounding, she ran, skidding on the muddy path and across the wet grass as she headed towards the Japanese Gardens, racing towards the central island over the wooden bow bridge.

'There's nowhere to run, Fran, you might as well stop now!' she heard Alfie yelling angrily as he charged along behind her in the dark.

Hoping to lose Alfie, Franny, panting, clawed her way up the large muddy mound of the gardens, crushing the delicate flowers as she did so. She slipped, falling down on her front in the wet earth as the rain started to pour down.

At the top of the mound, she leapt across the waterfall, her feet sliding off the slimy rocks, covered in green algae.

Making it across to the other side, Franny, soaking wet, pushed her way into the thick bushes, but almost immediately Alfie grabbed her and dragged her down through the dense, woody undergrowth by her hair. She felt every scratch from the twisted thorns and twigs as she fought to get away.

'Ain't no escaping me, darlin', you should know that by now.'

She kicked out, catching Alfie square on his knee then elbowed him in his face, but unable to fight him off completely, she felt the force of Alfie's fist smash against her face; the power of it knocking her to the ground.

Alfie sprang on top of her, his eyes void of any emotion. 'I'm going to kill you!'

'Get off me! Get the fuck off me!' she screamed at him, but he slammed his hand over her mouth, the pressure of it driving her head further into the cold, wet mud. His hand was heavy and hard on her mouth and she bit down on it, sinking her teeth into his palm, drawing blood.

'Fuck! You bitch!' For a second Alfie pulled his hand away, giving Franny the opportunity to push him off, pulling herself up onto her knees; but he gripped her jacket, causing her to fall down face first in the mud before he twisted her arm behind her back.

'Why did you do it, Fran? You sick bitch, why?'

'I . . . I . .' She wrestled beneath him, her face still pushed into the earth.

'Tell me! Tell me why the woman I loved would do that to me!' He flipped her round, turning her to face him.

Covered in mud and with her face swelling, colouring blue and red, Franny screamed back, 'I didn't know! I didn't know it'd upset you so much!'

Disgusted, he stared at her, then banged her head against the ground. She yelped. 'Didn't know! You saw how fucked up I was.'

'No, I never . . . I mean, I saw you stressed, but I thought, well I thought it was about Bree and about the coke you were taking, cos you were taking a lot of it. You never really told me how you felt about the letters until the other day. I wouldn't have written them if I'd known they were going to affect you the way they did.'

Alfie, still sitting on top of Franny, yelled at her, 'You should never have written them anyway! Do you know what you've done to me? Do you, Fran?' Alfie's eyes filled with tears. 'Look at the state of me. I'm a grown man and I'm fucking crying and you did that, Fran, you did that to me. Why couldn't you have left well enough alone?' He paused again, then wiping his face from the rain and his tears, he pulled out a gun from his jacket, pushing it hard onto Franny's temple. He spat his words at her, 'Tell me why I shouldn't kill you now. Go on, come up with a reason, cos I'm happy to pull the trigger. You know I will.'

Sounding breathless and her words full of pain, Franny whispered, 'Because of Mia . . . Who'll find Mia, if I'm dead? You don't even know what she looks like.'

Alfie shook his head, a multitude of different thoughts rushing through his mind. 'You're something else, you know? There's always something for Franny Doyle to hide behind, ain't there? Vaughn was right about you, you're a fucking snake, and you're a nasty bitch . . . and I hate you. You hear me, Fran? I hate you!'

Ignoring the fact that she was lying not only to Alfie but also to herself, Franny said, 'I only did it because I was worried about you. It was the only thing I could think of to do.'

'What? What the fuck are you talking about?'

'After Bree, and after she . . . after she lost the baby, I knew that you were upset. The first couple of days you just sat around and drank. I was worried because I've seen you spiral before, so I wanted you to get away, to take a break, but you wouldn't listen. You were having none of it. So . . .'

'So, you thought you'd mess my head up?'

'It wasn't like that, Alfie, I swear. Even before the stuff with Bree, you'd had a tough year. I just wanted you to go away and recoup.' She paused, then lying through her teeth, Franny added, 'Selfishly, I just wanted the old Alfie back. I know now what I did was stupid, but the letters, well that was just my way to encourage you to go.'

Bemused and still enraged, Alfie spoke through clenched

teeth. '*Encourage?* And that's how you do it? Fucking hell! You're a joke, Fran.'

'I'm so sorry, Alf, like I say, I had no idea it would affect you like this, it was only because I was worried about you that I wrote them, but it never seemed like it was bothering you. You hid it well.'

'Oh, so it's my fault now?'

'No, of course not. I just didn't know you were so upset. I mean, I don't know *anything* about this guy or why he's in prison. The only thing you told me was you helped get him put away.'

Distraught, Alfie shook his head. 'I ain't a grass – it wasn't like that.'

'I'm not saying you are, I just know when you told me last year that he was being released, you seemed jumpy, and frankly, a bit scared . . .'

'And you thought you'd take advantage of that by pretending the letters were from him, did you?'

Franny, shivering from the cold, stared up at Alfie. 'I'm not proud of it.'

With a faraway look in his eye, Alfie said, 'I really thought they were from him. I should be relieved that they're not, but . . . but for some reason it don't make me feel any better.'

Speaking just as quietly as Alfie, Franny asked, 'Who is he, Alf? Tell me who he is.'

The spark of fury came back into Alfie. 'So you can write another letter about it, play some more of your mind games?'

'No, of course not.'

Alfie's bellow caused the bird in the tree to flutter out the branch. '*I don't believe you!*'

'You've got to trust me, Alf. I'd never do anything to hurt you.'

Roughly, he grabbed her hair, pulling her head up inches away from his. He jammed the gun against her temple again. 'Since when, Fran? Since when?'

'Why don't you just try me?'

Tears pricked in Alfie's eyes. 'Try you?'

'Yeah.'

Bitterly, with pain encased in his words, Alfie said, 'Okay, I'll try you . . . You ready? You ready for this . . .? The guy I put away, twenty-odd years ago . . . he was a nonce.'

As Alfie moved from on top of Franny, to sit against one of the trees, she sat up and stared.

'What?'

'Yeah, a nonce.'

'How did you know him?'

Alfie shook his head. 'He was Charlie Eton's dad. Barry Eton.'

Franny stared in horror at Alfie. 'Charlie's dad? I don't understand. How did *you* get him put away?'

'You ain't getting it are you?'

Puzzled, Franny stretched out her arms wide. 'Getting what?'

'Me, Fran. He hurt *me* as well as Charlie, and it wasn't just the once. I was thirteen years old and I was too scared to do anything about it . . . I couldn't stop it. I tried to tell Charlie, but he was just a kid like me, so what could he do? And there was no one else to tell.'

Stunned, Franny whispered, 'My God. I'm so sorry, Alf.'

'I moved away from the area, got put away in a boys' home. It was bad, but it was better than being around Barry. Then some years later, Charlie tracked me down. Turned out he knew all along what his dad was doing to me.'

Franny gasped. 'And he never said anything?'

With his head down, unable to hold eye contact, Alfie shrugged. 'Fran, he was petrified himself. He was an innocent kid as well. Back then, there was still hope for Charlie. He wasn't like he is now. Anyway, he asked for my help. He had this one sister who was still living at home. She was having a terrible time. Cut a long story short, he needed me to give evidence against his dad. None of his sisters would go to court – they were too scared – and his mum, well she was a drunk, so that only left me and Charlie. And however tough it was, there was no way I was going to say no.'

'And that's why you and Charlie have an understanding?'

Alfie shrugged. 'I dunno about an understanding, but we've got that connection.'

'So what happened to his sister in the end?'

'Charlie never really talks much about it. I don't think he sees any of his family, but I wouldn't know; last time I knew anything about them was years and years ago. I couldn't even tell you their names. We were just kids back then. It's only really been this past year since we moved back up to Soho that I've spoken to him. Like I say, he's a different guy to the one all those years ago. After the court case we never spoke again. The only thing I do know about that sister is she was in and out of mental institutions most of her life then ended up overdosing in a back alleyway. She had a kid apparently. God knows what happened to her. The whole thing's a mess.'

Franny reached over to touch Alfie. He drew away. '*Don't fucking touch me*, Fran. I'm so angry with you . . . You know, the things Charlie's dad did to me, that never goes away. You just learn to live with it. That's all you can do, and that's what I did do until . . .'

'I sent those letters?'

And as the rain continued to pour down and dawn began to break, Alfie said nothing, only stared, and a tense silence fell between them.

It was a few minutes later before Alfie's phone rang, breaking the silence. Sitting in the mud, he wiped away his tears and after rubbing his face, he took a deep breath before answering the phone. 'Hello?'

Alfie listened to the caller, his face drawn. Then clicking his phone off, he turned to Franny in shock and disbelief. 'It's the club. There's been a fire. The whole place has been destroyed.'

19

Driving back to Soho Square, Franny trembled. She had plenty on her mind, the enormity of the past few hours hitting her and the fear of what to do about Mia overwhelming her, but her thoughts were interrupted by Alfie. 'Do you think we should go and see what's happened to the club? See if they've put the fire out yet?'

With her eyes firmly on the road, Franny shook her head. 'No, just leave them to it. What good are we going to be? They probably won't let us near anyway.'

Nodding but saying nothing, Alfie continued to gaze out of the window, but another thought came to him. 'What were you going to tell me about Vaughn? Back at the club, just before you realised Mia was missing, you were talking about Vaughn.'

Trying to seem as casual as possible, Franny shrugged.

'I don't know, Alf, I can't really think. I can only focus on Mia right now. That's all I'm bothered about.'

'I know, darlin', but it's weird. He ain't answering his phone, but he left me this message earlier. He was adamant he wanted to speak to me . . . Listen.' Alfie pressed his voicemail, putting it on loudspeaker, and a moment later, Vaughn's voice filled the car. *'Alfie! Alfie! For fuck's sake, pick up the phone! I need to talk to you! Call me back as soon as you get this. If you don't hear otherwise, I'll meet you at the club. Make sure you call me back!'*

Alfie swivelled round in his seat to look at Franny, seeing the raised bruise on her face. He felt ashamed. He'd never really hit a woman in his life. It just wasn't his style, and as much as it'd been fucked up – really fucked up, what she'd done with the letters – she wasn't to know Charlie's dad had abused him and she certainly wasn't to know even after all this time that the thought of Barry Eton turned him from Alfie Jennings, a face to be reckoned with, to the trembling little boy from all those years ago. And although most people wouldn't have done what she did, Franny just wasn't most people. She'd really only done what she'd thought was best for him. She'd been worried. Jesus, worried about how he felt about Bree leaving him – the woman he'd basically had an *affair* with. But that just showed Franny's strength. No matter how hurt she'd been, she'd still put him first. In his book that took some doing, and it also meant he had no right to be angry with her. 'So, what do you reckon, Fran? Have you any idea what he was talking about?'

After pulling up a few streets away from their house because of the surrounding roads being blocked off due to the police and fire engines, Franny rested her head on the steering wheel. Her body was tired, her mind even more so, but she had to keep going for Mia . . . But where was she? Who the hell could've written that letter and left it on the dashboard? She wanted to run to the police, get help, but after what the note had said about not going to the police, she was too scared to risk it. She had no idea where to start looking, and the truth was, she was terrified.

'Fran? Fran?'

'Sorry, Alf, what did you say?'

'Vaughn. What do you think he was on about?'

Franny took a deep breath, pushing down her emotions once again as she came up with something to say. 'The thing is . . . The thing is . . . Vaughn was ripping us off.'

Alfie looked shocked. 'What? No way! Not Vaughn. You must've got it wrong.'

'He was, I . . . I wanted to tell you before, but I didn't have all the evidence. That's why I've been a bit secretive of late. Anyway, I found out and I confronted him, and of course he didn't like it.'

'But why would he want to meet me in the club, then?'

Franny shrugged. 'Once he knew I was going to say something, I suppose he thought he'd get to you first. Get you to believe *him* rather than me. After all I did take your money before, so he probably thought it'd be easy to turn you against me.'

'I just don't get why though – we're all partners.'

Rubbing her temples from the pounding headache that

was beginning to start, Franny said, 'He thinks I owe him for the money I took from you both last year, and as you didn't force me to pay him back, I guess he saw that as some kind of betrayal from you, and he decided to take matters into his own hands.'

'By ripping us off?'

In full flow and starting to believe her own lies, Franny nodded. 'Yeah, but he didn't see it like that; he saw it as taking back what was his.'

Clearly not wanting to accept what Franny was saying, Alfie lit a cigarette. 'Vaughn may be a lot of things, but to go behind my back like that, well it's not like him. Are you sure you haven't got this wrong, Fran?'

Franny looked at Alfie evenly. 'I wish I had, but I think Vaughn's been laying the groundwork for a long time.'

'What do you mean?'

'All those digs at me, trying to make out like *I* was up to something. Basically, trying to get you to turn against me.'

Alfie stared at Franny. It was true that Vaughn had kept trying to lay the seed of doubt about Franny, and it *was* true that the books weren't balancing, but Vaughn, rip him off? It was so hard to believe, but then, when Franny had taken the two million pounds from them last year, albeit for good reason, *that* had been hard to believe as well. He supposed, when it came down to it, none of them were in this business because of their sainthoods. 'So, why were you in the club?'

Not wanting to answer any more questions, Franny snapped, 'Look, Alf, do we have to do this? The fact is I came to the club and we had a row. I found him taking the money out of the safe . . . as well as his passport. He's gone, Alf.'

'Gone? Where?'

'I dunno, but I guess he realised that once I told *you* what *he* was up to, then things would get very difficult for him. I'm sorry, Alf, I know it's hard to hear this. I was upset myself. After all, I thought we were all friends. I guess I was wrong.'

Franny smiled at Alfie, though her eyes were dark. When he was about to answer her, Alfie's phone rang again. He answered it, still processing what Franny had said. 'Yeah . . . shit . . . are you sure? . . . Okay, thanks.'

After a minute he put the phone down and looked at Franny, her whole face and body still covered in thick mud.

'That was my pal. He's heard some rumours. Apparently, even though it's still early doors, the word is the fire brigade reckons the fire at the club wasn't an accident. It was deliberate and by all accounts the fire was so hot it'll take a long time before they can determine the cause. They're still trying to put it out now.'

Keeping her gaze straight, Franny nodded again, showing no emotion. No pangs of guilt.

'And I know exactly who it was . . . There's no doubt about it. Charlie Eton started that fire. Question is, what are you going to do about it? But whatever you do, Alf, I think you should make it permanent.'

160

20

After cleaning herself up, Franny, unable to stand being cooped up in the house with Alfie asking more questions about Vaughn and her head swimming with thoughts of Mia, stood in the street, leaning on the railings as the rain continued to pour.

She couldn't really feel the chill of the air, nor the fact her clothes were soaked through to her skin – all she could do was stare, trance-like, at the passing cars and people, unaware of the noise of Soho, unaware of anything but the thought of Mia . . . Bree . . . and of course, Vaughn.

The pain in her chest was real. The panic she was fighting clamped down on her, threatening to overwhelm her. Crushing her.

'*What have you done?*' She spoke out loud to herself as she walked towards St Patrick's Church on the other side of Soho Square. It was a place that held so many memories for her, a place that, although she wasn't religious, she was drawn to.

In the foyer of the church, Franny did as she always did and lit a candle for her mother, the mother she had never known but had heard so much about. She lit another one for Mia, her hands shaking, then smiled as she lit one more, this time for her father, whom she missed so much.

She watched the flickering flames, mesmerised, wondering what advice her father would give her if he were still around. Undoubtedly, he'd tell her what happened was all *their* fault. Bree and Vaughn's. And she shouldn't feel guilty about what had happened, because they'd brought it all on themselves. He'd also tell her whatever she did, she shouldn't panic. *Keep calm, keep very calm. Don't let anything slip*. And have no regrets. Absolutely none – *what's done cannot be undone*. But mainly, he would tell her she shouldn't feel anything towards them: no sadness, no guilt, no nothing; and whatever she did, she had to keep one step ahead.

Sighing, she frowned and walked into the church itself, suddenly aware of how cold she was. She shivered, the gloom of the day made worse by the heavy stone of the building. Her footsteps echoed as she walked on the highly polished marble floor, under the large Corinthian column and past the two large statues of angels. She took a seat on one of the wooden pews.

She stared up at the gold dome at the front of the church. None of it was supposed to turn out like it did. None of it was supposed to hurt anyone. All she had done was try to help, hadn't she? If Bree had listened, if Vaughn hadn't wanted to bring her down, none of this would've happened, and she hated them for it. *Hated* them for putting her in this position. It was also because of them Mia was missing.

The pain came back in her chest as she started to shake. She still didn't have the first clue what she was supposed to do, where she was supposed to turn. Maybe it'd turn out that she *had* to go to the police after all. But apart from the letter warning her specifically not to go to them, the problem was the police would have questions about Mia. Questions that she didn't have the answers to, or rather answers she wouldn't want to tell them.

She'd never felt so helpless in her life. Never. Hopefully, whoever wrote the letter would be in touch. But it was the waiting that was the problem. Waiting on hope, not certainty. The waiting part was killing her.

'Franny? Franny?'

Turning around, Franny frowned as she saw it was the girl from the club. Wet and dishevelled and with half her front teeth missing. She scowled at her, irritated that the girl knew her name. Vaughn must've told her.

Angrily, she growled, 'Whatever it is, I'm not in the mood. Now I'd appreciate it if you'd leave me alone. I came in here to get a bit of peace.'

Dressed in only a tiny denim mini skirt and a long-sleeve thin red cotton top, and with holes in her satin dolly shoes, Shannon shivered as the rain dripped down her neck. She smirked. 'Not sure if praying will help. Maybe talking would.'

With simmering anger, Franny stood up from the pew, moving towards Shannon. 'Not with you it wouldn't. Now please, go away, and if you think you're getting any money from me, think again. Go and beg elsewhere.'

Clearly not in the least concerned by what Franny had to say, Shannon stared at her, full of hostility. 'Vaughn was right about you, you're a nasty cow.'

'You know nothing about Vaughn and you know even less about me.'

Not to be put off, Shannon chewed on her gum as she spoke. 'I know he's my friend.'

Pushing her long chestnut hair out of her face, Franny laughed. She couldn't believe that she was even engaging in conversation with this girl. 'Let me tell you something, Vaughn would never be your friend, so wherever you got that idea from, think again. Like I say, you don't know anything.'

Red-faced and trying not to let what Franny said hurt her, Shannon yelled, her voice echoing around the large, empty church. 'It's you who doesn't know anything . . . you don't even know where the baby is.' And without another word, Shannon turned away, stomping off down the aisle.

In the greyness of the day, Franny's face was a picture of shock. It took her a moment to register what Shannon had meant, but then with her heart pounding, she ran back through the church, catching up with Shannon in the foyer. She roughly grabbed hold of her arm. 'What did you say?'

Haughtily, Shannon shrugged. 'Oh, so you want to talk to me now?'

Shaking her hard, Franny hissed, 'You said, *the baby*. Tell me what you know about her.'

'Say *please*!'

Lunging at her, Franny squeezed Shannon's face between

her fingers as she pushed her against the stone wall. 'Don't play games with me, understand? So go on, tell me what you know.'

Pushing her off, Shannon spat out her words. 'I know that it's Bree's baby.'

Franny's head began to spin again and although she tried to keep her cool, she stuttered her words. 'How . . . how do you know about Bree?'

'There's a lot of things that I know . . . *Roses are red, violets are blue, we've got the baby, so what ya going to do?*'

Franny screamed, causing the old lady who was walking into the church to hurry away in fright. '*You!* You! You took Mia. Where is she? Where is she? I said, where the fuck is she? You better not have hurt her!'

Shannon shouted back, 'No, of course not, we're looking after her.'

Beside herself with anger, Franny pushed Shannon hard, banging her against the walls of the foyer as questions ran through her head. 'Who's *we*? *Who's we*? And . . . and that letter you wrote, it was . . .'

Shannon shrugged and interrupted, '. . . like the ones that Alfie had. Yeah, I know. I know all about them because I saw them.'

Confused, Franny quizzed, 'What? How?'

'I just did.'

Shaking her head, Franny said, 'I don't know how you saw them, but I do know you're a nasty little bitch! What did Alfie ever do to you?'

Shannon seemed surprised. 'Alfie! He ain't done anything. It's you! It's you who's the horrible cow.'

165

'This is crazy. I don't even know you, so just tell me where Mia is. You really don't want to mess with me.'

'I'm not scared of you. You can't do anything to me that ain't been done before.'

Franny's eyes darkened. She stepped within inches of Shannon. 'You'd be surprised what I can do to you that hasn't been done before.'

Still not backing down, Shannon said, 'Then you'll never know where *Mia* is, will you?'

'Just *tell* me.'

'It'll cost you.'

Franny sneered. 'Money? So that's what this is all about, though it doesn't surprise me.'

Shannon shook her head. 'No, it's about family.'

'Family? What are you talking about?'

'Well Uncle Charlie thought it'd be nice for her to stay with family.'

Frowning, Franny said, 'Charlie? Who's Charlie?'

Smirking, Shannon sing-songed her words. 'Oh, you know him well. I'm talking about Charlie Eton. He's my uncle.'

Franny looked at Shannon in disbelief. 'What?'

'Oh yeah, and there's you thinking I don't know anything. Looks like it's *you* who don't.'

Still in shock, Franny replied, 'And are you saying Mia's with him?'

Shannon laughed. 'With Charlie? No way, he hates babies. Can't stand the sight of them. No, Mia's with her granny. She's with Ma. Ma Dwyer.'

21

Outside in the rain, Franny paced about as she spoke on the phone. She'd never met Ma Dwyer, but she'd heard of her. Heard of the twisted relationship she'd had with her sons and heard how brutally she'd treated Bree. So, the idea that Ma had Mia felt worse than when she hadn't known where she was.

And on top of that, the other problem she now had was the fact that Charlie was Ma's brother, and she had no idea if Alfie knew that or not. Of course, Charlie and Alfie went back a long way, back to when they were kids, but when Alfie had spoken about Charlie's family earlier, he didn't seem to know anything about them. So hopefully, he could never put two and two together. *Hopefully* Charlie wouldn't speak to Alfie about Mia. Though again, it was all about hope and hope certainly wasn't going to help her now, especially as she'd blamed Charlie for the fire, which meant

Alf would be paying Charlie a visit one way or another very soon. Somehow she needed to stop him.

She rubbed her head, feeling a migraine beginning to kick in. 'Just give me Mia back, you understand, Ma?'

On the other end of the line, Ma Dwyer sat in her kitchen of the mobile home in Essex she'd once shared with her sons. She dipped the piece of white bread in the runny yolk of her fried egg before shovelling it into her mouth, leaving a dribble of yellow and white running down her chin.

'I'm afraid I can't do that, Franny . . . *Shut up, you noisy little madam!*' Ma turned to shout at Mia who screamed in the corner of the untidy room.

Distressed, Franny clung on to the phone. She spoke gently, appealing, desperate. 'Ma, *please*, please, don't shout at her. She's only a baby and she's probably hungry. Have you fed her?'

Nastily, Ma sniffed, burping as she spoke. 'Who do you think I am? Gordon fucking Ramsay? This ain't a five-star hotel.'

'I know, I know, but she still needs to be fed, Ma.'

Ma stared at Mia. 'Listen here, by the looks of her she's not only been eating too much, but she's clearly been spoilt as well. It'll do her good to know that when she cries people aren't going to drop everything to run to her. She'll soon learn. It never did my lot any harm sitting there all day. They soon get tired of screaming.'

Tears ran down Franny's face as she listened to Mia continue to cry. 'Ma, I'm begging you, just please, please pick her up.'

'I ain't a fucking forklift truck. Now do yourself a favour

– stop begging and start talking and maybe that way we can come to some sort of arrangement. Where's Bree anyway? I would've thought she'd be the one calling me.'

Keeping her voice even despite the fact she was trembling, Franny said, 'She's too upset . . . You took her baby, what do you expect?'

Scratching between the folds of fat on her neck, Ma sniffed. 'But it's not just her baby, is it? It's Johnny's. It's my son's baby as well, which means she's my granddaughter. And he might not be around but that don't mean I suddenly stop being her granny. And I know my son would've wanted me to have her.'

'You can't just take other people's babies.'

Ma snapped, 'Are you stupid or you just ain't listening? She isn't just *other people's*, she's my son's.'

Franny spoke firmly. 'Ma, she isn't though. Mia isn't Johnny's baby.'

It was the first time Ma sounded unsure. 'What do you mean? I may not be Einstein, but it doesn't take him to work out when Bree fell pregnant. She was still with Johnny.'

Franny sighed, her migraine now pulsating behind her eyes as she thought about what Ma was saying. She remembered that in the beginning Bree had never been entirely sure whose baby Mia was, mainly because of the slight crossover between Alfie and her husband, Johnny. But to her there was no doubt. She knew Mia was Alfie's. Watching Mia grow she could see her looking more and more like Alfie each day. Mia was the spitting image of her father.

A slight bit of hope came back into Franny's voice. 'No, Ma, Mia came early. She was premature. She's Alfie's baby, not Johnny's. Look at her, Ma. Look at her face. You know Alfie. You can see that she looks like him. Go and look at her, *please*.'

'But . . .'

'Just do it, Ma.'

'Okay, okay! Hold on . . .' Irritated, Ma stood up, kicking the large tabby cat out of the way as she waddled over to the corner where Mia was sitting in her car seat. Holding the phone, she stared at Mia, seeing Alfie staring back at her.

'Ma! Ma, are you still there?' Franny called down the phone, knowing she had to play this right. After all, Mia might not be Johnny's, but the fact was, Ma still had her.

Waddling back to her chair, Ma answered Franny, 'Of course I'm still here.'

'So, did you see? Can you see what I'm saying?'

Not wanting to admit it to Franny that rather than Mia being the image of her son, she was the image of Alfie, Ma tried to sound casual. 'I don't know what you're talking about. All babies look the same to me.'

'Maybe they do, Ma, but I'm sure the police would have something to say about kidnapping. Because that's what this is. Mia has nothing to do with you, but you still took her.'

Ma laughed, though she didn't feel as confident as she had done half an hour ago. 'That's ridiculous. You wouldn't call the police – that ain't what you lot do.'

Franny's voice was cold and hard. 'Believe me, Ma, I would do anything for Mia and I mean *anything*.'

Not liking how the conversation was going, Ma said, 'I

don't want to speak to you anymore, I want to speak to Bree.'

'Like I say, she's too upset to talk.'

'I'll be the judge of that. I already know where she lives. Shannon told me. So maybe I'll give her a knock.'

Franny's head once again began to spin. How Shannon knew where Bree lived, she had no idea, but what she did know is that she needed to stay as calm as possible. 'Do whatever you want, but she won't speak to you.'

'Then I'll speak to Alfie.'

'*No!*' The minute she said it, Franny knew in that one little word, she'd spoken too quickly, had jumped too soon, had panicked too much. She chewed her lip, closing her eyes, hearing the pounding of her heart and hoping that Ma wouldn't have picked up on her desperation.

A laugh came down the phone, loud and unpleasant. 'Why not, Franny?'

Franny could feel that Ma had her on a hook. 'Because, like Bree, he's upset. Wouldn't you be?'

'Well, maybe getting a phone call from me will make him feel better.'

'Don't do that . . . Just *don't.*'

Again, Ma roared with laughter, the sound mixing with Mia's distressed cries. 'He doesn't know, does he? He doesn't know about Mia.'

'Of course he does. He's her father, isn't he?'

'Or is it Bree he doesn't know about?'

'What are you talking about?'

Ma's voice dripped with scorn although she spoke quietly. 'Oh, Franny, who are you trying to kid? Something's going on, I'm no fool. Bree was always a sly little bitch, and it doesn't surprise me that you're the same. And for one moment there I thought you had me . . . For one minute I really thought I'd have to hand back this little snot bag to you. But it turns out for one reason or another you don't want Alfie to know what's going on.'

Unable to hold her temper, Franny screamed down the phone, 'Listen to me, Ma, you better just hand her over to me, you understand? This ain't got nothing to do with Alfie.'

'Why don't we let him be the judge of that.' The hoot of laughter from Ma incensed Franny more.

'If you phone him, you'll regret it. I'm warning you, Ma.'

'No, Franny, I'm warning *you*: if you don't give me what I want, then *you'll* regret it because I will be phoning Alfie . . . Now this is how it's going to go. I'm going to decide how much I want for Mia, and then I'll call and let you know. Understand?'

Paling and barely able to speak, Franny nodded her head. 'Perfectly.'

Ma chuckled nastily. 'Good. And in the meantime, I think I'm going to pay that little mare a visit. I think it's high time me and Bree had a chat about old times.'

And with that, Ma put down the phone, leaving Franny standing in the pouring rain. But a minute later, she began to run, jumping in her car and speeding off with only one thing on her mind.

22

Franny sat outside Bree's maisonette. Her head was whirling from the revelation but if she didn't lose it, if she didn't panic, then she could get it sorted and get Mia back. She'd tried to call Charlie, not that she knew what she was going to say, but she needed to get to him before Alfie did, though she knew that was dangerous. The minute Charlie Eton smelt weakness, he was sure to take advantage of it.

Sighing, she looked at herself in the driver's mirror. She could see the tiny line of stress forming between her eyebrows. She could see her skin was paler than usual and she could see the fear in her eyes.

'*Franny.*'

She whipped round, her heart pounding. She was sure she'd just heard her name . . . No, no, she was just being silly. Maybe it was the wind, or someone in the distance shouting . . . but it had sounded so much like her name and it *had* sounded just like Bree's voice . . . No, God what was she doing? She had to stop this. She was tired, that was all. She wasn't going to start letting her imagination play tricks on her. But . . . No, no, she was only going to think happy thoughts. Mia. Yes, she would think about Mia and what they would do together when all this was over.

Taking a deep breath, she got out of her car, and ignoring the fact that she'd begun to tremble, ignoring the fact that a cold chill of fear ran through her body, she walked towards the flat in Ruston Road, pausing a moment at the communal door before letting herself into the entrance hall.

At Bree's front door, her hands shook as she fitted the key in the lock. She paused again, forcing herself to breathe out. To be calm. To think of Mia. That's what she needed to focus on. Nothing else.

Then pushing the door open, Franny stepped inside.

Taking a sharp intake of breath as the darkness encased her, Franny quickly switched on the light, pushing herself against the wall as she closed the door, somehow trying to distance herself from the scene in front of her. The eerie silence surrounding her.

Bree's body was lying exactly where she had left it, but even in this short space of time, it had already started decomposing. Her skin had changed from porcelain white to a blotchy purple and red, her face no long slender, rather puffy and bloated, and Franny could clearly see that rigor mortis was setting in.

Not looking at Bree as she walked past her, Franny, still trembling, and swallowing down her wave of nausea, went up the stairs, getting the large suitcase out of the bedroom cupboard.

She began to collect all of Mia's and Bree's belongings, not wanting to leave any trace of them being there, and methodically but as quickly as she could, she went into all the cupboards and drawers, fridge and wardrobes, taking everything there was, leaving no evidence that Bree had been there at all.

Half an hour later and satisfied that everything was collected, Franny pulled on a pair of gloves and set about wiping everything down, and by the time she'd finished not only had it gone dark outside, but she'd also missed a call from Alfie.

After taking the suitcase and putting it in her car, which was parked directly in front of the flats, Franny hurried back, grabbing the roll of gaffer tape and thick plastic sheeting she'd picked up from a DIY shop on the way over.

Back inside the flat, Franny, quaking, leant on the door. She stared at Bree and right then and there Franny knew that the hardest part was just about to begin. Though as much as she didn't want to do what needed to be done, she knew that she just couldn't leave Bree's body lying there, *especially* as Ma might decide to pay Bree a visit.

Taking another deep breath and unwrapping the large, thick plastic sheet, Franny placed it onto the floor. Then with only a slight hesitation, Franny bent down, pulling Bree onto the sheet.

Bree's body was surprisingly light, though it was stiff, but Franny supposed that was to be expected after this number of hours. About to continue pulling Bree onto the sheet, Franny froze, staring in horror at the large bloodstain on the floor that had been hidden under Bree's head.

Panicking, Franny snapped herself out of her thoughts and ran upstairs, charging into the small kitchen set just off the lounge. She looked under the sink, quickly getting the scrubbing brush and a bowl full of soapy water before running back down to the private hallway.

Placing both the bowl and brush on the floor, Franny knelt by Bree just as her phone began to vibrate. It was Alfie. She'd already missed his call and even though she'd rather not speak to him, after everything that had happened, she reckoned it was best to have him on side, not wanting to add to any more of his suspicions.

She pressed answer at the same time as she began to scrub Bree's blood out of the carpet and with a great deal of effort to sound calm, she said, 'Hey Alfie, hey honey, sorry I missed your last call.'

Alfie's voice was monotone. 'Where are you, babe?'

Exhaling, Franny tried to keep it light. 'I just went for a drive. I couldn't sleep. My head's a wreck.'

'I don't suppose you've heard anything, have you? About Mia?'

Without being able to stop it, a shrill tone came into her voice. 'No, no, not yet but I'll let you know if I do. You'll be the first person to know.'

Alfie's concern was palpable. 'I'm so sorry, babe, this must be so stressful for you. I wish I could do more to help. Have you spoken to her mum?'

Franny sounded shocked. 'Her mum?'

'Yeah, Mia's mum, you need to tell her.'

A wave of relief hit Franny. She had to keep her head. She knew she was beginning to let panic dictate her thinking. 'Oh yeah, her mum. Yeah of course, I spoke to her mum and as you can imagine she's in a real state.'

'Who is she anyway? What's her name?'

With anxiety making her sound breathless, Franny continued to scrub the floor. 'What? What do you mean?'

'Fran, are you okay?'

'Yeah . . . well no, not really. It's just difficult to talk about it.'

Alfie's concern oozed down the phone. 'Yeah, of course, I understand. I was just wondering whether maybe it would do some good for me to speak to Mia's mum. I don't know, reassure her and take the pressure off you having to do everything. I just feel useless that I'm not doing more to help.'

Franny felt the sweat running down her forehead as she talked. 'No, no . . . no. I . . . I've got it covered, but thanks for the offer, Alf . . . Anyway, you don't know her so it'd be a bit strange. I mean, I was surprised to hear from her myself, you know when she asked me to look after Mia . . . She's someone I knew from way back, the daughter of my dad's friend. So you see, it's best just to leave it to me.'

'Okay, well if you're sure, but it's good you spoke to her. Hopefully whoever has got Mia will be in touch again to let us know what they're really after . . . It's going to be okay, Fran.'

Looking at the bloodstain on the carpet, which was no

longer so obvious, Franny answered quietly. 'Yeah, I think it will be.'

'That's my girl – and, Franny, I know I don't say this often, but I'm really proud of you. I'm a lucky man to have you.'

Feeling flustered and uncomfortable, Franny hurried her words. 'Listen, Alf, I've got to go. I'll be home later but I ended up driving all the way to . . . to . . .' she paused as she quickly thought of a place '. . . Richmond. Can you believe I ended up in Richmond?'

'Fran, baby, I'm worried about you. Are you sure there's nothing I can do right now? I can come and get you if you like.'

A thought suddenly crossed Franny's mind. She spoke carefully. 'Yeah, actually there is. I was thinking about Charlie.'

Alfie's voice hardened. 'Don't worry, I'll be paying him a visit. He won't even know what's hit him.'

'Well that's what I was going to say, Alf. Maybe I was too quick to point the blame at Charlie. We can't be sure, can we? We don't actually know if he started the fire.'

Alfie sounded adamant. 'Oh, I'm sure all right. More than sure in fact. The more I think about it, the more certain I am. Who else is it going to be?'

'Look, I know your mate said the fire was deliberate, but we don't know that for sure. Nothing official has been said yet. Why don't we wait? We don't want to make things worse with Charlie, do we? Promise me, Alf, you won't go and see him until I come back. *Please*, I can't cope with any more stress right now and an all-out war with Charlie is something neither of us need.'

There was a pause before Alfie said, 'Okay, if that's what you want.'

'I do, and not only that, but it's the right thing . . . I'll see you later.'

Franny put down the phone, but immediately it rang again. 'Hi, did you forget something?' There was no answer. 'Hello, Alf? Alf?' She pulled the phone away from her ear and looked at the screen. Rather than it being Alfie as she first thought, the number had come up as private. She spoke again, though much more tentatively. 'Hello?' Again, there was nothing and trying not to feel alarmed, Franny clicked off the phone, frowning and staring at it once more before quickly pushing it down into her jeans pocket.

Bringing her focus back to Bree, Franny, feeling a pain in her neck from the stress, began to roll Bree up in the sheet but the rigor mortis caused Bree's body to take on a strange and awkward shape; her legs were still angled and bent back from her fall. They were locked in position, making it impossible for Franny to straighten them out.

Unable to get Bree in the sheet as she was, Franny, chewing nervously on her lip, closed her eyes, steadying herself, then tried to think of nothing at all. With all her strength, she grabbed hold of one of Bree's legs, forcing it straight, forcing it down, listening to the sound of Bree's limbs cracking and breaking as she straightened her up.

Taking hold of the other leg, Franny again pushed down with all her weight on Bree's hip. She heard a pop as it dislocated out of its socket. A wave of nausea ran through her, sweet saliva rushing into her mouth. She slammed her lips shut, swallowing down her vomit, and with hands shaking she began to wrap Bree's now broken-boned body tightly up in the sheet, gaffer-taping it closed.

Wanting to finish the job as soon as she could, Franny stood up and ran outside, opening the boot of her car before wedging the front door partly open.

She checked up and down the street, and seeing it was deserted, she quickly rushed back into the flat and scooped up Bree's body, then after the count of three, Franny ran to her car, throwing Bree into the boot and slamming it closed.

She breathed out, bending over, resting her hands on her knees. Emotions washing over her as her whole body shook.

She stayed like that for a minute, letting the nausea pass over as she tried to get her trembling under control. She sighed, knowing that there was still a long night in front of her. But she also knew that she needed to keep going. There was no time to waste.

Gathering herself together, Franny ran back inside the flat and looked around, giving it one more check to see if everything was back in place.

She locked up carefully, shutting the communal door behind her before jumping back into the car and speeding away into the night. But what Franny Doyle didn't see was that someone was following her.

23

After spending the past half hour trying to get through to Vaughn on the phone, Alfie stood at the door of Charlie's club. He still couldn't believe Vaughn had left the way he had done. Okay, they'd been at loggerheads over Franny, and he'd been like a dog with a bone, but for Vaughn just to go off like that without saying anything, well if he was truthful, not only had it pissed him off, but it'd hurt too. Really hurt. They'd been through so much together and for it to end up like this felt like a real low-down blow.

He'd left a few voicemails for him, and no doubt Vaughn would eventually call back once he'd licked his wounds. Though of course, there was still the question of the money. According to Franny, Vaughn had been ripping them off, which was a pretty tough pill to swallow. But then, maybe Vaughn hadn't seen it like that. Maybe Vaughn had decided he was still owed over a million pounds and as he wasn't getting anywhere by asking for it, well, he'd just help himself.

And there was a part of him that didn't blame Vaughn. These past few months had been a mess. *He'd* been a mess, what with the letters and Bree leaving him; perhaps Vaughn had just had enough of all the drama and wanted to get away himself. He had to admit, right now the idea of disappearing seemed very appealing. Still, the fact that he saw Vaughn's point of view didn't mean he *wasn't* going to give him a hard time when he did eventually see him. A *really* hard time. Alfie style. For now though he had another little bird to catch: Charlie Eton.

Pushing himself back into the shadows, waiting and watching for Charlie's men to leave, Alfie braced himself and hurried in, going up the back stairs of the seedy club Charlie had been running for the past few years.

At the top of the back stairs, which were strewn with empty condom wrappers and smelt of urine, Alfie pushed open the large, metal fire door. He walked along the corridor to the far end, quietly going through another door, not wanting to attract attention.

'Oi, mate! Do you mind! We're busy in here! Now piss off!' A large, balding fat man sitting naked on a chair in the middle of the room sneered at Alfie as a young girl, who Alfie guessed was no more than seventeen, knelt at the man's feet, attempting to give him a blow job.

Angrily, Alfie strode up to him, clutching hold of the man's thinning hair, pulling back his head. 'Do you want to say that to me again, *mate*?'

Terrified, the man gave the smallest shake of his head. 'No, I'm sorry . . . no harm meant.'

Ignoring him, Alfie looked around the dark, bare room and seeing the man's trousers lying on the floor, he walked over to them, picking them up before going into the pockets and bringing out a brown leather wallet.

'Let's see how sorry you are, shall we?'

Opening it up, Alfie pulled out a wad of notes before walking back to where the man was watching him wide-eyed. He smiled at the girl who was still kneeling on the floor, and handed her all the money. 'Here, darlin', take this.'

'Oi, there's five hundred quid there. You can't give her that! She ain't even finished yet!'

As the girl got up and hurried out of the room, Alfie bent down, staring at the man square on in his eyes. 'Funny that, mate, cos that's exactly what I've just done . . . You got a problem with that?'

Reaching between the man's legs, Alfie grabbed hold of the man's balls, squeezing them hard and causing him to cry out in pain.

Alfie sneered. 'I said, have you got a problem with that?'

The man was barely able to speak. 'No . . . no.'

'Good, that's what I thought you'd said. Now where's Charlie?'

'Upstairs . . . he's upstairs.'

Smirking, Alfie stood up, wiping his hand on his trousers before leaving the pathetic, terrified man squirming about in agony.

As Alfie went up the stairs – lit only by a flickering red light – to the flat above the club, he thought again about the promise he'd made to Franny. He'd told her he wouldn't go around and see Charlie until they were certain about the fire, but when he'd put the phone down, he'd thought better of it. Jesus, this wasn't just a few threats here and there; this was a raging fire that basically had wiped out the whole building and most of next door's place. And okay, Franny had asked him not to go and pay Charlie a visit, but the way he saw it, what Franny didn't know couldn't hurt her.

He didn't even want to start thinking about how much money they were going to lose through all the damage caused by the fire, and that was even before taking into account any future earnings. Yes, they had insurance but until everything had been investigated, the insurance company wouldn't even think about paying out. It could all take months. And now with Vaughn gone, everything was going to be left down to him, which meant someone had to pay. And he was going to make sure that someone was Charlie Eton.

'Hello, Charlie.'

Charlie, having just come out of the bathroom, looked at Alfie in puzzlement. He wiped his hand on the small, grey towel at the same time as making a mental note to pull up his men for letting Alfie slip by them.

'What are you doing here? Though you look better than you did yesterday. That coke must've done you good.'

Alfie's face darkened. 'Let's just say things have taken a different turn. You know what I'm talking about, so let's not pretend.'

Charlie walked over to light himself a cigarette, keeping his gaze on Alfie. 'You're not being very nice given that less than forty-eight hours ago you were weeping like a baby on my shoulder.'

Angrily, Alfie screwed up his face. 'That's different, and besides, you know what I'm getting at.'

'No, Alf, actually I don't. As usual you're talking in fucking riddles, and I take it now your club's been somewhat *destroyed*, you're not here to talk about our deal, which is a shame. I was looking forward to becoming a partner in your business.'

Alfie, taken aback by what he saw as Charlie's brazenness, was bemused. 'Are you having a fucking laugh?'

Charlie chuckled. 'Yes, but clearly you aren't, though I'm glad I've seen you because I wanted a word about my niece. I understand you've been looking after her.'

'What?'

Blowing the smoke out of his mouth, Charlie laughed but at once he began to choke. Through splutters and spitting, he just managed to get his words out. 'Shannon. She tells me you and Vaughn were good to her.'

'Shannon's your niece?'

Red-faced and with tears in his eyes from the coughing, Charlie grinned. 'Oh yeah, for all the good she is. Ungrateful little bitch. By rights I should be pissed off that you nicked her from me but seeing as we're mates, I'll give you a squeeze. I hope she treated you well and didn't charge you too much.'

Still slightly shocked to hear about Shannon, and not wanting to think about what Charlie had put her through, Alfie growled, 'Firstly, we're not mates, Charlie. Get that into your head. And secondly, I would never go near Shannon. The kid's barely turned twenty.'

Charlie roared laughing. 'Is that what she told you? I have to give it to her, she's a hustler all right. She's barely turned sixteen.'

Alfie felt nauseous. 'Jesus Christ, she's still a baby.'

Charlie shrugged. 'Who gives good head.'

Alfie, unable to hear any more, charged into Charlie, pushing him hard and slamming him against the wall. 'What happened to you, Charlie? Don't you see? The man you hated most in the world, who abused you as a kid – well look, you've turned out just like him.'

Taken by surprise and seething with anger, Charlie clenched his fist, swinging it round into the side of Alfie's head. He ducked just in time, bringing his knee into Charlie's stomach before grabbing his hair and squeezing his face between his strong fingers.

Hissing with anger, Charlie sneered. 'I'm nothing like him! Nothing!'

Alfie leant into Charlie's face, smelling a mixture of alcohol and cigarettes. 'No, Char, that's where you're wrong. Look around you, look at what you do for a living.'

'No more than you.'

Alfie shook his head. 'I might be a lot of things and I may do a lot of things wrong. I may never get to heaven but what I do know is, I will always have a clear conscience when it comes to kids. Young girls. I don't know how you can live with yourself. Franny won't even have the girls near the club if she doesn't check their ID.'

With his face still squeezed tightly between Alfie's fingers, Charlie gave a scornful laugh.

'Franny! Don't talk about her like she's some kind of saint. You have no idea, do you?'

Letting go of Charlie, Alfie, puzzled, stared at him. 'Now who's talking in riddles? What the hell are you on about?'

Charlie looked at Alfie evenly, wondering whether or not to tell him all he knew about Franny, not that he knew an awful lot; Shannon hadn't known much and Ma had been pretty secretive, calling him up to ask him to leave it all down to her, and although he hadn't had time to ask her *exactly* what her plan was, he knew when it came to his sister it would be bound to be about money. For Ma, money was oxygen.

But then, if Alfie thought that it was all right to come around reeking of attitude then it was well in his rights to wipe the smile off his face. So maybe although he wouldn't tell him everything, he would just dangle a carrot, or rather dangle a word. One word . . .

'Bree.'

As Charlie had thought, Alfie's face dropped.

'Bree? What do you know about Bree? And what's she got to do with Franny? What the fuck are you talking about?'

Seeing Alfie on the back foot, Charlie shrugged, amused. It was only this year that he and Alfie had started speaking again after a very long time, twenty-odd years in fact, and he liked it that Alfie didn't know much about him anymore. Unlike him who knew everything there was to know – all about Alfie's relationship with Bree, courtesy of Ma – with Alfie not having a clue he was related to her and in a roundabout way, related to Bree as well. And that certainly amused him.

Knowing more than his friends knew, his enemies knew, always put him in a position of strength. That was the way he liked it, and he was going to keep it that way. 'Oh nothing, Alf, just something that Shannon said, though you can take it with a pinch of salt what some crackhead says, can't you?'

Alfie stared coldly. 'Can you, because either you're playing games with me or you're not telling me something.'

Just as coldly, Charlie, who was certainly not going to tell Alfie anything else, said, 'What is it you wanted anyway, Alf? Because I feel my time is being wasted here.'

Alfie strode back across to where Charlie was standing, his eyes full of hatred. 'Tell me about the fire, Charlie. Tell me why you did it.'

Charlie turned his head to one side. '*Me?* You think *I* started the fire?'

Alfie's tone was dangerously low. 'I don't think, I know you did, and in my mind, that's crossing a line. Everything has a consequence, and you're just about to find that out.'

Aware his employees must be otherwise occupied, leaving him alone, Charlie began to backpedal. 'Listen, Alf, you've got this all wrong. I didn't even know that someone had started the fire. I thought it was an accident. That's what I heard anyway.'

'Don't lie to me, Charlie.'

'I'm not, I swear! I'm not the one who's lying to you.'

'I don't believe you, and what the fuck is that supposed to mean? I don't like games.' Pulling out his gun from his inside jacket pocket, Alfie jabbed Charlie in the chest.

Charlie's face drained of colour and, full of fear, he put his hands in the air.

'Come off it, Alf, you ain't being serious. You can't kill me, not here, not like this.'

Angrily, Alfie said, 'Kill you? Who said anything about killing you, Charlie? That would be a little unfair, don't you think? Until I know for certain about the fire, I'm going to leave you my calling card as it were, a little reminder never to take me on.'

And as Alfie Jennings aimed the gun at Charlie's knee-caps, thinking about the fire, thinking about Shannon, thinking about all the other young girls Charlie had taken advantage of over the years, without hesitation, he pulled the trigger.

But as he walked away, hearing Charlie writhe and scream in agony, Alfie heard something else, something just before Charlie blacked out.

'*Ask Franny about the baby . . . Ask about Bree's baby.*'

24

Epping Forest was somewhere that Franny knew well. Her father had taken her on many occasions and not just for a walk in the woods. From her earliest years he had taught her everything he knew about the *business*. And one of those things was where to dispose of something so that nobody would ever find it.

So, it was here in the dark of the night Franny found herself driving as near as she could to the area of the woods she needed to be in.

With the rain still falling, blanketing the trees with a ghostlike mist, Franny pulled up, switching off the engine and the lights of the car. Surrounded by nothing but blackness, she waited a moment in the unsettling silence, letting her eyes adjust to the darkness.

She sat staring ahead, her body going from hot to cold. Her shivering turning into violent spasms and sweats. Her breathing was tight. She felt like she had someone's hands around her neck and the pulse behind her left eye throbbed as she covered her face with her hands, images of Bree and Vaughn rushing through her mind.

Overwhelmed, Franny sat motionless for a couple of minutes, hearing her own breathing as her tears ran through her fingers. But knowing she needed to get herself together, she slowly straightened up, wiped her face and took a long deep breath.

Forcing herself to get out of the car, Franny's hand hovered over the door handle then, hesitantly, she stepped out, walking to the boot and opening it up.

Trying not to think, Franny began to hum, desperate to disconnect herself from the moment. She checked around, more for herself than out of necessity. The area she had driven to was always deserted, a place her father had at one time or another brought his own baggage to 'dispose' of.

She could see how much her hands were shaking as, still humming, she dragged Bree's wrapped-up body out onto the ground with a loud thump. Next, she reached to the back of the boot, grabbing the spade that she'd picked up from the DIY shop, along with a packet of fox-deterrent powder; the last thing she needed were the animals of the forest digging up Bree.

Checking behind her once more and reassured there was no one around, Franny placed the spade and sachets of powder on top of Bree's body and began to drag her through the trees and bushes to the small area beyond the thickets where her father had always said was a safe, hidden spot.

With her whole body sweating already, Franny nervously

surveyed the space, grateful that it had rained so the earth was now soft, making it relatively easy for her to dig. With a weary sigh, she picked up the spade, but she stopped, frozen, hearing a noise . . . a voice. Someone was calling her name.

'Franny. Franny.'

She whirled around, trembling, staring through the mist, which was getting ever thicker. Her heart was pounding as she stepped forward. Suddenly she stumbled, tripping over Bree's body, falling down onto the wet ground. She let out a small scream and panicking she scrabbled, the sound of her panting filling the air, fear running through her as she used the gnarled tree next to her to pull herself up.

Her chest moved up and down in exaggerated movements as she pinned herself against the trunk, listening, watching . . . waiting. But the only sound she could hear was the pattering of rain against the leaves.

Jesus, she had to pull herself together. What was she thinking? She was being weak. Stupid . . . *again*. She was letting her mind play tricks on her. She of all people should know better. She knew there were always strange sounds and noises in the forest. Calls of animals and birds. An owl. A fox. A badger. It could've been anything making a sound. It was an easy mistake to make thinking that someone was calling her name, wasn't it? Because after all what else could it have been?

Nervously looking around, Franny took a deep breath. She rubbed her head, massaging her temples. Christ, it felt like she was losing it; this was so unlike her and she hated the way it was making her feel. Or maybe she just needed to sleep, put her head down and get some rest – perhaps that's all it was. After all it had been days since she'd had a proper night's sleep. Yeah, maybe that's all it was . . .

Determined to pull herself together, Franny picked up the spade and convincing herself her shaking was just from the cold and nothing else, she began to dig.

Two and a half hours later, having dug the shallow grave, which was much more difficult and took more physical effort than she had imagined, Franny rolled Bree's body into the grave. She winced at the thud of Bree's body hitting the bottom of the grave before shovelling earth back on top of it. Trying to push her emotions to one side, knowing this was the only way forward, Franny flattened out the ground surface, placing leaves and branches over it, then carefully undid the sachets of fox repellent and scattered the powder all over the area.

Exhausted but having finally finished, Franny picked up the spade and walked slowly through the mist-strewn forest, unable to shake the feeling that someone was watching her.

25

Walking back into the empty house in Soho Square, Franny headed for the shower. She bagged up the clothes she'd been wearing in a black bin liner, knowing that she needed to get rid of them as soon as possible along with the suitcase of Bree's belongings, which was still in the back of her car. There were a number of rubbish dumps just outside London, so getting rid of the stuff would not only be easy, but also totally under the radar.

As she stepped into the steaming shower, the water pounded down on Franny. She could feel the burn of the water on her chest. The sting against her skin, the pain of it scorching her body. She closed her eyes and sank to the floor, burying her head into her knees as she began to wail. As the water continued to buffet down, she scrunched her eyes tightly, desperate to shake the image of Bree's dead, staring eyes, and of little Mia.

'Fran?'

Franny looked up, brushing her wet hair away from her face. She gave a small smile as she looked at Alfie.

'Hey, Franny, what's wrong, darlin'?' Alfie, looking worried, stared at Franny. She couldn't really remember a time when he'd seen her cry like this.

Uncomfortable with her own emotions, Franny shrugged. 'You caught me feeling sorry for myself.'

Passing her a large, fluffy white bath towel, Alfie wrapped it around her as she turned off the water, stepping out onto the black marble floor. 'You look tired, Fran. You need to sleep. It won't help anything if you make yourself ill. Driving around Richmond isn't going to do you any favours either.'

Franny was puzzled. 'Richmond?'

It was Alfie's turn to look puzzled. 'Yeah, you said you drove there.'

'Oh God, yeah, sorry, I'm not thinking straight. I can't even remember what I was doing five minutes ago. I'm all over the place.'

'And you still haven't heard about Mia?'

Tightly Franny shook her head.

'What's that?' Alfie pointed to the black bin liner in the corner.

Sounding as casual as she could, Franny wrapped her long hair up in a bun before pulling on a clean, grey cashmere tracksuit. 'Just some clothes I'm throwing out. I was trying to keep myself busy by doing a bit of a tidy-up.'

As Alfie looked at Franny, he couldn't quite help but think she seemed different. He couldn't quite put his finger on it, but there was something strange, something distant

195

about her, though perhaps that was only to be expected after what happened with her friend's baby.

From thinking about Mia, Alfie's thoughts then shifted to Shannon, to Charlie, to what he had said about *Bree's* baby. He wasn't going to tell Franny what had happened to Charlie, after all he had promised her he'd leave well enough alone and the last thing he wanted was to add on any more stress. It certainly didn't look like she could handle it.

But not saying anything about Charlie didn't mean that it wasn't bugging him, eating away at the back of his head. How did Shannon know about Bree? And why would Charlie say to ask Franny about Bree's baby when there was no baby? Maybe he'd been talking about her daughter, Molly. But why would he call Molly, who was almost seven, a baby?

Though he supposed Charlie had always been a head-fuck. He'd always got off on playing games with people's minds, and maybe saying what he had done was just part of his amusement, knowing that it would wind him up . . . upset him, and it wasn't hard to work out how he'd found out about it.

After all it wasn't just Vaughn and Franny who knew about Bree's miscarriage. His ex-wife – who still had a lot of contacts in Soho – knew about it, and so did his friend, Lola Harding, and as much as he told them on countless occasions *not* to make him and his affairs the centre of their gossip, they had mouths like the Mersey Tunnel – big and wide – and they just couldn't seem to help themselves. Though even taking all that into account, it was strange, because something still didn't feel right in his gut, and over the years following his gut was what had kept him alive and on top for all this time.

Sighing and following Franny down the stairs into the kitchen, Alfie poured himself a drink of orange juice, still thinking about Shannon and Charlie.

'You're a bit quiet. Are you okay, Alf? Listen, I'm sorry if I've worried you recently and I know what I did about the letters was so wrong. We can talk about it if you like, if that will help?'

Alfie shook his head, not wanting to go there. 'I'm fine, but I did want to ask you what you know about Shannon.'

Franny held a fixed smile on her face. 'Who's Shannon?'

'Remember that girl in the club?'

Franny laughed, though her laughter seemed too loud in the large, newly fitted kitchen.

'We have so many girls in the club, Alf, or rather we did. I wouldn't remember all their names, sorry.'

Alfie nodded, watching Franny's reaction. Watching the way her eyes darted around, watching the way she played with her hands, something she only really did when she was nervous. So maybe he wouldn't push it with her quite yet, but maybe what he would do was go and pay Charlie Eton another visit. Take him some grapes and a magazine, and who knows what he might find out?

The ringing of Alfie's phone broke up his thoughts. He pulled it out of his pocket and answered it.

'Hello?'

Nodding and making humming sounds, he listened intently before clicking off the phone.

'Who was that, Alf?'

Lighting a cigarette, Alfie matter-of-factly said, 'The fire investigation team. Apparently they've found a body.'

Trying to keep her voice even, Franny feigned shock. Her heart began to race. Being here when they found Vaughn's body was never supposed to be part of the plan. She'd imagined she'd be in Norway, safely away from Soho, and the sooner she was able to make a run for it, the better. Everything felt like it was closing in. 'Oh my God, that's terrible. Do they know who it is yet? Have they done any identification?'

'No, I think that will take weeks.'

'What else did they say?'

Alfie shrugged. 'They didn't, they said they'd let us know when they had any more news.'

The silence between them felt like an enormous weight to Franny as she stood looking at Alfie. Her discomfort was only met by her phone ringing. She glanced towards where it was lying on the side, wanting desperately to take the call but unable to. It was from Ma.

'Aren't you going to answer it? It could be about Mia.'

Hoping it was just her paranoia that Alfie was looking at her oddly, Franny waved away the suggestion. 'No, I recognise the number. It's just one of the girls who worked at the club, no doubt wanting to know if she'll still be getting paid. Cheeky cow, doesn't she realise, no work, no money . . . Anyway, I'm starving – what do you say to going to get a Chinese for us?'

'Yeah, of course. I'll get the usual, shall I?'

'Great . . . And, Alf, thank you.'

Grabbing his wallet from the side, Alfie smiled. 'No problem . . . and I love you, Fran, I really do.'

Franny gave a small nod. Sounding strangled, she said, 'I love you too, Alf.'

Pulling up his jacket collar, Alfie shivered as he headed towards Chinatown, which was only ten minutes' walk from their house. His phone beeped, and he looked at the screen, thinking it was probably Franny changing her mind about crispy duck, though it simply read:

Ask Franny what she did.

26

The minute Alfie had safely left the house, Franny picked up the black bin liner to take to the car and grabbed her phone, dialling Ma straight back as she pushed down her anxiety.

'So, here's what I'm thinking, Franny . . . I'd like twenty thousand to start with as a down payment, and then I'll see how it goes.'

Franny spat her words down the phone but she was overcome with panic. 'You can't be serious. Are you kidding me?'

'Don't ask stupid questions. What do you think? Oh, and if you ain't here in an hour with the money, the deal's off.'

With her heart racing, Franny stared up at the clock. It was ten-thirty; the traffic would be bad at least till midnight and trying to get to Essex from where she was, well that would take her at least two hours if not more.

Her voice was high-pitched and strained. 'That's crazy,

Ma, I can't get it to you that quickly, and I don't even know if I've got that kind of money in the safe.'

On the other end of the phone, Ma Dwyer shovelled a piece of Victoria sponge into her mouth. 'Well that's your problem, it ain't mine. You have to ask yourself how much you want her. How much do you want Mia back?'

'You know I want her back, so don't start saying that. You just have to give me a little more time.'

Running upstairs to the guest bedroom where their personal safe was hidden behind a large set of white hand-carved drawers, Franny pushed the furniture out of the way. She bent down, punching in the code before opening the safe and beginning to count the money as she continued to listen to Ma talk.

'I don't have to give you anything, Franny Doyle. There are other bidders you know.'

Shocked, Franny froze. 'What are you talking about?'

Ma chuckled. 'Well Mia's a little girl. The sort of people I know would pay a lot of money for her. Babies don't come along that often.'

Losing all sense of composure, Franny screamed down the phone, 'No, Ma! No! Oh Jesus Christ, you can't even think that. Ma, listen to me, whatever you want I promise I'll get it for you. Anything. Just don't do anything stupid! Please, please!' Tears filled her eyes as she fell to her knees.

'Stupid? Getting a bit of money in my pocket ain't stupid, and wherever that money comes from, it don't bother me. Your readies are just as good or bad as the next person's.'

Rocking back and forth on the floor, Franny begged into the phone, her words hard to hear as her sobbing drowned them out. 'That's not what we agreed, Ma. This was about not telling Alfie, but I'd rather him know. I'd rather he found out all about it than you do this.'

'It ain't your call though, not anymore. And when you come, I want to see Bree; though clearly, she doesn't care that much about her daughter. I would've thought she'd have been on the blower to me already. So, make sure you bring her along, you hear me? Otherwise I might change me mind about doing business with you.'

As Ma cackled, Franny cried hysterically. She yelled, 'Ma, *please*! Jesus Christ, *please*. Bree's not here.'

'What are you talking about?'

Franny's words rushed out. 'She's . . . she's had to go away . . . She's . . . she's not well. She couldn't cope with the fact that Mia was gone.'

'You seem to think that I care about your problems – well I don't.'

In desperation, Franny shouted down the phone, 'I'm going to call the police then!'

Ma roared with laughter before her voice dropped into a dark, nasty tone. 'You listen here, Franny. Don't ever threaten me. Never, never do that. You call the police, I'll deny everything, and you will never see Mia again. Do you understand me?'

In the tiniest of voices, Franny replied, 'Yes, yes . . . sorry.'

'Now that's more like it . . . and, Franny, make sure you're here in an hour.'

In the remote countryside of north-west Essex situated just outside the village of Ashdon, close to Shadwell Wood, Ma opened the pink front door to the mobile home. She grinned at Franny who stood shaking. 'Where is she?'

'All in good time; now come on in.'

Franny stepped inside. It was hot, and two fat cats were lying on the sofa. Over in the corner, plates of food and empty boxes of cigarettes were discarded on the floor. 'It's a bit of a mess. That's what I miss most about Bree – she was a good little worker. Lazy at times, but nothing a good hiding wouldn't solve . . . Make us a cup of tea whilst you're there.'

Franny glared at Ma. 'I'm not here to socialise. I just want to see Mia.'

Ma sniffed, scratching her crotch through her tight, light blue nylon leggings. 'You're late.'

'I know, Ma, and I'm sorry, but there was no way I was ever going to be able to make it here within an hour.'

'Like I said before, that wasn't my problem . . . Have you got the money?'

Franny emptied her bag on the table, tipping out bundles of twenty- and fifty-pound notes.

'There's twelve thousand there, and I've also brought Alfie's watch. It's a solid gold Bvlgari watch, it's worth about twenty-five grand, so the total's more than you asked for.'

Sitting down at the small brown, kitchen table, Ma stared at the money and the watch and then up at Franny. 'It may be more in total, but it's *not* what I asked for. I don't need some poxy watch.'

Franny picked up the watch, pushing it towards Ma. 'For God's sake, it's worth a lot of money. Look at it!'

Ma pushed Franny's hand away. 'Like I say, I don't want

a watch. I already know what time it is, which is a good job I do, otherwise I wouldn't know how late you are . . . almost *double* the time I said.'

Trying her best to keep her temper, Franny sat down, scraping back the chair to sit opposite Ma. 'But I'm here now, that's all that matters, and what I've brought you is just the start. Once the banks open tomorrow, I can bring you the rest of the money in cash, and you can keep the watch as well . . . What do you say, Ma?'

Ma leant across the table, brushing her body into the discarded plate of cold, greasy bacon.

'I say, *too late*.'

Franny's eyes filled with tears, frustration and anger welling up in her. 'Ma, please, we've established I'm late but like I say, I'm here now.'

Ma stared straight into Franny's eyes. 'No, you don't understand. What I mean is, it's really too late. Mia's gone. Like I told you, there were other bidders.'

27

Shannon Mulligan took a long, deep drag of her roll-up. Her hands shook, and her lip trembled as she picked off some strands of tobacco from the corner of her mouth. She was angry and not just a little bit angry. The other thing that Shannon found herself feeling was sad, something she rarely let herself be or rather something the crack cocaine stopped her feeling.

She sighed, trying to fight back the tears as she stubbed out her cigarette on the wall, making her way back up the stairs to the sauna she now found herself working in.

None of it had worked out like she'd thought it would. Not that she'd really thought about it at all. Not at first. It had all happened so quickly. When she'd taken the baby, she hadn't imagined Ma would cut her out completely. Stupidly, she thought that Ma would be pleased with her. Kind to her. Proud of her even. Though that was the problem – she should've known what Ma was like, but for one crazy minute she'd convinced herself that her aunt would suddenly start to care.

Where she'd got that idea from, she didn't know. Her whole childhood with Ma had been spent either avoiding getting a beating or lying on her back earning her keep. Perhaps, it was because it'd felt nice, really nice when Alfie and Vaughn had been kind to her and she hadn't wanted that feeling of being cared for to disappear. But not only had Ma refused to tell her exactly what was going on with Mia, but her aunt had screamed at her when she'd asked to stay the night, refusing to even lend her ten pounds to get something to eat.

She'd had nowhere to go so she'd decided to go back to Charlie's, thinking that everything was back to normal and he'd forgiven her for staying away, but the moment she'd walked in, Charlie had pounced on her, giving her a black eye.

She'd fought back and had been lucky to catch Charlie in the stomach, managing to get away before he did her some serious damage. But now she knew that unless she wanted Charlie to put her in the ground, there was no way on earth she could go back to him.

On the way out of Charlie's she'd seen Alfie going in, but she'd felt too humiliated to go and say hello. She hadn't wanted to admit to him that yet again she had nowhere to go. But perhaps the main reason she hadn't gone up to Alfie was because she hadn't known what, if anything, Ma had told him about her involvement in taking the baby. The last thing she wanted was Alfie being angry with her. Taking

Mia had never been about Alfie; it had always been about Franny, but now it had turned into one big mess.

The only good news she'd had recently was she'd heard a rumour that Charlie was in hospital; though whether that was true or not she wasn't sure. The rumour mill of Soho had a way of exaggerating things but if he was, she certainly wasn't going to take him a bunch of flowers.

'Oi, Shannon, hurry up, you've got a client.'

Shannon glanced at Laura, a tall skinny blonde behind the desk whose body looked out of proportion due to her enormously large breasts. Shannon gave a small smile then looked at the monitor watching a small, stocky, well-built man walking up the stairs.

Sullenly, Shannon said, 'Who is he?'

'Just another perv who likes them young. He's only been coming a little while but he's not keen on me – he thinks I'm too old for him. He'll probably go for you . . . It's your lucky day, darlin' . . . Don't look like that, money's money.'

Shannon shuddered. She could feel her eyes beginning to prick with tears and it was stupid because she'd lost count of the amount of men she'd slept with over the years and she'd certainly lost count of the number of blow jobs she'd given. She couldn't even remember when she'd first lost her virginity, though she knew it was somewhere between the ages of seven and eight.

She had thought that getting a job in the sauna – which was situated behind Tottenham Court Road in a grimy, upstairs flat – would mean that there was a chance she could work behind the reception area making bookings; something she'd always dreamt about, or even cleaning the rooms; she wouldn't have minded that either. But it turned out apart from the owner having already told her that was never going to happen, the clients were even worse than they had been at Charlie's, and although she'd been there less than a day, she already hated it.

'What's he like?'

Blowing a bubble, Laura shrugged. 'Put it this way, all the girls here hate him. They call him Mr Weirdo. He likes it rough and when I say rough, I mean seriously rough. When I had to go with him, I couldn't walk properly for a week. I looked like I was doing an impression of John Wayne. I don't think my fanny could take a hammering like that anymore.' She cackled, then added, 'Anyway, just be careful. There's something not quite right about him . . . Go on then, say hello.'

As the man made it to the top of the stairs, Laura pushed Shannon – who felt nervous and ill at ease – forward.

Shannon stared at him in disgust. He was small and squat but strongly built and muscular. His face looked like he'd been in one too many fights and she didn't like the way he was looking at her, not once taking his eyes off her and not once showing any flicker of emotion on his face.

Grinning, Laura chewed on her now tasteless gum. 'You've got Shannon today. She's new but she'll look after you, won't you, Shan?'

Without answering, Shannon nodded as she walked towards room number two, biting on her lip to stop the tears rolling down her face.

Opening the door to the tiny room, which had a small

massage table in it, Shannon walked in, followed by the man who still hadn't said a word to her.

Feigning confidence, Shannon said, 'So, what do you fancy today, mate?'

Barry Eton stared at the girl. She was slightly older than he usually liked but then she was better than nothing. He had been going to pay his son Charlie a visit, not only to have one of his girls who by all accounts were prime and up for the taking, but also to give him a surprise; after all twenty-odd years in prison was a long time. But it turned out Charlie was in hospital, so it'd have to wait. He'd waited all this time, so what difference would another few days make?

He'd been out of prison for a couple of months now, but he hadn't been to see Charlie or even spoken to him. He'd been too busy reacquainting himself with all his old contacts. Though he'd seen and spoken to his daughter Ma a few times, and now they were going into business together, well they'd be seeing a lot more of each other. They were certainly birds of a feather.

Ma had always been different from his other kids who'd liked to complain. Even though she hadn't necessarily enjoyed certain things when she was a child, Ma had just kept her mouth shut, something he certainly couldn't say about his other kids.

The only one who hadn't given evidence against him, albeit she hadn't gone to court – too afraid according to his barrister – had been Ma. His other kids had turned against him, giving written statements along with Charlie's testament and Alfie's evidence. Oh yes, Alfie Jennings, that was a name he'd never forget. Alfie owed him big time.

He'd been found guilty because the jury, of course, had fallen for the bleats and whines of the hard-done-by Eton kids. Well it was a fucking joke. Anyone would think they hadn't had a roof over their heads. But it was more of a joke now because he only had to look at his kids and know that he'd done them a favour; if it wasn't for him, Charlie would never be on the path he was, earning good money and enjoying all the fruits that came with it.

And of course Ma. She had set herself up as a bit of a madam, and although when she was a kid he hadn't thought she'd come to much, she had proved him wrong; growing up into a woman he was proud of. Not only that, it seemed that family meant something to Ma. She'd taken in his granddaughter when her no-good mother had overdosed on smack in some back alley. He hadn't been sorry to hear of her death; in truth it couldn't have come quick enough. After all, if it hadn't been for her crying like a baby, making Charlie worry about her all those years ago, the court case would never have happened. So, the way he saw it was what goes around comes around.

Snapping himself out of his thoughts, Barry Eton lurched forward, grabbing the girl roughly by the hair. She squealed and the tears that had been threatening to come began to roll down her face.

'You little whore, take your knickers off.'

Shaking, Shannon stared into the man's eyes. There was something about him that didn't feel right, something more than the usual clients. She shook her head. 'I don't want to do this no more . . . I'm sorry, you'll have to get one of the other girls.'

Barry Eton scoffed. He knew he looked younger than his sixty-two years as his muscles – a consequence of working out every day in the prison gym for the past twenty-two years – bulged through his black jumper. 'If I wanted one of the other girls, I would've asked for them, so you're not going anywhere.'

He grabbed the girl between her legs, his powerful arms pushing her against the wall.

'Please, I don't want to do this.'

'I don't care what you want, so are you going to take them off or am I going to take them off for you?' His hand slipped to the top of her thigh and started tugging roughly at her knickers.

Crying, she shouted, 'Get off me! Just get off me!'

'I don't think so, darlin', and now I'm going to show you what I do to little girls who tease.'

Before Barry had time to start to undo his trousers, Shannon suddenly thrust her head forcefully forward, driving it into his face. She heard the crunch of his nose as her head-butt landed square on it and as Barry staggered back, Shannon took the opportunity to run.

She darted out of the room, hearing the man yell after her. She charged past a shocked-looking Laura who was still sitting behind the reception desk chewing her gum.

Taking the stairs two at a time, Shannon rushed out into the street. It was dark and raining. Dressed only in a tiny, thin white dress, she continued to run until she was certain no one was following her.

Slowing down to a walk, Shannon turned into Montague Place, brushing away her tears and heading back towards Soho.

Driving along in a trance-like state, Franny gazed out in front of her, trying not to make any more driving errors as the tears rolled down her face. She'd already driven through several red traffic lights, and almost knocked a woman over on a zebra crossing but no matter how much she tried, she just couldn't concentrate. She certainly couldn't think straight or get her thoughts in order. All she felt was shock, a strange numbness where she couldn't process what had just happened. What Ma had done to Mia . . . It seemed like she was in a dream . . . She couldn't get her head around the fact that Ma had *actually* sold Mia to the highest bidder, not only that, but she hadn't even known the man's name and had no idea where he'd taken her to.

As waves of nausea hit her, suddenly, Franny slammed on the brakes, almost knocking over a person who was running across the road. She glanced at them and immediately realised it was Shannon.

After quickly pulling over by the corner of Bedford Place, Franny stepped out of her car, feeling more than a little shook up. With the rain getting heavier, Franny wrapped her jacket around her as she called out. 'Shannon, hey Shannon!'

Shannon turned around, her expression turning into a scowl. 'Oh, it's you. What do you want?'

A strange look came across Franny's face. 'I was wanting

a word with you. Why don't we have a chat? Come and talk to me.'

Shannon looked around. It was dark, and the street was empty. 'No thanks, it's all right, I'm okay here.'

Franny continued to walk up to Shannon, her eyes dark and cold. 'What's the matter, Shannon? You had all the bravado the other day and now you don't want to chat. Come on, it's raining. I'll give you a lift.'

Shannon began to back away. 'Leave me alone. I ain't got anything to say.'

Rage rose up in Franny as she stared at Shannon. 'The problem with that, Shannon, is I know you have. I know you probably like to talk to all those little girlfriends of yours who haven't got anything else to do, and the thing is I don't want you to talk about my business, and I certainly don't want you to talk to Alfie.'

'I'm not going to, I promise, and besides, I don't even know what's happening. Ma ain't told me nothing, so I ain't really got much to say.'

As the rain continued, Franny pushed her hair out of her face. 'Why don't I believe that? I wish I could.'

'You can, you can!'

Franny shook her head as she stepped forward. 'No, Shannon, I'm afraid I can't. You're trouble – that's all I see when I look at you. Have you any idea what you've done? Right now, Mia could be anywhere, and you know something, Shannon, it's all *your* fault and I think we need to have a talk about that, don't you?'

Shannon began to back away as the rain drove down. 'Like I say, I don't know anything about Mia.'

Anger and hate spat out of Franny. 'But you still took her, didn't you? You still gave her to Ma knowing what Ma was like. What sort of person does that?'

Dejected and feeling ashamed of herself, Shannon gazed at Franny. 'I'm sorry.'

Franny laughed bitterly, her eyes burning with hatred. 'Sorry? Are you kidding me?'

'It's just . . . it's just that you were so mean to me.'

Clenching her teeth, Franny's eyes darkened. 'Mean to you? You stupid, stupid little girl!'

Naïvely, Shannon said, 'Look, I never thought it through!'

'Yeah, and that's the problem, and because you didn't, Mia's in trouble. Now I'll ask you again, Shannon, and if I were you, I'd think really carefully . . . Where is Mia?'

Shrugging, Shannon's eyes filled with tears. 'I swear, I don't know anything.'

As Franny stepped nearer and nearer to Shannon, Shannon began to run, darting across the road, hearing Franny chasing behind her, knowing she wasn't far behind.

'Shannon, you little bitch, you're going to pay for what you've done! Shannon!'

Not bothering to answer, Shannon sped along Bedford Place before turning into Russell Square. She was sweating and panting, having never run so fast in her life but she knew whatever happened she didn't want Franny to catch up with her. There was something about the way she'd looked that had frightened her.

With her heart thumping in her chest, Shannon continued to run as fast as she could, speeding past the bowling alley heading towards Southampton Row, feeling Franny getting ever nearer.

Not wanting to wait for the traffic lights, Shannon ran across the busy road, scurrying between the cars and taxis, ignoring the honks of the irate drivers' horns as she just managed to avoid being hit by a speeding bus.

On the other side, with the wind and rain making it difficult to see, Shannon jumped the railings. Her feet were hurting, and she was tired, but she knew she had to keep going.

Stumbling along she turned into Remnant Street, glancing behind her, and was relieved that she couldn't see any sign of Franny, but suddenly she felt somebody grab her, pulling her into the large office doorway. About to scream, Shannon turned around, ready to fight, but she stopped and grinned, a big gummy smile as she recognised the person in front of her.

'Hello, Shannon, where've you been? I've been looking everywhere for you, but I'm glad I found you. I've got a job for you, one that you might like. What do you say?'

With her face shining with joy, Shannon nodded, once more her heart pounding but this time with delight. 'Yes! Yes, I'd like that.'

'Good, but first how about I get you out of the cold and cleaned up. You look like you need a hot meal . . . Come on, but we have to be quick.'

And as Shannon, soaked to the skin, hurried along the street, no longer feeling afraid, a thought suddenly came to her: maybe life wasn't so bad after all.

28

Exhausted, having searched the streets for Shannon, Franny was almost able to taste her own fear. She walked into the kitchen of the Soho house she shared with Alfie, her face drained of colour, all fight having left her.

'Where've you been? I've been waiting for you for hours. One minute you're telling me to get some Chinese, the next thing you're nowhere to be seen. I was out looking for you, walking the streets like a numpty. What the fuck is going on, cos it's making me uncomfortable. It's like you're winding me up. Just talk to me, Fran.'

Franny stared into Alfie's face, handsome and strong but lined with worry. She could see he had genuine concern for her, and every part of her wanted to tell him what had just happened with Mia, with Ma, with Shannon, to share how she felt, to share how terrified she was, but no matter how much she wanted that, she knew that could never be an option. The only thing left open to her was to find Mia, but she had no clues, no leads and for all she knew it was already too late. Mia might be gone forever and she was terrified.

Alfie stared at Franny, wondering when the right time was to talk about Shannon, to talk about what Charlie had said, but looking at Franny, clearly it wasn't now. 'Fran, I'm speaking to you. I want to know what the fuck is going on.'

Trying to speak, Franny put her head in her hands and began to sob. Her whole body ached. Her head felt a mess. In fact, she'd never felt so helpless in the whole of her life.

'*Franny.*'

Quickly, she looked up, scooting around in her chair. Alarmed, she gazed around, her eyes darting about. She stared at Alfie, speaking in a whisper. 'Did you hear that?'

Alfie looked at her strangely. 'Hear what?'

Wide-eyed and scared, Franny looked at Alfie. 'It sounded like someone was calling my name, Alfie. Did you hear it? It sounded like a woman's voice.'

He shook his head, concern etched over his face. 'It's just the wind, darlin'. Listen, you need to get some sleep. This is exactly what I was like, thinking I was hearing things, thinking I was going mad.'

'That was different – you were taking all that shit, I'm not.'

'No, but you're tired and stressed, exactly how I was. Look at you, Fran. You haven't slept. That alone can send people crazy.'

Rubbing her temples, Franny's eyes pricked with tears. 'It isn't just that though.'

'Then tell me what's going on. Tell me where you've been. Like I said before, I can't help you if don't tell me what's going on. I thought you and me, well, I thought we were a team?'

Needing to believe it herself, Franny said, 'We are . . . we always have been. You know I've always told you everything.'

'Then don't stop now. Come on, maybe I can help.'

Franny gazed into Alfie's eyes. 'I thought I had a lead, with Mia . . . It turns out it wasn't.'

Alfie stood up, reaching for his cigarettes. 'Jesus Christ, Franny, that's exactly what I'm talking about; you should've told me. For God's sake, all this secrecy has to stop.'

Franny nodded. 'I know, I know, but I didn't want to get my own hopes up and whilst you were getting the take-away . . .' She paused to make sure her story sounded sincere, half believing it herself. 'Well that's when I got a call. I did try to get in touch with you . . .' She trailed off.

'From who? Who was the call from?'

She shrugged, beginning to feel uncomfortable with all the questions. 'Just someone I know.'

Taking a drag of his cigarette, Alfie watched the smoke rise into the air. None of this was making sense. He thought the reason they'd taken Mia was because of *him*, something *he* had done, somebody he'd pissed off without knowing and as it was common knowledge that Franny was connected with *him*, whoever it was had taken the opportunity to snatch Mia as some kind of ransom.

He'd truly thought whoever had taken Mia would get in contact with *him*, letting *him* know what they wanted. But the more he thought about it, the more it dawned on him: it wasn't about him at all. It never was . . . It was about Franny.

'What have you done, Fran?'

'What do you mean?'

'I mean what have you done? Who have you pissed off? Think about it. Who have you turned over?'

'What?'

Full of sincerity, Alfie said, 'Look, I ain't having a go at you. In this business there's always someone who's got a gripe, who ain't happy. It's obvious that the reason Mia was taken is about *you*, not me . . . or maybe it's about your mate. What have they done? For fuck's sake, Franny, think, because maybe that's the key to it all.'

Ill at ease, Franny shrugged again as she scrambled for words. Alfie was far from stupid. If she said the wrong thing, she knew that he would smell it a mile off. 'Her ex-partner . . . he's a face, from up north. She left him without saying anything so of course when Mia went missing at first she thought it was him, or at least one of his men, but it ain't. It's nothing to do with him.'

'What's his name?'

'You won't know him.'

'Come on, Franny, I might! Talk to me for fuck's sake. And if I don't know who they are then I can ask around. Why are you being so evasive? Why I am getting the feeling you ain't being straight with me?'

Franny raised her voice as she covered her ears. 'Alf, stop! Stop! Stop! Please just stop! Stop trying to fix something you can't. The point is, it's not him, it's not her ex . . . and . . . and she doesn't want him knowing about Mia going

219

missing, not yet anyway. So, you asking about ain't going to help with matters; it's just going to make it worse. But as you can imagine my friend is going out of her mind. She can't cope, Alf. It's like she's going mad. She's hearing things. She can't sleep. Can't eat. She has no idea where to turn, no one to talk to. It's a mess . . .'

'I'm sorry, Fran.'

With her eyes wide, Franny continued to talk, not hearing Alfie's apology as she was consumed by her own thoughts and feelings. 'Though what she does think – and it's only a guess, but it's the only kind of lead she's got – she thinks Mia was taken by . . . well that guy.'

Puzzled, Alfie asked, 'What guy?'

'Charlie's father. Barry Eton.'

Alfie couldn't have looked more surprised if he tried. The minute he'd known the letters were from Franny he'd no doubt ruled that out. To him, Barry Eton was out of the picture when it came to Mia. 'That's impossible, Fran. Why would he do that? No way.'

Franny, knowing much more than Alfie, vehemently shook her head, terror painted across her face. 'It's not though. Listen, I've found something out. I think Mia's been sold.'

Again, Alfie looked surprised. 'Hold on, hold on, what are you talking about? All this is news to me. Why would you or your mate think Mia has been sold? What the hell's going on?'

Feeling cornered and hating all the questions, Franny snapped, 'I just do okay, I just do. It ain't a coincidence that Barry has been released and Mia goes missing.'

Still in shock at the suggestion, Alfie took hold of Franny gently. 'You're grasping at straws, darlin'. I know you're worried, but unless you have any reason to believe he took her, which you haven't, then it's madness to think that. You've got to try to calm down, babe. It really is crazy.'

Her frustration at not being able to tell him about Ma turned to anger. After all, she was privy to the fact that Barry Eton was also Ma's father, and Shannon's grandfather, so it wasn't too unreasonable to think that Ma had sold Mia to Barry or at least one of Barry's friends – she'd admitted she knew people in that kind of world – but Franny's problem was trying to make Alfie understand without telling him the truth. She screamed at Alfie again, 'Why is it? Why is it such an extreme thing to say? Go on, tell me, why? Charlie lives here, so Barry still has a connection to this area.'

'Fran, sweetheart, stop. Just listen to me. Sshhhh, just calm down and listen . . . Charlie doesn't have anything to do with him.'

Franny's eyes flashed with anger. 'You'd be surprised what people don't tell you, Alf.'

Irritated himself now, and the discussion of Barry putting him on edge, Alfie yelled, 'What the fuck is that supposed to mean? What is that supposed to fucking mean?'

Franny pulled her hand away from Alfie. 'It means, stop being so naïve. You don't know everything that goes on and unless *you* can tell me for certain Barry hasn't taken Mia, then it's crazy to rule it out. And even if Barry isn't the one who actually took her, maybe he knows something about it.'

Alfie shook his head. 'Why would he know?'

Franny yelled in Alfie's face, 'Because the world they live in is a small world! He'd know if a baby had been touted about and sold . . . So, you need to help me find him, so I can ask him just that.'

Alfie began to back away, thoughts and images running through his mind. He shook his head, terror coming into his eyes. His voice trembled. 'I can't, Fran, I just can't. I can't do it . . . I'm sorry, but no.'

Franny grabbed hold of Alfie who shrunk away. Angrily she shook his arm. 'You've got to!' She paused, knowing that although she wanted to know where Barry was, and she needed Alfie's help with finding him, she certainly didn't want Alfie to *actually* speak to Barry. That was too dangerous. Who knew what he might tell him? Even asking for Alfie's help was risky but she really didn't have any other choice.

'Look, Alf, I understand that you don't want to talk to Barry or have anything to do with him, and I'm not asking you to, I just need you to help me find him!'

Alfie pushed past Franny, hitting one of the chairs out of the way. He slammed out of the door, striding into the front lounge, which was decorated in grey and silver.

Marching across to the bottle of whiskey on the side, Alfie unscrewed the top and not bothering to get a glass, he drank it down, feeling the burn.

'Alf, don't walk away from me!'

Wiping his mouth with his sleeve, Alfie turned his back on Franny. 'Leave me alone, Fran.'

Incensed, Franny stormed up to Alfie, her face marked

with anger. She snatched the bottle from Alfie's hand, throwing it down to the side where it smashed, shattering into tiny pieces. 'I'm not going to leave you alone because I need you to help me.'

Trembling, Alfie stared at her. 'No, Fran, I can't do it, and it's not that I don't want to, I just can't, I'm sorry.'

'What about Mia, Alf?'

'Look at me, Fran, just the mention of his name makes my head a wreck. I'd be no good to you anyway. You need to get your mate to sort it out. Get her old man to ask about. He's a face ain't he? So, he'll be able to find him just as well as I could.'

Franny poked Alfie in the chest. All that was on her mind was Mia. Anger and resentment ran through her. She hissed. 'You owe me, Alfie Jennings, you hear me?'

'What are you talking about?'

'I'm talking about Bree.'

'What?'

'You think just because I didn't say anything much when you and Bree got together, that it didn't hurt me? Then you're wrong, because it did. I hated you for what you did, you hear me? *Hated* you.'

Shocked, Alfie gazed into Franny's eyes, her face only a few inches away. 'I didn't know.'

Franny screamed at the top of her voice, 'Then you're a fool, Alfie, a fucking fool. How could you think it didn't hurt? I loved you. Loved you so much, and that was hard for me to do. You always knew how hard it was for me to feel anything, but I did, with you, yet you still got together with Bree.'

Pressed against the wall, Alfie gawped in amazement. 'What are you talking about? You left, remember? You took two million quid from me and Vaughn without so much as an explanation, so what did you expect me to do?'

The screech that came from Franny was heard outside. 'Not that! Anything but that . . . So now, like I say, you owe me, because now, I feel something else for someone else . . . I feel for Mia.'

Alfie looked at Franny strangely. 'You don't even know her.'

Holding back the truth, Franny snapped as tears rolled down her face. 'I know that she's a baby, Alf, and if you don't want Barry doing the things he did to you to Mia, then you'll do this.'

Ashamed at how frightened he felt, ashamed at the tears that ran down his face as well, Alfie whispered, 'I can't. I just can't. Have you any idea what you're asking me? I wouldn't even know where to begin to look for him.'

Suddenly, Franny slapped Alfie hard across the cheek. Her face was red and angry but she spoke quietly. 'Then I'll ask Charlie, and after that, we keep on looking until we find Barry, and when we find him, I'll make sure he tells me where Mia is, and then, Alf, for all the things he did to you as a kid, I'll kill him . . . I'll kill him just for you.'

29

Having been woken up several times by nightmares and only getting a fretful sleep, Franny, tired and stony-faced, sat in the car next to Alfie, who was in the passenger seat.

'You promised me that you'd leave him alone, and now you're telling me that you blew his kneecaps off? Have you lost all sense? Didn't I tell you that I didn't want any more trouble?' She glared at Alfie.

'Listen, I did what I thought was best, understand? I know that he caused that fire; I just know it. You should've seen what he was like. Cocky fucker, it was almost like he knew something that I didn't. He even said . . .' Alfie stopped, deciding once again he wanted to keep the information about what Charlie had said to him just before he blacked out, to himself.

Irritated and uneasy, Franny, sipping from a takeaway coffee, asked, 'He even said what?'

'Nothing, nothing . . . He just made out he didn't know anything about the fire.'

'Well maybe he didn't.'

As he spoke, Alfie pulled out his phone in his pocket, feeling it vibrate. 'You've changed your tune.'

'Yeah well, I already told you that maybe I was too hasty . . . Who's that?'

Alfie read the text on the screen; again the message was the same as the first, from the same number that no one answered when he'd called it back.

Ask Franny what she did.

He looked at Franny, the nagging unease that something clearly wasn't right, that something was going on right under his nose, but he couldn't quite figure out what, came back into his mind, and although he tried not to, Vaughn's warning that Franny wasn't to be trusted raced around his thoughts.

It was ironic because for all the agg, he missed Vaughn. He missed being able to run things by him and although there were times when they were at loggerheads, ultimately, when the shit really hit the fan, Vaughn was always there for him, which made the fact that he'd just got up and gone even more difficult to accept.

And he hated to admit it, but although he felt betrayed by him, right now he needed him. Needed Vaughn to help figure out what was going on, though he'd be damned if he was going to tell Vaughn that. He'd left enough messages for Vaughn, letting him know he wanted to talk, but if

226

Vaughn wasn't going to call back right now because of his bruised ego or some fucked-up rationale that everyone owed him money, well there was no way he was going to start to beg him. No way at all.

'Alfie, are you listening to me? I just asked who that was from.'

Tucking his phone back into his jeans, Alfie, as casually as he could muster, said, 'Just one of me mates wanting to know if I fancied going out for a drink.' He smiled, watching Franny watching him. Not giving anything away, mirroring Franny's neutral expression.

The silence lasted until Franny said, 'Okay, well you stay here then, and I'll go and speak to Charlie.'

'Are you sure you don't want me to come with you?'

Franny gazed at Alfie. She touched his face gently. Although when Alfie had told her about hurting Charlie she was initially angry, the more she thought about it, the more she realised it could work to her advantage. She could now use it as an excuse for not wanting Alfie to come in and speak to Charlie, something that otherwise might've been difficult to do without him becoming suspicious.

'Alf, I love you and thanks, I know this is hard for you, but he's hardly going to want to speak to you after what you did to him, is he? I doubt he's going to be your number-one fan. And to tell you the truth, I think if you did try to talk to him, it's more likely to put him off saying anything than if I went on me own.'

'If you're sure.'

Franny smiled, though her smile didn't reach her eyes. 'Yeah, I am.'

'Are you sure we shouldn't call the police? Don't get me wrong, it ain't something I'd normally do, but we have to think about Mia.'

Pensively, Franny said, 'Well that's the point and that's why we can't. Once the police find out it wouldn't be long before word gets out on the street that they're looking for her, so whoever has got her, would release. If she's too much of a risk to keep, they'll want to get rid of her as quickly as they can . . . and I mean permanently get rid . . .' She paused, choked at the thought, and then added, 'Look, you wait here, I'll see you in a bit.'

Inside the hospital, Franny sat and waited for the nurses to finish changing Charlie's bandages. She looked at her watch. She'd already been waiting for over half an hour, but she needed to speak to him today, the longer it took to get any leads on Mia, the less likely it would be to ever get her back.

For all she knew, Mia might not be in the country anymore. The trafficking of kids was rife, and big money passed through hands of small-time villains and large professional gangs. The vile demand was always there, and the number of children who went missing or were in some abusive situation was overwhelming.

She sighed, putting her head in her hands, trying not to let her imagination take her to dark places. She had to think positively, because after all, what else had she got?

She had tried to call Ma, but she hadn't answered her phone. She doubted Ma would be of any help, especially knowing how desperate Franny was. It probably amused her; Ma certainly liked to play games but if Ma wasn't careful, those games might turn on her.

The other person she still needed to speak to was Shannon. She was sure she knew something more than she was letting on. To her, Shannon was the weak link, and if she could get her to talk, maybe she could glean some more information, though one way or another, she was determined Shannon deserved payback.

'You can go in now if you like, but try not to be too long. He's very tired. I think the operation took a lot out of him.' The small, Filipino nurse spoke warmly to Franny and then walked down the corridor carrying a large sluice bag.

Without bothering to answer, Franny walked into the whitewashed hospital room, shutting the door quietly behind her.

A computer monitor sat on the wall behind Charlie, connected to a multitude of coloured wires that ran over his bed. A green oxygen wire ran to his nose. He was covered in clean, white sheets, but Franny could see through the silhouette of them that the lower part of one of his legs had been amputated.

Silently she walked up to Charlie, leaning down to his ear. 'Hello, Char, I need a little word with you.'

Charlie's eyes flicked open. A look of fear crossed his face but disappeared quickly as it turned into a snarl. 'What the fuck are you doing here?'

'Now that isn't nice, Charlie, and especially when I've brought you some flowers.' Franny threw the bunch of white lilies on Charlie's stomach. 'When I told the florist they were for someone ill in hospital, they told me not to buy them, cos apparently lilies are associated with someone's funeral . . . so I thought I'd bring them along just in case.'

Charlie swiped at the lilies, throwing them onto the floor. 'Get out! Get out!'

Franny shook her head. 'That's just not going to happen, and you don't look like you're in any position to throw me out . . . So why don't we just make this quick?'

'What do you want?'

'I want to know where your bastard of a father is.'

Charlie seemed shocked. 'I haven't seen him for years.'

Sitting down on the edge of the bed, Franny stared hard at Charlie. 'Not good enough, Charlie. I need more than that.'

'Listen, I've got nothing else to say to you. Does Alfie know you're here?'

Franny nodded. 'He does actually.'

Defiantly, Charlie, who looked pale and in pain, angrily said, 'Well you can tell him from me, he's a dead man. You hear that, Fran. He's a fucking dead man!'

Franny grabbed hold of Charlie's left leg, squeezing the amputation site through the sheet. He screamed out in pain, but immediately, Franny slammed her hand over his mouth. 'I wouldn't start threatening people, Charlie – those days are long over. Looks to me like your reign has come to an end.' She released her hand and through his agony Charlie screamed.

'Fucking bitch, how dare you come in here after your fella put a bullet through my leg. I won't let you get away with this. Either of you. You've ruined me.'

Dripping with sarcasm, Franny smirked. 'My heart bleeds for you, Char, especially after you've lived such a respectable life.'

Charlie snorted with derision. 'Oh, you think it's funny do you? Let's see how hard you're laughing when I let Alfie know about you and Bree. Ma told me that he doesn't know anything about the baby. I think he'll be very interested to find out, don't you?'

Franny raised her eyebrows at Charlie before she stood up and walked across to the oxygen tube. Taking it into her hands as she smiled. She squeezed it, kinking the tube and watching as Charlie began to struggle for air, his face turning from a shade of red to purple. 'I don't think that's going to happen, do you? I think that would be stupid of you to do that . . . What's that, Charlie? I can't hear you.'

As Charlie spluttered, banging his hands on the bed, writhing about, Franny kept hold of the tube and kept smiling. After several seconds, she let go, allowing the oxygen to rush back through it.

Taking a deep gasp of air, Charlie rubbed his chest, his words staggered as he struggled to speak. 'You stupid bitch! You're crazy . . . you could've killed me.'

'And if you threaten me again, I *will* kill you, just like that, and I won't think anything of it. You see, right now I've got too much to lose to worry about a piece of scum like you, so let's have no more talk of telling Alfie, shall we, and then you and me will get along fine . . . Now I want to know where Barry is.'

Sounding slightly panicked, Charlie shook his head. 'I

have no idea where that man is, like I already told you, I haven't heard from him for years.'

Again, Franny squeezed Charlie's leg, sending a shooting pain around his body.

'And is that the truth, Charlie? Because you know I'll come back if I find out that you're lying to me.'

With his face squeezed up in agony, Charlie nodded, barely able to get the words out. 'It is, it is! Jesus Christ!'

Watching the blood begin to stain the white sheets, Franny let go and nodded. 'Okay, but have you any idea where I might find him?'

Exhausted, Charlie shook his head. 'No, none of us are in contact with him. If Alfie has told you anything about him, you'd know why. I can't help you.'

Walking towards the door, Franny stopped. She gazed at Charlie for a moment. 'And, Charlie, not a word, you understand? Not a word about Bree.'

Having waited five minutes after Franny had left, Charlie reached for his phone, dialling a number as his hands shook. It was answered quickly. 'Hello?'

'Dad, it's me, Charlie. There's someone asking around about you.'

30

It had been over half an hour since Franny had walked into Queen's Hospital in Romford to see Charlie and as Alfie sat waiting, watching the people come and go, he suddenly froze. A wave of nausea washed over him. A wave of fear . . . Right in front of him, not even two hundred metres away, scurrying away from the main entrance, talking on his phone was Barry Eton.

Unable to keep the bile from rushing into his mouth, Alfie opened the car door and promptly was sick. He wiped his mouth on the back of his sleeve, closing his eyes for a moment to get his breath, then cautiously – though he doubted after all this time Barry would recognise him – he peeked around the back of the car, watching Barry stalk across the car park to where a grey Mini was waiting for him.

Physically repelled he watched the car move out of the hospital car park but as it got to the gate, Alfie – suddenly thinking about Mia and Franny – sped into action, pushing his fears to one side. He ran around to the driver's seat and began to follow. He put his foot on the accelerator and followed the grey Mini, swerving between cars, desperate not to lose sight of it.

At Aveley bypass he turned right, following the car down a long main road, heading towards Tilbury Docks. He continued to follow, pulling back occasionally to avoid being seen.

At the edge of a large industrial site, Alfie pulled up, watching the grey Mini stop alongside an abandoned warehouse. The lights of the Mini were turned off but he couldn't see who got out of the car or even how many people there were.

It was dark, and the rain began to turn into hail, banging down on the top of the roof. Still with his stare fixed on the car, Alfie pulled his phone out from his pocket. He pressed dial, listening to the voicemail click in, then speaking in a whisper, Alfie said, 'Fran, it's me, look, I had to take the car. I'm at a warehouse in East Tilbury. It's the disused shipping site – you know the old motor factory on the front. I'll explain all when I see you, but if you can get yourself here, I'd appreciate the back-up . . . but be careful . . . Listen, I have to go.'

Clicking off the phone, Alfie looked around before hovering his hand over the car handle, trying to force himself to get out. *'Come on, come on, you're no longer a kid.'* He spoke out loud, pushing himself on, trying to ignore the feeling of terror he experienced at the thought of Barry Eton only being a few feet away. Trying to ignore his biggest demon. Then taking a deep breath, Alfie opened the door, closed it silently behind him and headed off towards the warehouse.

As he crept along the side, Alfie couldn't see or hear anyone. The only sound was his feet crunching on the stony gravel whilst the long grass hid the shattered glass and rusting debris surrounding the derelict warehouses.

He could feel the adrenalin rushing around his body as his heart pounded faster, a thin trickle of sweat running down his back as he tried to steady his breathing.

Creeping along the wall, Alfie suddenly stopped, hearing voices coming from the other side of the crumbling warehouse. He strained to hear what they were saying but the noise of the hailstones hammering down on the discarded, rusty metal sheeting made it impossible to make anything out.

A sound directly behind him made Alfie begin to run, keeping low and next to the wall, hiding as much in the shadows as he could. At a small, metal side door, he paused a moment, then slunk inside unnoticed.

Inside the old warehouse, which seemed to creak with hidden sources of noise, Alfie tried to work out where he needed to be. He walked along the corridors, which were strewn with the remains of pipes and tubing, rubbish and bottles abandoned on the floor.

Cautiously, stepping along, conscious of not wanting to make any noise, Alfie saw a set of stone stairs in the far corner of the darkened warehouse. He headed towards them, walking up to the next floor, following another maze of corridors, looking over his shoulder as he went, stopping at every sound.

A man's shout from the far side of the warehouse made Alfie stop in front of a door with a large glass partition. Carefully, he peeked in and although he couldn't see anyone, there were shadows moving on the far side of the empty room.

Certain that was where Barry was, Alfie closed his eyes again, steadying himself as the unwanted images of what had happened came into his mind. He wiped away the sweat that was now running from his forehead, pushing himself into the pitch-black corner.

Hearing the echo of footsteps, Alfie crouched down before slinking away as quickly as he could, desperate not to be spotted . . . What were they doing here? It didn't make any sense. The place was abandoned but suddenly his thoughts were interrupted when another noise caught his attention . . . It was the voice of a child. The cry of a child.

Trembling, Alfie put this hand into his jacket pocket. *Shit. Fuck.* He'd left his gun in the car and the problem was, he didn't know who they were, or how *many* of them there were. Maybe the best thing he could do was go back to the car; at least then he'd be armed and would stand some kind of chance.

With his mind made up, Alfie darted back the way he came, but at the end of the corridor where the stone stairs were, he could see someone was down near the side door where he'd come in. Hurriedly, he backtracked, trying to find another way to get out, frantically running along the corridor, hoping to head towards the other side of the building.

At the end of one of the corridors, Alfie stopped. He

could hear the sound of the small child's crying getting louder, echoing around the building and he panicked. Alfie turned around, running as fast as he could to try to work out where the child was.

Drenched with sweat, Alfie felt like he was in a maze, the echoes of the different sounds making it almost impossible to work out where he needed to head to. A cry below him made Alfie run to the edge of the open landing and, horrified, he saw a little boy being dragged roughly along by a tall man, who looked to be in his forties.

The noise of Alfie's feet on the wooden boarding made the man look up, and on seeing Alfie, he picked up the boy and ran.

Charging down the stairs, feeling the tightness in his chest, Alfie yelled, 'Oi! Oi! Wait! Wait!'

Suddenly a shot was fired, hitting the wall, and Alfie threw himself on the ground, ducking down as the bullets ricocheted off the discarded steel drums. He rolled out of the way and then crawled along on his hands and knees, pulling himself back up at the door.

Dashing along, Alfie charged down the hallway. Although he wasn't armed, he was determined he wasn't going to lose them, but a clatter from nearby made him halt. Breathing hard, he pressed his body into the shadows again, hearing footsteps getting nearer.

He could feel his heart thumping as he waited to see if whoever it was, was going to pass by. But suddenly the footsteps stopped, and he could hear nothing but the sound of the hailstones outside.

As he stood, pinning himself to the wall, Alfie could

sense that whoever it was seemed to know he was there too. As he tried to hold his breath, not wanting to make a sound, he readied himself, then silently counted down before leaping out from the shadows.

The tall grey-haired man stood holding a little boy, no older than six or seven, but the man began to back away as Alfie ordered, 'Put him down . . . I said, *put* him down.'

'What are you going to do about it, if I don't?'

Alfie's eyes darted to the side of him and he quickly picked up a large plank of wood. 'Whatever it takes.'

The man, keeping his eyes on Alfie, slowly placed the child down. Then holding his teddy bear, the boy ran to Alfie, who held his hand and started to walk away but as Alfie turned to make his escape to the exit, he spun around, and suddenly froze. In the distance, at the bottom of the stairs, he could see Barry Eton.

His breathing becoming shallow as he continued to stare, feeling like the whole warehouse was beginning to spin, feeling the terror he had as a kid, but as he tried to pull himself together, a blunt object smashed down on the back of his head and a second later, Alfie Jennings blacked out.

'Alfie! Alfie! Are you okay?'

Alfie slowly opened his eyes to look into Franny's worried face. He tried to sit up, but a pain shot through his head. He touched it, and felt a mess of sticky blood in his hair, but suddenly a thought crossed his mind. He croaked his words. 'Where is he?'

'Where's who?'

Cringing at the pain, Alfie, still holding the back of his

head to stem the blood, managed to sit up. 'There was a boy here, a little boy. Where is he?'

In the dim light, Franny looked around. The place was deserted. She'd been lucky to find Alfie, though, after arriving in the cab. It had taken her over half an hour to do so. 'There's no one here, Alf.'

'I'm telling you, Franny, he was here with some guy . . . and Barry.'

'What?' Shocked, Franny stared at Alfie. 'Are you sure? Are you sure it was him?'

'Absolutely, I followed them from the hospital.'

Angrily, Franny shook her head. 'Charlie told me that he hadn't had any contact with Barry.'

Trying to stand up but deciding to leave it for a moment, Alfie said, 'I'm not surprised Charlie lied to you, but I *am* surprised he still has anything to do with his father. He hated that man, not only that but he was terrified of him as well. I just don't get it.'

'You said yourself though that Charlie's a different person now . . . Listen, are you okay? I mean after seeing Barry.'

Alfie's voice was full of concern. 'I didn't really see him properly but yeah, I'm fine.'

'Did he see you though?'

'I don't think so, he was too far away.'

'Look, are you sure you're okay?'

Alfie, seeming angry with himself, said, 'It's not me you should be worrying about. It's the little boy. I had him, Franny. I was holding his hand but then I froze. I saw Barry in the distance, and I just froze. I fucked up and now the boy's in trouble.'

'How do you know?'

Irritated and frustrated, Alfie snapped. 'Come off it, Fran, what the fuck else will he be? If Barry's got anything to do with him, then it's bad news. Look, do me a favour and have another look around will you? Make sure he still isn't here?'

'Alf, seriously, there's no one around. I already checked when I was looking for you. I think the best thing we can do is to get you back home. Clean up that wound – it looks nasty.'

'Forget about me. *Please*, Franny, just go. I saw the look in that boy's eyes and no doubt about it, the kid's in trouble.'

Having left Alfie in the car, Franny, with Mia heavy on her mind and with the constant feeling of sickness in her stomach, made her way into another of the warehouses. Like the other ones, it was empty and dark, crumbling and deserted and she walked along carefully, not wanting to nick herself on any of the sharp edges of the broken bottles, nails or rusting metal strewn around.

Certain there was no one about, Franny, guided by her phone torch and the moonlight, made her way confidently through the back corridor of the warehouse; the double doors creaking and swinging open. She peeked into all the rooms where weeds and grass grew in the corners and the sleet fell through from the broken ceiling. They were all empty and looked like no one had been in them for years.

Thinking she'd head back to the car in the next few minutes, Franny frowned as she thought she heard a noise. She swivelled around quickly but there was nobody there. She stared into the darkness, feeling a chill coming over her.

'Franny! Franny!'

Her chest became tight and she backed away, banging into a discarded sheet of metal, which was leaning on the wall. It tumbled to the floor, clattering and echoing around the large, derelict warehouse.

Alarmed, Franny squeezed her eyes shut, rubbing her head, trying to stop herself trembling, trying to stop herself thinking of Bree . . . She had to pull herself together. She had to think of what Alfie had said. *It was just the wind. It was just the wind* . . . Yes, that was all it was and allowing her imagination to mess with her head wasn't doing anyone any good.

Exhaling, she opened her eyes and began to back away, back to the safety of the car, back to Alfie. But her phone battery suddenly died, and the light cut out, leaving her standing in nothing but darkness.

'Franny.'

Franny spun around again, taking short, shallow breaths as she gasped for air. 'Bree?'

She grabbed for the wall, moving along, terrified as her eyes darted about and pricked with tears. The next moment she started to run; down the corridor and through a large door before racing around the corner, skidding and sliding on the wet concrete but as she got into the next room, Franny suddenly realised she'd gone the wrong way.

Panicking, she looked for another way out and at the end of the room she saw a small metal door, which she headed for, running through it as she tried to stop herself from screaming.

As she stumbled into the room, which was brighter and

easier to see in than the other one due to the long wide windows void of panes of glass, she stopped and stared. There was something over in the far corner.

She cautiously walked towards it, her heart thumping as she felt her feet brush through the wet leaves that had been blown inside. With eyes having adjusted to the dark, Franny could see clearly . . . There was a small, purpose-built platform and on it were toys, children's toys. A ball. A train. A small fire engine and a couple of pieces of Lego. She glanced down at the floor and saw a discarded pair of children's trousers. Seeing something else, looking like a dark stain, she bent down and touched it gently. It was blood. Spots of blood. 'Jesus.'

'Fran! You okay?'

Franny jumped, screaming and falling forward in fright. A rush of terror swept over her. Breathlessly, she rubbed her chest, her eyes wide with fear. 'Jesus, Alf, do you have to sneak up on me like that? Christ almighty. I thought you were . . .'

Alfie touched his head, which was still sore but at least the bleeding had stopped. 'You thought I was, who?'

Fractious, Franny shrugged. 'No one. You just gave me a fright, that's all.'

'Sorry. Sorry, I didn't mean to, it's just that you've been ages and I was getting worried . . . What's that?'

Franny stood up, a look of concern over her face. 'I found them. They're kids' toys, and . . .' She stopped, clearly unable to form the words to describe the little boy's trousers out loud.

Alfie's face paled as he looked down at the trousers. He

felt shocked and he was forced to try to steady himself against the wall, his words difficult to find. 'You think they belonged to the kid? You think . . .' He stopped, unable to say what he was thinking.

Glancing around, Franny answered gently, 'Usually I'd say we were jumping to conclusions, but look at that . . .'

'What is it?'

Franny walked towards the end of the room and shivered. 'It looks like some camera equipment, a tripod.'

'You think . . .' Again, Alfie couldn't find the words.

'That they'd brought the boy here to film him? And you scared them off? Yeah, I do. It's the perfect place. No one comes here and it's a long way from anyone. No one's going to hear you scream.'

Swallowing hard, Alfie nodded, closing his eyes as he saw the image of the little boy's haunted face.

'Alf, listen, I know this is hard for you. Let's get out of here.'

He shook his head. 'It's not hard for me, not really. For me it's over, but for that little boy, whoever he is, it's probably only just begun. We have to find him, Franny. Him *and* Mia.'

As Franny took Alfie's hand partly to comfort him and partly to comfort herself, she nodded in agreement. 'Yeah, and the first person we need to go back and talk to is Charlie Eton.'

31

Back at the car park outside Queen's Hospital, Franny stared at Alfie. Her thoughts were a muddle and it felt like she was spiralling. The pain in her chest was constant and she couldn't shake the sense of nausea away. Even to concentrate on everyday things seemed harder with each passing moment. All she could think of was Mia and it was all she could do to stop Alfie finding out but that didn't stop her wishing she could tell Alfie everything. To share it with him. To relieve her burden, but she knew that was impossible.

Panicked she shook her head. 'No way, you ain't going in to see him. You hear me, Alf? You've already made a mess of things. So, no, you ain't going in.'

Angrily, Alfie raised his voice, irritated and on edge. 'Don't tell me what I'm going to do. There's a kid out there who needs my help.'

It was like a firework had gone off in her head as she screamed at Alfie, unable to keep her emotions under control. 'There is, but there's also Mia to think of! Have you forgotten about her! Have you? Well have you?'

'Calm down, Fran, for fuck's sake!'

'No I won't calm fucking down, not until you listen! I'm not going to let you storm in there and ruin everything.'

Bemused as Franny burst into tears, Alfie snapped, 'What the fuck are you talking about?'

Trying to get her temper back under control, Franny took a deep breath and shook her head. Even though the stakes somehow seemed even higher now, she still had to keep her eye on the ultimate goal. Find Mia and then get the hell out. All along she knew that if Alfie ever found out about Mia and Bree, he would kill her, but more so now than ever.

He was angry and she'd known him long enough to realise that when he felt something so deeply, so passionately as he did right now, if he realised on top of everything else that his daughter, Mia, was out there missing, there'd be no talking, simply a bullet in her head; and then Mia would be certainly lost forever, if she wasn't already.

Whatever happened, whatever Franny had to do, she needed to keep Alfie away from Charlie as well as Barry. 'What I'm talking about is seeing you would be like a red flag to a bull. You should've heard him before – there's no way Charlie will speak to you. Jesus Christ, he's lost his leg, Alf. He's never going to walk properly again, and that's because of you. He's pissed, and you know something, Alf? I don't blame him.'

Furiously, Alfie banged his chest. 'He ruined our business. Burnt the fucking place down. So he needed payback . . . Don't look like that, Fran, I know he did it, cos who else would it have been?'

Uneasily, Franny shrugged, wanting to change the subject. 'Who knows? Who knows if he did and you didn't even wait to find out if it was him. I told you to back off and wait but you couldn't do that, could you? Anyway, the point is, he wants to kill you, so he ain't exactly going to start talking if he sees you.'

'But, Fran, it's not like he even told you the truth, is it? He blatantly lied about Barry, so what's going to stop him lying this time around?'

'I'll make sure he doesn't.'

'No, Fran, *I'll* make sure he doesn't, and if I don't get the truth out of him, well he can kiss goodbye to life as he knows it.'

Scrabbling around for excuses for why Alfie shouldn't go up and see Charlie, Franny quickly said, 'But if we both go, and Barry does come back here, then we might miss him; or if I stayed here and you went to see Charlie, that wouldn't work either. I don't know what Barry looks like. At least if you stayed in the car you could keep an eye out, and if he did turn up, I dunno, take down the car registration or something.'

'But what are the chances of him reappearing?'

Franny spoke matter-of-factly. 'Alf, any chance is better than nothing.'

Thinking about it, Alfie nodded his head. What Franny was saying made sense. And in truth, him wanting to go up and see Charlie had been more about his paranoia than Franny not being able to handle him.

For some reason he'd convinced himself there was a motive behind Franny not being keen on him going to see Charlie. It was ridiculous, because it was obvious that the only thing that mattered to Franny was trying to find her friend's baby and the only thing that should matter to *him*, was to somehow find out the whereabouts of the boy. Anything else shouldn't even come into it.

'Yeah, okay and I'm sorry, you're right. It's stupid for us to both go up there. I'm just a bit of a mess at the moment, head's all over the place. I'm not thinking straight. Thank God for you, hey? Left down to me, I think I'd probably fuck this all up more than I have done already.'

Franny gave a tight smile. 'Yeah well, it's tough for you – I know that. So, whatever I can do to help, then it's all good.'

'Yeah, all good. You and me, we make a great team.'

Alfie leant over to kiss Franny. He'd missed being close to her. These last few months had been crazy, and he kicked himself for not confiding in her from the start. She was what they talked about when they said: *behind every successful man is a strong woman*. She certainly was his strength. His everything. And the fact that he'd jeopardised all that for Bree, for anybody, was almost unthinkable.

Drawing away from her, he smiled sadly and asking a question he knew she wouldn't really have the answer to, but he needed to ask anyway, Alfie said, 'Do you think that we'll find them?'

Franny stared into Alfie's face, her voice a whisper. 'Yes,

I do, and you know why? Because we won't stop looking for them until they're safely back.'

Inside Queen's Hospital, Franny walked along the corridor to one of the lifts that took her up to the critical care unit.

The place seemed deserted apart from a few of the night staff and porters and for some reason Franny felt the whole place had an unsettling calm in the air.

At the door of the unit, one of the nursing staff, a tall young woman, stopped Franny.

'I'm sorry, visiting hours are over.'

'Can't you make an exception? I really need to speak to Charlie Eton.'

'I'm sorry, we don't allow visitors now unless it's an emergency and you're a close family member.'

'That's exactly what I am . . . I'm his cousin, so can you let me in?'

The nurse shook her head. 'I'm sorry, I can give a message if you like.'

Firmly, Franny said, 'No, this is something I need to tell him myself. You see there's been a death in the family, and as you can imagine I need to tell him personally rather than just on the phone or you giving him a message for me. I don't want to wait until morning; it's difficult enough for us already.'

Concern and sympathy suddenly showed on the young nurse's face. 'Oh yes, of course, I'm so sorry to hear that.' She stopped and glanced up at the clock on the wall. 'Look, I'm sure it'll be fine to go and speak to him, just take as long as you need. If I can get you something to drink, let me know.'

Franny smiled but it was cold, lacking any kind of warmth. 'No, it's fine but thank you for asking.'

'Not at all. Would you like me to show you where Mr Eton is?'

'Oh no, I know exactly where he is.'

In the darkness, Franny walked quietly into the hospital room where Charlie lay, still with tubes and machines surrounding him. He was asleep but the sound of Franny pulling back the trigger on her gun made Charlie's eyes open. She jammed the nozzle into his mouth, clattering and smashing past his teeth.

'I told you I'd come back if you lied to me, and what do you know, here I am.'

Gagging on the gun, Charlie stared wide-eyed at Franny. He went to pull the gun out of his mouth, but Franny's words stopped him.

'I wouldn't do that, Char – who knows, it might go off. It happened to someone I know recently. So, I'd be careful if I were you. *Really* careful.'

Trembling, Charlie slowly brought his hands down by his sides, staring at Franny, waiting for what she had to say.

'So, here's the thing, Char, you told me that you haven't seen your dad, yet I know different. I know he was here visiting you. Funny that, ain't it?'

Charlie shook his head at which point, Franny jammed the gun further into Charlie's mouth, causing him to reflex vomit. His mouth filled with lumpy sick, which dribbled out of the sides.

'Watch what you're doing, Char, you'll block my gun if you ain't careful.'

Charlie attempted to speak, but his words were incomprehensible.

'Don't bother trying to talk, Char, what you need to do is just listen. You see, what I think is, you obviously know something more than you're letting on, so I'm not going to leave here until I find out *where* Barry is, and as always there's the easy and the hard way.'

Without warning, Franny ripped the gun back out of Charlie's mouth, the metal smashing down on his teeth again. He squirmed from the pain, his face screwed up as he choked on and wiped away the vomit in his mouth. He spluttered out his words.

'I never lied to you! You asked me if I knew where he was.'

Suddenly, Franny backhanded Charlie across the face with the side of the gun, the crunch from his nose breaking filled the air as blood exploded from it.

She hissed at him, anger flashed in her eyes. 'Stop lying, don't play games because I have better things to do than be here with you, Char, and you're really starting to piss me right off. Are you really that stupid that you're going to deny it? We saw him coming out of the hospital.'

Through pain and fury, Charlie ranted. 'I never saw him though! Maybe when he came up to see me one of the nurses told him I had a visitor, maybe when you were here, he came and thought better of it.'

'But if you ain't in contact, how did he know you were here in the first place?'

Charlie sounded desperate. 'I don't know! I don't know, maybe someone told him. Maybe Ma let him know. Maybe she's in contact with him. She never tells me anything. For fuck's sake, Franny, I'm telling you the truth.'

'But the thing is, I can't believe you, Char. You already swore blind that you don't know anything, so I ain't going to believe you this time, am I?'

Arrogantly, Charlie shrugged. 'I don't care what you believe.'

'Then you must have a death wish, Char, either that or you get off on the pain.'

Franny walked to the end of his bed, throwing up the sheets to reveal Charlie's bandaged stump. Out of her pocket she pulled a lighter. She flicked the flame, which lit up the dark, bringing it close to Charlie's leg. 'Now, I'll ask you again, the hard way, or the easy way?'

Charlie's eyes filled with terror as he tried to pull himself up the bed away from Franny and the flame. He hissed angrily at her, 'You're a sick bitch, you know that! A fucking sick bitch!'

'Funny that, cos people have told me that before, but no, Char, I'm not. The thing is, I don't want to be here any more than you want me to be, but seeing as you're making this difficult for me, you leave me no option.' She put the flame near his bandages, immediately causing Charlie to say, 'All right! All right! I'll tell you . . . It's true when I said I never saw Barry. I swear I haven't seen him since the court case all them years ago. I ain't even had any contact

251

with him until yesterday . . . Apparently, he'd been round to the club but thanks to your fella, I wasn't there was I? Cos I was in here . . . But Ma, she sent me his number and either she or the people who work for me told him where I was.'

'And that's all?'

There was a slight hesitation from Charlie, which Franny picked up on.

'Yeah, that's it.'

'Why am I sensing something more, Char?'

With his eyes on the flame, which Franny was playing with nearer and nearer to his leg, Charlie shrugged. 'I dunno, cos there ain't anything else to tell you.'

'Where's your phone, Char? I *said*, where's your phone?'

Hesitating, Charlie cleared his throat, his eyes darting about. 'Okay, okay, look, I called him yesterday, but I swear I never knew he was here. I had no idea he'd come to the hospital until you said.'

Franny moved even closer to Charlie, bringing the flame up to his face, so near that she heard it singe the tips of the stubble on his chin. He sharply drew away as she spoke.

'What do you mean, *you called him*?'

'After you came. I called him. I said that someone was asking about him, but I never said who, I swear I didn't mention your name, and up until then, I hadn't spoken to him before that – that's the truth.'

Franny stared at Charlie with a mixture of confusion and hatred. 'Why? Why would you do that after everything that he's done to you? It doesn't make sense.'

252

'I just wanted to give him the heads up, that's all. I mean, whether I like it or not, he's family.'

'Family! Family doesn't go around doing what he did to you. He terrified you when you were a kid, he terrified your sisters, and have you forgotten that you got Alfie to give evidence against him? *You* gave evidence against him, yet years later, you're calling him, *warning* him. What's wrong with you, Char?'

Charlie closed his eyes and rubbed his head. Genuine confusion sounded in his voice as he spoke. 'Look, I know, you don't have to tell me it's fucked up. It's all fucked up, but you can't help who you're born to, and somehow you've got to work out ways to live with it. Come to terms with it, otherwise it'll eat you alive, and this is just my way of doing that.'

'But you don't have to help him. Char, you're an adult now, you don't need to have anything to do with him. You don't have to be involved with what he does.'

Charlie shrugged, squeezing the bridge of his nose with his fingers. 'At least I didn't mention your name, but it is what it is.'

'Not when he's still hurting people . . . I think he's got Mia, Char.'

Charlie opened his eyes and stared at Franny. 'Did Ma tell you that?'

'No, she wouldn't tell me who'd . . .' Franny stopped, unable to say the word, and it was Charlie who filled in the blank for her.

'Bought her?'

Franny nodded fighting back her tears again. Fighting back the panic that drowned out all her thoughts.

'I doubt he did, Fran. I doubt Barry would. Ma would know she'd never get a penny out of him, and money is what makes Ma tick. Plus, my dad's not into babies, he likes them a bit older.'

Franny shuddered. She felt ill at how easily Charlie spoke about it, as if they were simply talking about something as hum-drum as a shopping list. 'But maybe it was one of Barry's contacts, so although he didn't . . . well you know, take her, perhaps some associate of his did. He could've been the middle man, Char? It's a possibility, and it is a tight-knit world, and Mia would've gone for a lot of money.'

Unable to stop her eyes filling with tears, Franny clenched her teeth as she spoke. 'Enough! I don't want to hear that, I just want to find where she is. I know for certain he's involved with some little kid, some little boy.'

'What?'

'Alfie saw him with a little boy, no older than six or seven. Don't protect him, Char. *Please.*'

'I ain't. I swear I don't know anything about any of this, and I wouldn't have called him and warned him about you if I'd known.'

'But why else would I have wanted to speak to him? You must've known it was about Mia.'

Charlie snapped. 'How the fuck did I know that? You weren't exactly Florence Nightingale when you came in, were you? And we're hardly each other's number-one fans, are we? I didn't think, all right. If someone comes and threatens me like you did, then I'm not really going to feel like a frigging chit-chat, am I?'

'You don't seem surprised that Barry had this kid though.'

Full of sincerity, Charlie looked at Franny. 'Why would I be? Prison's hardly going to reform him, is it? He would've met a whole lot more people, just like him, in there. They could keep their fantasies alive, they could sneak phones in, photos, swap stories. The wing he was on would've been like a holiday camp for nonces.'

'Then if you feel like this, I need you to help me.'

'Franny, come off it.'

Franny's voice turned hard again. She stared at him. 'Easy way or hard way, Char?'

After a moment, his eyes matching the hostility in Franny's, Charlie said, 'Fine, what do you want me to do?'

'I want you to call him and find out where he is.'

'He's not stupid. He knows that I would never ask that. I've got no reason to.'

Franny sat down on the edge of the bed and began to think. The room fell silent and only the wind and rain on the hospital window could be heard. After a couple of minutes, Charlie suddenly said, 'I've got an idea, and I reckon it just might work.'

32

Barry Eton dragged on his cigarette as he sat in the small, untidy bedroom of the mobile home that was situated a few feet behind his daughter's. He enjoyed the solitude. After years inside, a lot of which was spent locked up for over twenty-three hours a day, having people around him constantly took some getting used to. So being on the private, secluded site, tucked away in the heart of Essex with Ma, was perfect.

Not that he'd seen Ma, apart from getting her to make the odd cup of tea for him and warm up the odd sausage roll. He liked to keep his privacy, and here suited him down to the ground. And there was no way Ma would knock on his door, unless of course she'd been invited to. No way at all.

For all the mouth she had, for all the front she had with other people, when it came to him, he knew that she wouldn't dare give him the smallest of cheek, or even look at him the wrong way. The discipline he'd given her as a kid had made sure of that.

He sighed and yawned, passing wind at the same time as he listened to his son, Charlie, on the other end of the line. He felt irritated by the unwelcome disturbance, and he was still slightly on edge from not only someone asking around after him, but also the near miss they'd had back at the warehouse.

He'd been told that it was a safe space, that no one ever went there and up until then, they hadn't. They'd been able to shoot a few films as well as live stream, but now they'd have to find somewhere else; though he supposed he was lucky that the security guard, or whoever it was who'd disturbed them, hadn't seen his face. Hopefully, they'd just assume it was a bunch of youths messing about in the warehouse, who'd got a bit out of hand.

Annoyed at the thought of it, Barry growled. 'What do you want, Charlie? I don't appreciate being disturbed. Twice in twenty-four hours; it's a bit much.'

'Well that's why I was calling. I . . . I got the wrong end of the stick.'

'What the fuck are you talking about?'

'Well they weren't so much asking around about you, rather asking about your products. I didn't realise that until just now. When they spoke to me, they weren't really clear, or rather I didn't understand what they were after when they talked to me, so I jumped to the wrong conclusion. You know, better be safe than sorry.'

Barry mocked nastily, 'Shut up, you muppet, so you're saying you got me looking over my shoulder for nothing?'

'Something like that.'

'You've always been a fucking idiot. What did I do to deserve such a son? So, what exactly does this person want?'

'They're customers of mine. I've known them for a while. They like to do the whole couple thing, and I think they've got tired of the girls I can supply, so they're interested in some of the products you can get your hands on.'

Barry pulled a face, reaching over for the packet of peanuts by his side. He tore them open, pouring half the bag into his mouth. He spoke aggressively, spitting bits of nuts everywhere. 'You see what I can't get my head around is, why after all these years of you not bothering to contact me, let alone fucking apologise for ruining my life, would you call and tell me that?'

'Things change.'

'Yeah, they certainly fucking do, like I've finally got my freedom. Have you any idea what it was like in that place? All because you and your sisters along with that mate of yours, Alfie, couldn't handle a few games.'

There was a long pause from Charlie as he swallowed down his anger, his hurt, his bile. He whispered the words: 'A few games? Is that what you call them?'

Barry smirked to himself. 'Oh, please tell me you ain't going to start whining and crying like a girl? I would've thought you'd done enough of that to last you a lifetime.'

Coldly, Charlie replied, 'I ain't going to cry. Never again. Not for you. Not for anybody. That's one thing I do know, you understand?'

Roaring with laughter, Barry started to cough as a crumb of peanut caught the back of his throat. 'That's more like it. That's my boy! Now, tell me again what it is you're after.'

'Not me, but I've got some clients. They're a married couple, who like their products young.'

'How young?'

'As young as you can get. They also aren't bothered whether your products are pink or blue. All that matters is that they're fresh. They're willing to pay a lot.'

It was Barry's turn to pause before he said, 'You do understand when I get a call from you like this, it makes me nervous, makes me wonder what you're up to. After all, I wouldn't say you were the most trustworthy of sons.'

'Listen, I've always had clients come and ask me for very young products, but until now, I've had my own business. I've had my girls and that's suited me, so I've never really bothered with anything else. But now, who knows how long I'll be stuck in here, and who knows if I'll be able to run the club anymore. I have to start thinking of other ways to earn money. I thought I might as well make the most of you. After all, we're family.'

Sneering as he stubbed out his cigarette, Barry said, 'It's a shame you didn't think that way when you decided to give evidence against me in court.'

There was another long silence on the phone before Charlie spoke again. 'Look, I ain't saying that we'll ever get to that point where we're going on a cosy fishing trip together. But what I do think is that we can work together. I've got a lot of people who want what you can provide, and I'll be able to guarantee that all of them are trustworthy. You won't have any problem with them because they'll only be people that I know personally. We can sort out the money properly later, but I'm thinking a fifty-fifty split . . . What do you reckon?'

Lighting another cigarette in the dark, Barry stared out of the window, not saying anything as he mulled it over, but eventually he said, 'Maybe . . . maybe it could work. Eton and son. I like the sound of it, and in actual fact, I have got a product that's just come my way. Six years old, blue, and as fresh as they come. So maybe, we should set up a meeting with these friends of yours, especially if they're willing to pay for a quality product . . . Call me tomorrow and I'll let you know more.'

In the side room at Queen's Hospital, Charlie clicked off the phone. He closed his eyes, trying to keep his own pain locked away in his head, the place where he liked to keep it; then he looked at Franny who'd been listening to the whole conversation. His head was pounding and his mind racing with unwanted thoughts. 'I think he's taken the bait. I'll give you the details when I know what's happening.'

'Did he say anything about Mia?'

Charlie shook his head. 'No, but he ain't going to talk on the phone about that. I can tell he doesn't trust me completely, so I didn't want to push it. But I'll find out more later.'

'And you reckon he'll meet us?'

'Yeah, I do. He's just come out of prison and although he has the contacts, he hasn't got the money. And that's what he'll be looking for, to build himself up again. But be careful when you go and see him.'

Franny looked puzzled. 'Why? You think he'll have men with him? You think there'll be trouble?'

'No, not like that, but who knows where he's keeping this kid. So, the thing is if you don't play the game right, and Barry suspects for even a minute that you ain't to be trusted, then you may never see this kid again. No one will, and you'll certainly never find out about Mia. Anything else, Fran, is up to you.'

33

It had been twenty-four hours since Charlie had called Franny back, letting her know all the details of where to meet Barry and one of his acquaintances, but as Alfie stood by the bed, watching Franny sleep, finally looking peaceful after her having woken up in the night several times screaming, he was loath to wake her up.

He glanced at the time. It was already six-thirty, and the meeting was supposed to be in less than an hour.

He knew Franny wanted to go and meet Barry by herself, chiefly because she'd told him she was worried that Barry would recognise him. But he knew there was no possibility of that. After all, he'd been a kid the last time he'd seen him, and when he'd given evidence against Barry, he'd done so from behind a screen. Still, he'd begrudgingly agreed to play it Franny's way.

Personally though, he thought the real reason she didn't

want him to go and meet Barry was because she presumed he wouldn't be able to cope with it. That he'd be unable to handle speaking to Barry. That was the problem with Franny: she cared too much about him and always put herself second. Though in part, he had to admit she was probably right. The idea of seeing Barry nauseated him, and the fear, although he knew it was irrational, often overwhelmed him.

But now it was time to think of more than merely himself. The boy. Mia. And of course, Franny. It wasn't right that she was going to have to deal with everything on her own just because he hadn't dealt with his demons. And although Franny was certainly her father's daughter, he was *still* Alfie Jennings. Face and name to be reckoned with, and as such, he needed to be looking out for her rather than the other way around.

Franny had been so tired, so stressed, and she needed her rest before it all became too much for her. Everyone had a limit. Even Franny Doyle. And whether she liked it or not, he was going to make sure she got her sleep.

Having made up his mind, Alfie quietly shuffled out of bed, picked up his jacket and tiptoed out of the room, closing the door behind him. It was his turn to take the lead, and the first thing he was going to do, hard as it might be, was meet Barry Eton on his own.

Opening her eyes slowly, Franny took a moment to wake and realise where she was. She stretched out in the warm, king-size bed, before suddenly glancing up at the clock. *Shit*.

'Alf! Alf! It's nearly quarter to seven! Alf! I'm going to be late!' She jumped up, rushed down the stairs, but stopped as she saw a note pinned to the front door.

Hey darlin', thought you should get some kip, so I've gone myself to meet Barry.
  But don't worry about me, I can handle it.
Love ya. Alf x

Alarmed, Franny tore the letter off the door and ran outside into the street just in time to see Alfie drive off in her car. She yelled after him, trying to wave him down, screaming at the top of her voice in panic.

'Alf, Alf, stop! Wait! No wait!'

Then watched as the car's rear lights disappeared into the darkness, leaving her standing in the middle of the street, a sense of foreboding creeping over her as she began to shake.

The run-down estate in Walworth, South London, was where Alfie Jennings found himself walking. The place was neglected, and the large grey tower blocks loomed overhead. The children's playground in the centre of the estate with its rusting swings and slides was full of a group of junkies noisily having an argument, and the boarded-up shops, complete with graffiti, ran along the bottom of the flats. The whole place was strewn with rubbish – empty bottles of wine, cans of fizzy drinks and beer – and Alfie couldn't remember the last time he'd been in such a grim-looking place.

The arrangement had been to meet Barry and his friend, Alan, in the pub that was situated on the edge of the estate. Barry had given a description of Alan to Charlie, who'd passed on all the details to Franny, so he knew *exactly* what lowlife scum he was looking out for.

Apart from that, he had no idea what else to expect. Whether the boy he'd seen with Barry would be with them or not, he just didn't know. This could just be an exercise for Barry to size him up, see if he could trust him. Though the one thing he knew for sure was that he needed to play it cool. He knew no matter how he felt, no matter what Barry said or didn't, there was no way he was going to mess this up. He *couldn't* mess this up, especially as he'd taken it on himself to go and have the meeting instead of Franny.

Taking a deep breath, Alfie, outside the White Lodge pub, leant on the wall. He could feel his legs trembling, which gradually took over his whole body, sending his muscles into spasms as if he were cold. He could also feel the sweat running down his back, and it seemed like he had ringing in his ears, and all because any minute now, he was going to have to face Barry Eton.

About to step inside, Alfie felt his phone vibrate. He pulled it out of his pocket, thinking that it would probably be Franny, but he frowned, seeing a text.

DID YOU ASK FRANNY WHAT SHE DID?

He stared at it, confused, the pulse on the side of his jaw beginning to throb. This was the third, maybe fourth text like that he'd had, and he still hadn't the slightest of ideas what it was about. He knew he needed to deal with it, speak to Franny, but at the moment, he couldn't take any more, handle anything else. His head was already all over the place as it was. And right now, it was the closest he had felt to Franny for a long time, and selfishly, he didn't want that feeling to end.

Stuffing his phone back into his pocket, Alfie took another long breath before walking inside the pub.

The place was dark, and it smelt of sweat. A few old men sat in the corner saying nothing to each other and a woman, who looked to be in her mid-sixties but wearing a tiny mini skirt and a tight blue low-cut blouse, sat at the bar on her own, knocking back the whiskey.

Glancing around, Alfie spotted Barry's friend, Alan. The description Charlie gave Franny was almost exact. He was small, barely touching five foot three, in his early thirties, and dressed as arranged in a blue shell Nike tracksuit and baseball cap with a red letter **A** on it. To Alfie, there was no doubt he was a smackhead. There was something about the way he was standing at the bar, jogging up and down on the spot, nervously looking around, his pupils wide and dilated, like he could certainly do with a fix.

Alfie, feigning confidence, walked up to him. 'Where's Barry?'

'He ain't here.'

It was with a mixture of relief and disappointment that Alfie said, 'But we arranged to meet.'

Sniffing, and agitated, Alan shrugged as he bit down on one of his dirty nails and spat it out on the floor.

'He thought it was best that I came first, check you out. Who knows, you could be the filth.'

Alfie leant in. 'Do I look like the Old Bill to you? This was arranged by his son, so it's hardly likely is it? I've known his son for a while, so he was vouching for me.'

Disinterested, Alan said, 'You can't be too careful these days, can you, mate? And Barry, well he likes to know exactly who he's dealing with before he goes into business with them. I'm Alan by the way.'

Alfie answered drily. 'I know but I ain't here to make friends. I want to speak to the organ grinder not the monkey.' Alfie said this as he slid himself with a threatening air of menace next to Alan, perching himself on one of the wobbly wooden stools in front of the bar.

Now chewing on another of his dirty fingers, looking more agitated than ever, Alan stared at Alfie. 'Look, he ain't here. Like I say, he sent me instead, so if I were you I'd be nice, otherwise I might have to tell Barry he shouldn't be doing business with you.'

Alfie looked at Alan evenly. He could feel his irritation and disgust towards this man rising. Every part of him wanted to give Alan a good beating, but instead, he spoke quietly.

'Whatever you say, but I ain't happy – you see it feels like you're taking the piss, like you're wasting my time.'

'Think what you like, mate, no one's forcing you to be here, are they?'

'No, I know that, but what's supposed to happen, now? When am I going to meet Barry? More to the point, when am I going to sort out this product?'

Alan licked his lips. He stared at Alfie for a moment before saying, 'The thing is, there's a lot of people out there who says they've got the money, but really all they want to do is have an eyeball at the goods. Barry needs to know you're good for the dough.'

'Of course I am, otherwise I wouldn't be here, would I?'

'Then Barry needs to see it.'

Alfie frowned. 'What are you talking about?'

'He's here. Barry's here, but he just didn't want to come to the pub himself, not yet anyway. So, think of me as his messenger. You give me a deposit, I take it to Barry and he'll come down and see you.'

Alfie sneered. 'I'm not going to do that, am I?'

Alan began to move away from the bar. He pushed his hands into his pockets. 'That's the way it works; if you don't like it, it's no skin off my nose, mate. I'm just here to tell you what you have to do. If you're not interested anymore, that's fine.'

Alan turned to walk away and against his better judgement, Alfie called him back. 'Wait! Wait! How much do you need?'

Alan blinked, and a nasty sneer on his face appeared. 'A monkey.'

'Five hundred quid?'

'It's going to cost you a lot more than that eventually. Barry needs to know you're serious but as I say, no one's forcing you. Say goodbye now.'

Nodding, Alfie thought of the little boy and Mia. This could be his only chance, so there was no way he could afford to let Alan just walk away. Barry wasn't going to give them another chance and if it meant giving this lowlife, Alan, some money to show Barry he was good for it, well that was fine by him. 'Okay.'

Alan raised his eyebrows. 'So, you'll give it?'

'Yeah, but I want to see Barry. Not tomorrow, not next week, *today*. You got that?'

'Totally. If I take it now, I can be back within twenty minutes and let you know how long Barry will be.' And with that, Alan scurried out of the pub.

An hour had come and gone, and Alfie was kicking himself for being so stupid. Alan was a druggie, and it was obvious by now that he had just taken his money and run. But then, what else could he have done? He could hardly have said *no* to him. If there had been a chance to meet Barry, he hadn't wanted to risk messing that up for the sake of five hundred quid, and as such, he'd *had* to put his better judgement aside. The other reason he'd given Alan the money was he'd hoped that it was true. He'd hoped what Alan had said about meeting Barry was true because it would've meant being one step closer to rescuing that little boy whose haunted eyes reminded him of his own, when he was around that age. But now, *now* he was steaming, and he wasn't going to leave the estate until he got his hands on Alan.

34

Driving around the back of the estate, Alfie's gaze darted about. Suddenly he slammed on the brakes as he caught a glimpse of Alan, wandering over an area of wasteland behind a large block of flats.

Pulling over as quickly as he could, Alfie jumped out of the car and sprinted across to where Alan – who'd just looked over his shoulder – was.

Fear was pencilled over Alan's face as he began to run, whilst Alfie screamed after him. 'Oi! Oi! I'm going to fucking kill you! You hear me! Alan! Alan!'

Terrified, Alan squealed like a pig as he headed towards the underground car park, hurtling along and slipping on the wet ground as he did so.

Coming to the entrance of the flats' car park, Alfie looked left and right, unable to see where Alan had gone. But he knew that he couldn't have gone far, and one way or another Alfie was going to find him.

Walking in, Alfie bent down, picking up a small scaffolding pole, which had been discarded along with a heap of household rubbish, tipped in the corner.

'Alan, mate! If I were you, I'd give up!' As Alfie spoke he looked under all the parked cars, tapping the pole in his hand.

'Come on, you know you can't get far, mate. You want a bit of advice? The longer I can't find you, the more pissed off I'll be, and you know what I'll do then, Alan? I'll take it all out on you.'

He continued to walk further down the slope towards another set of garages, his eyes darting around. The tiniest of noises behind him had Alfie spinning around. He stared into the shadows, working out where it was coming from. He listened again – yes, there it was, over by the lock-ups.

Slowly, he walked towards the sound. 'Alan? Give it up, mate.' There was no response as Alfie stood by the thin gap between the two garages. He couldn't see down it; it was too dark, but he could hear that someone was there.

Suddenly, in a hopeless attempt to escape, Alan sprung out, but not before Alfie's foot booted him hard, tripping him up and causing him to sprawl across the concrete.

'Going somewhere are we?' Alfie stood over Alan. He brought back his foot, kicking him in the ribs. 'Now, I want some answers. Where's Barry? And where's my money?'

Alan, who was groaning on the floor, shook, as the kids

on the estate – used to regular fights in the area – stood around barely interested, paying more attention to the smashing up of an abandoned car by the lock-ups.

'You owe me some money, mate. I hope you haven't spent it on that shit you like to take. You really picked the wrong person to mess with.' Alfie pressed his foot on Alan's back as he squirmed underneath him.

Covered in dirt, Alan stuttered. 'Listen, I'm . . . I'm sorry, mate.'

'I'm not your mate, and how about I show you just that, you piece of scum.' Alfie kicked Alan in the side again, the sound of cracking ribs echoing around the underground car park. Alan screamed out in pain, staggering for breath before curling up in a ball.

Alfie prodded him with the piece of metal scaffolding. 'That was just for starters, and if you don't tell me what I want to hear, you'll see what the main course is like. Do you understand?'

Alan nodded his head as he whimpered. 'Yeah, but I don't know much.'

'I'll be the judge of that. So, my first question is, was this just a setup to mug me off? Is this what you and him do? Get some punter and rip them off? Is that your game?'

'No . . . no. He did send me, but . . . but not to take your money. I was desperate.'

Alfie jabbed the pole in Alan's ribs. He yelled out in agony. 'Just answer the question! I ain't interested in any hard-luck story, you got me? I mean, where do you get off taking my money and going off to score?'

He stared down at Alan. He wasn't going to risk going

272

into his pockets, knowing that there was a good chance he might have a dirty needle in them.

'Turn them out.' Alfie prodded his foot against Alan's pockets.

'I swear I've got nothing, I spent it all.'

'Well then, you'll have no problem showing me, will you?'

Seeing he clearly had no choice, Alan eased his hand into his pocket, grappling for the money Alfie had given him.

Begrudgingly, clearly having hoped to keep hold of the money, Alan sulkily said, 'Okay, here, but it's not all there.'

Swiping the screwed-up notes from Alan's hand and taking a quick look around, Alfie crouched down. 'There you go . . . See, that wasn't too hard, was it? Now what might be harder is trying to get the truth out of you. Do you think that's possible?'

Alan nodded but said nothing else as Alfie continued to talk. 'So, is he here? Is Barry really nearby?'

Holding his ribs and still shivering on the ground, Alan muttered, 'No. He just called me up and asked me to come and meet you. He just wanted to make sure you seemed all right. Sometimes he does that, gets me to do little things like that for him.'

'Then where is he?'

Alan's eyes stayed firmly on the scaffolding pole Alfie was holding. 'I dunno, I ain't seen him, and that's God's honest truth. He just asked me to wait for you, so I guess he'll be in contact soon.'

Holding down his temper, Alfie asked, 'And if he isn't?'

'I dunno, Barry is a law unto himself.'

'Yeah, apparently so.'

Back in the car having gotten all the details from Alan, Alfie sat and stared, gazing up at the moon as his emotions overwhelmed him. What he'd heard Alan talk about so casually, so matter-of-factly, was something that he'd never forget, something that he knew would haunt him forever, and the worst thing about it all was that he knew this woman in Doncaster was just the tip of the iceberg.

And as he continued to stare up at the full moon, shining bright in the clear February sky, Alfie Jennings began to cry.

35

Having sat and waited nervously at the window, Franny finally saw Alfie driving up the street. Part of her didn't want to go and speak to him, terrified of what he might've found out, but she supposed it was better to face what she needed to. Not bothering to put on her shoes, Franny dashed out into the street, running through the puddles to greet Alfie.

Out of breath, she sprinted to where he was parking, and although she knew it might be her paranoia, her fear, Alfie's face looked strained. Breathlessly she said, 'Alf? Alf?'

Stepping out of the car, Alfie's expression was pained. 'Franny.'

Concern coated Franny's words. 'Alf, is everything all right? I mean, whatever it is, I can explain. I can explain everything.'

'What?'

She spoke rapidly. 'I know I don't know him, but I do know you can't trust what Barry said. He'll be telling you anything to get himself out of trouble. He'll be saying stuff that you can't take seriously.'

Slightly confused, Alfie said, 'I never saw him.'

Huge relief immediately passed over Franny. She let out a long sigh. 'Really? How come?'

Alfie, emotionally drained, shrugged, unable to tell Franny the story yet.

'So, where've you been? I was worried. I tried calling you. Like I say, I thought, maybe Barry, you know, had said some stuff to you.'

Exhausted from the evening, Alfie gazed at Franny, noticing the strain in her eyes. 'Like what?'

On edge, Franny chewed on her lip. 'I . . . I don't know, but I understand how difficult it would've been. Look, I just want to be here for you.'

Alfie smiled, feeling his own relief at seeing Franny. It was exactly what he needed. He kissed her on her head before bringing her in to his chest, holding her close. 'I didn't see Barry, but I'll explain everything later. You know the other guy we'd arranged to meet, Alan? Well he was there. Piece of scum. But I think we've got a lead.'

Franny drew away from Alfie's embrace. 'About Mia?'

He shook his head, and spoke sadly. 'No, not yet anyway, but I'm sure once we go and speak to this woman, we can get some proper answers.'

Breaking down, something she hated to do in front of Alfie, Franny sobbed. 'Where is she, Alf? Where's she gone? I'm so scared I'll never see her again . . . I mean, my *friend's* scared she'll never see her baby again, and of course, I feel responsible.'

'Maybe I should meet this friend of yours. Speak to her, let her know that we're doing all that we can. Perhaps she has some ideas herself. Maybe it would take the strain off you if I did.'

Alarmed, Franny shot down the suggestion quickly and firmly. '*No!*' She took a breath and, composing herself, lowered her voice. 'No, thank you, but no. Like I've said before, it's hard enough already for her. We'll sort it ourselves. It'll just make it worse for her.'

Although Alfie wasn't sure why, a strange feeling came over him again, which he couldn't quite understand. It wasn't doubt, it wasn't suspicion, but something just didn't feel right. Then as he had done so many times lately, he pushed it away to the back of his mind, then he smiled warmly and noticing Franny standing shivering, he spoke gently.

'You're going to catch your death. Come on. I picked up something to eat. I know we have to go and see this person tomorrow, but I need you to eat. I've got to start looking after you because you're clearly not doing that yourself.'

Alfie walked to the back of the Porsche, pressing the key button as Franny came around.

Franny immediately froze, staring in horror at the back of the boot. She glanced at Alfie then back at the boot before saying in a tiny whisper, 'Where are they? Alfie, where did you put them?'

'What are you talking about, put what?'

Walking even nearer to the boot, Franny continued to

stare, realising that somehow Bree's belongings as well as her own bloodstained clothes she'd worn *that* day had gone. 'In the back. There was . . . there was a black bag full of clothes and a suitcase. Remember, when I was having a shower, I told you I was doing some clothes sorting?'

Alfie shook his head as he lifted the food bags out. 'I dunno, darlin', I never saw them in there.' He shrugged and turned away, heading for the house, but Franny, beginning to panic, grabbed hold of his arm, her eyes full of terror as once more her voice cracked into hysteria. 'You must've seen them, Alf. Where did you put them?'

'Fran, baby, stop! Stop. Just take a deep breath. What are you getting yourself worked up about? Come on, it's cold, come on in.'

'But you must have moved them. Think, Alf, think! Yesterday? Maybe you moved them yesterday?'

Not understanding why Franny was becoming so hysterical, Alfie spoke soothingly. 'This is the first time I've used your car in a while, Fran. Look, you must've made a mistake, they're probably still in the house. And anyway, I thought you said that it was old stuff, so who cares if you don't know where you put them.'

As Alfie walked away, Franny stood, cold and barefoot in the rain, whispering to herself as she began to tremble violently. 'I care, Alf. You have no idea how much I care they've gone.'

36

The drive to Doncaster on the M1 was long and gave both Alfie and Franny more time to think than they would've liked.

'What have you done, Franny?' Alfie's voice broke the silence, and Franny, uncomfortable with the question, turned to look at Alfie as he drove. She tried to keep her voice light as she asked, 'Done? What do you mean?'

Thinking about the texts he'd been receiving, Alfie asked again, 'I mean, if you've done something, and you were worried to tell me, whatever it is, you can. The point is, look at me: I've fucked up so many times in the past myself. Bree . . .'

Franny cut in, 'We've already gone through that, and I told you how I felt. *What's done is done.*'

'I know, and I'm grateful that you forgave me. I don't deserve it, so if there is anything that you want to tell me, then you can. I'm hot-headed, we both know that, but we're a strong team and I know we can get through anything as long as we're truthful.'

Once again Franny's smile was tight. 'Where's this coming from, Alf?'

Quickly glancing across to her, Alfie smiled before gazing back at the motorway. He knew that maybe he should mention the texts right now, especially as he was talking about being truthful, but each time he came to it – each time he was about to tell her about them – something held him back. 'It's not coming from anywhere. I just thought that everyone has their secrets.'

Franny, pale and feeling ill, stared back out of the window, her thoughts crossing from Mia to Bree to Shannon. She'd been trying to find Shannon since she'd seen her that day in the street. She'd asked around but nobody knew where she'd gone. With Charlie's club closed she'd probably had to move on, find work elsewhere. Though in truth, she still would feel happier if she got to *talk* to her. 'I don't, Alf. I don't have any secrets; maybe that's just you.'

She glanced at him, giving another weak smile before the two of them fell silent again, retreating into their own thoughts.

An hour and a half later, the weather had got worse. A combination of heavy rain and sleet pelted down on the car as they drove through the centre of Doncaster, South Yorkshire.

It had been a while since Franny had been here, watching

the races at the famous St Leger. But they had been happier times. With her father, with her uncle. Times where life seemed to be so much easier than it was now.

With a heavy heart, she watched as they drove along West Laith Gate, turning left into the busy Trafford Way. She supposed she should be pleased that Alfie was so on-board now, albeit she had to be careful, but she had a sinking feeling that since he'd seen the boy in the warehouse, this determination to find Barry was less about Mia and more about him and the young child. And as such she wanted to scream at him, wanted to let him know how much not knowing where Mia was, was slowly killing her.

Every day, every hour, every minute that passed felt like a painful, torturous eternity, but no matter how much she wanted to tell him, no matter how much she wanted to free herself of the burden, she couldn't. She just couldn't.

Sighing, she pulled down the passenger mirror and looked at herself, but suddenly her gaze caught sight of something, some*one* behind her. She screamed. There in the mirror, sitting behind her, was Bree.

Panicking, Franny unclicked her seatbelt and spun around, kneeling up, her breathing laboured as tears came to her eyes.

'Fuck's sake, what's wrong! What's wrong? Jesus, Fran, you nearly gave me a heart attack.' Alfie, having got a fright from Franny's sudden outburst, reached across and touched her whilst keeping his eyes on the road.

'I . . . I . . . I thought . . .' She stopped and gawked at the empty back seat.

'Thought, what?'

She answered in a whisper, 'Nothing . . . nothing . . .' She trailed off as she continued to stare at the empty back seat. It was stupid. What was she even thinking letting her mind play tricks? She was stronger than that? She could keep it together . . .

'Franny, talk to me, baby.'

Tensely, Franny said, 'Sorry, Alf, I just thought . . . I thought you'd hit a rabbit.'

'A rabbit?'

Sliding back into the cream, leather seat, and doing her belt back up, Franny shrugged. 'A rabbit, a small dog, I dunno, it sounded like you hit something.'

Not saying anything, Alfie frowned as Franny huddled up, rubbing the side of her head as they continued to drive along; passing the mosque, heading towards Carr House Road, which took them past a row of small shops and houses, and on to Leger Way where the racecourse loomed large.

Gathering herself, Franny spoke calmly as she clenched her hands together. 'How long now, Alf?'

Alfie glanced at the GPS, worried that it was all getting to be too much for her. 'I reckon we can be there in about ten minutes, maybe five . . . I tell you something, I ain't looking forward to it, Fran.'

Franny nodded, briefly touching Alfie's hand. 'Me neither – to tell you the truth, I'd rather be going anywhere else but here.'

* * *

On the eastern edge of Doncaster, Alfie and Franny came to Armstrong, a sprawling urban village with row upon row of terraced houses and bungalows. The roads were quiet as they drove along slowly, coming to Cleveland Street and turning into Rand Street, which was a long road made up of red-brick houses.

'I never expected it to be like this, Alf.'

Alfie gazed around as he drove carefully along, much slower than he normally would've done as he tried to hold off the inevitable. 'Me neither. It looks so normal. It looks like a place where you'd be happy to bring up your kids.'

'I guess it is, but I suppose it's a case of what goes on behind closed doors. You never know who your neighbour is, not really.'

'You never know who anybody is, Fran, so thank God I've got you.'

Franny fell silent, feeling her stomach twist up into a knot, feeling the guilt press down on her chest like a dead weight and feeling the loss of what they used to have together.

At the end of the road, Alfie pulled up outside a small block of flats.

He stared at them. 'This is it. Are you ready?'

Franny shook her head. 'No, Alf, I'm not, but then, I don't think I ever will be.'

Inside the flats, the place was clean. Cream walls matching the cream square floor tiles, smelling of bleach and polish. A large potted plant stood in the corner and letters for the various residents were neatly stacked on a wooden shelf.

Alfie and Franny walked up the stairs and at the top landing, Alfie turned along the corridor to the end, followed by Franny.

Hearing the sound of a baby crying, Franny whirled around to look at Alfie. Her eyes pleading. 'Do you think that's her? Alfie, do you think that's Mia? It could be her.'

Alfie gazed down at Franny, his heart going out to her. 'Listen, darlin', it would be nice if it was, but I don't want you to get your hopes up. Alan said nothing about Mia. For all we know this could be another wild goose chase. This woman, whoever she is, might not even know Barry.'

In the quiet of the hallway, Franny frowned, hearing herself sounding desperate. She knew she needed to keep it together. 'But I thought you said that she would know who he was. Where he was. I thought that's why we came here.'

'I did say that, but we've only got a smackhead's word for it. I'm sure he was telling the truth, but I'm just scared that if she doesn't know him or she doesn't know anything about Mia, then it'll be tough for you.'

Franny hissed through her teeth, letting her emotions speak for her. 'You know what I think, I think that you're forgetting about Mia in all of this. I think that this is somehow your crusade against Barry, against your demons, and you just don't give a fuck about anything else.'

Hurt, Alfie shook his head. 'How can you say that? I would rather be at home, having a beer, having a laugh with my mates. Do you really think if I had any other choice that I'd come looking for the man who nearly destroyed my life? Every time I think of him, I get sick. I can't tell

284

you how many times I was up in the night, throwing up. I'm terrified, Fran, and that's something I'd never admit to most people. I feel ashamed of my fear. I feel ashamed I haven't dealt with it before, but I just couldn't . . . Though I can't let it beat me, because if it does, then Barry's won and that little boy, and Mia, and all the others suffer. I won't let that happen, not if I can help it. So don't you think for a minute I don't care about what happens to Mia, because I do. I'm just not good at talking about this.'

Franny pulled herself together. She gazed steadily at Alfie as she spoke with genuine remorse. 'I'm sorry, Alf, I shouldn't have said that. So why don't we go and find out exactly where this scumbag is?' She went into her pocket and pulled out a small gun. And with that, Franny walked towards the door.

Standing either side of the flat, Alfie and Franny had put on gloves. Alfie held his gun against him, knocking on the door with his foot as he nodded to Franny. There was no reply, so he tried again. This time harder.

A moment later, they heard a woman's voice. 'Piss off!'

He banged once more with his foot, not saying anything, and once more the woman shouted through the door. 'I said, piss off!'

Alfie called back, checking up and down the corridor as he did so. 'Alan sent me. I need to speak to you – it's important.'

The woman's voice held a strong Yorkshire accent. 'I don't know anyone called Alan, so it can't be that important, can it?'

'Well, he sent me. He said maybe you could help.'

The woman coughed. 'I don't know what you're talking about, so if you don't mind, *piss off*!'

There was a pause before Alfie, choosing his words carefully, said, 'I just wondered if you had any spaces in . . . your crèche.'

There was silence then the sound of several locks opening. A second later, the woman put her head around the door. She was small, and looked to be in her mid-fifties. She was grey-haired with a tight perm and her face had deep wrinkles running all over it. Her eyes darted down the hallway and she spoke to Alfie, who hid his gun behind his back.

She spoke in a hushed tone, looking nervous. 'I don't know who you are, and I don't know who this Alan is, but coming to my door like this isn't how it goes. So, I'd be grateful if you could leave.'

Alfie bent down to her, his face inches away. 'No, I'm not going anywhere because I'm at the right place, aren't I?'

Nervously, the woman stared at Alfie. 'Whoever this bloke is, he had no right giving out my address. Like I say, that's not how it works. You could be anybody.'

The woman tried to close the door but Alfie jammed his foot in it as Franny stepped next to him. His voice was low and threatening. 'I just want a word.'

'*Sally, what's going on?*' a man's voice from behind the woman called out. He appeared briefly, but seeing Alfie, he frowned then suddenly darted back.

Alfie pushed the door open with force, slamming the woman out of the way, who fell to the floor screeching.

Following Alfie, Franny ran inside, closing the door behind her, but she stayed with the woman as Alfie charged into the bedroom.

Seeing the man trying to climb out of the window onto the small balcony, Alfie, still holding his gun, ran across, grabbing hold of the man's legs, dragging him back. He grappled with him as the man fought hard. He took a swing at Alfie and picked up the chair in the corner, throwing it across the room before trying to make his escape over the bed.

Alfie pointed his gun. 'I'd stop right there if I were you.'

The man just stared at Alfie then slowly reached down and picked up a toddler who'd been asleep in a cot.

The man smirked. 'You might as well put the gun down, because you and I both know you're not going to shoot.'

Alfie said nothing as he watched the man back out of the bedroom carrying the young child. But not having seen Franny enter the flat, the man stepped into the hallway where Franny quietly walked up behind him, hitting him hard over the head, knocking him out cold as Alfie ran forward to catch the falling child.

37

It was another half an hour before the man, who Sally had informed them was called Anthony, regained consciousness – though when he did so, he found himself tied to one of the kitchen chairs.

Pulling at his hands, which were bound behind him, Anthony glared at Alfie. 'Untie me now! I *said*, untie me now.'

Alfie walked up to him and shook his head as he stared back at Anthony, who was sitting next to Sally – also tied – to another chair.

'Are you having a laugh, mate? You're tied up and you're trying to tell me what to do? If I were you, I'd wind my neck in and keep quiet. Don't make this any worse than it is already.'

Anthony made a snorting sound, bringing phlegm into his mouth. He smirked, then spat straight at Alfie whose face curled up in disgust. Wiping the spit off his blue cash-mere top, Alfie sneered.

'You've really made a mistake now.' He brought his fist back, then struck Anthony hard across his face, causing his nose to pop and blood spurt out. Alfie pulled up a chair next to Anthony, straddling it backwards and sitting down to light a cigarette. He stared, full of hatred, blowing the smoke into Anthony's face.

'I want some answers, Anthony, because I'm not here to talk, I'm here to listen. So, come on then, tell me everything you know about where I can find Barry.'

'I'm not telling you anything, so you can sing for all I care.'

Alfie smiled nastily then grabbed Anthony's hair, pulling his head up higher, forcing him to look. 'I think by the end of the day, it'll be you singing.'

'Piss off!'

Alfie laughed though his eyes were cold. 'It must be a northern thing that makes you lot so stupid, ain't that right, Sally?'

Alfie glanced at the woman who began to screech with anger, 'Fuck off! You heard what my husband said – we haven't got anything to say to you because we don't know anything. So, you can do anything you like to us, you still won't learn anything new.'

'Is that right?'

Sally nodded defiantly. 'Yes, it bloody well is!'

Alfie, finishing off his cigarette, stubbed it out on the carpet. He looked around the small flat. It was tidy and clean. Flowered wallpaper adorned the room and the blue leather couch was strewn with large velvet cushions. The polished wooden floor was semi-covered with a thick cream rug, and the fake fireplace bounced with flames. And whether it was because he knew what sort of people Sally and Anthony were, he thought the whole place with its spotless, dust-free shelves and furniture held a sinister air.

'So, you're saying whatever I do, you won't talk.'

'That's right.'

'Okay.'

Alfie stood up. He winked at Franny who sat in a chair holding the toddler who had gone back to sleep, then Alfie made eye contact with Sally again. He grinned as he pulled out his belt from his jeans. 'As in *anything* I do, Sally?'

The confidence in Sally's voice seemed to disappear. 'Yeah . . . yeah . . . that's what I said, isn't it?'

'Even this, Sally?'

Taking Anthony by surprise, Alfie looped the belt around Anthony's neck and began to pull it tight. 'How about now?'

Beginning to panic as she watched Anthony's face turn red, his eyes bulging, Sally screamed, 'You're hurting him!'

Alfie chuckled and jarred and pulled the belt even tighter as he stood staring at Sally. 'And how about *now*?'

'You're going to kill him!'

'And now?' Alfie bared his teeth, pulling the belt with all his might.

'Stop! Stop!' she cried. '*Stop!*'

'Why? I thought you'd said I could do anything, so it's pointless me stopping, ain't it?' Alfie began to whistle as Anthony, starved of oxygen, started to judder.

'Okay, okay! I'll tell you, just leave him alone!'

'That's what I thought you'd say!' And with that, Alfie released the tension in his belt before kicking the chair Anthony was tied on over onto the floor, causing him to smash down on his side as he coughed and spluttered for air.

Feeding his belt back through the loops in his jeans, Alfie sat down again, resting his foot on Anthony's head, who was having difficulty breathing.

Angrily, Sally said, 'Look what you've done to him. You bastard!'

'I could do more. I could do the same to you if you want? I usually don't lay my hands on women, but I could make you an exception to the rule. You want me to show you?'

Sally, her eyes full of fear, shook her head.

Alfie grinned. 'Good, I'm glad we've got that sorted out. So now, what I want from you are answers, and if I think for a moment you're not telling me the truth, you and Anthony here will be spending a painful afternoon with me? Do you understand what I'm saying?'

'Yeah, yeah.'

'So first off, who does this baby belong to?'

Sally glanced across to the toddler who Franny was still holding. 'He's . . . he's my grandson.'

Alfie put his weight into his foot, crushing and pressing down on Anthony's skull. As Anthony let out a scream of pain, Alfie leant in towards Sally. 'Wrong answer. Try again, and this time you better get it right or your husband here is really going to suffer.'

Sally's eyes darted about. 'Okay, we've been looking after him, for a friend.'

Alfie shook his head. 'You really are testing my patience.' He raised his foot to bring it down again on Anthony but as he did so, Sally began to speak again, her words rushing out.

'No, don't! Stop! I'll tell you, just please don't hurt him anymore . . . The kid belongs to a couple, or he did.'

Alfie, already feeling ill and not really wanting to ask any more questions but knowing he had to, said, 'What do you mean, he did?'

'They sold him, and we're just looking after him until the new owners come and get him. I swear he's fine. Look at him – he's well looked after. He's a happy boy. I always change him, I always . . .'

Alfie bellowed, cutting into the woman's words. 'Shut up! Shut up, you warped bitch! Do you hear what you're saying to me? Do you understand what shit is coming out of your mouth? You're talking about him as if he's just about to go to Disneyland instead of going to be abused by God knows who for God knows how long.'

'It's not always like that!'

With his face curled up with hatred, Alfie hissed, 'I don't care if it's like that only once. Once is too much, you hear me?'

'I'm only saying.'

Alfie lunged out and grabbed Sally's face. He squeezed it hard between his fingers, fighting back the tears. 'Don't push it. Don't push *me*. Because I am so close to putting a bullet in your head. Do you understand?'

Terrified, Sally nodded as Alfie let go of her. She continued to talk. 'What I mean is, sometimes we look after kids who are simply changing hands. You know, someone can't afford their kid, or don't want them and the dealers buy them and then ask us to look after them until the new parents are found.'

'You make it sound like it's all rosy.'

Sally shrugged. 'I'm just trying to explain the difference, that's all.'

'And what about the others? Because, fuck me, what you've told me is bad enough, but what about the other side of that coin? What about this kid here?' Alfie nodded towards the toddler and as he did so he caught a glimpse of the strain on Franny's face. He tried to smile at her, but he couldn't manage it; what Sally was saying was too unbearable.

'He'll be all right. The person who bought him lives in Japan. They'll give him a good home . . . but there are the others who get sold for other reasons.'

Alfie rubbed his head, which was now pounding with a migraine. 'What is wrong with you? How can you live with yourself?'

'It's money, ain't it? We all have to earn our keep.'

Alfie stood up and began to pace, anger and disgust running through him in equal measure. 'I could be starving on the fucking street and you would never get me to come even close to doing what you do. I would rather die.'

The woman's eyes flashed with irritation. 'It's not like I'm the one who's abusing them though, is it?'

Alfie charged up to Sally, inches away from her. Everything in him wanted to put his hands around her neck and throttle her, but he held back as he felt the tears cutting at the back of his throat. 'You might as well be, because you're part of it. You know what's happening to these kids, yet you're still willing to be involved.'

'At least I look after them properly! At least they get food and a bit of care. Sometimes it's more than they've had in their entire life.'

Roaring out in anger, Alfie smashed his fist against the wall, resting his head against it as he tried to breathe and shut out the enormity of what Sally was saying with such aloofness it felt surreal. He spoke in a whisper. 'Franny, I can't talk to her anymore. You do it, because otherwise I'm going to fucking kill her.'

Franny, placing the sleeping toddler in the cot in the corner, nodded. She walked across to where Sally sat, reassuringly touching Alfie's back as she walked past him.

Her voice was icy cold as she spoke to Sally. 'Let's talk about Barry, shall we?'

'I don't know who he is.'

Incensed, Franny slapped Sally hard across the face. 'Don't play games with me. I'm not like he is – I won't just kill you, I'll make every second as painful as I can too. Now, tell me about Barry Eton.'

With Anthony still on his side tied to the chair and Alfie resting against the wall with his eyes closed, Sally spoke, the tension in the air between the two women palpable. 'I've only done business with him a couple of times. He's just one of many clients that ask me to look after one of their products.'

'How do you know him?'

'My husband was in prison with him. Not on kiddie

charges, he's not into that either, but for GBH. Anyway, he met Barry and they got talking, and Anthony told him what we do.'

Franny stared at Sally. 'How long have you been doing this?'

'A long time. I mean, before the internet really became popular we did it, but it was much harder. Now it's easy. People from all over the world are on the dark net, and there's always a supply and demand with this.'

Franny felt revolted, as she was sure Alfie did, but she didn't let her emotions show. 'And what about a baby? A little girl, she was . . . she *is* four months old. Blonde curly hair, the palest of skin, blue eyes. She's beautiful, really beautiful. Have . . . have you seen her? Recently, it would've been recently.'

Sally shook her head. 'No.'

Franny exploded, her face turning red. She shouted as she trembled with anger. 'You're lying! You're fucking lying.'

Seeing the rage in Franny, Sally, becoming frightened, began to stutter her words. 'I . . . I . . . I don't know. I'm telling the truth!'

Overcome with emotion, Franny's voice cracked with hysteria, rage and hurt, panic and fury rushing through her. She pulled out her gun and pressed it under Sally's chin. 'Then where is she? Where's Mia?'

Petrified, Sally shook her head. 'I don't know . . . I don't know!'

A manic look came into Franny's eyes. 'That's no good to me, Sally, because I have to find her. You hear me? I have to find her so scum like you, scum like Anthony, like

Barry can never, *never* put their hands on her. Do you understand that?'

'Yes . . . yes.'

Still with the gun underneath Sally's chin, Franny leant down and hissed, 'Then tell me where she is, *Sally*.'

Sally's eyes filled with tears. 'I can't tell you, because I don't know. I don't. I promise I don't.'

'Save the tears and don't fucking insult me. Don't insult those kids you took in, don't insult any of us with your crocodile tears, because I don't care, and I have never hated anyone so much in my life as I hate you right now.' Franny paused, images of Mia flashing through her mind. She took a deep breath before saying, 'Carry on telling me about Barry.'

Trying to regain her composure, Sally's tone was edgy. 'Well, it's only recently he's got out of prison; he hasn't been trading long, though I'm not sure if he's really got the money to.'

'What do you mean?'

Sally shrugged, sighing and sounding like a woman defeated. 'Unless you're the middle man, which he isn't anymore, a lot of the contacts he did have, well, he would've lost touch with them. Then if that happens, you have to shell out for the products – the kids – yourself, before you can sell them on. Plus, sometimes you have to pay people like me if you don't have a buyer straightaway.'

Franny glared at Sally. 'I was under the impression Barry did filming, streaming, rather than just buying and selling.'

'I dunno, but if he does, he won't be the main player. He'll be working for someone else just to earn a few bob.'

Hating the conversation, Franny said, 'Why doesn't he do it himself though?'

Glancing down at her husband, Sally said, 'Because you really have to know what you're doing to set yourself up on the net. Of course, if you're computer savvy then it's easy enough and you can make yourself a fortune, but otherwise, the police will be able to track you straightaway, and I don't think Barry wants to end up inside again.'

'So, what's his game?'

'From what I understand, he wants to be a dealer.'

'So, has Barry paid you a visit recently?'

Taking a deep breath, Sally nodded. 'Yeah, he was here yesterday. He came to collect a little boy I was looking after for him, though the kid was only here a couple of nights.'

Franny, almost unable to look at Sally, asked, 'So where's the boy now? What's going to happen to him?'

'Look, I shouldn't be saying any more.'

Without hesitation, Franny raised her voice. 'Just *tell* me!'

'If people find out they can't trust me, I'll be in trouble.'

Franny pushed up against Sally, her eyes blazing. 'Listen to me, Sally, these *people* will be the least of your worries if you don't continue talking, so you might as well tell me.'

Gazing up into Franny's face, Sally simply said, 'There's going to be an auction. Barry's going to auction off the boy.'

38

Alfie, having recovered slightly, sat staring at Sally. He spoke to her as Franny fed the toddler – who'd woken up hungry – a bottle of milk.

'Have you a photo of this boy?'

'No.'

Alfie – his patience non-existent – kicked the legs of Sally's chair. 'I said, have you a *fucking* photo of this little boy?'

Nervously, Sally nodded. 'Yes . . . yes, it's on my phone. We don't usually take photos. It's too risky but . . .'

'But what?'

'Barry wanted me to because it was a way of drumming up business. He thought that as I know the right people, maybe I could ask about, see if anyone's interested. You know, show them the photo because obviously the more people go to the auction, the better for him. The more money it will generate.'

Alfie spoke, but it was more of a statement than a question. 'And you'll get a cut of that. A bonus.'

Sally nodded as Alfie continued to talk. He spoke thoughtfully. 'Let me see the photo.'

With only a slight hesitation, Sally said, 'My phone's over there. The code is 7, 6, 9, 7, 4, 1.'

Alfie stood up and strode across to pick up Sally's phone. Still wearing gloves, he punched in the numbers. He scrolled through Sally's photo album, shaking his head at the inoffensive pictures on it. Seaside snaps, holiday snaps, fun days out that only emphasised to Alfie the horrific reality of the whole situation.

Suddenly he stopped. His whole body froze as he stared at a photo of a little boy sitting on a couch. The same little boy he'd seen in the warehouse, with his same haunted eyes – the same look of fear in them. He whispered to no one particular. 'That's him . . . that's the boy. I think we've found him.' He quickly showed the photo to Franny before turning his attention back to Sally. 'This is the boy Barry brought to you, isn't it?'

'Yeah, sweet little thing. No trouble. Didn't cry once. Come to think of it, he didn't say anything.'

Snorting in derision, Alfie snapped, 'Are you surprised? He was probably terrified . . . What's his name?'

'Taylor.'

'And who does he belong to?'

Sally blinked, looking more uncomfortable than she did already.

Alfie tilted his head and, frowning, spoke with dangerous menace. 'Who, Sally? *Who* does he belong to?'

'Alan.'

Shocked, Alfie stared at Sally. 'Alan? Barry's friend?'

'Yeah. He's a druggie and he's known Barry for a while. Anyway, Taylor's mum went off when the kid was a baby and Alan had him.'

'What about what he went inside for? I don't get it. Surely, social services must've known he's not safe to be around kids?'

'Don't ask me. From what I understand they thought he'd been rehabilitated. You know, saw the error of his ways. So, he got the kid back and moved away from the area. I suppose the authorities lost touch with him. Happens a lot.'

'So, Alan sold Taylor to Barry?'

'Yeah, for a thousand quid. No doubt Alan's already pissed it away on gear. But Barry's quids in. A kid like Taylor will go for a lot of money.'

Alfie sat down, letting the information wash over him. He couldn't believe what he was hearing. It was one thing being a drug addict and another thing being a cruel, heartless, calculating monster. A thought came to him. 'But hang on, you said, the more people *go* to the auction. He's not doing it online?'

Sally spoke flatly as Anthony lay motionless at her feet. 'No. A lot of people who aren't big players prefer to do it more discreetly. That way they know who they're dealing with. Online, it could be anyone, anywhere in the world, and like I mentioned, you really have to be sophisticated, know what you're doing, otherwise the police will be knocking on your door before the auction's even over.'

'So where and when is Barry holding it?'

'I don't know.'

Alfie sneered. He bent down to Anthony, putting the gun against the man's head. 'Come off it, Sally, you said yourself that he wants you to drum up business, so all it will take is a call from you to let him know a regular client is interested in Taylor. Either that or I do what I've wanted to do since I walked in here. What's it going to be?' Alfie undid the safety latch on his gun. 'Your choice.'

'All right . . . all right. It's going to be held in a couple of days' time at a warehouse in East London. I don't have to call him though because you just need to take an entrance ticket and they'll let you in.'

'And how do I get one of those?'

'They're over in the drawer. That large drawer under the television.'

Alfie walked across to the far side of the room and bent down to open the drawer. He frowned and looked at Sally. 'Is this some kind of fucked-up joke?'

'No, that's what you need to take. That's your ticket to get in. That will get you into the auction.'

A wave of nausea rushed over Alfie as he bent down, taking a blue dummy with a blue ribbon tied to it out of the drawer.

39

Having called the police anonymously from outside the flat, and having waited and watched them arrive, Franny and Alfie drove back to London in silence, both of them traumatised and wishing they could turn back the clock and un-hear what they'd been told in Sally and Anthony's flat. But both of them realised what they'd heard would stay with them for the rest of their lives.

By the time they arrived in Soho Square, it was the early hours of the morning and tiredness hit them.

Outside the house, Alfie turned off the engine and just sat and stared ahead, and it was a number of minutes before he spoke his first words in over two hours. 'We need to sort this.'

'I know, but how?'

'It's too risky to leave it for the police; by the time they've done their investigation, Barry will be long gone, so I'm going to go to that auction. *We're* going to go.'

Rubbing her temples and taking a quick sip of her warm can of Coke, Franny, feeling exhausted, asked, 'But what about Sally and Anthony? What if he hears something?'

'If Barry *does* hear anything about Sally and Anthony being arrested, he certainly won't think it's anything to do with him. He'll probably just be pleased he took Taylor out of there before there was a raid. Though I expect word won't get out for a few days, if not more, and by that time Barry would've taken Taylor to the auction.'

'So, what next?'

'We're going to go and bid for him. However much it takes. Whatever it takes, we're going to make sure we get Taylor back. And once we've got him, I'll take him to my friend Claire. She fosters kids and stuff, you know through social services, so she'll know exactly what to do with him. If we do that he'll be safe, but we'll be able to keep our names out of it. She won't say anything about us.'

Worried, Franny stared at Alfie. 'That's all fine, but ain't you jumping the gun a bit? The auction's tomorrow night – you won't be able to lay your hands on enough money that quickly. Things have been difficult.'

'Like I say, whatever it takes, I'll do it. We've got a good few grand in the safe and . . .'

Franny cut in, knowing that she needed to tell Alfie she'd taken the money albeit she certainly wouldn't tell him she'd taken it and given it to Ma to keep quiet about Bree and her.

'We haven't.'

'Yeah we have, there's about ten or fifteen grand, and I know it won't be enough but it's a start.'

Franny spoke intently. 'But that's what I'm trying to tell you, we haven't. Not anymore.'

Alfie's face darkened. He became agitated. 'What the fuck are you talking about?'

'The money in the safe, I . . . I had to use it.'

With the tension between them electric, Alfie fell silent as he stared at Franny in disbelief, and it was only after a few moments he said, 'Why the fuck didn't I know about this? And more to the point, why did you use it?'

Franny, the panic swirling around her again, snapped. 'I don't need to run everything past you, Alf. In case you've forgotten, we're a team. Sometimes we'll do things together and sometimes we'll do things individually and know the other person has got our back and won't question what we do.'

Alfie tilted his head, menace coming into his voice. 'You haven't answered the question.'

Franny's mind raced as her eyes darted across Alfie's face. 'Vaughn.'

'Excuse me?'

'I had to give the money to Vaughn. Well rather, I had to put the money back in the business to try to balance the books. I didn't want to say. You were so stressed.'

Alfie shook his head, his stare piercing. 'Hold on, I'm not following you.'

Keeping her cool like she'd always been taught, Franny leant in to Alfie's face. Her tone was cold. 'I know we're both tired but it's not difficult to understand what I'm saying . . . I told you before, Vaughn was robbing us from right underneath our noses, and when I found out I confronted him, and he tried to turn it round to make it look like I was the one stealing money.'

Alfie held Franny's gaze and with a strange look in his eye he said, 'And you would never do that, would you?'

Feeling uneasy, but certainly not letting it show, Franny shook her head. 'I know what I did about the letters was wrong. I should never have written them, but no, I would never do anything to hurt you or our business.'

Alfie nodded slowly. 'Because you've got no secrets, have you, Fran?'

Tightly, Franny replied, 'None.'

'That's right, because you've already told me that, haven't you? The girl with no secrets.'

Alfie smiled, but it was as icy as Franny's tone had been cold. Everything in him wanted to believe Franny, but everything in him wanted to shake the truth out of her, because right then, he knew she was lying . . . *Lying* about putting the money back in the business. And the reason he knew that was because *he* had in fact put the money in the safe, the morning *after* Vaughn had left. The morning after the fire. So, what Franny was saying was impossible. But why she was saying it and why she had taken the money without telling him was an entirely different matter. And maybe, just *maybe*, there was something in the anonymous texts he'd been getting that was nearer the truth than he'd wanted to believe. Perhaps, after all, Franny *had* done something and perhaps she really did have a secret.

He took a deep, long breath. He had to keep a lid on it. Whatever it was would have to wait. He needed to keep his mind on Taylor, and he wasn't going to risk being distracted for something he could deal with later. But he would deal with it. He would eventually get the truth out of Franny, *one way or another*.

Franny, wanting to break the strained silence, said, 'You need to get some sleep, Alf – we both do if we're going to be any use to Taylor . . .' She paused before adding, 'And Mia.'

Alfie nodded, feeling a pain in his chest, though he wasn't entirely sure if it was physical. He loved Franny so much and he was afraid that when he did eventually find out what she was hiding, his heart might get well and truly broken. 'You get some rest. As for myself, I've got to go and sort some money out, as well as pay someone a visit . . . Will you be all right, Fran?'

Exhausted and on the verge of feeling like she was going to lose it, Franny nodded. 'Yeah, I'll be fine. Who are you going to see?'

'Alan. I'm going to pay Alan another visit. It's about time him and me had a little chat.'

Trying only to concentrate on the matter at hand, Alfie made his way across the estate towards a group of kids huddled in the corner smoking joints.

He nodded to the oldest-looking kid, who Alfie didn't think could be much more than fourteen. 'I'm trying to find Alan. I dunno his second name, but I reckon he lives around here.'

The kid, taking a large drag of the joint he was holding, stared at Alfie, his eyes full of disinterest. 'Can't help you, mate.'

Alfie went into his pocket, pulling out a twenty-pound note. 'How about if I give you this? Can you help me now?'

The kid shrugged but took the money. 'Depends. What does he look like?'

Alfie thought of Alan, he could almost taste the disgust in his mouth. 'He's small. He barely touches five foot three, and he's probably in his early thirties. When I saw him last time, he was wearing a blue shell Nike tracksuit and baseball cap with a red letter **A** on it. His face is probably a bit messed up at the moment, oh and he's a total smackhead.'

The boy nodded. 'Yeah, I know him. A proper nonce.'

Alfie frowned. 'Why do you call him that?'

The boy, who had a thick cockney accent, pulled a face. 'Cos he is. He's proper snaky. He's always watching the younger kids down here. Always trying to make friends with them. A couple of months ago he took a kid into his flat. Nothing happened cos the kid's dad went looking for him and found him before it did. Geezer gave Alan a right battering. I think he even called the police, told them he'd beaten Alan up and the reason why, but the Old Bill – instead of nicking Alan, they ended up nicking the kid's dad.'

Alfie shook his head, imagining just how the scene would've played out. 'And is it true that Alan's got a son?'

The boy raised his eyebrows. 'Yeah. His name's Taylor, though I ain't seen him for a bit. But usually he's out here on his own, even when the weather's pissing it down or it's snowing, Taylor will be out here without a coat. Even my mum ain't that bad, and she's shit.'

Having got the details of where Alan lived, Alfie made his way to the large block of flats on the west side of the estate, noticing that most of the CCTV cameras were either hanging off the wall or had been smashed.

Getting into the lift – which had a used syringe in the corner lying in a pool of urine – Alfie tried to hold his breath, not wanting to inhale the stink of alcohol and faeces that sat heavily in the air.

At the top floor, the metal door opened with a shudder and Alfie marched along the corridor, making his way to the end flat. Without bothering to knock, Alfie began to boot the front door down, causing tiny splinters of wood to scatter everywhere. Then with one final kick, the door swung open, and Alfie casually walked in.

The place lay in darkness, the curtains closed and, as Alfie's eyes adjusted, he could see the whole place was a mess. Going towards the bedroom, Alfie's attention was suddenly drawn towards the far side of the room; something – or rather somebody – was there and, without any doubt of who it was that crouched and hid in the corner, Alfie leapt at the figure, pounding his fist into any part of the body he could find. He spat out his words.

'How could you do it? How could you sell your own flesh and blood? How could you sell your little boy?'

Alan screamed. 'What difference does it make to you?'

Enraged, Alfie bellowed back. 'Are you having a fucking laugh? You do know Barry's auctioning him off?'

Confused, Alan stammered. 'Yeah . . . yeah, of course I do. What else would he do?'

'But that's your kid!'

'So?'

Incensed, Alfie rained down harder blows, which made

Alan scream out in agony as he felt his front teeth being jammed back by the force of the punches, with a pain shooting through his eye like a needle had been thrust straight through it.

Panting, Alfie stood up, still attacking Alan with his feet as he kicked him in the side.

'Why didn't you tell me that Taylor was your son before? Why didn't you mention anything about him?'

Terrified, Alan muttered, blood and saliva bubbling and frothing out of his mouth. 'You didn't ask, and what difference would it make? And besides, you were looking to find where Barry was.'

'You're scum, you know that? *Scum.*'

'I don't understand, what have I done wrong? I told you where to find Sally, didn't I? I helped you out. I told you she would know where Barry was. It's not my fault if she didn't tell you.' As Alan stopped talking, Alfie grabbed hold of a clump of his hair, tearing it as hard as he could away from Alan's scalp.

'Seriously? You think this is just about me finding Barry?'

'Well if it's not then what is it about?'

Alfie rubbed his chin in shocked bewilderment. 'You really don't get it, do you?'

'No, cos I've told you everything I know.'

Alfie, still holding Alan's hair, shook his head. 'It's not about that now. It's about Taylor. It's all about Taylor now.'

Alan lowered his voice, his eyes becoming dilated. He licked his lips. 'Are you going to buy him then?'

'What?'

'You are, aren't you? You're just like me. We have the

same tastes.' Inexplicably, Alan grinned and was immediately kicked hard in the back by Alfie.

'What the fuck are you talking about? I'm not like you and never will be. You make me sick to my stomach, Alan, and now I'll tell you how it's going to go.'

Alfie walked over to the curtains and pulled them tighter together, causing clouds of dust to rise from them. He walked over to the door and shut it before turning to look at Alan and pulling out a rope from his coat pocket as he did so.

On seeing the rope, Alan, still in pain, began to back away fearfully, shuffling along the floor.

'What . . . what are you going to do?'

Full of hatred and not wanting to hear anything more out of his mouth, Alfie ran at Alan. Roughly, he grabbed Alan's arms, expertly tying them behind his back before slipping the rope down and round Alan's ankles, then around the base of the radiator on the wall, making sure that the knot was tight.

Out of his other pocket, Alfie pulled a black roll of tape. 'You ready for this?'

'No . . . stop, look, maybe we can come to some agreement.'

Alfie sneered. 'You have nothing I want.' And with that, Alfie began to bind the black tape round and round Alan's mouth.

Once he'd finished taping up his mouth, Alfie stared at Alan. 'So, what I'm going to do now is say goodbye. I won't be seeing you again, but then, Alan, nobody else will be seeing you either, so make the most of these last few hours.

At about seven o'clock tonight, friends of mine will be coming to pay you a little visit, and make no mistake, they enjoy what they do, and they'll take you somewhere that no one can hear you scream. And do you know what their speciality is, Alan? Burying people alive.'

Alan made muffled sounds of protest through the tape, and with a smile on his face, Alfie retorted, 'That's right. And the best thing about it is that you'll have a lot of time to think . . . Enjoy the journey. Oh, and, Alan? I'll see you in hell.'

40

Back at the house in Soho, Franny was frantically running around, pulling out cupboards and drawers, going into each and every wardrobe. She dragged out bags and shoes, pausing every few moments to rack her brain to see if she'd made a mistake; if in all the stress she'd absentmindedly brought in the suitcase of Bree's belongings and the black bin liner full of her bloodstained clothing, rather than leaving them in the boot like she'd thought.

But the more she tried to think, the more she couldn't. Every day, every memory seemed to merge into another. It didn't make sense. She was certain that she'd left them in the car. She had to think . . . *Think*. When and where had she last seen them? But each time she came back to the same answer; she'd left them in the boot and now they were missing.

Trembling, she put her hands to her face, feeling the tears dripping through her fingers.

'Franny. Franny.'

Terrified, she screamed and looked up, spinning around. She shook her head then scrambled over to her bedside cabinet, pulling out the gun from the drawer. She pointed the gun in the air. 'You leave me alone, you hear me? You leave me alone?' She whirled around, hearing the wind and the rain pick up outside.

'Franny. Franny.'

As Franny backed against the wall, she burst into manic laughter, loud and frenzied. 'I know it's not you, Bree. It can't be you . . . I know you're not real.' She continued to shake as she glanced around the room but as she spun round, Franny screamed, thinking that she'd seen someone behind her. She began to shoot; firing off bullets, shot after shot, emptying the cartridge on her automatic weapon, but then she froze. Her breathing staggered and hard, she stared in upset confusion, realising that she hadn't been shooting at anyone at all, only her own reflection in the large mirror on the wall.

'What's going on?' Alfie, holding his phone, walked into the bedroom, shocked at the sight of the place strewn with clothes and the mirror shot out. He looked at Franny in disbelief. 'Franny, what the fuck has gone on here?'

Wide-eyed, Franny stared at Alfie. 'Leave me alone. You hear me? Just leave me alone.'

She tried to run out of the room, but Alfie grabbed her, drawing her in to him. 'You are going to tell me what is going on because I'm not leaving here until you do. You've been lying to me, haven't you, Fran?'

Silently, and with her breathing still short and shallow, Franny nodded.

313

'Are you going to tell me about it?'

Shaking, she stared at him, tears rolling down her face as she nodded again.

'Is it bad?'

Again, Franny nodded, but this time she managed to whisper the words, 'It's really bad, Alf, it's really bad and I don't think you'll ever forgive me. I can't even forgive myself.'

Such concern filled Alfie's eyes that Franny had to glance away. 'Fran, how about I make a deal with you. If you tell me now, then we leave it here, within these walls. Whatever it is, I promise I won't bring it up again. We don't have to talk about it unless you want to. Even if it's killing me inside. I give you my word, I'll make sure it won't break us.'

Franny sobbed. 'Alf, once you know what it is, it can't do anything but break us.'

'You're scaring me now, Franny. Is there someone else? Is that it? I know I said I could never forgive you if you cheated on me, but I could get over it. It might break my heart, it might bruise my ego, but to keep you, I would do anything.'

Franny took in Alfie's handsome face. She took in his care and love, and briefly and gently she kissed him on his lips. 'I wish it was that, but it's much worse.'

Alfie gave her a sad smile. 'Worse than that?'

Again, Franny nodded.

Alfie only half joking said, 'Killing someone ain't even worse than that.'

Franny gave a lopsided smile. 'It all depends on who you kill.'

Alfie frowned. 'Well have you? Have you killed someone? I mean that's part of the game we're in. Look, whatever it is, I reckon you'll feel better when you tell me, because it's clear that it's eating you up inside.'

Full of sincerity, Franny nodded. 'I think you're right. I can't go on like this, Alf. But before I tell you, you have to understand it all started off with good intentions, but it just got out of hand, and the more I tried to stop the snowball from rolling, the bigger it got. Does that make sense?'

Alfie, agreeing, said, 'Of course. What's that saying . . . *The road to hell is paved with good intentions.*'

A flicker of alarm crossed Franny's face. 'Don't say that.'

'I was only joking.'

'Well don't. Just don't.'

Alfie nodded. His voice was warm and loving as he said, 'Okay, I won't . . . So go on then, tell me.'

Taking a deep breath, Franny began to talk. 'It really all started when Br . . .' She stopped and closed her eyes, then trying again, she said, 'When Br . .'

'Sorry, darlin', I'm so sorry but I have to take this.' Alfie glanced at his phone, which was vibrating; a call coming in. 'I wouldn't take it if it wasn't urgent, but it's about sorting out some money for the auction.' He paused and looked at Franny, his eyes pleading with her to let him take it.

'Yes, of course, you have to take it.'

'Sorry. Just hold on to what you were saying, okay? I want to hear it.'

Alfie answered the phone, keeping his eyes on Franny as he listened to the caller talk, but he mouthed the word, *sorry*, to her before he spoke into the phone.

'So what time should I be there, mate? And are you sure it can get sorted . . . good . . . yeah . . . okay, I'll see you then.'

Clicking off the phone, Alfie turned back to Franny. 'I think I might be able to sort a bit of money for the auction. I need to go and see them in a little while, but I've still got time to listen to what you were saying.'

Franny blinked and stared at Alfie. What had she been thinking? What the hell had she just been about to do? Jesus. The idea she had been seconds away from telling Alfie about Bree, about his daughter, Mia, was unthinkable. This was exactly what her father had warned her about: emotions. She had let her emotions get the better of her. She had nearly ruined everything because she had allowed her emotions to dictate her sense. And telling Alfie about Mia would've been the biggest mistake of her life . . . or rather the end of it.

And although she acknowledged that she'd just had a lucky escape, now she had to make sure that there weren't any more emotional outbursts like the one she'd just had.

Of course, if things were different she and Alfie would have a future because she did love him, there was no question about it, but she refused to let love be her weakness and make the wrong choices. And that's exactly what she had to do: she had to choose, whether she liked it or not, and she chose Mia. And when she found Mia, and she would find her, then she and Mia would leave Soho, leave London, leave England and start a new life.

She smiled and simply said, 'No, you need to go and sort this out, it's more important.'

'But what about you? I can't just leave you like this.'

'Just see it as a moment of weakness.'

'But it's obviously important. You said yourself you lied to me, you said . . .'

Franny placed her fingers on Alfie's lips. 'Sshhhh, baby. Stop, it's okay, we can talk another time. Neither of us are going anywhere, are we? Right now, the only thing we should be thinking about is Taylor and Mia. And please don't worry, Alf, I'll be fine. Even this talk we've just had has given me clarity . . . Everything will work out the way it should . . . I love you, Alfie.'

Alfie, putting Franny at the back of his mind, made his way across to Chinatown, pushing past a group of tourists taking photographs on Shaftesbury Avenue. He walked down Wardour Street before crossing the road to turn into Lisle Street.

He strode along for a moment before pulling up the collar on his jacket to protect him from the chill of the air.

Halfway along the street, at a large Chinese restaurant, Alfie walked down the stone stairs into the basement and knocked on the door twice.

It was opened by a man, who nodded at Alfie and let him in. Alfie smiled at the same time as taking a deep breath. Taylor needed him, so if it meant borrowing money from the infamous Triad clan, a gang of people he would normally stay away from, a gang of people no one in their right mind would do business with, well that's exactly what he would do.

41

Alfie sat at the table with Mr Huang in the basement of the restaurant. The room was silent apart from the noise of the restaurant-goers above.

He'd known Huang for a long time, though interestingly he'd never learnt his first name, but as far back as he could remember, Huang and his family had been living in the heart of Chinatown, running a gambling business, drug trafficking, money laundering as well as – rumour had it – people trafficking. He was also a loan shark. Fierce and ferocious, Huang certainly was not someone to be messed with.

Huang was part of, or rather the head of the clan of Triads in the area. A huge crime organisation, which still had its ties in China and Taiwan. In the past Alfie hadn't had a good relationship with the Triads, mainly because he'd been trying to set up his own gambling club over in Soho, something they hadn't taken too kindly to. In fact, he had the war wounds to prove it when they'd come into his club threatening him, cutting off part of his finger to give him a *friendly* warning to stop running the club.

What had followed had been a bit of a turf war, but eventually they'd settled their differences and given each other a respectful understanding. Though there was certainly no love lost between the parties; neither of them particularly liked each other, though it wasn't a question of liking, it was a question of business. And when the interest they charged on any loan was three hundred per cent – along with a pound of flesh if need be – then he knew they would do business with anyone. Even him.

Huang, a slender-faced man in his late sixties, with a head of thick black straight hair, pushed his round glasses up to the top of his nose as he stared at Alfie in bemusement. 'Mr Jennings, we've known each other for a long time, and I would say you're certainly a successful businessman. I would also say you knew how to run your firm with fairness, as well as knowing a good deal when it came your way. The one thing I wouldn't have said about you though, was that you were a fool. Mr Jennings, what you've just said to me now is what I consider foolish. Our rates are high and our consequences for not paying are even higher.'

Alfie nodded. 'If you know all that about me, then you'll also know I haven't taken this decision lightly. You'll know that at the moment, you're my only option.'

Huang looked at Alfie before pouring himself a cup of green tea from the delicate china pot that sat on the table.

'Maybe that should worry me. If we're the only option, then things must be really bad.'

'No, not bad, I'm just in a hurry. I need the money by tomorrow and I've had a cash flow problem because as you know, the club has been shut down due to the fire. But that doesn't mean I'm not capable of paying you back.'

'So how do you propose to pay us back, bearing in mind the interest we charge?'

'On a re-mortgage. The house in Soho Square, I'll re-mortgage that.'

Huang shrugged, pulling a face. 'But I've always been under the impression that house was Ms Doyle's, given to her by her father, Patrick.'

Irritated by all the questions, Alfie couldn't stop himself from snapping, 'Look, I don't ask you how you keep your books in order, so I don't appreciate you asking me.'

Huang gave a nasty smile. 'Mr Jennings, the difference is, I don't come and ask you for half a million pounds.'

'I get that, but I can pay you back.'

'You do realise that the reason I'm saying all this is for your own good. That I'm just making sure you have the resources to pay the loan back because I would hate to have to get my men to *force* the money out of you. After all, we go back a long way.'

Alfie's voice was firm. 'With respect, I know what I'm doing and there won't be any need for extreme measures. Like I say, I'm good for the money, and if for any reason that proved to be untrue, then, Mr Huang, I'm willing to take the consequences of any decisions I make.'

Huang nodded. He remained silent for a few moments

before pushing the piles of money, which were sitting in the middle of the table, towards Alfie. He stood up and walked to the door, turning back to look at Alfie. 'It's all there, Mr Jennings, and I do hope for your sake what you're saying is the truth.'

After Huang had left the room, Alfie sat there with the money in front of him, wondering quite what Franny would say when he told her she'd have to re-mortgage her house.

42

The next morning Alfie, who hadn't bothered going to bed because he knew he'd just be up all night worrying about the auction and Taylor, smiled at Franny as she walked into the breakfast room. He studied her face. She looked slightly better than she had yesterday, though maybe that was the sleeping tablet she'd taken. However, he was sure that when he told her about the deal he'd made with Huang, she probably wasn't going to look so calm.

Deciding to make herself a drink to stop feeling nauseous, Franny switched on the coffee machine. The smell of fresh beans wafted into the air. She spoke quickly, an array of thoughts rushing through her mind. 'How did you get on yesterday? Is everything set for today? I thought maybe I'd go and see Charlie again, ask him about Mia.'

'I thought you said he didn't know anything.'

Franny shrugged. 'That is what he said, but in light of

everything, I'd like to speak to him again, see if there's anything – even the smallest of things that might help try to find her. Sorry. You didn't say how you got on . . .'

'I sorted it. Hopefully we'll have enough, more than enough, but you never know with this kind of thing. With any luck, because Barry's a small fish, the auction will only attract the scum with no money, rather than the scum *with* money, because that's when it becomes a problem. Once I'm outbid, there's nothing I can do. I've asked myself a thousand times if I should get the police involved, but I know it will only make it worse for Taylor.'

'And Mia.'

Alfie lit a cigarette, drawing on it deeply. 'Exactly. Barry will dispose of Taylor the minute the police go sniffing around, so it's just too risky. And the tragic thing is, nobody would miss Taylor. Barry could dig a grave in Epping Forest and nobody would ever know.'

Franny shivered, becoming tense. 'Jesus, Alf, what's wrong with you?'

'It's the truth.'

She stared at him as images of Bree came into her mind; as if she could hear the noise of Bree's limbs breaking and the sound of her body being dragged through the forest. 'You still don't need to say it though. We both know what will happen if we don't deal with this properly . . . So, go on then, how much did you manage to get? Who lent it you?'

Alfie exhaled before he said, 'Half a million. I got it from Mr Huang.'

Franny could almost feel herself paling. She raised her

voice, furious and frustrated. 'Are you fucking stupid? You went to the Triads to get money, and not even some money, but half a million pounds. You have lost your mind, Alfie. You need to give it back. You hear me? You need to give it back.' Franny slammed her fist on the table, sending her cup of coffee onto the floor.

Raging, Alfie stood up, flipping the table over in anger, sending it crashing across the room. 'It won't make a difference, will it? Even if I took the money back now, I'll still have to pay the interest. You know that as well as I do. The minute I walked out of that place with it, then *bang*, I owe them.'

Franny spat her words. 'Then why did you do it?'

'Because I had no other choice! I had no fucking choice. It's not as if I could go to the auction with a frigging IOU, is it?'

Franny flew at Alfie, slapping him hard across the face. He grabbed her arms as she screamed at him, 'And how are you going to pay it back? Go on, tell me – oh, and whilst you're at it, tell me what kind of interest they charge.'

'Three hundred per cent.'

As Alfie let go of Franny's arms, she stared at him in horror. 'Three hundred?'

Frustrated, Alfie kicked the kitchen cabinet. 'That's what I said, didn't I?'

'So, you have to pay back *one and a half million pounds* to the Triads.'

Alfie's face curled up in a snarl as he leant in nose to nose with Franny. 'Yeah, yeah, I do. And if I don't, I know what happens, but you know something, Fran, I'm willing to take that consequence. I'm willing to do that for Taylor, because I won't have a life anyway if I can't save him.'

Franny spoke slowly. 'But they must've asked you about collateral.'

'They did . . . and I told them . . . I told them that it would be on the house.'

'*This* house? As in *my* house?'

'Well what other house am I talking about? I'm hardly talking about Hansel and fucking Gretel's house, am I?'

'You want me to re-mortgage this house that my dad gave me?'

Still furious, Alfie glared. 'It's bricks and fucking mortar, Fran. What we're dealing with is worth more than that, so what's the problem? And fuck me, let's face it, it's my life we're talking about here. If I don't pay them, well I'm a dead man.'

Franny stayed quiet as she thought about what Alfie was saying. The problem was, or rather the problem *Alfie* had, was that she'd already spoken to the bank about re-mortgaging the place. She hadn't signed on the dotted line, but the bank had been only too willing to lend her some money against it – not that she had any intention of paying it back. They could repossess the house for all she cared, because like Alfie had said, *it was only bricks and mortar*.

But what it meant was when she left with Mia, she would also be leaving with a couple of million pounds, which ultimately meant she and Mia could lie low. And if she was careful with the money, she'd be set up for several years.

Nobody could find her; she could just fade into obscurity. She could even become someone else, assume a new identity. No more Franny Doyle.

But even if she did all that, she knew Alfie would still come looking for her, wanting to know why she'd gone, wanting to know why she'd just disappeared without a goodbye.

And of course, very soon the police would be starting to ask questions about the fire in the club, and certainly by that time she needed to be gone.

Perhaps she would even leave the area before she found Mia. She could still search for her. She didn't need to be here in Soho – and in reality, the sooner she got away the better. She'd already messed up by letting her feelings get in the way. And yes, yes she'd miss Alfie, and if she let it, it would break her, tear her apart, because God she loved him, but that love would cause her to make the wrong choices. She'd already seen love destroy her father, and she certainly wasn't going to let that happen to her.

So the more she thought about it, well, the more she realised that maybe Alfie borrowing the money from Mr Huang wasn't so bad after all. Maybe, it would play to her advantage. That was of course if she stayed focused on Mia and she didn't let her feelings ever get in the way again. And as much as she wouldn't have chosen this for Alfie herself, him not being able to pay back Mr Huang could save her a lot of grief in the long run. It certainly would bring finality.

'I know it's only a house, but the problem is . . . the problem is . . .' She stopped for a moment and worked out what she was going to say, wanting her story to sound as credible as possible. 'My dad put this house in a trust for me. One of the conditions of it is I can't sell it, or even re-mortgage it.'

Alfie's face turned ashen. 'What . . .what are you talking about?'

'This house is in a *trust*, Alf. Dad obviously knew the game we're in is precarious; money laundering, drugs, clubs, illegal betting, it's so easy to lose everything overnight. He wanted to make sure that I'd always have a roof over my head, for the rest of my life. Putting the house in a trust was his way of doing it . . . I'm so sorry, Alf.'

Suddenly looking unwell, Alfie sat down hard in his chair. His voice quiet. 'Why didn't I know this before?'

'It just never came up and, to tell you the truth, I haven't even thought about it until just now.'

'What am I going to do, Fran?'

As Franny refused to let herself feel anything – no love, no care – her eyes were cold and calculating, but it went unnoticed by Alfie who rested his head in his hands.

As she watched him sit in silence, she knew that one day her decision might pain her, but some things were worth the sacrifice. And Mr Huang disposing of Alfie, mainly because of his own recklessness for taking such a huge loan out with such a notorious gang, was a sacrifice she was willing to make, and a sacrifice Alfie had no option *but to make*, especially as it meant she wouldn't have to look over her shoulder forever. And besides, it wasn't all bad – this way Alfie could still save Taylor with the money he had because ultimately, that's what it was all about.

Saving the ones you loved at whatever cost. Whatever it took.

She touched his back gently and kissed his cheek, closing her eyes as well as trying her hardest to close off her heart to him. '*What's done is done.* You'll think of something, Alf, because if you don't pay him back, you're a dead man walking.'

43

Having waited outside Queen's Hospital for Franny to pop up and see Charlie again, Alfie sped through the traffic, clenching down on his jaw, trying to tell himself that the only thing he should be focusing on was Taylor. However, this was proving to be somewhat difficult.

'Alf, slow down, you're going to be pulled over and then you're really in for it. We've got this far so it's not worth messing up when we're so close to getting Taylor back.'

Breathless, Alfie, still pale and wishing that he could think about more than Mr Huang, nodded. 'Yeah, sorry, Fran, I've already fucked up enough, but I can't mess up with Taylor.' He took his foot off the accelerator, his stomach twisting into knots.

'Try not to be too hard on yourself, Alf. You borrowed the money for all the right reasons.'

Giving a wry smile, Alfie said, 'Yeah, but I'm not sure

I'll be thinking that when I've got me hands tied behind me back at the bottom of the Thames, will I?'

Franny swivelled around in the passenger seat to look at Alfie. 'Listen to me: there are a lot of things that might happen in life or have happened that we don't and won't understand, but above all, Alf, I want you to know that I'm *genuinely* sorry I can't help you with the house.' She looked at him knowing what she was saying was the absolute truth, because she *was* sorry that she couldn't help, but there was simply no way she could pay off Mr Huang instead of using the money for a new life for her and Mia.

Alfie sounded sad. 'Thanks, darlin', I appreciate that. You've always been there for me when it matters.'

Franny quickly turned away, watching the cars and lorries go by as they headed towards the A13. She and Alfie were aiming to get to the edge of Essex before nightfall. As much as she knew what needed to be done, as much as this was the only way, sometimes none of it felt easy. The betrayal, the guilt . . . even the love she had for Alfie made it difficult to come to terms with what she had to do. *What she had done*. But then she supposed her feeling sentimental was just her being weak. And anything other than strong wouldn't get Mia back and help her start a new life.

After a moment she asked, 'Would you still have borrowed the money if you'd known I couldn't help you?'

There was a long pause as Alfie thought about it, changing lanes as he did so. Eventually, he said, 'You know what, Fran, yeah, yeah, I think I would. I couldn't have done anything else. How could I leave that kid there knowing there was something I could've done about it?

Nobody was there for me when I was around about his age, but I can be there for him.'

'Well that's exactly it, Alf. You've summed it up right there. Sometimes we have to do what's wrong to get to what's right. The decisions we make aren't always the best ones, but if they're for the right reasons, I guess we just have to learn to live with them.'

Alfie raised his eyebrows. 'Or not, in my case!'

Fighting to push any sentiment as far down inside her as she could, Franny shook her head. 'Alf, it's not over yet.'

Taking a deep breath, Alfie said, 'Yeah, you're right, and anyway, I can't do anything about Huang right now, but I can do something about Taylor. I'll think about that lot tomorrow, when Taylor's safely back.'

'You'll be all right, especially as we know now from Charlie that Barry isn't going to be at the auction himself. It might be easier for you . . .' Franny didn't add that it certainly would be easier for *her* knowing Barry wouldn't be there, instead she said, 'I can't imagine anyone with a higher bidding power than you, either. Not at the level Barry's operating at, though I understand you can't be too careful. But it'll be okay, I'm sure of it.'

'I hope so. Did Charlie say anything else? Did he say why Barry wasn't coming?'

'No, when I went in to see him they were just about to take him down to theatre again. Something about stopping a bleed, so he didn't have time to say much. But I guess it's safer for Barry not to be there; I doubt he'll want to do another stretch. Maybe he's feeling edgy.'

Alfie frowned. 'Does that mean Taylor won't be there?'

'I don't know. I'm not sure how it'll work. But I do know, well according to Charlie, that it's all going ahead and it's a genuine sale. No bullshit, no messing about. Barry is looking to earn some money, and using Taylor is perfect for that. He got him cheap, and Alan doesn't care what happens to him as long as he gets his money for gear . . . By the way, I forgot to ask, did Alan go for his little trip with your friends?'

Alfie gave Franny the briefest of glances. 'Yeah, I got a call from them. It all went to plan. They said they made it painful and slow. They also said he cried like a baby, which is pretty ironic considering who he is . . . rather who he *was*.'

Franny, pleased at the news, nodded, then turned her attention back to the auction. 'And are you sure you're all right that I'm not going to come in with you? The idea of going into that place sickens me.'

'Yeah of course, I understand. If you wait outside and take all the cars' registrations as planned, then once we've got Taylor, we can send the info on to the police. That way no one who'll be there tonight will get away with it, but at the same time there won't be any risk to Taylor. And hopefully, if all goes well, within a couple of hours that boy will be safe for the first time in his life.'

Having driven for over an hour, Franny and Alfie found themselves in Essex. They followed the GPS, which took them through quaint country villages and long winding roads until they got to an old disused farm and warehouse on the outskirts of the village of Boxted, where they drove slowly along Lower Farm Road, looking out for the turning.

They continued along in silence for a few more miles, crossing over the river Stour, heading towards Dedham. Suddenly Alfie slammed on the brakes, peering through the darkness and towards the copse of trees to see a barn lit up.

'I think that's it.'

Franny spoke in a whisper. 'Yeah, I think you could be right . . . Look, over there, you can see a load of cars.'

Alfie stared but as he did so, a sudden wave of nausea rushed over him. He quickly opened the driver's door, and retched, vomiting up the contents of his stomach.

'Alf, are you okay?'

Wiping his mouth with the tissue Franny handed him, Alfie answered quietly, feeling his body tremble. 'I will be once this is sorted. It's just difficult because . . .' He trailed off.

'I know, Alf, I know. You don't have to explain, but let me tell you something: I think you're really brave. You should be proud of yourself. You've conquered things you didn't think you would . . . And, Alf, no matter what happens, never *ever* forget I love you. Always hold on to that.' She stretched across, kissing him gently on his cheeks, once more having to close her eyes and fighting back her tears as a wave of love for Alfie crashed in on her and it was another couple of moments before she eventually opened them and said, 'Do you want to wait another minute?'

'No, let's do this. I'm ready.'

44

At the entrance of the old barn, Alfie could see the place was well lit and a crowd of men stood or milled around.

'Ticket.' The man at the doorway stared at Alfie. He was well built and looked like he was in his mid-sixties, with deep-set eyes and a pockmarked face, and he blocked Alfie's way, repeating what he'd just said. 'Ticket.'

Alfie tightened his fist in his pocket. Everything in him wanted to throttle the man, but instead he pulled out the blue dummy along with the blue ribbon from his pocket, passing it to the man who nodded and stepped out of the way.

Alfie walked in and was greeted by smiles and nods from the other men who looked just like him. Just like his neighbour. Just like his barber. Just like the man on the street. And it made him want to throw up. He wanted to scream. He wanted to take the gun that was in the back of the car and blow them all away, but that wouldn't save Taylor, and that's what he was here to do.

He could feel the sweat dripping down his back as he looked around. The old crumbling walls of the barn decorated with fairy lights and paper lampshades, a wooden table full of bottles of wine and paper cups, a murmur of chatter all around; so normal, all so seemingly innocent, yet so twisted and dark.

Alfie walked to the back of the barn, and although he knew it was a cold and chilly night, he felt like he was burning up. He pulled at his shirt, trying to loosen an already loose top, and wiped the perspiration from his brow.

'Are you new?'

Alfie spun round and came face-to-face with a cheerful-looking man in his late forties, smartly dressed, with olive skin, and wearing a wedding band.

The room began to spin and Alfie reached out and leant on the damp, stone wall for support. 'Excuse me?'

The man smiled again, apologetically and politely – so polite to Alfie it seemed surreal, as if he were asking the time. 'Sorry, it's just that when I noticed you come in, I thought I hadn't seen you before. Often in these places you get to see regular faces, although most of the time you never get to know anyone's name, so let me introduce myself, I'm Rupert. I'm very much looking forward to this, aren't you? Apparently this product is well worth bidding for. Young and fresh, though not so sure about the fresh – often by that age they've already been broken in.'

Rupert laughed as Alfie swallowed down his bile. He

knew he should say something, *anything*, as he didn't want to draw any more attention to himself than necessary, but the words wouldn't come out. He felt his legs beginning to shake, and the tightness in his chest felt like it was crushing down on him.

'Are you all right? You look a bit peaky.' Rupert stared at Alfie with a concern that only made the moment so much worse for Alfie. It was vile, twisted, perverse. The caring attitude Rupert showed was abhorrent because any minute now, Rupert would start bidding on Taylor without care or concern.

Forcing himself to say something at the same time as he swallowed hard, making sure he wasn't going to throw up on Rupert, Alfie, knowing he didn't even sound like himself, spoke in a small, strained voice, 'I . . . I had something to eat on the way over; it hasn't agreed with me. But to answer your question, yeah I'm new here, I've never done . . . I've never been to an auction before, I usually . . .' He stopped, unable to bear what he was saying, but seeing Rupert looking at him with interest, he continued. 'I usually sort it out another way. Through clubs and parties, though often the . . . the products there are older. I'm a friend of Sally and Anthony, by the way.'

Rupert grinned, his upper-class voice at odds with Alfie's. 'I haven't met them, but I hear they're good people, and how exciting for you that this is your first real auction; well you're in for a treat. The action can get very heated. Though it's a shame they're not actually bringing the boy here because when they do, even if you don't win the bid, if you're lucky, often you're able to . . .'

Alfie cut in, 'Sorry, sorry, I don't feel very well . . .' And with that Alfie ran out of the side entrance to be sick.

He dropped on the ground to his knees, feeling the wet grass as he leant his head against the large, stone wall of the barn. He closed his eyes, trying to stop himself from shaking. He didn't know if he could do it; he didn't know if he could go back in there.

The tears rolled down his cheeks and he watched them drop onto the earth. What was wrong with him? Why couldn't he just pull himself together? '*Come on, come on, you can do this, you can beat this.*' He spoke out loud to himself in a quiet whisper, hating himself for being so weak, hating the fact that Taylor needed him to be strong yet here he was, crying. Here was the great Alfie Jennings crying, but then he wasn't so great, was he? If he couldn't do this without turning into a trembling wreck, what use was he to anybody? To Taylor. To Mia. To Franny. Shame not greatness was the only thing he felt.

'Gosh, make sure you give me the name of that restaurant, won't you? Then I can make sure I never go to it.' Rupert stood above him, chuckling at his own joke.

Alfie turned his head, wiping his tears. He stood up and nodded and with a cold look he flatly said, 'Yeah, sure.'

Rupert spoke in a clipped voice, brimming with excitement. 'Anyway, just thought you'd like to know the auction's going to start at any moment. The screen's all set up.'

Alfie frowned. 'Screen?'

'Yes, the wonders of technology. Barry's going to FaceTime in; he'll be projected on the wall by all accounts.

A larger-than-life Barry, who'd have thought? Marvellous isn't it? Come on . . .'

Taking a deep breath, Alfie followed Rupert inside the barn. A feeling of dread crept all over him as he prepared himself to sit and watch a larger-than-life image of the monster who'd haunted his waking dreams.

45

With the bag of money on his lap, Alfie held on to his chair, squeezing it hard as the projector threw the image of Barry onto the massive screen at the far end of the barn.

He watched and listened, hearing Barry talk – the first time he had done since the court case all those years ago.

Barry waved and grinned as he sat in what Alfie thought looked like an empty room, purring with pleasure as he FaceTimed the awaiting crowd of bidders. 'Pleased so many of you could make it. As you know I haven't been around for a while. I was a bit busy, you know what her majesty's like – likes to take her time, likes to do things at her pleasure. Twenty-two years of fucking pleasure!'

The crowd laughed while Alfie paled, trying to keep his shaking to a minimum whilst Barry continued to talk. 'Anyway, I'm delighted to be back, and I'm hoping that I'm going to be around for a while this time. You'll be seeing a lot more of me . . . and my products.'

The crowd broke out into applause and Alfie bit down so hard on his lips that he could taste the blood in his mouth.

'Anyway, enough of my chat, gentlemen – let the bidding begin. But before we do, I'm sure you want to see exactly what your hard-earned money is going to buy. Am I right?'

A resounding cry of, '*Yes, yes, show us!*' was heard around the room.

Barry grinned and from the side of him and off camera, he pulled Taylor into shot.

On seeing Taylor, seeing his haunting, bewildered eyes look out at the crowd, look out at him, the bilious, nauseous sensation engulfed Alfie again. He rubbed his eyes, wiping the sweat that had trickled down into them away, and he fought the urge to run.

Barry, chuckling, and still holding on to Taylor's arm, said, 'Whoever is the lucky winner, let me tell you, you won't go wrong with this product. Quiet and no trouble at all. And the best thing, gentlemen, is that the original owner of this product is comfortable with the deal. It's a clean slate, so once it's yours it's yours. In other words, no one will be looking for it. So, with that in mind, who wants to start the bidding? Any takers for fifteen thousand?'

'Fifteen here!' A man Alfie couldn't see properly raised his hand over in the far corner.

'Twenty-five!' A louder shout from the front caused the crowd to titter with laughter as he waved both hands in the air enthusiastically.

The room fell silent causing Barry to intervene. 'Come on, twenty-five grand – that's a giveaway.'

'Fifty.'

A couple sitting in the shadows raised their hands and Barry giggled. 'Now that's more like it. Do I hear sixty?'

A large fat man, who was as well dressed as Rupert, raised his hand. He spoke with a Scottish accent. 'Here, I'll offer sixty.'

Rupert who was bouncing on his seat with delight and sitting next to Alfie, suddenly shouted, 'One hundred thousand pounds!'

Around the room, oohs and ahhs were heard, and Rupert, smelling of expensive aftershave, smugly leant over to Alfie and whispered in delight, 'I reckon he's mine. I know none of this lot will go that high. I tell you what, when I pick him up, you can come with me if you like, have a bit of fun.'

He squeezed Alfie's leg then winked at him to which Alfie said, 'No thanks, *mate*, and I'd appreciate it if you'd get your fucking hand off me. Wouldn't want it broken, would we?'

Rupert's face drained of colour. He looked taken aback and retreated into his seat.

'So, at a hundred thousand pounds, going once, going twice,' Barry shouted out to the crowd.

'One hundred and fifty!' Alfie's voice boomed out as he waved his hand in the air and from the corner of his eye, he could see Rupert looking agitated, an expression of fury on his face.

Rupert called out, 'Two hundred thousand.' He side-glanced Alfie with a sneer.

'Two hundred and fifty.'

As Barry's face was projected on the screen it was clear to Alfie that Barry couldn't believe his luck.

'Three hundred thousand!'

'Three-fifty!' Alfie shouted again, hoping Rupert would back down, desperate for him to.

'Four hundred thousand!'

Alfie turned to stare at Rupert, feeling the whole crowd looking at them with interest and amusement at the spectacle. 'Four-fifty. Four hundred and fifty thousand pounds.'

Furiously, Rupert hissed at Alfie, 'You better make sure you have the money. I've seen what they do to people who don't pay. They check you know, so whatever's in that bag of yours, make sure it's enough.'

'Oh, don't worry about me – I've got the money all right. The question is, have you?'

Haughtily, Rupert turned his nose up at Alfie. 'Damn right I have . . . Four-eighty!'

The tension rushed through Alfie. He had only another twenty thousand before he reached his top bid and ran out of money. Taking a deep breath, he called out, 'Five hundred thousand! I offer five hundred thousand pounds.'

A scream of excitement sounded somewhere in the room as Rupert leant in to Alfie.

'Whenever anyone starts to go up in twenties, I'd say they're running out of money, wouldn't you?'

Alfie shook his head, speaking quietly through the side of his mouth. 'I think you're speaking about yourself there, Rupert. I'm just being sensible. How about you?'

He held Rupert's gaze as his heart pounded in terror – this was it. There was no more, and he couldn't even pretend there was. Panic stifled him as he watched Rupert raise his hand in the air, a wide smile spreading across his face. 'Five hundred thousand . . . and . . .' He paused and rummaged in his pocket, pulling out a ten-pound note. He glared at Alfie then shouted. 'And ten pounds.' The crowd cheered but Alfie buried his face in his hands as the room began to spin, his whole body beginning to shake. He'd almost done it, he'd almost saved Taylor, but now what would become of him? In horror he listened to Barry count down as well as listening to Rupert giggling next to him. 'Five hundred thousand and ten pounds, going once, going twice . . .'

'Wait! Wait! Wait!' Alfie yelled out as he suddenly remembered the change he had in his pocket. Frantically, he jammed his hand into his jeans pulling out a ten-pound note along with some pound coins. He called out again, his voice tinged with slight hope. 'Five hundred thousand and . . . and . . . thirteen pounds.'

He glanced at Rupert, whose smile had dropped, replaced by an expression of fury as he hissed, 'I'm out. All out.'

And as Rupert stood up and stormed towards the exit, Alfie once again buried his head in his hands listening to Barry count down the bid. 'Five hundred thousand and thirteen pounds from the gentleman at the back, going once, going twice, going three times . . . Sold!'

And with that, Alfie Jennings was promptly sick again.

46

Alfie drove with his foot right down on the accelerator as he sped through the villages, heading towards the outskirts of Ongar in Essex, to the disused airfield.

As he took the corners at speed, anxiety mixed with adrenalin rushed through him. He knew he couldn't be complacent now. Until he had Taylor, he couldn't relax.

After the auction they'd checked his money, making him give half of it there and the rest he had to give to Barry when he handed over Taylor, in less than twenty minutes.

Hitting ninety miles an hour, Alfie concentrated on the road ahead, knowing that taking the roads this fast with the rain pouring down was dangerous, but there was nothing else he could do. They'd warned him if he were late, then there was a chance Barry might not be there, and not only would he lose his deposit, but more importantly he would lose Taylor.

'I think we'll be there in about fifteen minutes,' Franny said as she looked at the inbuilt GPS. 'Take the next right, Alf, it's coming up in half a mile.'

Going too fast, and concentrating too hard to answer, Alfie nodded as he focused on the dark, wet road ahead, part of him knowing that having to work so hard on driving would stop him having to think; think that within the next twenty minutes, he'd be coming face-to-face with Barry.

The disused airfield was down a long country track with dips and potholes and Alfie now drove slowly, steadying his breathing as he dipped his headlights. The rain continued to lash down and the windscreen wipers worked overtime.

Looking at the time, Alfie saw it was just past midnight and at the end of the track, he turned the engine off. In the pitch-black he spoke to Franny. 'I'll go, you stay here.'

Anxiously, Franny said, 'Are you sure? I don't mind. I mean, perhaps it's better for me to deliver the money and get Taylor.'

'No, I have to do this on my own.'

'I'm worried that you might blow it. For all you know he might be in there with someone else, and well, if you can't just get in and out of there without having a conversation, then I'll do it. Think of Taylor, Alf. See sense.'

Nodding, Alfie contemplated what Franny was saying. 'I get that, but I have to do this.'

With tension in the air, Franny grabbed hold of Alfie's arm, her eyes imploring him. 'But you don't – you really, really don't.'

Alfie stared at her. 'What is it you're afraid of, Fran?'

'I'm afraid . . . I'm afraid you're going to muck this up, let your emotions get the better of you.'

'I won't, I promise. I'll get Taylor, and that's all. I'll just go in and go out, I swear, and I can deal with Barry another time. How about that?'

Knowing there was no way she was going to persuade him not to go, Franny spoke quietly. 'Okay, okay, but no conversations, Alf, because that's when, well that's when it'll all go wrong.'

'No conversations, you have my word.'

Franny sighed as she handed Alfie the bag of the remaining money along with a small handgun. 'Make sure you bring Taylor back safely. Nothing else.'

'I will do, make no mistake about that. I'll see you soon.'

Alfie walked through the long grass, using his phone as his torch. He waded through the mud and thick grass, feeling the water go into his shoes as he headed towards the abandoned air shelters and buildings of the World War II airfield.

Standing by the crumbling watchtower, and with his eyes adjusted to the darkness, Alfie looked up the field and saw a light coming from underneath one of the rusted corrugated-iron-roofed air raid shelters. Immediately he knew *that* was where Barry was.

He closed his eyes, lifting his face to the sky, feeling the rain fall on him as he realised not only was this a chance to get Taylor back, but it was also a chance to face up to his own nightmares. And with that thought, Alfie Jennings began to walk towards the shelter.

Coming up close to the air raid shelter, he could see

there was no door, just a thick covering of hanging ivy and evergreen. He pushed the plants to one side, dipping down his body to get in as he forced himself through the knotty and twisted ivy stems.

Inside it seemed colder than out, and the roof leaked, rain dripping down from the rotting ceiling, making puddles on the concrete, which was strewn with weeds.

Alfie raised his eyes to the end and there, looking terrified, shivering as he sat on a plastic crate next to a small, portable spotlight was Taylor and by his side stood Barry Eton.

He stared at Barry, willing his legs to move, willing himself not to turn into that frightened boy he once was.

He strode up to Barry, holding his gaze for a moment, but as he got nearer, Alfie couldn't look at him anymore, and he glanced away, giving a small smile to Taylor. He spoke gruffly.

'Barry, they said I'd find you here.'

Barry sniffed loudly, the end of his nose red from the cold. He scratched his stomach, which hung over his belt. 'Have you got the rest of the cash?'

'Of course.' Alfie opened the bag, feeling like he was on automatic pilot. He could see his hands shake as he showed Barry the money. 'It's all here, but I'm happy for you to count it.'

Barry shook his head. 'I don't know many people who would've paid that sort of dough for a kid like this. You must've really wanted him.'

Casually, Alfie shrugged, still not holding eye contact. 'Not really, it was more that I didn't want Rupert to have him. That man has a lot to answer for.'

Barry laughed. 'That man has a way of rubbing people up the wrong way. How do you know him?'

'I don't. I met him tonight, but that was enough . . . certainly enough for me.'

Again, Barry laughed, and this time Alfie stared at him, his eyes and his heart full of hatred. His breathing became short and shallow. Without even thinking, Alfie roared, 'Shut up! Shut the fuck up. None of this is funny, you twisted son of a bitch.'

Barry, shocked, spluttered, 'What the fuck did you just say to me?'

Alfie stepped in closer. 'You heard me, but I can repeat it if you like. *Shut the fuck up.*'

'Who the hell are you?' Barry's eyes darted around.

'I'm not the Old Bill if that's what you think. Why don't you look closer?'

'What are you talking about?'

'Look at me, Barry. Go on, keep looking, who do you see?'

Barry looked at him strangely. 'The only thing I can see in front of me is a cunt.'

Alfie snarled. He placed his face inches from Barry's. 'Wrong answer. Look me in my eyes. You've seen me before, and this close as well, remember? Remember what you did to me, Barry?'

Barry shook his head and stepped back, knocking into a small pile of bricks, which clattered to the floor. 'I don't know what you're talking about.'

Alfie's face flushed red with anger. 'Don't you? . . . Taylor, why don't you go outside and wait for me? You think you

348

can do that? Just through those plants. I know it's raining but I won't be long, and you'll be okay there, cos I know you're a good boy.'

Taylor stared at Alfie. He blinked, and a tiny smile came to the corner of his mouth. He spoke with a small lisp. 'Yes, I'll wait outside, cos I'm a good boy.'

In that moment, Alfie was crippled with heartache. He felt the pain for Taylor rip through him like a razor. The only consolation was that he knew from now on Taylor would be fine. He watched him trot out, sucking his thumb as he ran, and once he was sure he was safely outside, Alfie turned back to Barry who stared at him.

'How did you know his name was Taylor?'

'I know a lot of things. About you, your life, your friends and what you do, but mainly I know you're a piece of scum, and you like to prey on kids; frighten them, make them hurt in places where they should never hurt, make them have nightmares for the rest of their lives, make them terrified of every sound, make them fear putting the light out, make them wet their bed until they're well into their teenage years. That's what you like to do, isn't it, Barry? You piece of shit – that's what you do. But I'm not a kid anymore and you're no longer the monster to me that you once were; you're just a pathetic, twisted old man.'

Barry tilted his head and gazed into Alfie's eyes, and it took a minute or so for Barry to say, 'Fuck me, if it ain't Alfie Jennings. I wondered when you'd crawl into the proceedings. I've heard a lot about you recently but my, my, haven't you changed. Look at you, you're built like a brick house now, not like the runt you used to be who'd freeze when I said *boo*, who'd freeze when I made him give me a kiss . . . I suppose there's no chance of one now.' Barry made kissing sounds then burst into a nasty laugh, prompting Alfie to charge at him, smashing him against the wall, clenching his fist and hitting him hard in the side of his head, causing Barry to stumble and fall, crashing his skull on the pile of bricks.

Standing over him, Alfie could see blood running out of Barry's ear. He could also see his eyes rolling to the back of his head as he struggled to talk. 'And . . . and there's me thinking . . . thinking we . . . we're going to be . . .' Barry trailed off as the life began to slip away from him.

Alfie crouched down by his side. 'If you're about to repent your sins, save it. I ain't a priest and to tell you the truth, I think it's too late for you.'

Barry, grappling for air, managed to give a crooked smile. 'Ma said you were an arsehole . . . You know my daughter don't you? I understand you've had . . . had a few dealings with her.'

Alfie was puzzled, but he sneered in contempt. 'Even at the end Barry, you're talking shit. I've no idea what you're on about.'

'Ma . . . Ma Dwyer, she's my daughter, Charlie's brother. I thought . . . I thought he would've told you that.'

Alfie reeled, trying to get his head round it. If Ma was his daughter that meant Bree, who'd been married to Ma's son, Johnny, was in some strange way related. 'Ma? Ma's your daughter? Then did you know Bree?'

As he tried to laugh, he began to cough, rasping and wheezing, his nose beginning to bleed from his fractured skull. 'Not personally, but Ma . . .' He stopped, the effort of speaking overwhelming him as his body began to shut down, succumbing to hypoxia as his life dwindled on a thread, but he tried again, sounding confused and disorientated. 'Mia . . .'

Barry closed his eyes but hearing the name, *Mia,* Alfie lifted Barry up by his shoulders and shook him. 'Don't fucking die on me now, you bastard. What about Mia? What about her?'

Muttering inaudibly, Barry's eyelids twitched, and Alfie was forced to put his ear over Barry's lips in an attempt to hear what he was trying to say. 'Ma . . . Mia . . . Ma . . .'

'Ma had Mia, is that what you're trying to say? For fuck's sake, Barry, is it? Is it? Barry! Barry!' But as Alfie sat up to shake Barry again, he realised he was already dead.

Getting up, Alfie grabbed the bag of money and ran outside to see Taylor crouched down trying to shield himself from the rain.

Alfie smiled at him, picking him up to carry him to the warmth and safety of the car. 'It's going to be all right, Taylor, you hear me? Everything's going to be all right. You're such a good boy, you know that? And I promise you from now on, you'll never have to be frightened again.'

And as Alfie hurried to the car with Taylor safe in his arms, everything else faded into insignificance, everything apart from Ma, the person he was about to go and see.

47

'You can't, that's crazy!' Franny stared at Alfie in horror as Alfie drove at speed, racing along the roads towards the home of Ma Dwyer.

'Shh, keep your voice down, Taylor's asleep. You wanted to find Mia, then we need to get there now!'

'But what exactly did Barry say?'

'Well he was trying to tell me something about Mia, something about Ma having Mia. I dunno, he wasn't making sense at the end.'

Panicked, Franny shook her head. 'Why would he tell you about that?'

'I don't know, but he said it, or at least that's what I think he said.'

'Well there you go then, you don't know for certain. Alfie, this is crazy – let's go home. Please, let's just go back. It's been a long day. We can talk about it in the morning.'

Alfie sped around the corner. 'This is the closest we've got to a lead. It might be your opportunity to find out where Mia is. Come on, Franny, it's worth going to see Ma, even if it's a dead end. I know you're scared to get your hopes up about Mia, but we can't wait till tomorrow. Every second counts.'

Franny spoke urgently, her words rushing out. 'What about Taylor? He doesn't need us to be doing this. We need to take him to your friend Claire so she can get him cleaned up and get some food inside him and make sure he has a safe night's sleep, and like you say, she'll know the right authorities to contact in the morning. Who knows, as she's a foster carer she might be able to take him in, but we have to get him there. Come on, Alf, just turn the car around.'

'No, Fran, say what you like but I ain't going back. Taylor will be fine – he's warm and he's asleep. Christ it's probably the most peace he's had in his life; so lying there for another couple of hours ain't going to hurt him, but what will hurt is missing this chance. If it's too much for you, I'll deal with Ma. You can stay in the car, but if it's the last thing I do, I'm going to help you find Mia.'

Outside the mobile home site of Ma Dwyer, which Alfie knew well from when he'd been there with Bree, he parked the car by the hay barn, pulling out the gun from the bag of money.

'You stay here with Taylor.'

Franny shook her head, her face stricken and pale. She licked her lips, which were dry, panic running through her. 'No, I'll come too.'

353

'I think it's probably best if you wait for me.'

Franny snapped, 'I'm coming. Mia's my . . . my friend's baby, so if Ma has anything to say, I want to hear it.'

'What about Taylor?'

Fran stared at Alfie. 'You were the one who said he's fine, so just lock the car and put the alarm on. He'll be all right.'

Without waiting for Alfie to answer, Franny opened the door, jumping out and running towards the north side of the traveller site, hearing Alfie shouting after her. 'Fran! Fran, where are you going? Fran, you don't know your way around. Just wait!'

Franny ran frantically through the rain and wind, heading towards Ma's mobile home, knowing that she had to get to her before Alfie did. She remembered her way from when she'd come before, and she hoped for her sake that Alfie was still well behind.

Seeing the pink door of Ma's caravan coming into sight, Franny ran faster, charging through the mud, fear and dread crushing her.

At the door she gave a quick check over her shoulder, making sure Alfie wasn't in sight before she began to hammer on the door and on the sides of the caravan.

'Ma! Ma! Open up! For fuck's sake, open up!' Hearing nothing coming from inside, Franny kicked the lock, raising her foot and smashing it down, trying to force the door open. But it didn't budge and, desperate, she tried again to open it, this time slamming her shoulder against the door. 'Ma, it's Franny! Ma, if you're in there, open up! *Please!*'

As she raised her foot to kick the door again, it suddenly

swung open, and there standing in front of her wearing a flowered blue dressing gown, holding a metal baseball bat, was Ma Dwyer.

Without hesitating, Franny pushed inside, shutting and locking the door quickly behind her. 'Ma, you've got to help me.'

Ma's bemusement turned into a cackle. 'Help you? You must've lost the fucking plot.'

Franny's eyes were wide open with fear. She spoke quickly and breathlessly. 'Please, because any minute now, Alfie will be at that door looking for you. He wants to know about Mia.'

Ma raised her eyebrows. She sniffed and sounded amused. 'Well that will be an interesting conversation, won't it? Shall I go and put the kettle on?'

Franny grabbed Ma by her dressing gown. 'This isn't funny!'

Ma glared at her, full of hostility. 'If I were you, I'd let go, especially if you want me to listen to what you have to say.'

Franny dropped her hold and began to pace, talking in an agitated manner. 'You've got to help me. You've just got to, and you owe me. You hear me, Ma? You owe me.'

Ma roared with laughter. 'And how do you make that one out?'

Red with fury, Franny spun on Ma. 'Because you knew that I was coming for Mia that day. None of this would be happening if it wasn't for you. I could've been gone, I could've been out of here, but no, you wanted to play games, even though you knew I was good for the money, you let her go.'

'You were late!'

Franny's face curled up in a snarl as she held herself back from attacking Ma. 'I got here as quick as I could.'

'Not quick enough though!'

'Have you any idea how it feels knowing Mia's out there somewhere? Have you any idea how much that hurts?'

Ma, placing the baseball bat under her arm, shrugged. 'No, and I don't care either, but you know what I find really odd about this whole thing? You doing all Bree's dirty work. I mean, where is she? It's almost like she disappeared off the face of the earth.'

Franny pushed Ma in her chest. 'You leave Bree out of this. Why do you think she ain't here? She can't cope with it, and she doesn't want to see you, does she? She told me how you treated her but not only that, Ma, you sold Mia to someone you didn't even know the name of! So, don't ask why Bree's not here – it's pretty obvious.'

Ma's face darkened. 'I'm in the business to be making money, not making friends. I already told you I'd sell her if you didn't show up on time, and I don't need to know names.'

'*Ma! Ma! I want a word! Ma! Come out wherever you are!*' Outside, Alfie's voice was loud and aggressive as he searched for Ma.

Fighting the tears, Franny began to tremble. She whispered to Ma, 'Please, you've got to help me. He'll be here in a second, and he can't find out about Mia and Bree.'

'I'd say that was your problem, wouldn't you?'

Ma stepped forward to open the door, but Franny

356

blocked her way. 'Don't do it! Ma, please! Listen to me – I've got money. There's some money in the car. I won't be able to bring it to you until later, but I promise I will. I'll come back with it.'

Ma narrowed her eyes. 'How much are we talking?'

'One hundred grand.'

'You really are desperate, aren't you, Franny? Make it one-fifty and we have a deal.'

A hammering on the door made Franny jump, she leant her body against it as Alfie shouted, '*Open up Ma! Otherwise, I'll kick the fucking door down!*'

Terrified, Franny nodded, whispering in panic, 'Okay, okay, but he can't find you here.'

'You better be good for the money though.'

'I will be. Now hide! Just hide! I'll be back later, I promise. Just give me a few hours.'

As Franny watched Ma waddle down the hallway, she waited for a moment before unlocking the door. 'Alf!'

Alfie frowned, surprised to see Franny standing there.

'Hi, sorry about that, Alf. I locked the door because I didn't want anyone coming in.'

'Is she in there?'

Franny shook her head. 'No . . . no, I checked every-where. It looks like she might've gone away.'

Alfie glanced behind Franny, looking up the carpeted hallway. 'Then how did *you* get in?'

Franny's voice trilled in an odd sing-song way. 'Me? How did I get in? I . . . I . . . oh for God's sake, Alf, that's a stupid question. Can't you see where I kicked the door? It must've been badly fitted because it came open almost straightaway.

It can't have been on the latch properly. I dunno . . .' Uneasy, Franny trailed off, holding Alfie's stare.

'But how did you know which caravan she was in?'

Franny's words came tumbling out. 'When . . . when I came around the corner, there was a guy. I asked him which caravan. I'm surprised you didn't see him actually. He told me Ma was away, but I didn't believe him, so I thought I'd check. You know, be vigilant, because when I thought about it, you were right, Alf, we needed to check this out, and now we have done, we won't ever wonder, will we?'

Alfie looked at Franny strangely. 'Are you all right?'

'Yes . . . no . . . not really. I know I shouldn't have done, but I got my hopes up. I thought Ma might be here, and we could've got some answers . . . Look, let's go. Let's get Taylor to your friend's house.'

'Okay, and I'm sorry, Fran, I thought we were on to something too. But like you said earlier, it's not over yet.'

'That's right, it's not over yet.'

And with that Franny gave a tight smile as she stepped out of the mobile home, closing the door behind her, knowing that she needed to leave London tonight.

Outside Claire's house, on the south side of Muswell Hill, Franny gave Taylor a big hug. She crouched down as she spoke to him, smiling and speaking with warmth. 'Listen, sweetie, these people are going to look after you, and I know you're going to be really happy from now on. Really, really happy. I just know it.'

Taylor answered shyly, his big blue eyes full of mistrust. 'Am I?'

'Yes, baby, you are. You really are.'

She gave him another hug before standing up, watching him walk into the house, holding Alfie's hand.

As Franny turned away to get into the car, she heard Alfie call her back. He ran up to her, a look of concern on his face.

'Are you sure you're all right with me staying here awhile, Fran? I just don't want to leave Taylor straightaway.'

'Absolutely. You do what needs to be done, Alf.'

'And you'll put the money in the safe for me? Maybe I can talk Mr Huang around. Maybe he'll let me give him half of it back without the crazy interest.'

'Maybe . . . Look, I'll see you.' She turned back to walk to the car, but stopped and spun around, rushing up to Alfie and throwing her arms round him. She squeezed her eyes closed, stopping the tears from falling, nuzzling her head into his neck.

Surprised, Alfie said, 'This is lovely, Fran, and I could stay here all day with you like this, but what have I done to deserve it?'

She looked up at him, giving a sad smile. 'I just wanted to give you a proper goodbye, that's all.'

Alfie sounded worried. 'Fran, what's going on?'

'Nothing, it's just been a difficult day.' She stood on her tiptoes and gave him a kiss on his cheek. 'I love you, I love you so much – never forget that.'

And as Alfie watched Franny drive away, he felt his phone buzz in his pocket. He pulled it out and looked at his screen. The text read:

FRANNY CAN'T BE TRUSTED.

48

Franny sped along Soho Square, her thoughts racing and her heart pounding as she pulled up outside her house. She turned off the engine and ran to the front door, knowing she had to be quick. This was her chance to get away, though she still had to be careful. She had no idea how long Alfie would stay with Taylor, but she certainly knew by the time he got back, she needed to be gone.

She'd take some clothes and a few essentials, grab her passport and of course, take the money left over from the auction – and once she'd found somewhere to stay, she'd sort out re-mortgaging the house from afar.

Her hands shook as she put her key in the door. She switched on the light, then froze. She stared around in horror at the sight in front of her. Hanging all around the hallway were Bree's belongings. The belongings she'd kept stored in the missing suitcase.

In shock, Franny pushed herself against the wall, shaking, her breathing becoming laboured. '*No . . . no . . . no . . . no!*'

She spoke out loud, not understanding, not comprehending what was happening, her eyes darting around and, unable to stand the sight of them, she leapt forward, grabbing at Bree's belongings, pulling them down off their hangers, collecting them up in her arms.

She charged through to the lounge but stopped in her tracks and let out a small whimper as she saw her blood-stained clothes dangling from the ceiling. She spun around looking for something, *anything* that would give her an explanation.

Breathing hard, she backed away, cowering in the corner with her eyes transfixed on the bloody clothes that hung above her. It took her more than a couple of minutes to force herself up, force herself forward.

Pulling a chair to under where her clothes hung, Franny stepped up but suddenly the lights went off and the sound of a child's music box played out from the hallway.

She screamed in terror, crying, calling out, her voice shaking, panic racing through her veins. In the pitch-black she stepped off the chair. 'Hello? Hello? Whoever's there, it isn't funny now. Whoever you are, you can stop . . . You hear me? You can stop.'

'Oh, I hear you, all right.' The lights came on and standing in the doorway was Shannon.

'It's you?'

'Yeah, it's me.'

'You little bitch, you did all this?'

'No, that was me . . . Hello, Franny, surprised to see me?'

361

Stepping into view, Vaughn Sadler stood next to Shannon, holding baby Mia in his arms.

Stunned, Franny stumbled back, and held on to the chair for support as her legs gave way. Covering her mouth she sobbed into her hand, 'Mia . . . Mia, oh my God, Mia – but you, I thought . . .'

Vaughn interrupted, 'You thought I was dead? Disappointed, are we?'

Franny held her head, pacing around in a circle as her whole body felt like it was going into shock. 'But they said . . . they called Alfie and said . . .'

Vaughn scoffed. 'They said they'd found a body in the club? Yeah, that's right they did, but I asked them to call him. I asked them to say that. You know, it's amazing what people will do when you pay them enough. It seems everything is for sale, even your soul if you're willing to pay enough, wouldn't you agree, Fran, or did you never have one in the first place?'

'Get out! Get out!' Franny ran towards Mia. 'Give her to me! Give her to me! She's mine!'

Vaughn twisted away, holding Franny off. 'But that's the thing – she ain't yours, is she? We all know whose baby she is.'

'Why are you doing this?'

Vaughn laughed scornfully. 'Why am I doing this? Franny, seriously, you need to look in the mirror, darlin'.'

Franny, staring at Mia, shook her head. 'I don't understand where you got her from. Ma said she'd sold her.'

'That's right, she did. And you're looking at the happy buyer. I paid a lot of money for her as well because when

Ma told me you were trying to get her back, well of course, I couldn't have that, and I couldn't have anyone else taking her either. It was easy because you know how much Ma likes her dough.'

'I can't believe it was you!'

Vaughn handed Mia to Shannon, walked across the room and poured himself a large glass of scotch. 'Shannon filled me in on everything. She told me she'd seen Mia in your car and taken her, though she didn't know it was me who'd bought her from Ma. I thought the fewer people that knew, the better. She only learnt that later, when I needed her to look after Mia.'

'What? You got her to look after Mia?'

With a threatening air, Vaughn laughed. 'Well I had to get someone – after all there was the small matter of me having to recover from what you did. Bullet wounds take time to heal – maybe you need a reminder of that?' He stared at Franny, hatred oozing from his eyes.

'I don't need this – just move out of the way and let me leave. You have no right to stop me, and you have no right to hang on to Mia, especially as you let this crackhead look after my baby.'

Vaughn smiled nastily. 'Your baby? Your baby, Franny? I think you're losing the plot, darlin".'

Franny snapped. 'You know what I mean.'

'Get this into your head. Mia has nothing to do with you. *Nothing*.'

Franny shook her head. 'I don't want to do this in front of her.' She pointed at Shannon who responded by sticking her tongue out as she rocked Mia gently.

Vaughn shrugged. 'Why not, Fran? Cos she knows what you're like? She knows what a dark, evil bitch you are? You see, she watched you, Fran, after she'd taken Mia. She hid and watched you take that petrol can out of the car. I wouldn't be here now if it wasn't for Shannon pulling me out of that fire. Unlike you thought, Shannon *is* my friend, and I'm hers. And friends look out for each other, hey, Shan?'

Shannon blushed with delight, her happiness complete as she grinned a toothless smile.

Turning his attention back to Franny, Vaughn said, 'But then you wouldn't know that; you wouldn't know about friendship, would you? I mean, look what happened to poor Bree.'

Franny pointed at Vaughn, her voice on the edge of hysteria. 'Don't you dare, don't you *dare* talk about Bree. You don't know anything.'

Vaughn took a quick gulp of the scotch, enjoying the burn at the back of his throat. 'I know enough, and I know anybody who gets close to you, Franny, ends up getting hurt.'

Franny, still shaking, glowered. 'Get out of my way, Vaughn.'

'Oh no, not this time. I'm afraid I can't do that because we're waiting for a visitor.'

Franny blanched. 'What are you talking about?'

'They should be here any minute now.' Vaughn grinned as he looked at his watch. He began to count down, mouthing the numbers, when suddenly there was a knock on the front door. He winked at Franny. 'Bang on time . . . I'll be back in a minute.'

Leaving Franny standing there, Vaughn rushed out of the room, but a moment later he returned, followed by several police officers. He pointed at Franny. 'That's her, that's Franny.'

The tallest police officer walked up to her, trying to pull her hands behind her back. 'Franny Doyle, I'm arresting you on suspicion of murder . . .'

She pulled away from the officer. 'What? No! No, there's been some mistake. Vaughn, you know it was an accident, you know it! Vaughn!'

'. . . You do not have to say anything, but it may harm your defence if you do not mention when questioned . . .'

'What's going on?' Alfie stood at the door, a look of shock on his face. He stared at Franny and then at Vaughn, and then at Shannon who was holding a baby whilst a police officer roughly grabbed Franny's arms behind her back, putting her in handcuffs as she fought against him. 'I said, what the fuck is happening? Why are you arresting her?'

Ignoring Alfie, the police officer continued to read out Franny's rights as she struggled '. . . something which you later rely on in court. Anything you do say may be given in evidence.'

Alfie turned to Vaughn. 'Tell me what the fuck is going on.'

'You should've asked Franny that. I did try to warn you . . . *Ask Franny what she's done.*'

Alfie frowned. 'The texts, they were from you? Why? Vaughn, for fuck's sake, why are the Old Bill taking her in?'

'For murdering Bree.'

It was Alfie's turn to stumble back. He rested against the wall, staring at Franny. 'Fran, what's going on? What the *fuck* is he talking about?'

Vaughn smiled at Alfie. 'I'll tell you everything later . . .'

'No, you tell me now! How the fuck can she have killed Bree? She didn't even know where she was; nobody did. Tell them, Fran, tell them!'

Franny stared at Alfie, tears running down her face. 'I never killed her, I swear.'

Alfie, incensed, raged, 'You see, she never killed her! Listen to what she's saying. She just told you, so let her go! Let her fucking go!' Alfie began to rush towards Franny but Vaughn held him back.

'Alf, calm down, please. Please, mate, we'll talk later, I promise, but first I want to introduce you to someone . . . Meet your daughter, Mia.'

Vaughn gently took Mia from Shannon, placing her in Alfie's arms as Franny began to scream. Alfie gazed at Vaughn. 'What, she's mine? How can she be mine? I don't understand? I . . .'

'You will do, you will do, but I just need to say a quick goodbye to Franny.'

Vaughn turned and walked towards Franny, who screamed at him. Her face red and wet with tears.

'You bastard, you fucking bastard, you know I didn't do it! I didn't murder anyone.'

As Alfie stood in the centre of the room in shock, unable to speak a single word, unable to process quite what was happening, Vaughn leant in, whispering to Franny as the police began to drag her away. 'I know that, I know you didn't kill her, but they don't know that. I even know where you buried her. Try to get out of that one, Fran. You'll be going away for a very long time.'

Franny's face screwed up as she tried to pull away from the policeman who dragged her down the hallway towards the waiting police car. 'You'll never get away with it! You hear me, Vaughn? I will come after you, so you better watch your back! This isn't over yet! This isn't over!'

Acknowledgements

As always a huge thanks to the wonderful and supportive team at Avon but especially to Katie, my editor, who gives such positive encouragement and fantastic ideas, even getting me to write in more hugs! A big thank you to Darley, my agent, who gives the best advice on books and life – I'm lucky to have him in my corner. Thanks as well to Pippa – another year of answering my emails with patience and kindness! And a huge shout out to my readers and love to those around me. Lastly, to my wonderful 4 legged friends of the equine, canine and cavy variety – without them my life wouldn't be complete.

As the old saying goes . . .
Keep your friends close . . .
And your enemies closer . . .

Available now.

Before, there was just bad blood running
through her veins.
But now, there is poison . . .

Available now.

An eye for an eye,
A tooth for a tooth.
A daughter for a daughter . . .

Available now.

Sometimes love is toxic . . .

Available now.

Karin
Slaughter's
Killer Reads

Exclusive to
ASDA

EXCLUSIVE ADDITIONAL CONTENT

Dear Readers,

This next read is a gangland thriller full of lies and betrayals, focusing on a woman who will do anything it takes to keep her secrets safe.

Having been brought up by London's hardest gangsters, Franny Doyle will do all that is necessary to protect her family. But when innocent children get caught in the crossfire, Franny and her partner Alfie are dragged into a dark underworld – where past demons threaten to shatter all they hold dear…

Gritty and gripping in equal measure, there's one thing for sure: *Sinner* will have you on the edge of your seat all the way through.

Karin

READING GROUP QUESTIONS

Warning: contains spoilers

---

1. What three words would you use to describe *Sinner*?

2. Franny and Bree chose to keep baby Mia a secret from Alfie so that she wouldn't grow up in a life of crime. Do you agree with their decision?

3. Did your feelings towards Franny as a character change throughout the novel? Were you always able to understand the motivations behind her actions?

4. What character did you identify the most with and why?

5. Franny is fiercely protective of Mia, despite not being her biological parent. What comment do you think this serves on the meaning of motherhood?

6. What is your main takeaway from *Sinner*? Have the three words you selected for question one changed after this discussion?

A Q&A WITH JACQUI ROSE

Warning: contains spoilers

Throughout the book, there are many vivid descriptions of Soho. Is this a setting that holds personal importance for you?

Setting in books have always been so important to me, whether that's me reading a book or writing one. I like to think of the setting as an extra character. It can bring so much richness to the text, adding light and shade. Creating the world for the characters to live in is so much fun, especially if the place is real, like Soho is. I've always loved Soho, the eclectic mix of people and cultures, the dark side of it versus what tourists see. Soho was one of the first places that I lived in when I moved to London as a teenager, so it holds a special place in my heart, and I have lots of memories there, both good and bad. It was really important to make sure that I depicted the real vibrancy, noise and sometimes chaos of Soho with authenticity, so it can resonate with the readers who know the area, and the ones that don't know it can picture the sights, sounds and smells of the place.

This book deals with distressing themes, including child abuse and sexual violence. How did you ensure that you handled these themes sensitively?

As an author telling stories which often deal with difficult subjects, I feel I have a real responsibility not to sensationalize or be gratuitous. Being sensitive, especially in topics such as child abuse and sexual violence, is hugely important to me as I'm aware of how triggering it can be. If I haven't personally had lived experiences, then I make sure I speak to survivors and hear and respect their stories. It's vital to show a reader the truth of the impact that traumatic events can have on people's lives, but for me anyway, there's always a line you don't cross over. I want to make readers think and feel the impact, the consequences, the damage that people can do to each other, with care and sensitivity as I'm just not interested in writing books for the shock value.

How did the story evolve as you wrote it? Did you decide on all the twists and turns before you started?

I've started to plan out my stories now, but with *Sinner*, I definitely was a panster, which is basically writing by the seat of your pants! It's fun writing that way, as twists and turns come up as you write, but sometimes you can write yourself into a corner!

Is it difficult to write villainous characters such as Barry Eton and get into their psyche?

I love writing villainous characters, but I think it's really important not to write them as two dimensional, otherwise you make them pantomime villains. You have to really know how they tick, what motivates them, so I ask myself questions such as 'what would Barry do in this situation?'. I would say that on the whole, it's more fascinating than difficult to write such characters.

How did you start your career as an author, and what advice would you give to aspiring writers?

I actually fell into my career as an author. I was an actress for a while, and then I started to write plays myself. I had a conversation with Lisa Jewell, and I was telling her about wanting to write a book, and she encouraged me to do so . . . and the rest is history.

Franny is a strong female character. What comment does she serve on femininity and gendered expectations?

Franny is everything that society says a woman shouldn't be. She's strong and unapologetic, she takes on traditionally masculine roles and she often does those roles better than the men, yet she owns her femininity with pride. She won't change for others or toe the line because of expectations of society.

Charlie Eton and Alfie Jennings had similar upbringings and are connected by their shared childhood abuse, but they have very different characters. Are they foils of one another?

Yes, exactly! I thought it was a good way to show how a shared circumstance can affect people differently. I thought it was great to show and highlight Alfie's strengths, and really get an understanding of him and his motivations/behaviours.

When you are not writing your own books, what kind of fiction do you love to read?

I love to read historical, sweeping sagas, which I know is the antithesis of what I write, but I can't get enough of them!

THE INTERNATIONAL No.1 BESTSELLER

KARIN
Slaughter

GIRL,
FORGOTTEN

A small town
hides a big secret...

The
book that
inspired the
#1 NETFLIX
HIT

Who killed Emily Vaughn?

A girl with a secret . . .

Longbill Beach, 1982. Emily Vaughn gets ready for prom night,
the highlight of any high school experience. But Emily has a
secret. And by the end of the evening, she will be dead.

A murder that remains a mystery . . .

Forty years later, Emily's murder remains unsolved. Her
friends closed ranks, her family retreated inwards, the
community moved on. But all that's about to change.

One final chance to uncover a killer . . .

Andrea Oliver arrives in town with a simple assignment:
to protect a judge receiving death threats. But her assignment
is a cover. Because, in reality, Andrea is here to find justice
for Emily – and to uncover the truth.

Before the killer decides to silence her too . . .